3 1331 0   W9-COH-666

FEB -- 2016

"The collapse is already here, it's just not evenly distributed. *Graft* is a compelling, fast-moving work of austerity science fiction. High tech rubs up against low lives, battered Britishness struggles to get by in the face of imminent inhumanities. A powerful neo-noir."

Matthew de Abaitua, author of The Red Men *and* If Then

"England as a wasteland ruled by crime, car jacking as a doorway to love and morality, and plenty of body horror to mix with your posthumanism: *Graft* is a brilliant eulogy for our ruined future."

Edward J Rathke, author of Noir: A Love Story

"*Graft* is exactly what science fiction should be right now: it's brutally dark, twisted at its heart, with an incredible sense of foreboding about where we could end up if our mistakes aren't put right. Beautifully written, engagingly compulsive, it's one of the best books I've read in a long time."

James Smythe, Author of The Explorer

"Brilliant in its execution… Hill has devised a magnificent universe, clever concepts and enthralling characters."

Bad Cantina

"A memorable debut with pathos, dark humour and true heart."

Interzone

NO LONGER PROPERTY OF
Missouri River Regional Library

"Captures the smell and essence of Britain through its main character, his desires, addictions and strange courage. Written with direct vividness that keeps one inside its totally realised world."

Stephen Fry, Dundee International Book Prize judge 2012

Missouri River Regional Library
214 Adams Street
Jefferson City, Missouri 65101

BY THE SAME AUTHOR

The Folded Man

MATT HILL

GRAFT

ANGRY
ROBOT

ANGRY ROBOT
An imprint of Watkins Media Ltd

Lace Market House,
54-56 High Pavement,
Nottingham,
NG1 1HW
UK

angryrobotbooks.com
twitter.com/angryrobotbooks
Armed and ready

An Angry Robot paperback original 2016

Copyright © Matt Hill 2016

Cover by John Coulthart.
Set in Meridien by Epub Services.

Distributed in the United States by Random House, Inc., New York.

All rights reserved.

Angry Robot and the Angry Robot icon are registered trademarks of
Watkins Media Ltd.

This is a work of fiction. Names, characters, places, and incidents are
the products of the author's imagination or are used fictitiously. Any
resemblance to actual events, locales, organizations or persons, living or
dead, is entirely coincidental.

Sales of this book without a front cover may be unauthorized. If this book
is coverless, it may have been reported to the publisher as "unsold and
destroyed" and neither the author nor the publisher may have received
payment for it.

ISBN 978 0 85766 499 0
Ebook ISBN 978 0 85766 500 3

Printed in the United States of America

9 8 7 6 5 4 3 2 1

To Suze and Albie

Y

With a voice, she was too human. So that's what they took away first.

One maker plucked something gristly from her throat. A second stood by, thumbing the catch of a surgical gun. A third maker, holding her chin, nodded. The second leaned close and marked a dotted square on her neck.

With a name, she was still a person. So when they'd sent her under, had her feeding off the machines, a harridan came by her cradle and scrubbed it out. In its place went a Y, suffixed with a screed of glyphs. When their work was complete, the makers would wake her, tell her. Call her Y for short.

With memories, Y was tethered to a life before. So when her time came in the queue, the makers vandalized her hippocampus. Scraped away her sense of self. Cleaned out her mind almost whole.

And with her standard muscles, Y was too cumbersome, too slow. So when she'd had her modifications, her augmentations, her transplants and transfusions, the makers started her on a regime of hard hormones. They pumped in bags and bags to make sure she grew.

Finally, the makers came for Y's hair. Because with a bald head, she'd be unmarked, easier to sell. So when her muscles and ligaments had been repaired, and the makers were certain the immunosuppressives had taken hold, they sheared her clean. Laser-treated the fast-growth areas. Matched her face type and shade to a suite of wigs. And documented it all.

Then, with such things done, Y was ready for training. So that later they could take her, demonstrate her potential, and send her on.

ONE

Ask Roy what he believes in. Ask if he's going to hell, or if there's just a blank space after all this, and he'll say what he always says. He'll say: "Jesus is a friend of a friend."

That way suits Roy. That way he doesn't have to worry about forgiveness. But sometimes – while he's on the job, sitting in stolen cars, lurking in empty car parks, suspended between unkept bushes and rust-fused trolleys – he wishes there were someone, something, to deliver him. Because the waiting gets boring. And after so long dealing with people, or waiting to deal with people, it's boredom that does his head in most.

Hiding here in twilight, Roy wishes he were already at the Rose. His comfy chair at the back. Half a shandy, two bags of peanuts. He yawns, keeps yawning, keeps wanting to pack it all in and go straight over there. How much was tonight's job even worth, anyway? He coughs, startles himself. There's no doubt he used to enjoy all this sneaking about – the window-watching, the note-taking. It's just that now it feels so glamourless.

One eye on the target. One eye on the time –
But what else can he do?

So Roy sips from a flask of tepid coffee, smokes a pair of prison rollies back to back. He flicks through an offnet mobile rammed with porn. Checks his mirrors. Tries to rub away the comedy circles around his eyes. He rolls three more cigarettes in as many minutes. He scratches his groin. And then he tries to focus. He takes out his revolver – an import from the former Yugoslavia, an officer's gun – and chambers a pair of cartridges.

All as he watches and waits and watches and listens. Then waits some more.

He thinks: *All this time on your own can't be good for the soul.* He thinks: *What soul?* Maybe, despite the cash his handler stumps up, glamour's the wrong word anyway. Not for Roy: a fixer, tinkerer. Your man-down-the-pub.

And yet Roy's become so *skilled* at waiting. These days he breathes for this concrete – these car parks, the levelled terrain behind disused bingo halls, demolished shops, abandoned malls. He lives to wait. Because suddenly it's worth it – all the patience, all the rituals:

When his mark steps out of the squat, a woman in tow.

Roy opens the car door. Unfurls, stretches. He turns to his mark and tilts his head; watches the couple as they move across the tarmac.

Walking just ahead of the mark, the woman strikes a match for a cigarette. She seems to exhale her first drag for a long time. Her hair's updoed, beehived. She smokes with teen surl.

The mark looks concave, harried – feeble light betraying a run of misspent years. He catches up with her again and they walk in step, half-committed somehow, not quite hand-in-hand.

Roy approaches them, the revolver stuffed in his coat pocket.

"Evening," he says. He's far enough away that the wind might easily carry it off, yet close enough for the tone to register. The two of them pause and double-take.

"Evening," he says again, and cracks a smile.

The couple squint. They take in the man before them: shining bald, a heavy winter coat, with something like claw marks running across his scalp.

The mark speaks first. "We know you?"

Roy keeps coming. "Me? No. Not yet."

The woman turns to the mark. Roy's seen it all before. He knows her heart will be going – that her throat's catching when she swallows. From her stance he'd say her legs have seized as well.

Roy scans left, scans right. Nobody else, only the husks of burned-out cars. A road sign spitting error messages.

The mark pushes a shoulder in front of the woman and puffs himself up.

So Roy counters – quickens his pace. "Keep still for me," he says.

The mark edges forward to eclipse the woman. Possibly still wondering if Roy means him. "You what?"

Roy reaches for his revolver. He imagines a crack running from his feet to theirs. He knows at this range, them standing this way, he'd likely tag them both with one shot. He can almost feel the revolver's kick – the violence of it running through his forearm, absorbed in the elbow, triceps. A warm feeling, rare but addictive.

The woman murmurs something. Her dry lips catch and roll up on her teeth.

"Elbows or knees?" Roy asks.

The mark raises a hand. Can't work this out.

Roy shakes his head. "I don't do fingers."

The mark looks upset. "What's up with you, pal?"

The woman drops her cigarette and darts.

"That your missus, that?" Roy asks, tilting his head towards her.

"N-nah," the mark says. "Just some bird–"

Roy nods slowly, watching her go. Then he says, "Are we going elbows or knees?"

"I don't get you," the mark says.

So Roy raises his revolver and fires once into the air. The crack splits the night, sets distant dogs barking.

Now the mark gets it. It spreads over him like glue. He falls to his knees and goes rigid. Roy finds it oddly brave – this acceptance the mark's past has come to find him. That his past has teeth.

Roy looks beyond his mark to the woman. She's out as far as the car park boundary, the scrub that fringes a denuded petrol station. "Fast her, isn't she?" he says. She vanishes, and Roy shrugs. "Anyway. You know why I'm here."

The mark nods without looking up.

"And you know who sent me?"

The mark nods again. "Think so. Yeah."

Roy frowns – all he can do to look sympathetic. "Alright," he says. "Doesn't make it easier, though. Just means I say less."

The mark deflates. "It was self-defence," he says. "I swear down. We were off our heads. He comes up through the window and we get jumpy, so I pull my cannon and–"

"Listen," Roy cuts in. "I'm not judging. I don't care what happened."

The mark quietens. He rocks forward, a confessor baring his neck.

"Alright," Roy says again. "Let's get on with it. You left or right-handed?"

"L-left," the mark tells him.

Roy shakes his head. "Cack-handed as well? Christ, man. How's about we do your right? That way you can still write our friend a sorry letter."

The mark wilts. He gazes up at Roy with his elbows in the gravel, his hands twisted together.

Roy kneels by him, scans once more for trouble. The car park's still desolate. The mark is silent, slack. A trolley train creaks. No life in the squat. Lost carrier bags skiffle across the concrete. Roy, knowing now that deliverance won't come today, puts a fatherly hand on the mark's head and his pistol in the crook of the mark's right arm, and says to him: "Sometimes we've got to learn the hard way."

The mark mewls.

"Let's count to three, yeah? You and me together."

And the mark nods, nods, nods along –

"Good lad. Ready?"

Roy and his mark say it slow:

"*One–*"

But Roy being Roy he fires on two.

The North Wales coast under boundless sky. Two children, a boy and a girl, poke at dying fish with twigs, the ocean swell leaving grey foam between their toes. The fish are bland, silver-flanked. The boy's organized his in a line. Nudged by the foam, a few of them still twitch in the sand.

The girl – Melanie – has scored the head off one of hers, and it stares up dumbly. She decides it looks miserable like that, so she flicks the head away.

The boy feels weird in his stomach. Melanie keeps

threatening to remove her own glass eye, mainly because she can.

"Don't you want to see?" she keeps asking him. "Don't you, don't you?"

The children have just met. Their parents are somewhere nearby – one of the group laughing deeply, taking pictures with a loud camera, a big camera. His father, most likely. The boy is itching. Melanie's pasted with cream. The parents don't see. Once more she threatens him. Once more he squeals and looks away.

Finally Melanie puts her fingers to her face.

"Look," she tells him. "It's not scary."

The boy pleads and smells the salted air.

Melanie laughs. She's done it anyway. Her fake eye has popped out, is cradled in her hand.

The boy looks at her socket. He can see the insides of her head.

In the new Manchester, 2025, you have to find new ways to make ends meet. It's why Sol and his partner Irish drive about in a recovery truck looking for donors to steal.

Their little scheme goes like this: you see a driver, you scan their car, you agree to tag it. You go out early on your first run – early when commuters are preoccupied with getting in safely; getting in without getting jacked. And because it's bitter in the city – autumn on the turn – the weather helps too: wipers smear in the misty rain, and damp interiors easily steam up the windows.

Of course, nine times out of ten your commuter will park somewhere safe, somewhere sensible. Maybe the city's underground car vaults, or the caged walk-to-work pens.

But Sol and Irish are patient men. They know the odds. And they'll do their worst on that tenth.

This morning they lap a route not far from their workshop in Old Trafford, barely a mile outside the city centre. You'd think they're shitting on their own doorstep, but their unmarked recovery truck barely raises an eyebrow – it's as battered as everything else.

After a good few laps, they see a woman parking an anonymous Korean hatchback at the end of a row. Lady Luck's feeling kind – the driver's even left enough of a gap for their truck in front. Sol noses them past; laughs uneasily as Irish rolls down his window, leans to pip the horn, shouts something crass.

They lap the block twice again, just to make sure the woman has gone.

"We having it?" Irish asks.

Sol nods. There was a time he might have felt sad or sorry for what they do – but as Irish often says, "Guilt doesn't pay the rent." You can practise indifference, he's found, and now practice has made perfect.

The men park and pull on their caps. Roll out their hi-vis vests and bail. Out of the truck, they each signal to make sure the other has spotted a nearby CCTV rig whose lens case is dangling off its mount. Sol pauses there, the broken camera like some stranger's flowers – withered, browned – strapped to the railings at the scene of an accident.

Irish kneels, unracks the trolley. Sol pulls their wooden chocks from the passenger seat footwell.

"Excuse me," comes a voice.

Sol swivels. A man in the door of a terraced house opposite.

"What's all this?"

Off to the side, Sol hears Irish swear under his breath.

He feels instantly hot; starts patting his pockets.

"Sir…" Sol starts.

The man leans off his step on a beige crutch. Older, white hair. Straining to see through jamjar glasses. For some reason he strikes Sol as being only half-loaded, scrambled, so that now on his plain skin you can see his raw code poking through.

"I asked what's going on," the old man says, pointing at the truck. "Bloody jobsworths – you best have a good reason for all this."

Sol finds what he needs. He drops the chocks and crosses the road, a thin wallet in his hand. He straightens his cap and flicks the wallet open. Mounted inside is a passport photo with a fake name and some bumf about licensing. A decent approximation of the council's logo. "We're cleaning up," Sol tells him. He holds it out, trying to steady his hand. "The car's wanted."

The old man resettles his glasses and pulls Sol's ID into his face. He whispers as he reads, moving Sol's hand back and forth through his focal length. Sol can smell his breath.

After ten seconds, the old man clears his throat. "I better apologize. It's just that–"

"No need," Sol tells him. "Honest. It's nice to see a bit of community spirit."

The old man blinks. Vacant expression. "They just come and go as they please…"

Irish bounces over, cap off, forehead glistening. He winks at Sol, acknowledgment his partner isn't blessed with a natural blagging nature, and says to the old man: "Ever see any nice motors out here?"

The old man shifts his weight. "Oh, every so often. No one local, mind. Must be earning a fortune up some tower to drive the daft bloody things they do."

Irish frowns. "Not the safest place to park, though, is it?"

As if on cue there's a rumble behind them, increasingly loud, before a ferocious-looking motorbike burbles past. Riding pillion behind a rider in racing leathers, a smartly dressed woman pulls on an open-faced helmet. Sol watches her, fully absorbed: she's so still and composed, looking dead ahead. Then he winces as the bike tears away. Only aftermarket parts could make a machine so noisy.

"No, no," the old man says distractedly. Sol doesn't even remember the question. The old man's eyes follow the bike, its passenger. Then he looks back as if someone's behind him in the house. "Are they *gangsters*?" he whispers. "These ones you're after?"

Sol and Irish share a look. "Something like that," Sol tells him, shrugging with one shoulder. Then another pause as they hear the motorbike downshifting some distance away.

"Oh dear," the old man says. "It's really gone to the dogs, hasn't it?" Sol smiles, and the old man continues: "Listen, I don't suppose you gents fancy a cuppa at all. Kettle's not long gone. The granddaughters bought me some of those filter efforts."

"We're good, cheers," Irish says. "Places to go, people to see."

The old man nods. "Then I'll leave you to it."

Irish salutes him casually. "Appreciated. You take good care now."

The old man holds up a bronchial hand and turns to go inside.

Sol shoots Irish a look.

"What?" Irish says.

"Nothing."

"What's up with you?"

"Doesn't matter. Let's crack on."

Irish chuckles. "Don't like what you can't plan for, do you?"

Back in the road, Sol loads the chocks under the hatchback's tyres, making a mallet of his fist to wedge them in. Irish, still chuckling, stretches out on the trolley before disappearing under the car to shear its handbrake cable.

"Give us a hand then," Irish says, wiggling his feet.

Sol takes his partner by the hems of his overalls and pulls. The trolley slides cleanly, and Irish comes out beaming.

"I'll grab the winch," Sol says, stepping away. But as he's walking off, he hears Irish freeze.

"Sol."

Sol looks over. "What's up?"

"Check it out."

Sol follows his gaze. "What?"

"*Look*."

Down the road, a bright silver saloon is pulling out of a parking space. A Lexus, probably a 2012 or 2013 model. A little too early for a conversion, which means it'll cost a fortune to run, but still blessed with smooth, clean lines. Tinted windows. Non-standard alloys. From the looks of things it's even fitted with run-flat tyres.

It's a rare sight, a car this nice. And judging by its registration plates, which start RA, it's not local either. *RA*. Sol jogs his memory. *Carlisle*?

Irish nods at Sol as if to agree with something essential. "Piece of piss," he says.

And Sol can read his partner's mind. He shakes his head. "Don't even think about it."

"Call it community service," Irish says. He pulls his

cap visor low. "Care in the community."

"Not with someone in it. We're not jacking–"

"Opportunity knocks," Irish tells him. He points at the Korean hatchback. "More guts in that Lexus than fifty of these fucken sheds."

"Irish…"

The Lexus is being driven unsurely, tentative. The men can sense it's unfamiliar to the driver.

Then it begins to accelerate towards them, and Irish has broken away, gone, sprinting up the pavement.

"Get in the truck!" he shouts back to Sol. But before Sol has time to react – to appreciate the lines Irish is crossing, to fear the mistake his partner's making – he watches Irish salmon-dive off the pavement and up the saloon's bonnet. A sickening crump, and the Lexus skids, stalls. Irish rolls off it.

"What the *fuck!*" The driver's out already, a stocky build, dark leathers. Sol unconsciously connects the motorbike to the car for an instant, then hears his partner yelling madly. He opens the truck cab's door; watches heart in mouth as Irish springs up and shoves the driver. The driver falls gracelessly, shocked by the speed of it all.

Sol takes his hands off his face and climbs into the truck, head buzzing: *We jacked it. We jacked it. We jacked it.*

The Lexus screams past, and Sol follows. He can see Irish's silhouette through the car's rear window, his shoulders jerking up and down with laughter. Just as they turn, Sol glances behind – sees in his mirror the driver staggering up the road.

Two streets over, Sol's skin liquid, he spots one of their fly-posters flapping on a lamppost:

WE BUY OLD BANGERS FOR SCRAP.

•••

Mel's the only person shopping in the supermarket. The cameras follow her mercilessly down each aisle – their controller a sweaty security guard wrapped in fitted mesh.

Behind a till, also watching Mel, is a teenaged girl wearing a filigreed salwar kameez and circus-bright makeup. Mel's noticed this look more recently: neon fairyland by way of raver chic. It seems hollow as far as counterculture goes – childish revolt, permitted if only because it'd be so easy to crush – but it makes her feel oddly grateful: at least someone's burning bright in the gloom.

As customers go, the security guard doesn't have much to watch. He thinks he's got Mel down pat: a slight but cunning woman, a stray with a limp – like a past operation only did so much. The lights don't do much for her complexion, either. Regardless, he amuses himself with crass scores – *hips and lips and arse* – for something to do when he's not enforcing his own brand of corporal law.

Mel is oblivious to the guard's rotten gaze. She's here for the essentials: wet wipes, baby oil, tea bags, cotton pads. Desperate for the cash, she'd slipped a twenty from last night's takings.

That said, Mel doesn't intend on paying for much. She's already squirrelled a few items up her sleeve, shrewdly putting cheaper items in the basket as cover.

"Looking for anything, miss?" the checkout girl calls between the aisles. Mel knows it's the girl's job to sound suspicious, but it rankles.

"Vegetables," Mel calls back. "Broccoli?"

They share a sad little laugh.

"There's powdered stuff," the girls says, pointing. "Round there."

"Not proper though, is it?" Mel asks. She actually tastes broccoli for a second. Salted, buttered. The texture of a stem crushed between her back teeth.

The girl frowns. "Heard of it, but I never ate it."

Mel goes towards her. "How old are you?"

"Eleven."

"Eleven?"

"Yeah, why?"

Mel smiles. "I'm being daft," she says. "Eyes aren't up to much... But look at you. You're beautiful, aren't you – nothing to worry about there. Can't believe you haven't tried broccoli, though. It's only been missing a few years..."

The girl shrugs. "That powder smells rank anyway."

The thought of being so young again makes Mel touch a hand to her belly. A dull pain there, radiating. Some failure of empathy. When she refocuses on the girl's features it's like she's seeing the composited faces of every woman employed by the Cat Flap. That this girl's eleven but appears sixteen says something – and the closer Mel looks, the more she sees a worldweariness etched in her expression. Suddenly, Mel remembers herself lying with him – *him* – in their old bed, morning sun turning the windows into luminous squares, and vocalizing that trite old question: *But what kind of world would we bring them into?*

Mel blinks. Mel remembers needles sliding home. A series of bad decisions entwining, a blackened spaghetti of mistakes–

She shakes her head. The shelves around her are empty, their backlights fuzzing.

What if my girls have lied about their ages?

She stumbles.

"Miss?" the checkout girl says. "Miss?"

Mel snaps back. Striplights waning. "I'm alright, love," she says, and turns away. More empty spaces. A basket of used meat cartridges, donated, beneath a handwritten sign reading FREE MEAT JUICE.

Mel snakes round to the supplements. She stacks her basket and pushes more boxes up her sleeves, their edges catching on old scars. Each item justified with a hypnotic refrain: *this is my way of looking after things*. In the next aisle she does the same for toiletries, rolling packets around her thin arms to disguise their shape.

Satisfied then, she moves for the till. It's all rehearsed, this – pulled off at so many other shops before. She unloads the basket and tuts loudly, then makes a show of patting down her pockets. A song and dance about tipping out her bag. A pained face to the checkout girl. Lastly she says: "Gone and forgot my bleeding purse, haven't I? What. A. *Pudding*."

The girl looks stupefied. Copper bolts through her hair. "That's OK," she says. "You can… you can leave it here if you want. I'll keep an eye on it."

Mel smiles slowly. She touches the girl's arm. "Would you?"

The girl nods, reveals a cautious smile of her own.

Mel checks her watch, mindful of the boxes piled up behind it. "See. Knew you were a gem. I'll nip back in a bit, yeah?"

The girl nods.

Mel taps the girl's hand and goes to leave. Just before the sliding doors, though, she hears a whistle.

"In a rush?"

Mel clocks the security guard in his mesh wrapper, grinning yellow teeth. He points up and she looks into his camera. He whistles again.

"Come over here."

Mel goes to him, hands in her pockets. "I'm not a dog," she spits, mindful of the checkout girl. "You whistle at a fucking *dog*."

The guard steps out of his cage and motions to her sleeves. "What you got up here, then?"

Mel scowls. "My bloody arms."

He's a big guy, the guard, and before she even realizes he's locked off her wrist, twisted it up and back. He pulls her into him, and she smells his mouth, sour and livid. She wrestles to look back, but the checkout assistant can't see them. There's a tattoo on the inside of his forearm – a bird, feathers pluming, falling, with crosses for eyes.

"Clever little tealeaf, aren't you?" the guard says. "We lopped off hands for less in Afghan. Had this kid once, right – rooting through all our stuff he were…"

"I'll scream," Mel tells him. "And then I'll make sure you never piss standing up again."

The guard shows her a black tongue. "Screamed out there an' all. Specially when your first cut didn't go right the way through…"

She squirms against him. "Let go."

But the guard simply shrugs, unfazed. "Only doing my job," he says. "Doesn't have to be like this."

"You're not wrong," she whispers.

The guard pretends to look hurt. "Don't recognize me, do you? Were only after a discount – a freebie if you're being nice. I do you a favour… you do me a favour."

Mel stops struggling. She looks at him levelly.

"Course I know who you are," he says. "Everyone does. Should probably pay more attention to your regular johns, though – not the best customer service otherwise, is it?"

Mel nods. Wary now. The guard's grip slackens and she yanks free, rubs her wristbone. A punter? The stolen goods have travelled up her arms and started scratching the furrowed skin of her elbows. Irritating more scars. "You're right," she says.

Yet the facts feel wrong. And the main fact is this: in her house you respect the punters as they respect you – but it's hard to spot the worst of them.

"Now hop it," the guard says. "And warm up a spot. I'll be round to see you all soon."

Y

Y emerged from induced coma into the cruellest light: a space so bright she had to shut her eyes and scream to offset the burn. Her heart jumped at the shift in reality, and she remembered to inhale – stole a breath like it was her first.

Her senses cycled. She tuned in; knew she'd been absent, knew she was flat on a sterile-smelling surface, and that it was uncomfortable and cold. Oddly she couldn't remember the word for this surface – nothing came to mind, or quite matched the experience. With this dissonance came a throbbing pain in one shoulder, and the sense she couldn't lift her arm. She felt hollow. She took another breath and weighed her unease. It was relief, too, she decided. Finally – *finally* – she'd escaped her recursive dreams, the vast emptiness of them. Finally she'd escaped the grey box that'd encased her for so long. The looming black tower had gone, and with it a mass of dread.

But soon she realized her new box was much worse – While Y recognized her skin, its familiar texture, it was tight and hairless, and the forms sliding beneath were alien. There was a solidity to her muscles that somehow told her everything was different. And when she reached to massage her sore shoulder, she found she couldn't understand the joint of it – couldn't fathom her own body – and felt the lurch of freefall. She didn't know who she was. Her name was absent. Her past and all the ideas she had hadfor a future. She'd dissipated – gone. And as she ran her hands over her head, she found raw skin there, too.

In fact, Y was sure of nothing but the certainty she'd lost herself. That before there was a named woman in this goosebumped skin, and that now she inhabited a stranger.

She held her breath, an instinctive way to slow the whole world down for long enough to find another moment of clarity. And that was this: she lay alone on a plinth in a plastic case.

Her panic was absolute.

Y tore herself up and clawed at her bonds. Adjusting to the white-out, she saw they were bunched cables and lines filled with a black, viscous liquid that moved into her veins. There were drip-bags, bloodied rags, swaddling. It revolted her. And she screamed and fought and bit and clawed in vain, and the sounds she made were the stranger's, came from another body, and the fear they inspired only made the terrible light brighter. Here she was, trapped in some kind of incubator, a nightmare folded within a nightmare, and her interior world was returning as a vapour, not dream-vague but livid and real, and all around her were the grey walls again, their images double-exposed on the incubator's reflective surfaces, and above, projected onto the ceiling, the black tower had returned. It was waiting.

Y spiralled into herself. She took in brushed metal surfaces and the seamless machinery that attended her – the clamps on her ankles. She observed her body numbly, the tightly wound bandages around her swollen arm. She caressed the incubator walls – suedey to the touch, heated by a network of visible filaments inside. A crushing limbo persisted: she was imprisoned in a body between the wakeful and the dead, and nothing that came from her mouth matched her thoughts.

She wanted to be sick.

"Stop struggling."

It was a woman's voice. Stout and clear but not unkind.

Y locked up, a startled animal.

The ceiling flickered, and on it a grey square appeared. Y watched as the square jerked into rectangles. Now separated, the shapes began to circle each other and duplicate, tessellating as they went.

Y said something, but her throat garbled it.

"You'll learn," the woman said.

The shapes began to lose their order. They re-merged and spat fractals. Then a fierce geometric form came together from all the disparate pieces and detached from the ceiling; dripped down to meet her. Y winced and closed her eyes, but even there she saw its pattern, a vivid tableau imprinted on the reverse of her lids. The shape vibrated, had its own resonance.

"You're cooked," the woman said. "Ready. Done. Dinged."

Y was sweating, panting. The shapes grew more volatile. Next came a hissing sound. Y tried to push open the unit. Nothing budged. She could've been entombed in concrete. And then the woman said: "We've worked hard on this. You're something of a triumph."

Y didn't reply. She couldn't. Her throat simply burbled and popped.

"Do you like pain?"

Rising horror. The concept seemed to mean something.

"Pain…"

Something twinged in Y's feet. She felt warmth, saw a bright corona, and watched a knot of snake-like machines descend from the incubator ceiling.

"Not pain?" the woman whispered. Y screamed in her way, roiling in her own meat. The metal snakes began to constrict her legs, dislocated their geared jaws as if they meant to swallow her feet. Y tried to kick out, but the ankle clamps held fast.

"Or do we try pleasure?"

With this, the incubator became oily. The snakes disintegrated and a tropical dampness closed around Y's skin. It was filmy – a liquid fleece that shifted over her. "You must never forget who controls what," the woman said. "Who controls *you*."

Static hissed. Hermetic seals broke. The world grew noisy. "Welcome to Cradle Suite Three," the woman said. "It's about time you met your brothers and sisters."

Now the incubator chamber rose away, smoothly pulled from seals around the cradle. Y sat up as best she could, drawing wretched, ragged breaths. At the foot of her cradle was a masked woman in a tight bodysuit. And all around, in rows that ran forwards and backwards from her own, Y saw hundreds more cradles, identical cases hanging above each and every one.

"Your training begins tomorrow," the woman told her. "Out on the lawns." Y was faint from sitting, and her back was weak. She felt herself trying to nod, and, despite resisting, found it wasn't a reaction she controlled. The woman's ears moved upwards, and her eyes creased above her mask. She was offering something, Y realized.

The woman came to her side. She pressed an object into Y's hand. Through layers of swirling colour, pulled far into the distance, Y saw it was a pendant – a pearl fragment, so tiny and glossy, that hung on a slender chain. If she recognized it, the connection was faint. It had a hint of something deliberately forgotten, or severed.

"Wear it unselfconsciously for him," the woman said. And then she glided away.

TWO

Roy heads for Emerald City – a warren of box shanties in the Celtic Park, Stalybridge, east of town by ten miles as the crow flies. His destination is a local football team's sad legacy: two parts homeless shelter, two parts refugee camp. A stadium whose pitch has been clusterbombed with rickety prefab structures.

Roy turns in. The entrance a triple barrier topped with sharpline and flanked by watchtowers. He stops the car, cranks the window. The barrier guard seems polite enough – requests a name as he checks his sectors. No eye contact. From the towers, lasers rove across the gateline.

Roy wonders if they'll bother to recognize him some day.

The guard buzzes the first gate. The second won't open till the first is sealed. Same for the third. Roy knows the setup's strong enough to halt a suicide wagon doing eighty.

Inside the compound, the smell hits him full force. Sewage, plastic fires, incinerator chimneys. A sweet, rotting scent that sticks to your clothes, that clings to your nostril hairs.

He parks on the shale and steps out.

"Sexy! Sexy mister!"

Roy turns from the car. A woman scamping his way. She's isn't much more than skin and bone, whittled into spindles by addictions or worse. A metre off she bares stark ribs, top yanked up to the underwiring of a hollow bra. Roy fishes for spare change but finds only lint. "Nothing on me today, kid," he tells her, and shakes his head.

"Not even a peck?"

Roy thinks he might recognize her, some wraith of alleyways past. "No," he says. "I'm celibate today."

With this, Roy turns quickly towards the stadium's main entrance, thick as a pressure hull, and doesn't break his stride. He hears the woman curse him gently; her heels travelling away. Acknowledges the film of sweat spreading across his back, a tension stringing him out. Then he pokes the buzzer and blanks his face for the scan.

An impassive voice comes through a speaker. "Irises are fine. Password?"

Roy sighs. "Bananarama?" He looks around sheepishly.

A cough. Then, "That were last week's."

"For fuck's sakes–"

"Nope. One go left."

Roy could punch the speaker unit. He grinds his fist into his leg.

"Well?"

Roy clears his throat. "Is it milk organ?"

"Bing," the voice says flatly. The door pops to reveal a bank of flaking turnstiles.

Inside, Emerald City becomes a warren. Roy fingers a

crumbling wall covered in markered names and arrows. Properties here change hands often – it'll be a good day when he remembers the way without directions, even if the old part of him, a callused centre, doesn't want to be there when he does.

The route takes him down and out through the old players' tunnel, a concrete corridor splashed with inert radio-graffiti. On each side are the children of Tameside: a mother slumped, feeding her infant from the breast; baleful dogs in the shadows, licking puddles and the carcasses of small birds; and a young man, wrapped in damp cardboard, picking scabs from marbled legs. The confined space seems to concentrate the smell – urea and sweet decay. It's a site of outstanding natural entropy.

Roy emerges onto the pitch. The apartments – mostly breeze-block and tarp, or some configuration of corrugated steel sheet – spread out before him. Beyond, the spectator stands thrum with market stalls, gambling tables, makeshift chemists and clinics.

Roy traverses the grid counting homes – twenty-one, twenty-five, twenty-nine – and stops at thirty-one. He blinks, hesitant, before knocking on the door.

The Reverend answers. He's a large figure – always bigger than Roy remembers – with cartoonish features that remind Roy of food: a face of corned beef, torn prunes for eyes.

"Hiya," Roy says, and manages to hold the man's gaze.

The Reverend grins and beckons Roy inside. Roy enters without a word and watches the Reverend waddle back to his chair. As the man sits, his stomach spills from his shirt and settles in the crotch of his jogging bottoms. Apparently he's in a jovial mood, which counts for something. A pile of bountiful love –

"Welly-well-well," the Reverend says. "Look what our Lord Almighty's dragged in. And what aberrations do you bring before Him today?"

Roy takes out his revolver and touches it against his stomach. "I think I took a man's elbow in vain."

"Oh, that's fine," the Reverend says. "Jesus still loves you – it's only me who thinks you're a cunt."

Roy smirks uncertainly and looks at his feet.

"You may sit down," the Reverend says, nodding at the tatty Winchester in the corner.

Roy takes a seat. He places his gun on the chair's arm.

The Reverend leans over for something. Fat bunching. Finger podge. He lifts up an ornate collection tray and tilts it towards Roy. It's covered with powder. "Snozzle?" he asks, the *ess* like a dentist's drill. "*Un petit peu?*"

"No ta," Roy says. "Working today, aren't I."

"I don't know," the Reverend says. "Are you? You usually only bob in when you're high or dry…"

"It's quieter at the moment, yeah," Roy says, nodding too much, too defensively. "So if there's stuff going I'm up for it."

The Reverend suddenly heaves his bulk across his chair. "Darling?" he shouts down the hall, mock falsetto. It often manifests this way, his imitation of class. "Fetch our planner, will you?"

Roy hears a rustling sound in the far room.

The Reverend rolls back. "You found yourself a ladyfriend yet?"

Roy hesitates, then shakes his head.

"A male companion, perhaps?"

"No, Rev. Hard to even swing one way at the minute."

The Reverend cocks his head. "You're missing out, dear boy. But you know I can always arrange a treat for you. A little bonus. And the night terrors?"

Roy shrugs. "Now and again."

The Reverend snarls. "Liar. Don't fucking *lie* to me. What was it last time – drowning animals? Oh no, no – that's my other man. I know yours, Royston. *Clouds* laced with *visions*... the cry of that scumbag under those bootsoles of yours... Ha! Do you remember him? Do you? Do you remember what we said about the way we left his face? And let's not forget your *birds!*"

Roy lowers his head.

"And what of drinking? That sinner-man's crutch... that foul putrescence, those fibs you tell yourself about a better way, like the instructions might be lurking behind the label–"

"All things in moderation," Roy cuts in. "It's just one of those things, Rev. One of those things. And what's that, anyway?" he adds, meaning the collection tray. "Blomp?"

The Reverend dismisses Roy with a wave. "Blomp? Have some respect, young man. Now, hold out a hand for me. Come on."

Roy does as he's told, and the Reverend leans towards him.

"Oh, just regard these pianist fingers for a moment. *Ruined* by hard work. And yet the shakes have gone – there's hope yet! How far you've come – so *atypical* these days, Royston. Not that wreck we once knew. Now, I wonder about – no, I *marvel* at – your brain. Ought to test you, really. See if you're a psychotic yet, or whatever the trendy word is these days..."

Roy goes to speak but the Reverend's wife appears in the doorframe with what looks like an offcut of carpet in her hand. Roy realizes he doesn't recognize her – reminded that the Reverend's wives seem to come and go. "Win some, lose some," as the Reverend will often say.

"Star," the Reverend says, taking the item and stroking it. He opens it, revealing it to be a clothbound tablet, and starts tapping on its screen. Its keyboard sounds are still on.

Roy sniffs uneasily and fidgets in his chair. The Reverend glances up and winks as if to signal he's heard Roy's thoughts. Without looking he pats his waiting wife on the thigh. "Thank you," he says to her quietly. Then to Roy: "Darling, darling – you sit and admire her all you like. She *is* a doll."

Time passes as the Reverend writes on the tablet. At one point – Roy doesn't seem to notice – the Reverend's wife disappears into the back again, leaving Roy to listen to the key sounds clacking sharply in the stillness of the room, the Reverend's death-rattle breathing. Despite himself, he imagines the Reverend's fat cells strung together in phlegmatic strings, a yellowy gossamer stretched over the barrel of his throat.

Roy swallows deliberately, in part to check his own throat still opens.

The Reverend glances up. "Dealt with any garages recently?" he asks.

Roy tenses. "What kind? As in cars?"

The Reverend smiles and flips the tablet to show Roy a picture of a militarized half-track. "Of course not. As in pigs. Conversions. *Armour*."

"Nah," Roy says. He looks at the revolver. "Not really my bag."

The Reverend ignores him. "I recently got wind of a chap in Old Trafford who handles the type of project I'm managing. Fine craftsmanship guaranteed, apparently. And we've a brand spanking new client willing to pay handsomely for the connection."

"Same old, same old, then," Roy says.

The Reverend closes his tablet and slaps his enormous thighs. "Look, why don't you come and sit on your Reverend's lap?"

Now Roy imagines the man's head coming off in gibs, the revolver stuffed down his neck. "Give over, Rev," he says. "Just give it a rest for five bloody minutes."

The Reverend's expression crashes into a hard glare, eyes dark and empty as space, and Roy clenches. Then the Reverend laughs. "More than enough of me to go around," he roars. "Plenty, plenty." He turns towards the back room, shouts again. "Isn't there darling?"

"Give me the address, and a price," Roy says. "Can look over the rest on the bounce."

The woman comes back in. She says something to the Reverend under her breath.

"Get this man some paper," he replies. "*Pay*-per, yes."

Roy looks at his hands and clenches until the joints go numb.

"She's learning all the time," the Reverend says. "But anyway. You're right about business being quiet, Royston. Reminds me of those official recession days, much as I liked them. This environment picks off the weak, the chaff. Rewards the smartarses. And you're a smartarse, aren't you?"

Roy does his best to nod.

"You know what I've *always* said," the Reverend adds. "One man's apocalypse is another man's opportunity. Now take down this name. You'll meet him at the Rose like normal. Don't involve me any more than you have to – I don't care for the dirty details on this one, just as I don't expect you to let me down. But satisfy him, please – I think he has rather a lot of money, and we could both do with a new account on the books. A southerner, no less. Are you ready?"

Roy's pen is hovering.

"Havelock," the Reverend says. "Oh, Havelock, God bless his cotton socks."

Sol's headtorch burns white through the workshop's inspection pit. He pulls a spanner from the Lexus' guts, taps a few welds and heads for the ramp. He's calmer about the vehicle's provenance now; fairly confident there's no tracker – no immediately traceable lines to the workshop, or to them – but he can't help being jittery about the implications for business. The hatchback would've been easy, a good job well done. Jacking the Lexus, a high-value car, was new territory for them – and he can't shake the feeling someone will be looking for it.

From here they'll need to quickly break the car into salvage for the parts library. There's lots in the engine bay to attract wealthier clients, and even the useless bits will earn plenty on the weighbridge. He's confirmed the tyres as run-flats, too – far too good for a yard fire.

Irish insists on calling this "agile business", or "just-in-time". They work this way because there's no other option – unless you're willing to go straight and take a council contract, you'll eventually lose the battle with time and a supply chain missing most of its links.

Sol and Irish aren't exactly ignorant, either. They know the workshop's reputation is long since down the pan. To survive, they steal what they can to keep their promises. Or they break their promises and lose custom. It's simple, and it's brutal, but in the new Manchester, you make your way or you die. Whereas once you were told to sell the sizzle and not the sausage, now you try to sell the frying pan as well.

Sol's out of the pit and cleaning up when Irish bulldozes in, a plastic bag swinging from his hand.

"That's fucken war booty," Irish says, pointing first at the Lexus then across the workshop to a purple Transit hiked up on the MOT lane. "And that's our real work."

Irish's real name is Pete. Wiry and strong, flame-haired in his youth but greying now. He and Sol are the oldest of friends, so familiar they often communicate with little but their eyebrows, especially when the radio's up loud. Love won't tear them apart.

Sol turns off his headtorch. His face is a picture – smudged lines, hooded eyes. And he realizes Irish is angrier than he sounded.

"Serious here Solomon," Irish says. "Got to be first come, first served. Keep your boner for the nice motors, aye, but don't just pilfer the jobs you fancy."

Sol puts his hand on the Lexus' bonnet. "Had to sweep it for trackers. You know that."

"So what if it's tracked? Fuck all that. Anyone asks, it came in for a once-over before sale. *We* don't know where it came from."

"And the truck?"

"What about the truck?"

"You think he didn't see it? The massive white truck we drive about in?"

"You'd parked there, Sol, Lord above. He'll only remember the ginner bastard that flew up his bonnet!"

"It'll come back on us, your moment of bloody madness. A car this immaculate…"

"And if it does, the bastard'll be filed down, in bits, already sold on. We take chances like that now. We have to."

Sol shrugs. "Either way, I already tried with the

Transit. No clue, other than it idles rough as anything."

Irish softens. "Well what parts we got in? We need a new donor for it? No good quoting for jobs we can't do anyways."

"Few bits in the yard," Sol says. "Body panels. A sunroof somewhere."

"Checked the tensioners? Valves? Injectors? Air filter might be wet – they hate this time of year, these Mark 7s."

"Aye, obviously. It's none of that."

"Diagnostics?"

"That too."

"So we go for the stripdown. Remember how your pa'd tell us?"

Sol doesn't say anything.

"Bollocks, you don't know. You worshipped that old man. That line he always had. What was it – he'd go, he'd say..." and Irish puts on his best West Indian accent, which is beyond insulting: "You can't find what's wrong wiyit you pull dat all down and you clean it hard and you put it back together again. Five time out of ten it work every time – he he he."

Sol smiles awkwardly. "Be turning in his grave if he saw what we'd done with the place."

Irish grins but Sol isn't wrong. Sol's father was a master – four decades at Bentley before he came to Manchester to marry Sol's mother and set up alone. He knew how to upholster. How to strip and rebuild any bay system you could name. He'd fit your tyres in seconds, but he'd change your car's oil in hours, preferring to let the last drop fall from the sump than rush the job. He read Haynes manuals like newspapers. And by way of cataloguing his knowledge, he photographed his subjects with macro lenses – liked to capture the wear and tear, the slow death of steel, the burnish and heat of a still-hot engine. He kept files of these images, hidden albums maintained with reverence, and slotted the parts list behind each picture as a record of his encounter.

At weekends, Sol would play in the workshop while his father worked. He still remembers the smell of fresh-baked paint from the booth; the sound of the booth's extractors; that year's mucky calendar on the wall; and the jars of Coffeemate, not far off their synth-milk now. He remembers the day he peppered his knees with fibreglass while taking Polaroids on the damp cardboard beneath an unpainted bodyshell. The endless itching and lumps. And he remembers sheets of crisp, clean tarpaulin, on which Sol's father laid out something like exploded-view diagrams: an engine block and its parts all deconstructed, toothbrushed, hot-breathed, wiped down, and so many fasteners, so many little pieces of the whole. The puzzles that Sol's father took otherworldly pleasure in solving.

Irish circles the Transit van. "Give me a day on this. Sometime this week."

Sol shakes his head. "Fine. Whatever. And I'll crack on with the work that actually pays. We need that Lexus broken down and flogged, fast." Sol points to the bag in Irish's hand. "You gonna tell me what's for dinner?"

"Chippy," Irish says, holding up the bag. "Half a fucken hour I walked for these."

"Curry sauce?"

Irish winces. "Now don't be a heathen as well, Solomon. You want the squits again? It's gravy this, Jesus above. I'll be bollocksed if you're a proper Northman, the stuff you come out with. Curry sauce!"

Sol rubs his hands together and claps Irish on the shoulder. Habits die hard when it comes to food –

and even now, even in his forties, chippy is often the highlight of Sol's month. They eat in the staff room, lost in the sharp smells of salt and vinegar, puddled oil and rust, old sofa foam. Their oily fingers tearing at wet paper, salt stinging in the freshest cuts, both chewing with their mouths open, gurning through a kind of shared nostalgia. Sometimes you could be glad some things haven't changed. Glad some things never change.

Afterwards, Sol washes his hands with sand-soap, and the sinkwater runs black.

Irish sits back, burps loudly. Licks his fingers and rolls an anaemic cigarette. He holds up what's left of the chippy wrapper and leans in. "Storm's due," he says.

"Yeah," Sol replies. "Still need to get us a water butt for the yard."

Irish pecks out his cigarette, only quarter-smoked. "Waste of money," he says, tracing a shape in the air. "Soon enough it's all going underwater."

The garage falls quiet. They listen to the ticks and trickles of the old equipment that scrapes them a living.

Sol taps his head. "I know what I meant to tell you. We got a decent lead in before. Motor in Liverpool worth checking out – a recovered Ferrari, black auction. Some bellend parked it in the Leeds-Liverpool canal."

Irish's eyes widen. "And it's driveable?"

Sol adjusts himself through his overalls. "Doesn't matter. Someone'll have the bits off us."

Irish smiles. "Yesterday a Lexus. Tomorrow a Ferrari. Not doing half bad, are we? You wanna draw straws for the pickup? Flip a coin?"

"We can sort it in the morning," Sol says.

Irish flips one anyway. "Heads or harps?"

"Let's just wait and see what comes in tomorrow."

They get up and clock back on. Pointless, another unshakable habit. The rest of the afternoon they work side by side in silence. Around seven, Irish clocks off for home, moaning about a sore stomach. Sol still has an exhaust to swap; two dented wheels to hammer and rebalance. Maybe another crack at the Transit. "I'll probably stay late," he tells Irish, opening a tool chest to find the right-sized socket for his ratchet.

"You're gonna die staying late," Irish says by the roller door. "Dead. And you'll never get your end away again."

Sol laughs, hears Irish leave, and looks into the drawer. The set he's after is partially covered by an old receipt, and its shadow gives a strange finish and depth to one of the sockets. Sol peers in at it, surprised, and is immediately struck by a likeness, a jab of recognition. The moment enlarges, and the socket becomes the polished sphere, gently warped, of an eye, an artifice, set into the lines of a scowl, and finally a whole face, held in shadow but still irrepressible. It all slithers from the recesses, then – a shame, the enduring ache of her like stubborn residue – and he slams the drawer closed and needs to steady himself on the counter.

Even now, even now, Melanie still finds ways to see into him.

Mid-afternoon, a man visits the Cat Flap. Men often do, of course, this being the place it is, the time of things, the city they're in. It's just that this man is distinctive – and that makes Mel nervy.

For starters he's wearing a suit. You'd reasonably say it's tailored, pricey. You'd recognize a Didsbury-cut if you knew better. The man's hair is parted, shaved up the sides; a timeless look, almost jarringly neat. His hairline's receding slightly, elongating a narrow but not ill-proportioned face. He's tanned, too – a natural-looking sheen. Impressive if it came out of a bottle. Earned a long way from here if not.

When he mounts the pavement he doesn't break his step. His shoulders are relaxed, pulled back. A good posture – a clue he doesn't work with his hands. And you'd be nitpicking to find anything wrong with his shoes. Smart, black, military-glossed. No matching tie, no worries.

Unlike most men, however, he doesn't open the door. Instead he knocks on it firmly.

Mel inhales and holds the breath there. She goes through the entrance hall and opens it.

"Welcome to the Cat Flap," she says.

The man doesn't even blink. "Melanie?"

Behind him, there's another man watching from a car over the road. Mel can't see him properly, but it looks like he's got his face pushed right against the window. He's wearing sunglasses – odd given the weather.

"Ignore him," the visitor says. "I'm Jase."

"Jason," Mel says. She can't place his accent.

"Can I come in?"

Mel steps back. He shuts the door behind him.

"Disappointing weather," Jase says, and Mel can't tell if he's making a joke. They enter the waiting room. "How's business?"

"Cut the crap," she tells him. "What you after?"

"Just a chat."

"Well, I'm not here for that, sweet. Got a business to run."

The man fingers a piece of laminated A4 on the front desk. He seems vague, slippery. "This your menu, this? You do OK here, don't you?"

Mel fumbles for her cigarettes. She's not meant

to smoke inside but lights up anyway. "We look after ourselves, yeah."

Jase looks into her false eye – fixates on it. Mel feels like it's deliberate: a tactic to wrong-foot her. "And that's why you paint numbers on their bellies?"

Mel blows smoke towards an extractor fan that hasn't worked in years. "Common practice," she says. "The punters expect it. And if you know anything in our game, you know the punter's always right..."

Jase raises his eyebrows. "And tell me, Melanie, where do find your employees?"

Mel taps her cigarette. "Listen, I don't need the Inquisition. If you're council, fine, but I won't answer daft questions like that. You're here, you know my name. You know what we do. What's up?"

"Melanie, I just want your business today."

"My business."

Jase nods once. "I'm with a company that specializes in enabling fine experiences for discerning punters – people of all persuasions alike. We're already working with your colleagues throughout the region, and I think you'll be interested in what I've got to say."

Mel looks across the waiting room. Its cheap panelling is desaturated, damp-damaged. It's still early, so most of the women will be home catching up on sleep from last night. With their children. Working their second jobs. Or just working out. Doing whatever needs to be done.

"Well we're fine as we are," Mel says. "So you can save your breath."

"But I think you'll want to hear–"

"They'll be in soon," Mel interrupts. "And they don't like seeing me in a mood."

"Oh, Melanie. Come on. What are your margins like? How much do they really pull in?"

"Bloody Nora. I told you. I'm not here to–"

"Because we're in business to make your business more profitable. Fact is, punters happily pay top whack for experiences like yours. I've done my research – you've great taste. But you could be offering that same *quality* with a better ROI. And at the same time, you could be *diversifying*."

Mel huffs. "You talk like they aren't actual people. I pay a damn sight better than half the bleeders round here'd pay them. And they want to be here, remember. They aren't victims; they don't want rescuing. That's how we do things. It's their job, and they work same as anyone else works. Same goes for me."

"I understand that. And actually, I commented to my colleague just this morning that you're one of the few independent houses left. But what if you had staff in who simply didn't need paying?"

Mel grinds her unfinished cigarette on the top and blows the ash towards him. She pushes past and picks up the reception phone. "You digging for something? Because I swear, you don't want to find out who I've got on the end of this."

Jase coolly brushes the ash from his jacket and reaches inside it. "We've got this catalogue, see."

"Jason."

"It's Jase, Melanie. Please. Jase. I have to insist on that. And let me just ask you something. Let me just say–"

The door goes. It's the second man, wearing a suit just like Jase's. He's shorter, wider, much rougher round the edges. There's a waxy quality to him.

Mel shifts her weight. A bad feeling crawls up her neck.

"This is Jeff," Jase says. "That's Jeff with a J. Actually,

Jeff's all part of the bargain. He could be the key to your new income stream."

Jeff stands in the doorway. He's expressionless, face mostly concealed by his glasses. He raises a hand.

Mel shakes her head. "I'm going to call them now–"

"No," Jase says. His voice has tightened. "You're not. Let me explain."

Mel tries to keep her unease from showing. Twitch fibres bristling. She thinks: *Fuck off*. She says, "So do your bloody pitch, then."

"Like I said," Jase starts, not missing a beat. "I mean, let me just ask you. Where do you make toys?"

Mel doesn't answer.

"Go on." He shows her his nice white teeth. "Have a guess. Where do you think they make toys?"

"In workshops," Mel says.

"In the olden days, maybe. But now?"

Mel sighs. "Brazil? India? I don't–"

"*Factories*." Jase smiles. "Automation's a wonderful thing, no? What they built the foundations of this fine city on, you could probably go as far as to say. So what if I showed you how certain... let's call them assets... could be made to order? And what if those assets, over their whole lives, costed very little to run, needed less investment... and could be retired much later?"

Mel shakes her head. "I'm not sure I'm following."

"OK, but your posture says you're listening. Think economics, Melanie. You're a businesswoman, aren't you? Cheaper labour means you can lower your service prices, doesn't it? Which ultimately means you get more punters through the door..."

"Alright, look. You're starting to peck my head now. Aside from you acting all superior, I don't have a clue where you're heading with this, so let's just call it a day.

If you pair can clear off, now, I'd appreciate that."

Jase stands there smirking. His perfect hair, his perfect nails. His stubble just so. He pushes his brochure across the counter. He taps its cover and says, "Take a look at this. Overnight if you have to. Tomorrow... or whenever you get a chance. Maybe when you're quietest – and our observations say you're quietest from about, what, now till... five?"

"Will you just sod off, please?"

Jeff starts to laugh. Hearing it, Jase turns to him, shoes squeaking on their heels. "We like to say our products sell themselves," he tells Mel. "Don't we, Jeff? And we know Melanie's long-range plan isn't going to hold up."

"God's sakes," Mel says, picking up the brochure. "If I hold on to this, will you leave me alone?"

"You won't regret it," Jase replies, clearly in his element. Mel could swear he winks. "Have a quick flick through and we'll be in touch. Let's say... how's later this week?"

"Whatever." Mel shelves the brochure below the counter and clasps her hands.

"And remember," Jase adds. "We're talking significant savings over ten, fifteen, even twenty years... Not to mention room for growth on your new venture, if and when you take it."

"Twenty years?" Now it's Mel's turn to smirk. "Sweetheart, listen. I'll be long dead and buried by then."

The Rose sits in a hernia of the M60 – Manchester's orbital motorway. It used to be a sandwich trailer called Mega Baps but grew so popular the owner added a roof and four walls, and finally a bar. Together these things made it a rarity before the troubles. Now it's almost unique: a roadside pub that sells a half-decent

homebrew. Its relative distance from the city means it's
stayed more or less the same, with a brisk trade round the
clock. But instead of benches outside, there are dozens
of armoured haulage vehicles, half-tracks and courier
bikes in disarray – their engines and bonnets steaming
from harsh trips up the country. There's even the odd
luxury marque with statement wheels – a blunt signifier
of gangsters on safari. To Roy it's always seemed like the
perfect illustration of things. Caught in dusk, seen from
beneath the pub's awning, the car park resembles an
aftermath.

All this makes the Rose a preferred spot for Roy, who,
while anonymous here, has his corner, is left well alone.

A few windows were broken earlier this evening,
and the chill is noticeable. At the bar, glass fragments
winking from the carpet, the regulars tell Roy that a
dozen lads turned up on motorbikes and tried to raid
the place. Has he heard the rumour, they ask, that a
gang of orphans living in the old city tunnels have
turned bandit? Roy smiles at such a romantic idea; he
knows the real marauder gangs make their cash out
in the fortress suburbs – Didsbury, Hale – or the even
smaller towns deeper into Cheshire, as well as farther
north. The best have got out of Manchester entirely –
left the reins of the city's underbelly to the Wilbers: a
local slaver-gang, which, with its well-paid privateers
and brutal reputation, has all but monopolized the local
labour market, and benefits from most of the petty
crime too.

Roy sips his half, ruminating. In the olden days,
journalists would've had a field day with a story like
that. Like they did in South Yorkshire after the drone
raid in the hills. But then, he knows better than most
that there's no arguing with what people will do if

they're desperate. How fast those blacks and whites can smudge to grey.

In this Manchester, you do what you can to get by.

Roy watches headlights scanning the bar top – traffic coming and going. He only glances elsewhere when the doorbell goes, and a man wearing tweed strolls in.

Roy knows it's the client immediately. He can tell the man's unacquainted with the pub layout; that there's southern money, import power, in the fabric of his coat. Beneath his hat, behind the horn specs, his eyes are flighty.

Roy lifts a little finger, signal enough, and follows the man's silhouette as he takes off his hat and scarf and orders a bourbon – another symptom of a foreign body. *Nob*. It's so obvious the barman cocks an eyebrow in Roy's direction as he hands over the change.

Finally the man approaches. "Cold out," he says.

"Not wrong," Roy agrees, nodding at the broken windows. "Cleans out the pipes, though. Decent journey?"

The man sits down and speaks quickly: "The quick brown fox jumps over the lazy dog."

Roy smiles. Not an icebreaker so much as a quirk – make the client feel silly and they'll know who's boss. The Reverend taught him that. He pushes his nuts across the table. "Protein?"

The man looks offended. "I've no time for games."

Roy stops smiling. "I wasn't even playing yet."

The man pushes Roy's peanuts back to him. "It's Havelock."

"Pleasure," Roy says, ignoring Havelock's hand. "Our mutual friend reckons I can help."

"That rather depends."

"On?"

"How good a middleman you are."

Roy grins again. "I fix what can't be cleaned."

"So we hear," Havelock says, "which is why we're sitting in your squalid little world and not mine. For your sake, let's hope I'm not picking glass out of my brogues tomorrow."

"Listen," Roy tells him. "I'm not here to take the piss. You want something sorted, I'll get it sorted. Otherwise you can do one back to your floods. I don't need your money."

Havelock rocks back. "No?"

"Nah. Hobby, this. What we do for fun round here. So don't be coming out with the big-man shite, saying what's what. You lot have your own muck to roll around in."

Havelock smiles. "Yes, we do. But given the state of the union, I'd wager there being more on tap in the capital for someone as capable as you."

"I'm not thinking about relocation," Roy tells him. "Hate wearing wellies, for starters. Now let's not cause a scene, Mr Havelock."

Havelock hunches forward, smirks. "No scenes. Though it's worth knowing that if you *were* to try anything…" Havelock nods to the space on Roy's right, and Roy feels something grip his thigh. His stomach turns over.

He's sitting next to someone in a cloak-suit.

Havelock laughs. "Never trust a Mancunian, they told me. Even your boss said to keep that in mind. You're all bluster, aren't you?"

Roy sits back, tries to hold his nerve. "And you reckon your gimp here's the only one with a shooter? Turn round. Get an eyeful. You've got most of Manchester's roughnecks sitting up at that bar."

Havelock turns, takes them in. Turns back. "Pond scum," he says.

Roy looks sidelong as if he can actually see Havelock's bodyguard. He puts out a hand, probing, till he finds the slick, damp fabric of the cloak-suit, moulded over the bodyguard's skin like wax. "New model, this, or what?" he asks. "Nice feel, innit. None of that ribbing you normally get. Must make yourself some enemies to need it." Roy shifts his gaze to where he guesses the bodyguard's head must be. "Hope you don't need a slash tonight, kid."

The bodyguard makes a pleased sound. "I'll make sure it goes down your leg if I do," she says.

Roy looks back at Havelock.

Havelock simply smiles.

"Fair dos," Roy says, his hands up. "Fair dos."

Havelock clears his throat. "Do these unconscious biases often land you in trouble, Roy? Your handler said you were precocious."

"He doesn't know me at all," Roy hisses.

Havelock grins. "Well, business, then. You may already know I need an adapted vehicle. We're up here on a recruitment drive, and hope to return to London safely with our new employees. For this reason the vehicle must fit my specification precisely, and be produced quickly. I need high standards – not something one can afford south of Birmingham at the moment, I'm afraid to say."

"And you tried the chop-shops in Calais?"

"I prefer to support local industry," Havelock says.

"But you can't go direct."

"Busy man, Roy. Busy man."

The cloaked woman to Roy's right nudges him. A paper-thin tablet has appeared on the seat between them.

"Go on," Havelock says. There's an urgency in his voice now.

Roy puts the tablet on the table. He dims its brightness then prods the only icon on the screen. An app explodes into numbers.

Roy reads facts and figures. Thinking, he looks up at the Rose's artexed ceiling. Then back at Havelock. "What kind of people are you transporting," he says, "in boxes? And is that a bloody fridge in there?"

"It doesn't matter," Havelock says. "What matters is my assets travelling securely."

Assets. Roy shakes his head. "I'll have to do some digging," he says. "But let's sort the most important thing now: how much cash are we talking?"

Y

Y was locked in the diurnal cycle: a daily sequence of panicked waking and furious panting as predictable as her view of the pink mountains at the edge of the world; the thick mist that rolled over the mansion lawns, blue in the morning's amethyst light; and the rising sun that burned it all away.

By now, though, days themselves didn't matter. At first she had measured time by chewing her fingernails until they bled – counted the units of her sentence through the stages of her body healing: the stinging heat of the first day, the scab of the second, the abscesses that sometimes bloomed on the third, the lancing by makers on the fourth. But soon it was impossible to keep up. Instead, she followed more seasonal shifts in her behaviour. She knew, for example, that she'd resisted the makers more at the beginning – in part to test her new capabilities: the extra load bearing, her new power and grace. They had laughed and mocked, told her she must've "been a handful" in whatever had passed as her preceding life. But even they didn't bother her so much any more. She was growing more confident in her sharpness, her new agility, and it almost embarrassed her to think of how she'd once fought them off, running on instinct, thrashing about. Back then, she'd regularly injured herself out of raw animal frustration – not understanding the changes they'd made to her body. This, too, was rarer now.

There were dark spells, however, in which Y wished the makers had gone further. Regardless of her progress, every morning still felt like the first morning she woke, and she often felt bitter they hadn't taken more of her away. Her remnant mind – it must have been that – had undeniable power, and she lamented that they hadn't severed more of the connections; wondered if it was a deliberate policy. On these occasions she envied the brothers and sisters who never left the suite; whose open mouths leaked black fluid; whose every need was catered to by their cradle's arms. And she still sought a way to escape the black tower from her dreams, just as she struggled to apprehend the meaning of the pendant she found around her neck each morning.

In her brighter moods, though, she was simply grateful to know there'd once been more of her. It gave her the power to imagine something beyond the mansion – and with this surged a hope that she could eventually rediscover her previous self, wake up one morning and remember it all, every last bit, and undo this project, their training, all of it. Sometimes, when she was still and clear-minded, certain images came and went – ghosts of a life before. She just had to remember more – find an easier way to enter that state. She just had to repel their last tweaks and adjustments, their deep moulding of her. She wouldn't let herself love them. She wouldn't…

Explanations for the physical training were scarce,

and for the most part she was isolated. Unlike the people either side of her, forwards and backwards of her, in their rows of life-sustaining cradles, Y had no designated vocation but exercise. And when her brothers and sisters were taken off to the kitchens, workshops, classrooms, boudoirs and laboratories to put their modifications to good use, to train and develop their extras, to have their hands roughened in special machines with sandbelts, to prepare for the new lives the makers promised them, Y was usually kept in her cradle for hours.

It often felt like the makers kept Y separate to punish her, to mark her out. None of the brothers and sisters she met wore a pendant like hers, and none adhered to anything like the regime imposed on her. It meant that now and then she might catch a brother or sister giving her an odd look – a mixture of pity and fear, mainly – and then occasionally something else. Something closer to awe.

Regardless – or perhaps because of this isolation – she soon assigned a secret duty to herself: to comfort her youngest brothers and sisters as they sobbed in their sleep. It had begun to suffocate her, the urge to help them. It made her hot inside, fraught and restless, and so she acted when she could listen no longer, or when no one else came to silence them. Carefully, she'd remove her lines and tie off the drip bags to preserve their nutrient levels, careful not to knock over the additives measured out for muscle maintenance or repair. And then she'd swing out of her cradle and prowl across the suite, edging through the darkness her eyes had been mysteriously tweaked for, received images grainy and green-tinged, and stroke the brother or sister's face until they slept again.

In their daytime whispers, their tight-knitted circles,

Y became the cradle suite's night-comforter whose name they dared not mention, but who in the morning they always remembered.

On one particular night, it was a girl three rows forward and nine cradles down. Y went to her, fluid through the wire nests, the gridded cradles and cabling; a dancer *en pointe*. She felt certain the cameras hadn't followed her.

The girl was bruised, bewildered. Y didn't know if the girl could see her, or if Y was simply a blank shape against the background, her shadow dulling the cradle's arms and attachments.

Y offered a hand, which the girl squeezed against her chest. Through the gloom, Y could make out the girl's face: shining cheeks, a black-matted but glued gash in her hairline, and a seam of puffiness along her jaw. The girl was shivering, so Y pulled up her cover and tucked it under her chin. She couldn't see any obvious modifications; wondered what they might be making her.

"He watched me," the girl whispered to Y from cracked sleep, sniffling quietly and apparently delirious. "He watched me."

Y stroked the girl's hair, the girl's cheek, and absently squeezed her pendant. The girl's words made little sense, even as they unsettled her.

"He kept watching," the girl said. "He said he was my father."

At the foot of the cradle, which had been set to curve upwards, there was a pile of clothing. Y made out a shattered square pattern – didn't recognize it as digital camouflage – and boots spattered in mud. On top lay a crumpled beret. With greater awareness, Y would have recognized the smell as the residue of heavy weapons.

But knowing exertion more than anything else, Y could only identify the girl's sour sweat.

There was something else in the pile. A rolled piece of fabric, tied closed. And when the girl dozed off again, her chest less frenetic, Y moved to the foot of the cradle for a closer look. She rolled off the tie and unfurled the sheet. She could see it was the outlined torso and head of a person, boxes in ever-decreasing sizes, with the smallest a single square over the figure's forehead. There were little holes burned into it, which Y didn't understand, and there were stains on the fabric, still damp, and Y didn't understand these either.

She dropped the fabric, unexpectedly scared, and snuck back to her cradle past the suite's central hub – a mass of electronics and monitoring equipment.

Back in her cradle, she discovered the sticky dampness was still on her fingers, so she wiped them on her cradlewear, lined herself back in, and tried her best to sleep.

In the morning she found a deep maroon smear down her front. An hour later, it would earn her a thousand extra pressups.

THREE

The Transit job's a time-sink. It's why Sol hardly notices the car pull in. The tall, easy-limbed man who steps out. And despite the car door slam, feet on gravel, the headlight glare, Sol only really reacts when the man's shadow spills across the workshop floor.

Sol downs tools and checks the van's bonnet catch. Looks once, thinks twice, and picks his spanner back up. Is this it? Is this the man in bike leathers?

The stranger seems to fill the whole gap under the roller doors. He's completely still.

"Alright in there pal? Pete about?"

Sol looks at his watch. Late evening. "Sorry," he says. "You just missed him."

The stranger shrugs. "It's Solomon, yeah?"

Sol squints into the diffuse. Raises a hand to shield his eyes. It's tricky to make out the man's features, odd to hear his full name from a stranger. He looks down, vision smeared purple. He unpockets a rag and wipes his face.

"You alright mate?"

Sol steps forward. "Yeah," he says. "Yeah."

The stranger takes note of Sol's awkward stance: feet inwardly turned, one hand concealed. He reads it as a sign, a vulnerability, and steps inside. "Hiya," he says. The workshop lights pick out channels in his clean-shaven head. "What's a big lad like you doing being timid around me? Put it down, eh? We're all friends here."

Sol's grip tightens around the spanner.

"Got a reputation, this place," the stranger tells him.

Sol laughs nervously. "I dread to think."

"Hard to find, mind. Wouldn't know you were here, all the holo-boards you've got plastered on the fence."

"They pay the bills," Sol says. "We rent out the ad space."

The stranger smiles with a fraction of his mouth. "Can't pay you that much, though, can they? The LEDs are knackered on two of them." He motions to a chunky powerpack in the corner. Its thick cable runs the whole length of the far wall, then disappears through it. A shoddy hack job if the stranger knows better. He smiles again. "If you pay your bills at all."

Sol walks over and holds out a hand. "What you after?"

The stranger leaves Sol hanging. "We've got a vehicle swinging by for mods. Two or three days. Did my boss call ahead?"

Sol racks his brains, eyes rolled upwards as if to petition some god of memory. The problem is that Sol works with so many bosses, has met so many of these lackeys.

"Who's your boss?"

"Doesn't matter," the stranger says. But something about his response nudges Sol's primal tripwires.

"No," Sol says back. "I guess it doesn't."

The stranger sits down on a pedestal of part-worn tyres. He picks at a pricing sticker near his crotch. "Work must be nice and steady for men of your talents."

Sol wobbles his head. "Not too bad if you know where to look. Listen, though. Not being funny but I want to get off home soon. What's the project?"

The stranger doesn't skip a beat. "Security."

Sol looks at his free palm, thoughtful. "Attack or defence?"

"Bit of both."

"We don't build tanks, Mr–"

"No names!" the stranger snaps. "All you need to know is that my client's got a cross-country journey to finish in one piece. A to B on some less-than-pleasant roads."

"Southerner, then? Isn't he better off flying?"

The stranger doesn't respond.

"Maybe you don't get it," Sol tells him. "Ballistic glass isn't cheap – or even easy to come by. Pete's waited two months for secondhand stuff before now. Then there's sheet composite for linings... bespoke mouldings... Unless you've got an industrial printer and CNC you're gonna be at the mercy of your suppliers. And they're shipping most of this heavy gear overseas anyway."

The stranger rubs his thumb and forefinger together. "All about this, though, innit? Wouldn't be right if we didn't put our boys first. But seriously, it's worth your while. And we've got some guys abroad who like dabbling in a bit of supply and demand – a nice networking opportunity for you."

Sol looks outside. Sky the colour of a wet scab. He can feel himself wavering – a feeling deep-set in his shoulders. His mouth's dry. Then he grins. A sensation comes over him like the rush of relapse. It's not like he needs an excuse to stay at work, anyway – to avoid the lonely flat, his attempts at living a wholesome life there. "You want to come through, then? I'll stick a brew on–"

The stranger shakes his head. "Very kind, but I've got more errands to run."

"Right," Sol says.

The stranger reaches inside his jacket; produces a roll of dog-eared paper. "Just have a scan of this before I go." He launches the bung like a javelin.

Sol makes the catch. "These blueprints? Bit retro, isn't it?"

"Plans, yes."

Sol rolls off the elastic band. Opens the first page. His smile is gone.

"What?" the stranger asks.

Sol shakes his head, flicks through the sheets behind, accelerates to the last page. "We don't – can't – build *tanks*," he says. "We don't work to this kind of spec. And if this is for a *car*... seriously. Chiller units? Backup power? These harnesses? What's he hoping to carry, your man? None of our equipment is..." He fumbles the words. "We'd never get the tolerances right."

The stranger comes forward and passes Sol a card. "I've done my research. Seen some of the kit that rolls out of here – pig-rigs, armoured limos. Drone-proofing. That mad trike thing you did – the one with the turret."

Sol nods slowly. "That was Pete's stuff."

"So I know you're good for it," the stranger says. "Get on and call me when the parts turn up. Boss is hands-off, but likes to hear about progress. Goes without saying he likes a nice result as well. The base vehicle gets here within the week. And me, I don't really give a toss how you get the gear. Just sort it fast and we're all happy bunnies."

Sol scans the card – nameless, numbered. When he looks up again, the stranger's pointing at the Lexus. "And this little beauty over here," he says. "On the market, that, or what? Quality, that – smart-looking."

Sol turns to the Lexus. It's meant to be stripped down, sold on. And yet he finds himself nodding. *Opportunity knocks*. It might be in great shape, with plenty to salvage for resale straight off the shelf – but get rid now and they've made a few quid fast. Not to mention the fact he can't shake his jitters about having it here.

"Make me an offer I can't refuse."

"Two?"

"Two ton? It's worth at least a grand. Run-flats alone'd get two... and there's hardly anything on the clock."

The stranger chuckles. "Give it a good wash and I'll think about five."

Sol mulls it, shakes his head. "Nah. And to be honest, I don't deal with people whose names I don't know."

The man holds out his hand. "It's Roy," he says. "Just Roy."

"Roy," Sol says, and takes Roy's hand. "You can have it for nine."

An afternoon off. Hands slanted into her coat pockets – one round a can of pepper spray – Mel goes south through the city. She threads between the ghosts of Deansgate before cutting down past Castlefield's reconstituted Roman fort, now a makeshift camp.

On foot, over time, she's created more and more of these shortcuts – delighting in her personal map as it grows more complex; as she links her old Manchester with its reshaped topography. With every walk, its new pathways are becoming shorter, its new structures more recognizable, its developing enclaves more delineated.

The changed environment as she first found it, seen with fresh eyes, coloured with new smells, cavernous spaces where grand buildings once stood – is segueing to familiarity.

Despite the violence of previous years, it's still cobbled under the arches of the viaducts that pass over here, and the homeless in their sleeping bags cluster round the pillars as petals. Water drips from these structures almost constantly, and after dodging their streams Mel emerges into the canal basin proper: Catalan Square. Here the warehouses and bridges and quay markers create a unique space before her: an openness rarely found elsewhere in the city. She doesn't break pace.

On the water sit many barges, most owned by runners selling their paper-bagged goods to hazy figures who emerge as stereotypes from the shadows, from the doorways, only to slink away again. She smells food, infused cooking oils, woodburner smoke. What she can see of the canal water is widow-black and seemingly surfaceless, light sucked in and held in place. Mel passes a barge selling books, their wrinkled spines packed against its windows. "Classics!" the hawker shouts at her. She grunts at him, raises a hand. Now that work is everything, reading seems frivolous. Even daydreaming feels wasteful, conceited.

"Won't get anywhere without them!" shouts the hawker, fading fast. "The future's in these pages!"

And Mel walks on.

Down in Castlefield there's often a sense of being watched – because usually you are. Squatters live in these mills and warehouses – knocking through old conversions to create broken utopias – and the building entrances are well fortified. Look up, and you might glimpse a lens flash from a pair of binoculars, a camera, even a telescope.

Knowing this, Mel finds a bench this side of Merchants'
Bridge – the bouncy bridge, as they call it – that's out of
sight. Unfortunately it's tufted over and looks wet, so she
moves across to another bench on Castle Street. This one
overlooks Lock 92, where the Rochdale Canal narrows
and drops into the basin. A place to think, scheme, or just
recall. She sits and pulls out Jase's catalogue and a fresh
packet of cigarettes and takes in the sounds of running
water, the sparring of well-natured haggling, and the
fires crackling on the barges behind. Dead ahead is the
main span of Bridgewater Viaduct, with its distinctive
off-white struts like the balusters of a parapet. Just left
of that, the timeless-seeming hole where the Beetham
Tower once stood.

For Mel, coming to Castlefield is an almost spiteful
act – a deliberate effort to reclaim a territory as her own.
When you separate from someone you love, your shared
spaces so often become exclusion zones, force-fielded
from your future self by painful memories. Break back
into them, replant your flag, and you gain strength, put
yourself back in control. Even if that means writing over
something – double-exposing the film.

That said, there are spaces she's yet to reclaim – a
spot on Winter Hill, above the city, beneath the old
transmitter tower, where the Manchester conurbation
smears out under its own haze. Here Sol had proposed to
her after a McDonald's in her car. Not the romantic sort,
was he, with the smell of barbecue sauce on his fingers;
black oil forever like tattoos under his nails. And then
Werneth Low on the other side of the basin, another fine
view of the city, where they'd fumbled around until a
man with a dog whistled and shone his torch through
their steamed windows. A lot of embarrassment because

her backside was right up in the air, and Sol in hysterics because Mel farted out of fright.

Mel shivers. Even now the memory of his laugh is infectious.

Still, none of it matters anymore. The past doesn't exist. So Mel crosses her legs and lights a cigarette and starts to read the catalogue.

The editor's note is written in English, but not with many words she knows. To her it almost has the feel of academic marginalia – words thrown in for words' sake. She flicks through to find close-up shots of different people, set against dark backgrounds. The images seem like old clippings, post-coital portraits, and they give Mel a strange thrill. It feels secret, fascinating, almost arousing, to study their perfect contours, however desensitized she might be to their function. But it's weird, too – there's something clinical about their presentation, and the captions are couched in jarringly familiar terms: *punter this*, *punter that*. They'd done their research, for sure.

Objectively, Mel isn't ashamed to concede that there's a kind of frontier here, expanding behind the scenes. It makes sense, given the march of things. Similarly, and despite Jase's heavy-handed sales pitch, she can also admit that looking ahead is no bad thing. *After all*, she thinks, *to save money can mean surviving*. And even from a human perspective – a *feeling* perspective – a warped moralization, bringing in extra revenue could mean feeding the women and their dependants for longer. And wasn't the point of all this to get by? She remembers Sol saying something similar to her once, channelling his father's politics to justify yet another late night at the workshop, and now his voice rings through her head again: "Ambition is the force behind everything," he's saying.

Suddenly overwhelmed, she lights another cigarette and decides to walk the longest way home.

She thinks: *If it's only a trial.* She thinks: *You can be rewarded in the next life.*

In the workshop office, Sol spreads Roy's plans and pins down the corners. It's too late, but now he's committed, he's excited by it – it's exactly the kind of job that keeps him away from his flat.

First up, the parts. Owing to dead mobile networks and a council-controlled, council-rationed, council-monitored internet connection, Sol's invested in an encrypted landline switch for making the workshop's orders. It means routing into a proxy hub and back out through several landline handlers, each more deeply buried in concrete than the last.

Sol's primary contact has a local voice. Buried beneath the city, the tunnels, or maybe even a bunker. From the cross-chat – ghostly voices that occasionally waft in and out of the call – Sol concludes that this handler also looks after some pot growers up on the moors.

The second handler is out in the Channel. Sol's heard it's a derelict sea fort from the Second World War – a hacker commune whose business involves getting information out of Europe without lines of black marker through the juicy bits. An island province, guarded by mercs whose only task is protecting the server farms that pay their wages. The handler there talks to him impassively, unfazed by the request.

Sol's third connector is somewhere back on land, or at least some way beneath it – a common theme. She has a neutral accent, a colder manner, and a reliable line.

The fourth handler is somewhere more exotic: apparently Argentina.

The fifth – Sol's actual contact – takes the call from a repurposed killbox at the heart of the abandoned SAS complex in Hereford. Here they're anxious about security, and understandably so: their station is more like a nation state. Sol hears the connecting clicks, a series of antiquated modem sounds, and finally a voice, crisp as an October morning, with a Swansea accent.

"Mr Manchester?"

"Miss Wales," Sol says, confused by how she can tell. "You know I can't stay away long."

"Been a while since we last heard off you, hasn't it?" He can hear her smile. "Missed that voice of yours I have. Shaky down there are you? Getting giddy?"

"Has been time. Can't say no to easy money though. How's tricks?"

She chuckles. "Don't laugh and you'll cry. Four tells me you're after heavy comps, eh? The market's a bit crap, to be honest. Dire for months now."

"Shit," Sol whispers. "Not even ceramics?"

"Dismal, babe. Unless you've got a trowel, a field and a few spare years. Saying that, if you've got cash spare for a courier and a guard we're good for blast film. You're looking at steel, steel, or rewelded steel."

Sol sighs. "Who's shifting it?"

"Old plant north of Cambridge. Handful of ex-council boys moved there – they did a lot of the riot conversions down that way. Not been running materials for long, mind, but doling out DIY kits since Birmingham kicked off."

Sol picks his nails. "Is the steel all stripped out?"

Miss Wales pauses to look over something. "Yep. Says structural here. And God knows how, but I know they got hold of some dumper truck buckets recently…"

"Balls," Sol says. Thick or no, stripped-out metal

means dirty metal – sometimes without serial numbers filed off. Put another way, people get whisked off on state holidays for less. It's exactly the kind of shipment they send drones out hunting for.

"Timeframe?" Sol asks.

"How long you got?"

"Till yesterday."

Sol hears paper rustling, a pen clicked on. "Let's have a look. I'll be with you now."

Sol waits.

"You there?"

"Yep."

"It's a few days at a push," Miss Wales tells him. "Be a bin truck that drops it, so you'll have to cover fuel."

Sol looks at the ceiling, does the maths. "Fuel, yep. Right."

"How many heads you want with it?"

"Fewer the better."

"I can book it in with a driver and guard for now?"

"Yeah OK – and what's the insurance on that?"

"Let's see… vanilla… No letters. One CS. And our standard drone waivers – nothing's insured if they have a pop, etcetera… The usual drill."

It's enough. The essentials. These are the risks of the motorway network.

"And you're sure I'd be waiting for anything else?"

"Definitely. We've got MoD bods coming straight to us, it's getting that ropey."

"Christ. Well, I'll send a pigeon over with your bonus. Thanks for the help."

Miss Wales laughs. "My pleasure, treasure. Paygate's open when you're ready."

"Go for it," Sol says. "And cheers again."

"Don't be a stranger."

Static.

Sol paces over to the Lexus as he waits for the automated voice to cut in. He runs a hand over the car's roofline and thinks back to earlier – two hundred quid? That Roy was a cheeky sod. He stands by the bonnet, rubs away a streak of muck that looked like a scratch. The payment confirmation tone rings out. "Charge accepted," the robovoice says. Then, to finish, a cartoon fanfare telling him the funds have gone.

Sol hangs up and puts the phone on his belt loop. He feels anxious to get going – knowing he won't be satisfied unless he does a good job. It's always this way when they take on a new client.

He stops by the Lexus' boot, distracted, deciding to clean it out now before he goes home.

He opens the boot.

He looks in.

And the workshop spins out, disintegrates –

The pieces all fall away –

Black and purple, heat, dizziness –

Nausea –

Because in the boot of the Lexus.

There's a body.

Y

The driller came to Y's cradle side. He said, "Wakey-wakey!" and, "Guess who's got his hat on!"

Y opened her eyes. She was learning to suppress the terror now, to embrace the dark tower that stood sentinel through the night. The driller was looming, enormous. He glowered at her. "You kids have it all in here – where's your get up and go?"

Y pulled away her sleep feeds, patted down her cradlewear. She hissed at him, her version of a sigh. The driller smiled vacuously. "Come on, flower. Let's turn that frown upside down. Get out of that pit and get warmed up…"

His voice went through Y. The sentiment was metallic, grating. Almost sarcastic.

Y got ready while he watched. It didn't bother her. The whispers about brothers and sisters in dark rooms downstairs made it seem easy, and in any case the driller was dispassionate, his eyes dull with a doctor's seen-it-all glaze. He was actually making notes on the development of her frame. Live-tweaking his drill routine.

Y wore a black vest, black shorts, and the pendant. Her feet were bare. The driller stood her to attention and they set off through the cradle suites, out through an impressive corridor whose walkway shivered with uncanny radiance. On the way, they passed bustling kitchens, a bowling green, engineering workshops, a cavernous shooting range. Guard squads marched around in single file, so close to each other their movements looked mechanized. The floors were cold and bitty. To Y these rooms beyond her cradle suite felt permanently askew.

Intrigued, Y looked into the last area for a second or two – enough to recognize the shapes stretched across a target board. A moment more and the truth hit her: the boards weren't static at all. At the far end of the range, whimpering on a leash, was an enormous bovine creature with fabric pinned to its flanks. Printed on the fabric was the outline of a man.

"No rubbernecking," the driller said. He took her shoulder and hurried her along. "We'd never waste someone like you on senseless violence like that."

He watched me. He said he was my father.

As they continued, Y heard a barrage of shots. The sounds – high-pitched, rattling – made her jump. When the noise was over, she couldn't hear the creature whining.

Now they reached the cavernous atrium, marble-walled and gilded. Her footsteps carried in here – echoed upwards to a vaulted ceiling. Y listened to the liquid sounds of water fountains that caught light and sent resonant wave paintings cascading up the walls. Ripples of colour and texture, no two the same. Behind them, a red staircase led away into the mansion's upper tiers. Its bannister appeared to be made of bone.

The driller took her through the double front door and into the grounds.

Outside, a realm away from Y's cradle cooling systems, it was early but already sweltering. Over the hot season, the lawns turned a crisped heather colour, and the milking animals rallied themselves against the perimeter fence for a few feet of shade. The colours beyond this perimeter ran from gold to bronze, striking next to the purple sky. The driller often said it was the best view in the world.

He sniffed the air. "Smashing day for it!" he said, as if to suggest every day wasn't exactly the same.

Y started down the steep steps to the lawn. She knew what "it" meant. Together they crossed a slim natural bridge over a pond, the prickle of dry grass under her feet. In the water, slender metal snakes spiralled and snapped at each other, and her ankles pulsed in response.

She should be used to this by now. The exertion, the sun, the sweat. She'd done it for a long time, after all. But every session felt like a fresh trial. And despite the searing heat, the ragged blisters on her hands and feet, she was drilled again and again – heavy muscle stretches, body weight exercises, toning, free weights, contortions, circuits. It went on for two hours before she was allowed to rest.

"One, two, I'll break you!" the driller screamed in Y's face, keeping up his relentless pace. "Three, four, you're good for more!"

A hundred pressups, a hundred more. Lunges, squats, burpees – until it seemed it wasn't sweat but a certain future dripping out of her. Her body bristled beneath the blazing sun, and the pendant sat boiling against her skin. Nothing but reps and sets, and her driller's lust for more. Y hated that sun. Every second, minute and hour she was in it. The tingling afterwards. Her stinging lips, cracked and sore. Her shaking arms and cramping legs.

As the session went on, several other pairs – brothers and sisters with their own personal drillers – filtered from the mansion into spaces on the lawn around her. She noticed, when she was able to, that they all did the same thing at the same time. There was a click-track to keep rhythm, and the drillers screamed the same motivational lines in unison. The coordination amplified their words; transformed their orders into an enveloping white noise that came from all directions.

"One, two–"

Breathe in with the rep...

"Three, four–"

Breathe out with the neg...

Until the click-track stopped, and the drillers marched their projects to a nearby water fountain.

Y's driller placed her sweaty palm on a reader which blooped and screened a message: <GOOD DRILLING, USERNAME>

"Better to be nobody out here," the driller told her. Y blinked at him. "Now drink," he said. "Half a litre. We don't want any bloating, do we?"

Except Y could drink to drowning. She stood there, rapt by the water's sound, wishing she could squeeze herself out of her skin, a tube of tenderized meat, and lie in the fountain pool. That she could be left to soak there, absorbing the liquids, a shuddering mass in osmosis–

She drank like a thirsty dog.

"Enough," the driller said. "You're drinking *his* water, remember."

And in that moment, she thought she hated removing her mouth from the faucet more than she hated the star in the heavens above.

"Very good," the driller said. "Now. Inside to bathe, please. As hot as it'll go. Then stretch out, with emphasis on those quads. When you're finished, return to your cradle for repairing nutrients." He said this last line like an advertiser, smugly pointing at her, standing in a vulgar pose. "I'll see you again in forty-eight hours – unless our father wants to see you first."

FOUR

Once upon a time, Mel looked like a stickman scribbled out. You could rest your pint in the recesses of her collarbones; sharpen pencils between the ligaments of her wrists. Her hospital bed bleeped. The room thrummed with it – pipes and lines, drips and cables. So many tubes. And a strange thing happened to time there – as though Mel existed in an endless corridor from a filmed sequence, her bed in motion as her heart was massaged by the machine cocoon.

Sol didn't look much better. Far too long sitting there beside her. He saw it in the mirror when he washed his hands: his brow wrinkles deepening by the hour, his eyes retreating into his head.

Sometimes, he'd take Mel's hand – cold and oilless, the skin soft but undernourished and yellow. She had such smoker's nails, he thought, and in the dark he squeezed her fingers as he mumbled his sonnets, his tired apologies. He wept quietly whenever he acknowledged the question that seemed to linger in the room with them: *Did I put her here?*

Sol would've prayed for Mel if he thought it might save her. But the doctors said it was too late for intervention, and it felt like God had already given up.

Instead, he apologized some more. Of course he did. And then at other times, his sentiment changed. Of course it did. Because *she* should be sorry and *he* should feel sour.

The truth, of course, was that they shared responsibility. Her trackmarks – the scabs on tried-and-tested holes – came from a third party: an unseen incubus that stalked their relationship. The incubus gave her livid bruises, took her fingernails down to the quick. And the same incubus fed Sol's ego – filled the vacuum whenever there came an inkling he gave more attention to the vehicles at work; smothered a fear he'd abandoned her to this fate, just as Sol's father had his mother.

Nurses swept through the room. There were bed washes to prevent sores. Sol felt like he only ever said, "Any news?" He worried they'd grown bored of his voice, its moribund inflection, and, distracted, he often forgot what they told him.

There are things you think you should do in hospital. Behaviours you've learned from old TV, or from other visitors and relatives. And there are things you think you shouldn't: nod at other families; pay too much attention to the monitors.

There were also things Sol could say to Mel that he never imagined saying to anybody. He told her he thought death was close for her. And he would pick out details – comment on the fact she still had her earrings in. Small things like this reminded him so powerfully of their past selves; of two people cohabiting and setting out their boundaries. He knew that after a late shift at the garage, after he'd collected some milk on the way home and they'd eaten food together, they'd go to bed and she'd take out her earrings and false eye and reach over his chest to put them on the side.

Time had done such things to them. Their relationship was being stubbed out. Scratched out. And increasingly, obsessively, Sol came to believe that the best thing about eyes – whether you had one, like Mel did, or two, like he did – was how they gave you the option to look away.

One morning he couldn't bear the kind way the nurses looked at him. They'd been nothing but sympathetic and diligent, and yet he felt embarrassed to be seen there with Mel. They were endeared to his vigil, he knew, but this didn't shift an uncomfortable feeling they judged him; that they thought he lacked the will to prevent this happening in the first place. That wasn't him, he told himself. It wasn't the man he thought he was. Sol spent his life fixing things, and here lay something wretched – no, some*one* wretched – he lacked the capacity to fix. She had pushed him to see the outer limits of his personality; confronted his flaws, his pure weakness. He hated how it made him feel. And so, in an act of arch selfishness – shrinking from the opportunity to make himself a better partner – he leaned in to Mel with a fattening tear hanging from his nose. It'd been too long, he told himself, already dismissing his self-analysis. Too much had changed, and too much was still changing.

Something frayed had finally snapped.

"Mel," he said to her, and watched the tear fall and splash from her chin into the channel of her neck. "I love the bones of you. But I'm going now."

And that was how he left her.

•••

Roy's life is full of codas. So while the names, objectives and cover stories change, he considers repeatedly the unspoken rules of engagement in his transactions – in the debiting and crediting of life and limb.

One of the critical rules is this: don't expect the truth. When Roy takes contracts from the Reverend, he can expect just enough to run with, just enough to let his imagination fill the gaps, or paper over his reservations. It's why, as he leaves Sol in the workshop to return to the Rose, it's confusing that Havelock told him so much, and so earnestly. It said lots about the things Havelock wasn't saying.

Roy lights a cigarette, opens the window. Takes in Manchester air, its scent and taste. The smog and ceaseless drizzle. The ratty bars and risky streetfood.

What's that bastard up to?

Roy has to be careful: he knows you can seriously overthink this stuff. Drive yourself barmy. And does he really care as long as the fee clears? As long as there's food in his guts by the end of it? These are the pressing questions, most of the time – albeit two questions the Reverend would punish him for asking.

Ahead, the sky's shod in black-blue bruise. In his mirrors sits the lone headlight of a motorbike. Beyond, the dark jags on the horizon where the moors and gritstone tors run stitches between counties. Closer, he sees the silhouetted, attenuated servants of Manchester: her cranes and towers, her surviving chimneys and masts, all wanting to drag Roy back into the past. To a single dark day up a crane gantry –

But don't go there. Distract yourself.

Roy uses a pocket shortband scanner to keep an ear to the ground. It's one of the more useful things about the council returning to old tech. As long as you dodge the lev-bikes, which run on a different network, it's a good way to get gossip. Most of the time the scanner garbles things: fragmented sequences, clicking, Morse code signals. Occasionally, though, there'll be something juicy. Something to listen to, and simultaneously avoid...

Tonight, though, there's nothing.

Another glance behind. Roy wonders if the motorbike is trailing him. It could've overtaken a dozen times already, and the way the rider hangs back reeks of someone trying too hard to appear normal. He shakes his head. Probably it's sleep deprivation – the wrong instincts flaring.

Distract yourself, Roy.

Roy pushes his cig dimp through the gap in the window and watches the sparks burst. The biker reacts, swerves, before pulling up alongside the car. Roy sees his own face warped across the rider's mirrored visor. He raises his eyebrows. The biker lingers fleetingly, then powers ahead.

Roy exhales.

Distract. Yourself.

Now he thinks about this evening's job – his visit to the workshop. On the passenger seat his roadmap is still open, overwritten so thickly in biro that its planview city resembles a snakes and ladders board.

The workshop was southwest of town, Old Trafford, a place on its arse long before the rest of the city. That side of Manchester is a pain to access: nationalist insurgents had previously bombed a hole in the Mancunian Way, and without public funding allocated to fix it – or the mock beneficence of a megacorp with pocket change to spare – the road's stayed closed. A brutalist sculpture coming out in weeds.

The diversion had taken him down Deansgate from the far side. Not a pleasant option, but more or less his only one, unless he risked a dicier jaunt through Salford. He thinks about the filthy people who'd glanced up from their foraging to casually process his potential worth. Further along, he'd seen how the Beetham memorial lamp, turned off during the riots and blackouts of 2018, was now reduced to nude superstructure. When he'd started to see bodies, he was grateful for his nondescript car.

These bodies of Deansgate intrigued him a lot. There was no ignoring them: the majority were left in situ as grim markers, warnings against something vague and oppressive – the descent of man, or a viral form of neglect. Their stillness fascinated him – though when he considers what he does for a living, he knows in his heart it shouldn't.

Perhaps it unsettles Roy that the bodies hadn't been his marks. It's almost like he's forgotten people can die without his involvement – without a fee or a motive. In this alone, he knows death has skewed him. Just as he knows death sat alongside him as he watched Deansgate's bodies being scoured by human carrion – that death pointed to the skeletal children, the husks, as they scavenged trinkets and treasures to sell on the markets.

How do you help these people?

Roy knows the answer: you don't. That just like the garage man he went to see, just like anyone trying to put food on the table, Roy and the rest of them are too busy finding their own way forward, no matter the internal cost or conflict.

Eventually he'd found the workshop. Its doors were open, so he'd deliberately parked his car with full beams facing inwards. Yes, that was a good move. That was him at his best, and the Reverend would've approved. He'd got out, checked his pockets and zipped his coat to the neck.

Inside the workshop, Sol had been working on a purple Transit hiked up on a lane. Roy had cleared his throat and stood there on the threshold, a vampire asking to come inside.

The body in the Lexus is wrapped up like leftovers. A woman. It's hard to tell if it's the light or the clingfilm that makes her skin so grey, but under the sticky layers, Sol can see welts on her naked skin; the brown flakes that form a patina on her legs; the rings of bruise around her wrists. She's faceless, depersonalized – her head covered from the neck upwards in tape, with two lengths of tube exiting the mask at the nose.

Sol is shattered by it. He gawps down at her, disturbed and helpless, his lungs compressed. He closes his eyes, watches constellations die, a deafening ringing in his ears. Nausea grips and sends the workshop spinning: a blur of products and tools and banal fixtures.

He looks back at her and finds himself gripping the boot lid. The woman's utterly alien – a splinter in the real. Something inserted here from a world infinitely crueller.

On her torso, on her tin ribs, there's a folded note. He leans closer to find it's monogrammed with a distinctive symbol: two circles intersecting.

Then he screams.

Sensing his closeness, hearing his noise, the woman's body spasms.

She isn't dead.

As movement ripples through her, every muscle seems

to contract and relax. Each sinew carved out, inked into place. The cords that model her swell to capacity; her veins and tendons standing, shuddering, and settling by turns. He wonders, so briefly, if her laser-thin waist was machined to size.

And then there's the bottle. Sol takes it out, confused to find a thin white paste in the bottom. Food, he guesses, logical, deductive, until the searing realization: she's had to take it through her nose tubes. He retches then, and his eyes begin to water. The thought loops back – *through her nose*.

He says, "God help us," and the woman thrashes silently in the boot. "No, wait, no," he pleads, and when she squirms on to her side, Sol sees something else.

A third arm.

Now Sol goes faint, field of vision pinched.

Reeling, he dares to look again. Narrowed eyes. Right there: a third arm that looks as naturally articulated as the others, connected to a thicker joint on one side. He fixates on the deltoid muscles flaring around it, stretching out the clingfilm.

He says, "Shit," and touches her side. "*Shit*." This time she freezes under his hand. His voice breaks, squeaks, as he flounders for the right thing to say. "You're safe," he tells her. "You're safe."

The woman rolls on to her back and tries to reach out; tries to burst from her wrapping.

Sol reaches in and pulls her head to his shoulder. She's heavier than she looks. He sits her up on the boot sill and holds her upright by the shoulders, simultaneously horrified by her sliminess – yellow moisture trapped between her skin and the clingfilm – and ashamed by his disgust. If he lets go, she'll slide away from him like unset jelly.

Sol prays Irish hasn't forgotten his keys. That no one else will see...

He eases the woman down to the workshop's cold floor. Laid out, all three arms cable-tied behind her back, it's more obvious that the woman is unusually short. Stocky is also the wrong word – too vulgar – but he can tell she has a carefully restrained power. Her shoulders carry such definition, hewn tone. A wildness that, coupled with the blankness of her mask, scares Sol no end.

He props her up against the Lexus bumper. This time she holds herself. He darts away as if she's a lit firework. Think. *Think.* There – a felt rag covering an engine block by the tool shelves. He shakes it out, smells loosened dust. He doesn't know where it's been – if there's glass fibre caught in the material, metal filings or damp oil – but it's all he has to hand. His mind is fragmenting. He returns and carefully wraps her. "Your mask," he says, and touches her head with two fingers. She flinches, but he holds them there and with his other hand starts to unpeel her, trying carefully to ease the pressure on her face.

Only the mask won't come, and the woman stays silent and still. There's a relief that she's alive, and a fear she might now die here, like this. Self-preservation, maybe – and with that a flash of anger that she's even here at all. *What has Irish done?*

"Let's get you warm," he says, though he can see his breath and his fingers are frozen. He tears the film between her calves and stands her up, the idea being to take her into the workshop's break room. She's clearly disoriented, leaning into him, solid to the touch. He does what he can to keep her inside the felt rag. They amble, his ribs supporting her.

When he tries to move a box of ignition coils from the break room sofa, it turns out she can't stay on her own two feet.

The woman crumples into a pile, chest first. Her head lolls forward. She lets herself go; a bladder held for too long. Fluid not caught by the clingfilm streaks off towards the break room door, the inspection pit beyond.

"You're OK," he says, mining for platitudes. "You're OK." He takes her shoulder and brings her towards him. "What we're going to do, right—"

What are you going to do?

Sol kneels there, simply looking at her, until his thoughts coalesce. "What we're going to do right, is we're going call for help, an ambulance, the council, as soon as we've got all this off your face."

Again Sol pulls at the tape. Again no luck – and the momentum makes the woman slump further. She tries to move herself, and the felt sheet comes away, exposes her powerful back. Her muscles flutter as she tries to release her bound forearms. It pains Sol to watch. And now he can see the next problem: gashes in the crooks behind her knees. Sol tries to scaffold her as they move. They could be some fused-together creature, jerking towards the sofa. "Christ," he mutters at one point, as if he suddenly paused to take in the scene.

"Roll on to your belly," he says, now they've crossed the gulf. "Let me get at the ties." No response. He decides to demonstrate what he means – tugging at the plastic wrap, making popping noises. Slowly she comes to understand him, and with pliers, cutters, and brute force, the ties and clingfilm come away. Her hands, all three, cold and blue, fall limp by her sides. He takes her fingers and squeezes them; whispers again: "We'll get you sorted, OK? Your head now. Let's sort your head now."

Strung together, he can't help thinking his words sound exactly like something he'd say to a customer.

Y

Y hadn't experienced the cradle suite's deep cleaning cycle before. It was apparently no small feat – each subject being woken and ejected from their cradle and sent to one of the subterranean vaults to wait. With a subject absent, the makers could methodically drain and flush food lines, steam the cradle pods, refit worn padding, and, if necessary, adjust doses for the next stage of a subject's development.

For Y it meant an early rise, a rending away from the dark tower that now felt more like her dream-protector, or at least a sanctuary from the casual horror of her days. She woke to the driller's smiling face and burning eyes – rubine in the lowlights – suspended above her own. His breath was metallic.

"Deep cleaning day," he said. "The suite's making its way down to Canteen Five for a treat. Full meal, they tell me, with no controls. The harridans will see to you there. Thank you very kindly indeed."

Y was intrigued, if wary. She undid her lines, pulled out wires, tugged at monitoring pads. She hated the canteens like she hated the sun – the homogenous food, its lingering smell. The matronly women the makers called harridans. And the waiting. But the thought of no controls was tantalizing.

"Careful," said the driller, watching Y disengage. "Expensive, those."

Y slipped into her daywear. A gown. Shorts for underwear. The driller nodded politely and made a show of looking away when he was meant to – again to maintain the illusion of dignity. She took the opportunity to skim-scan the tablet in his hands:

SUBJECT: Y-----
PERSISTENT CRADLE OVERRIDE SUSPECTED. REQ: WETWARE REBOOT AND SECURITY UPHAUL. WEAPONS Y/N/DISENGAGED. ISOLAT–

"Oi!" the driller said.

Y jumped.

"Got my eyes peeled," the driller told her. "You little monster. Now off you pop. There's a good egg."

The driller moved on to the next cradle. Y heard his patter, identical lines, as she drifted into the lane and latched onto a small group heading the same direction. Together they marched over glowing arrows; took heed of a flashing screen at the boundary of the suite. This had their tags illuminated, with more arrows showing the route. Realizing Y was with them, the others slowed to let her pass. She ignored them and followed the arrowed route all the way to a service corridor, its walls daubed in yellow-black hatching. The air turned chilly.

Here the arrows pointed down a narrow gantry. The lights came on as she walked, clicked off again behind her. This shuttering went on for a while before she reached the cage-door of a service lift. Y went in, descended.

The doors came open at last. Y stepped out into an archway twice her height – a sort of tunnel entrance. The floor arrows flickered again, and she followed them through a heavy curtain designed to keep the cold out, where immediately the sound swelled: a busy vault before her, hundreds of her brothers and sisters in there – more than she had ever seen in a cradle suite, come to that. The fuggy smells of cooking, the clash of cutlery, the bustle of brothers and sisters. Discordant music cut through: a nocturne teased from a tuneless grand piano by a hunch-backed harridan in the corner. Its agonizing melody ran in a circular pattern.

Surely they couldn't be cleaning out every cradle on her floor at once.

An old harridan sprang from nowhere and took Y's shoulder, span her round. She wore a third eye. Y recognized wet-tech: reader optics set flush in her forehead, unlike her driller's full-eye implants.

"Hand," the harridan said.

Y showed her palm.

The harridan huffed and sniffed at Y. She chewed her tongue as if tasting something. "Cleanup, eh? Filthy urchins, the lot of you. And will you eat?"

Y didn't know how to react.

"Hmm?"

So Y nodded. In truth the thought of real food made her queasy now she was here. But choice… the very idea of choice –

The harridan scowled. "No manners, either?"

Y shook her head. She felt confused.

"Disgusting creature," the harridan said. "Bestial. You youngers have it so easy. You want to try being a settler! Still, it seems you're on strict calories, so you'll get what you're given. And now I must ask: have you seen our little friend RF?"

Y shook her head. She'd never even heard the name.

The harridan's third eye flared: she cupped her hands and beamed into them a shaky image of a face, turning slowly in a red orb. The orb spilled lines like a star during a solar storm. "This is RF," the harridan said, "who escaped during drills. In time we shall discover him, if the Slope or the guards don't claim him first. But should you learn anything…"

Y shook her head. She'd hadn't heard of the Slope, either.

The harridan glimpsed the chain around Y's neck, and pulled out the pendant from Y's shirt. Her third eye ebbed out, opacity returning quickly. "Oh," she said, holding the pendant in her palm. "Well, go on then. You can see the queue. And please be mindful."

Clutching her pendant, Y joined the food queue seething along the vault's left side. Brothers and sisters nearby were sharing stories about this boy called RF, some more outlandish than others. He'd given his driller the slip after a violent assault. He'd sprung over a perimeter wall. He'd shattered his cradle casing and strangled his driller one morning. He'd fled down the Slope, across the Slope, and into the fringelands beyond.

It went on and on. Everyone in the line. Everyone in their huddles and gangs and cliques.

Something flapped in Y, though. It excited her to think you could escape. That you could be submitted to the mansion's persuasions, and still possess the temperance, the will to leave.

But no one spoke directly to Y about the escapee. And those who noticed her, those who saw her angling to be invited into the conversation, simply looked away, gawped at her pendant, or unsubtly turned their backs.

At the counter, Y pointed to the most colourful, appetising foods. Fresh items, brilliant-coloured vegetables, gleaming seeded fruits. A platter of thinly sliced meats from a larger joint that sat shining in its juices.

The server caught Y's eye and said something under her breath – almost like she recognized her. The server lifted a plate and shook her head. Then she slopped out a runny mixture from a separate container. A thin, grey gruel. There was the faintest hint of pity on the server's face as she handed it over.

Y blinked. The server didn't budge. "Your calories," she said.

Y went like a pariah between the tables. She slammed down her plate when she spotted a gap. Several others were talking there, but as she wiped her spoon against her gown to clean it, they stopped.

Y nodded at them. They looked at each other.

And they moved.

No one else joined Y. She sat in silence, shovelling the tasteless food into her mouth. Despite the food's thinness, its texture was lumpy, and as she chewed there was the occasional crunch – fragments, shell perhaps. It hurt her teeth, made her doubly careful. The next time it happened, a spike that electrified her whole gumline, she became fearful of it happening a third. She began sifting through every small mouthful; filtered the gruel against her palate. She realized she was trembling; that her breathing had changed. She wanted to stop eating but couldn't risk the response to that, either.

The noise around her seemed louder than ever: histrionics and nonsense, tattle and blather. Two more spoonfuls and she knew she couldn't go on, tortured by the shining vegetables on what looked like every other plate, the despairing colour of what stared up from hers.

Until there was a booming noise, and the music stopped, and hundreds of spoons and forks and knives fell to the tables.

"Brothers and sisters!" the door harridan shouted, glee in her voice. The diners wheeled excitedly in their chairs. The piano's last note rang out and died on the air.

"Brothers and sisters: your Manor Lord!"

There were gasps, and a sudden flatness came over the room. Y looked up as a tall figure emerged from the canteen archway. The figure stopped there, feet pushed together, and gestured at the congregation with an extended arm and a flat palm, as though he were scything crops.

Y took him in. This man the harridan called their Manor Lord wore ceremonial dress, richly red, regal, a self-styled emperor in velveteen trousers, asymmetric shirt, and a floor-length cape detailed with luminous thread. He scraped an oversized sceptre along the floor, its head an unfamiliar skull.

"Children," he said quietly. "I am home again."

Y had never seen or heard of the Manor Lord before now; knew nothing of his importance or role. But as he stalked the tables closest to him, stooping to inspect his subjects' plates, the halting atmosphere gave way to a charged, nervous energy. Nobody could look at him. Nobody seemed to even breathe.

By a young boy's table, the Manor Lord picked up a slice of meat, sniffed it, and dropped it again. He scoffed at the boy and said, "There's nowhere in two worlds I'd rather be."

The boy looked at him.

"Did you hear me?" the Manor Lord asked him, voice measured. "My boy?"

"Yes," the boy said. "Welcome home."

Y felt a disconnect, a shift.

"And what is it you do for me?" the Manor Lord asked him.

"I will be a soldier," the boy said. "I will fight. I'll kill."

The Manor Lord lifted the boy clean from his chair by his collar, held him aloft. The boy didn't resist or cry out. He simply hung there, neither limp nor alert.

"An exemplar," the Manor Lord said, rotating the boy with his other hand. "Obedient, polite. Young and already strong."

Y thought the boy's eyes might have been closed.

Then the Manor Lord placed the boy back into his seat and tapped him on the head. "Fight bravely. For our enemies are massing."

The Manor Lord continued through the tables, inspecting the plates, pausing to consider a row of women, Y's age or older, before nodding curtly to a harridan nearby. On this signal, inscrutable, two of the women stood up and began to recite a poem or song in another language. It was a murmuring, disorientating sound, and someone at the back released an anguished squeak.

Y wanted to turn, to see. To understand. But the Manor Lord was drawing closer to her table, and the weight of his presence was crushing.

Closer, he was weirdly youthful, with small features crowded into the middle of his smooth face. It was like some kind of suction had pulled them away from their starting points. His hair was slicked back, the longest layers bunned up at his crown, and his cape produced a strange rubbing sound as he walked.

Closer still. He stood at end of her row. For a few seconds, he looked directly at Y, directly into her, then down to her neck, and the pendant, where his gaze remained. The world might have stopped for that instant, frozen on its orbit. Y knew, then, that he recognized her – even if she didn't recognize him. The shivers came automatically, impulsively, but she managed to keep it together.

He looked away again, just as the women finished their recital. He passed Y, turned on his sceptre and rounded her table. This close, Y could see the cape in full. On its outside were set hundreds and hundreds of little stones, off-white in colour, glossy in the light. She gripped her pendant, understanding it was formed of the same material, and with her other hand dug her fingers into her legs; had to stifle a noise.

The stones weren't stones at all. They were teeth.

The Manor Lord snorted. "You'll rise for me next time," he said. His voice carried to every corner; there was no need to shout. Again he used his strange, flat-palmed salute to gesture at the harridan standing stiffly by the entrance – a paragon of obedience. "And you should learn from your elders," he added.

The stress was palpable. Y's hairs were all on end –

"Did we all enjoy our food?" the Manor Lord asked. "We're so lucky to have such talented chefs looking after us while our makers clean out our sties, aren't we?"

Silence.

The Manor Lord plucked a plate from the nearest table and angled it to the room. What was left there slid off and splashed around his boots.

"I said, did we enjoy our food?"

"Yes, father," the room said. Y felt her throat vibrate involuntarily.

"And aren't we lucky?"

Another murmur.

"Good," the Manor Lord said. He was beaming. "Because, as I said to my chefs earlier today, it's not often we have an escapee on the menu."

He let it settle in. He watched their faces. And by the time the first of them had vomited, the Manor Lord had spun one-eighty on the fulcrum of his sceptre and walked straight out again.

Stunned, Y turned to the chef's hatch – tried to see the woman who'd served her.

It was like the server had been waiting. She was staring right back. Y couldn't be sure, but it looked like she mouthed something to her. Then another chef pulled down the shutters, and the whole canteen erupted.

In the midst of their minor riot, Y stayed completely still. The line was drawn. The link was clear. And she could've been wrong, hoped in some way she was, but the chef's whispered word had looked a lot like "Tomorrow".

FIVE

Jase and Jeffrey come round to the Cat Flap.

There are niceties. There are contracts. And there's a deal.

Jeff sits in one corner while Jase and Mel go over the fine print.

"Remember it's a trial," Mel says. "And only Jeff. Only for now."

"Course," Jase says. She thinks he's trying not to smile. "Just see our Jeffrey as a little hired help. A way to attract a different clientele. He's been with us about six months now, and already proved quite adept. And if he's not busy, you know, at first, you could have him do your odd jobs. Give this place a clean for starters. He's more than a decent physique, despite the average face. There's strength in the head, too. Intelligence. And there's always the doors to think about. He'd make a fine minder."

Mel looks at Jeff over in the corner.

"It's all no obligation," Jase tells her. "And if you're not fully satisfied we'll simply take him back."

"I can't promise anything," Mel says. "Money comes and goes."

"Course." Those teeth again. "Nature of the beast. But you'll be surprised. Pleasantly surprised."

"Are there instructions?"

Jase smirks. "No, no need for any of that. He's like us, you understand. But imagine a hip replacement, yes? Now extend that idea. Imagine you could sprint a hundred miles without a single sore ligament..."

Mel nods.

"All we ask is that you advertise. That you give him a good run. Outcalls, incalls, whatever makes sense."

"And what's to stop him going berserk or something, hurting one of us? A place like this runs on trust, see. That's the game."

"He won't do anything unless you want him to," Jase says, and winks.

Mel's stomach flipflops. She tries to stop a thought blossoming: the violence of it; the root of Jase's assumptions. He's closing on her now. She knows he's *closing* on her.

"And how long we talking?" she asks. "For the trial?"

"Say a month tops, to give you an idea of how we train them. He's completely self-sufficient. And there's absolutely nothing to stop you, you know, trying yourself. A test drive, let's call it. You'll find everything's engineered for performance..."

Mel holds up a hand. "Don't push your luck. I'll need a full breakdown of the costs, too, with a couple of days' grace while he finds his feet. Girls'll stress about someone new hanging about all day. It's a big change, something like this... a change to their environment."

She's annoying herself now, talking like this. It feels too much like sinking to his level. To bartering. She'd steadily got used to haggling for stuff on the markets – grains and dairy if the farm delivery hadn't been seized en route – but she's never felt entirely comfortable with it. Plus business now is never quite as simple as spitting in your hand and shaking on it.

In the corner, Jeff takes off his glasses. He's wearing what Mel can only guess are contact lenses. They turn his eyes into jewel-like orbs that shatter the light and send rainbow chips sprawling, vibrant, across the chipboard panelling. They're astonishing.

Jeff stares back at her. The effect is hypnotic.

She turns to Jase. She says: "A month."

Killing wasn't always so easy. Roy had to learn. And when you learn, you make mistakes.

Roy had messed up one job in a big way. And sometimes, spellbound by insomnia, he replays the error on whichever ceiling hangs above him.

It was a dark and stormy night…

The client had turned up at last orders with a pre-agreed codeword. Roy remembers him being nervy, wan, rank with bad health.

"Grab a pew," Roy said. "Make yourself cosy."

The man sat and picked at his cuticles.

Roy pushed his peanuts across the table. "What's mine is yours. What can we do for you?"

Lover spurned. Love rival. Love rat. It wasn't the point; he didn't remember this – the details didn't matter. "There's business to be had in the sorting of squabbles." That's how the Reverend put it. Even then, even with his mind falling apart, and the Reverend applying pressure to a certain part of him, he agreed; saw that clear as day. The collapse was the opening. Its yawning tract was actually a foundation. And sitting there, even with so much lost, even with so much of what made them civil gone or going, Roy understood there was a living to scrape out from the cracks.

Naturally the client had concerns, for which Roy had stock answers: *No trace. Don't be daft, I'm in with the right people. Nah, the cars always go to the scrappers afterwards.*

And then – only then – had the envelope been passed under the table.

"Jesus, I feel like I'm in a film," the client said.

A wink from Roy. "You could be," he told him. "You could well be."

A ringing bell broke the moment: "Last orders!" the barman sang.

The day after the meeting, Roy stole a large estate car and drove hard to Leicester. Over the Woodhead, windlashed, through the holes punched into England's twisted spine. Down through the M1 barricades, through gun checks, patdowns, all under drone watch. The odd rebel staging post, untouchable enclaves. He cruised past armoured convoys, citybound in the opposite lane.

People say it's bad now, but it was really bad back then.

Unusually, Roy didn't need to bribe anyone at the city's ringroad. The inner checkpoints were also clear. And then he was parked outside the mark's hotel, where the local operation ran a valet service which doubled as security. Nothing to do with courtesy: just practical; preferable to carjacking, the fastest-growing business of their time. Roy smiled, handed over the key. He wore leather gloves, a gift from the Reverend, and kept an eye on the car's rear lights as they illuminated a route towards another vehicle to steal.

Roy was tired after all the driving. It should've been the first warning. But he was also bolstered by how easily he smarmed the receptionist. He went in bleary, slower than usual, but still remembered to pulse the reception camera. Then, after deliberately catching a lift two floors too high and walking back down the stairs, heart beginning to clap, he shorted himself into the mark's hotel suite, found the bedroom, and got a surprise. A nasty scene:

Not the mark, but the mark's wife.

And their child.

Roy remembers all this through the details and the smells. She was in the shower, and she was singing. The little boy was on the bed, propped up on scrawny elbows with his feet dangling off the end. A lovely looking lad, he was, with superheroes on his pyjamas. The scent was sweet Sudocrem and shampoo. Steamed mirrors. A rose-patterned carpet and a golden chandelier. Leicester's interminable, siren-shot night. Curtains that looked so insubstantial in the breeze.

Roy ducked into the room. Roy remembers thinking, *Just be brave, little man, and this'll be fine.* He supposed it was a scene from a life he might've had – a kind of reverse premonition.

Backed against a wall, Roy edged across, hands splayed, as though on a ledge. He went deeper into the shadows, grateful that the TV flooded the room with sound.

Then the woman opened the bathroom door.

Roy flattened himself then, just off the angle. He stayed down and hoped and hoped –

At last he looked – no danger – and used the long mirrors to watch them.

The woman was patting her hair with a small towel. Not a clue. Her lad rolled over, his pyjama shirt open and chest fully white.

"Oh!" the woman said. "You big sausage. Why've you got that all over you?"

The boy looked awkward. Sort of distant and sad. He put a hand in the pasty mess and started crying. "You told me Sudocrem fixes everything," he said.

"Silly apeth," she said, and pulled him into her.

"I want to go home," the boy told her, muffled in her flesh. "Daddy's never here even when he brings us with him."

Remarkably, this filled Roy's throat.

The woman held him then, and her towel came away as she sat on the bed.

Roy was too tensed, lost his balance, felt a joint crack.

The woman span.

Roy cleared his throat, got up to leave, whispered, for some reason he'll never understand: "Excuse me."

The boy nearly hit the ceiling. But he didn't scream.

The woman baulked, wet hair across her face. She did.

Then the suite's front door opened. Timing or what.

The woman stared at Roy, hand on her mouth. Her eyes were glassy. Her scream echoed down the corridor –

The mark ran in, saw his family, then Roy. He went, "You?"

Almost like he knew him.

So Roy being Roy took out his revolver and shot all three.

The woman's mask comes into Sol's hands with a sucking noise. Like papier-mâché off a balloon. The tubes come out with a gout of phlegm. She gags, but there's nothing to bring up.

Artificial light –

And so much to take in at once: Sol looks into her drawn eyes, bigger than average, and dead-glazed, each staring loosely back; an uncanny luminosity to them. Her nose is crooked. Her head's shaved bald. There's dry blood caked on her chin, a dotted square tattoo on her throat. And her mouth is stapled closed.

Sol simply shakes his head. Unreality. You can imagine horror, conceive horrific acts, but being confronted with it, and so intimately, dismantles the world around you – kicks you in the guts and leaves you swaying on the flimsiest of bases. A savage reminder that people are at their most inventive when they want to hurt each other.

From her face, he guesses the woman must be in her early twenties. Nameless, voiceless – caught now between some hidden ordeal and the cold walls of Sol's knock-off shop.

"Are you OK?" he asks, a hand on his face.

She peers into him, eyes sharpening. Working him out, maybe. Then she's looking past him, focusing on the far wall. He clocks that she's seen something – it's there in her expression, a twinge, a shift. Her eyes snap back to him, and she seems to hold her breath. And then it all changes again.

Just like that, just as fast, the woman's fugue evaporates. She lunges at him, collapses on to him. Only the sounds of nasal breathing, scuffling, as she claws at his head and face. Caught off guard, he's quickly overpowered. The blows come sharply, and while he parries what he can, she's too powerful – so scarily quiet and committed. Her hairless head remains still, neck strong, and she doesn't seem to blink at all.

"Stop," he manages. "Stop!" Sol grabs a wrist, tries to drag it across him to decentre her weight. But the woman has him straddled, and each time he pulls, her third fist finds a gap.

"For God's sake, stop!"

The woman stops. She glares down at him.

"I swear I'm not," he tells her. *Not what?* "Please! I swear it."

She slits her eyes. She grabs him roughly by the jowls and pins his head back, rotates it. With her third hand, she points to a faded calendar on the wall.

He shakes his head as much as he can, looking between the calendar's naked model and the dashed tattoo on the woman's neck. "What? No – you've... It's nothing that, I swear – just... just a bit of fun."

The woman shakes her head quickly, mocking his paralysis. She tightens her grip until he can't move his head at all.

"What is it?" His voice is strangled. "What? The calendar? That's nothing! It doesn't mean anything at all! I don't know what–"

The woman shudders. She flops away from him, claps her three hands on the barrel of his chest. She makes him look at her; pulls at her skin – her elastic neck, stomach, arms – until he is grimacing, wincing with imagined pain. She points at him, accusatory, goading him to watch. In some way she's flawless, but she's panting and clawing at herself, and her eyes strobe with ire. Sol watches her, mute and embarrassed. In the half-light of the workshop, this little room, with all the electrics humming, it's as if every inch of her is covered in scars.

Y

This maker was called Chaplain, and he worked in the production suite. His name was more of a misnomer – he didn't have much spirituality about him, but instead a kind of smokiness. He trailed a smell that made you wonder if he carried a hunk of something rotten in his pocket.

Chaplain wasn't gentle, Y found. And that morning he woke her with a giddy shake.

Y snapped from her grey dreams and expected the Manor Lord's face to be bearing down, expressionless and infinite, forcing into her the taste of bitty gruel. It took a beat to register Chaplain's features – the unmistakable implants that glittered in his face; the subtle rainbows that danced over his brow and into the folds and pits of his cheeks.

She suppressed her panic, as usual. She remembered nothing new, as usual. And just as she'd tried for hours the night before, she attempted to rip the tooth pendant from around her neck.

"Hey, that's permanent," Chaplain told her, loud

enough to wake three cradles each side of her. "Don't be such a disappointment." He gazed over Y's glistening forehead, her greased head stubble, pausing to admire the nexus of her shoulders and collarbones, the sculpture of her stomach. "You're ready," he told her. "All this work, and today we make you a hero."

Y squirmed and stretched out. Wearing the chain and pendant was now a sentence of its own: it felt like a collar, a sign of someone's ownership, a ligature that only grew tighter as she fought it, and one that was cutting her invisibly at that. She spat in a funnel marked SPUTUM, and swore she'd get it off somehow.

Unlike the driller, Chaplain didn't pretend to look away while she pulled on her robe. He looked her up and down and handed her a large pill. "You'll have to let it dissolve as it is. No water yet – apparently one of the vaults needed a lot of cleaning…"

Y remembered the server. *To-mo-rrow.* She snatched the pill and kicked it back in one.

"Steady," Chaplain said. He gestured to the cradle suite's exit. "We're in the bowels."

Y followed Chaplain down there. Eventually they entered into a long, narrow rat run, lined with cheap wood and wiring. She'd heard of these studios – had sometimes heard Chaplain introduce their output between supper feeds and lights-out – but she hadn't expected them to be so basic.

Every few metres sat a turret-style camera rig with its lens disappeared through a slat in the walling. The red recording LEDs from each unit dotted these walls on both sides, and stretched well into the distance. They made the corridor look more like a runway at night. Y attuned to the rhythm of these blinking lights; intrigued as they fell into rows, blinking in harmony for two or three flashes before tumbling back to chaos. As Y moved through the hooped wires, around the powerpacks and tripod legs, the cameras conjured a strange image: the cannon of old ships on rough seas, their barrels pushed out through gunports.

Y bristled at this – the image was stark but fleeting. It seemed at arm's length, like her other memories, forever turning a corner just ahead of her. A reminder something had been taken from her that she couldn't retrieve. It made her ache, and it added to her confusion at what she'd managed to keep: this internal language, her ability to understand her makers, these truncated memories of before. How cruel that they'd left her with the stubbornness to know things hadn't always been this way. Because how could you be homesick for a home you couldn't remember?

The corridor only seemed to get longer, and Chaplain being ahead afforded Y a few stolen glimpses through the camera slats. The gaps were tight, so she couldn't see much – quick flashes of skin tone, exotic textile, the movement of lurid wigs. If she saw the Manor Lord now, would she react? Would a night of building rage finally combust?

Then Y tripped, and Chaplain heard it. "Y," he said, pausing. His eyes, catching the red lights, were like cells of fairies.

Y slackened, relented. Chaplain's use of her name was warning enough.

Eventually they came to a door. Chaplain knocked, and a woman appeared.

"You're late," she said. Y didn't catch a name – distracted instead by the trolley of clothes on the other side of the room. Its props and mirrors. Her guts were restive. She'd sat through screenings of these productions, but...

But nothing. The room was misting around her. A floral changing screen that covered silhouettes in the corner. Y knew there was something missing. Its absence rendered physical by a numbness that encroached from the corners. For the first time she noticed her vision was doubling and redoubling. Was it Chaplain's pill?

He guided Y with a hand on her back. The rainbows from his eyes travelled across the room's sterile-shiny surfaces. Over there, the woman tended to the clothes like they were plants, sliding hangers that dripped with strange garments from left to right. Centre stage was a seat fashioned from a stuffed animal's body. The animal had glossy brown fur and six legs, and its torso had one panel of ribs missing to accommodate a person sitting. Though the fur had clearly been restitched by a skilled crafter, the work was so faultless it looked like the creature was born and bred for comfort. Beyond where you'd naturally rest an arm, the fur and flesh beyond the neck was also missing – it revealed the top of the spine, ornately pinned with golden fixings, and the creature's long collarbones. The neck flowered into a death's head – a monumental skull angled down, as if the creature was grazing, or servile. Y stared at the skull's sockets: their distinct, odd shape, and at the four sharp horns curling out from its snout. It was a much larger version of the skull she'd seen on the Manor Lord's sceptre.

"A bursor," Chaplain said. "Wandered over from the fringelands – from the plains we will not and cannot go." He was still smiling. "Fascinating things. More or less vegetarian despite the fierce look. We're told the horns help it strip bark from trees, get at the sap. There's always bits of tree in their fur, you know? The synthesis is astonishing for its size – and a specimen of this size is almost as rare as you. One of our trolley teams brought it here with that chunk missing. We still don't know what could've taken such a bite…"

"Is she ready?" the other woman asked. She'd pulled a slick-looking mask over her nose and mouth.

"Sit down, please sit," Chaplain told Y. "Try to relax." He gestured to the woman by the rack. "Yes," he said.

The woman came towards Y. She held a luxuriant shawl in her hands.

Y looked away. Set in the far wall of the room, a camera lens twisted. The bursor loomed monstrous on its convex glass. Was he there? Was he behind it?

He watched me. He kept watching.

Y slumped into the bursor's fur; found its seat so accommodating. She felt herself melting into it – the fur even softer than it looked, the rear panel of the seat a kind of endless yawn. She was sleepy, and the surfaces were coming unstuck. The encroaching edges had enlarged, risen up. They were curling in.

Sounds came from somewhere else now – Chaplain or the wardrobe woman, she couldn't tell.

She heard: "Systemic protection… designed not to… selective… amnesiac…"

Y croaked. A rising noise that hung, reverberating, above everything else in her head. A droning. She'd never wanted to say something more. Her heart rate was soaring now, but her eyelids were heavy and falling. She began to feel angry again –

Still the voices spoke. More people in the room now. Fleshy. Medical overalls? The camera lens tightened on her. The red dot blink stopped for nothing. "Exquisite specimen… and the price? Bargain, really. Sold to an anonymous bidder, hence the demo, and ready for shipment tomorrow if all goes well–"

Y felt a set of hands move across her head. Fingers

picked at her shawl. Pushing, goading.

To-mor-row –

Y collapsed into herself, supernova, a universe folding right up. The figures came towards her until everything became the red dot. The singularity. And in her bursor seat, the loving fur, Y accepted the fugue, the focusing lens, and crawled right in. The room's corners crashed over her.

Inside the folds, there was only rage.

Y felt herself expand, her muscles thrumming with blood. At last, beyond the point of bursting, she stood tall and exploded, a fresh impulse compelling her. The figures in the room recoiled, remonstrated, but she didn't care.

They would come apart in her hands.

Him. Them. All of them.

SIX

A few days into the trial, Mel approaches Jeff from the reception cage. He's been sitting in the foyer since the morning, sunglasses on despite the drizzle.

"Quiet mouse aren't you?" she says.

Jeff shakes his weighty head. "Small talk's pointless," he tells her. "You should measure my abilities by tips."

Mel frowns. "So far it feels like I'm paying you to sit there in a corner and put people off. Jason know you're on a jolly does he?"

Jeff doesn't reply.

"Rude as well. Didn't they squeeze manners into that big head of yours, or what?"

Jeff leans, puts his mass to bear. "Would you prefer me to record your feedback and pass it to my supervisor?"

"You daft bugger. I'm not a grass, for starters. Just… just try and make yourself useful, right? Could try getting you on some outcalls if you like – save you sitting here all day. And think about taking them glasses off, will you? You seen it out there?"

The front door opens. Mel turns quickly, as if she's

been caught doing something. A dark shape moves across the hallway's tinted glass, and a pale, lanky man blunders in through the second door. He looks about awkwardly, a bracing draught all about him.

"Salaam," he says. A nasally voice. A thick plastercast round his right arm. His features are small and ratty, and untreated acne has cratered his chin.

Mel raises her eyebrows. "Hi," she says.

The man's visibly trembling. Some punters do.

Mel smiles and fetches the menu, watches as the punter picks through its laminated sheets.

"You're actually a bit early," Mel tells him. "If you want to wait, you're welcome, but I'd head back out for a wander if I were you."

The punter smiles, shifts. Clearly doesn't know what to do with himself.

"A drink?"

"What you got?"

"Glass of water?"

The punter shrugs, takes a seat. "Safe, yeah." He crosses his legs at the knee, more for the warmth than comfort. His jogging bottoms are soaked to the shins. "Heard decent things about this place."

Mel doesn't respond. She pours filtered rainwater from a jug and watches the punter struggle with the menu; his one good hand just about dextrous enough to flip the pages. She hands him the glass.

"What you done to that arm then?"

The punter blanches. He swallows a mouthful of water so fast his throat squawks. "Got jumped."

"Your wrist?"

"Elbow." The punter holds up his glass, furrows his brow. "Shot me. One round, like. Doc reckons I'll be picking fragments out of my chest for months... Sorry love, sorry – this water's got bits in it."

"Jesus," Mel says, ignoring his complaint. "They get anything off you?"

The punter downs the rest of his water. He swallows noisily again. "Did they fuck."

"And you reported it?"

The punter smiles and shakes his head. Puts his glass on the floor. "No." Mel looks sidelong at Jeff. "But they say it'll never stop hurting. Like an ache, innit."

"So what you thinking, then?" She nods at the menu.

"In here? Vanilla, to be fair."

Mel points to a picture on the open page.

"Safe her, isn't she?"

"That our number four?"

"Yeah. Nice one. Looks mint, her."

The punter notices Jeff staring now – goes to speak, decides against it. He opens his hands, somewhere towards a shrug.

"You heard?" he asks Mel. "Them nerds at the uni got the web destricted again."

"Derestricted, you mean?"

"I'm just saying. Better than the council doing it, innit? Gets you on most sites now. Like the old days. Had a few tins at home last night and got on the old networks and everything. Didn't even need a proxy."

"Haven't tried," Mel says. "Not for ages."

The punter nods emphatically. "You should. Honest. Your shop's on a site I found."

"What kind of site?"

"Directory of parlours and that. Can't argue with it. And I goes to my missus, 'No way man, they've been updating this while the rest of us had no bloody connection!' Know what I mean? The privileged few."

"Council bunch get all the perks," Mel tells him. "Still get a few in here on their tablets from time to time."

The punter nods, gawky.

Mel shrugs. "Will you want to pay up front or afterwards? If it's afterwards, I'll need your keys."

"He pays half up front," Jeff says from the corner.

The punter glances at Jeff then up at Mel, expectant. She can feel Jeff's eyes on her. "Shut up," she says, not looking over.

The punter doesn't know what to do. A strange silence settles. The walls flashing with skin.

"What are *you* here for, mate?" the punter asks Jeff.

The big man coughs. "I work here."

The punter throws his good arm up. "Chill, man, chill. Was only asking."

"Keeping an eye on scum like you," Jeff adds.

Now Mel glares at him.

The punter points a thumb. He whispers to Mel: "Who's he with?"

"Ignore it," Mel says. "Elephant in the room."

Jeff chuckles, taps his nose. "Just saying. I've got my beady eyes on you."

The punter stands up, and the brothel's air seems to shift, break. "How long you say I'm waiting again?"

"Not long," Mel tells him. "Any minute, really."

"Safe, safe."

Mel isn't far wrong. Somewhere out the back a bolt slides, and a cold lock rattles.

"That's Cassie," Jeff says.

Mel pouts. "You reckon?"

"You can smell her," he says.

Mel isn't sure she's heard him right.

"Hiya!" shouts a woman.

"Jesus," Mel says. She can't even look at Jeff. Then,

with mock brightness, she shouts: "Through here, Cass!"

Cassie bounds in. "Oh, lots of you," she says. She undoes her coat. An old band T-shirt, faded black with lurid green print. As she takes off her bag, the T-shirt's hem catches and rises, reveals the lower curl of a three tattooed on striated belly. She winks at Jeff, unfazed by the room's strange mood. "Who's first, then?"

The punter clears his throat. "You don't look nowt like four."

"But three's your lucky number," Cass says back. "Just have to let me get some slap on first."

The pair of them disappear. There's a rattle of door beads. A slam.

"What the hell was all that about?" Mel asks Jeff, fuming. She snatches the menu off the bench and goes back to the counter.

Jeff comes over to the mesh, leans on it. "It's only vetting. I can help while you get me some work. I won't get in your way."

"Vetting? This isn't a frigging job shop, Jeff. It's a business. My business. And that means I decide who's welcome and who's not."

Jeff ignores her. He lowers his sunglasses. Hard-cut diamonds shine out. "Call it market research," he says. "It's key. Tweak this, tweak that. It's how you make more money. And I want to fix up that missing letter and give the place a polish. You'd be a premium leisure destination. All tastes catered for."

Mel clenches her jaw.

"Are they all like him?" Jeff asks. "The punters?"

"Who – that fucking no-mark in there? No. Not all. I mean you even get couples sometimes."

Jeff nods down at Mel's arms. "We all have secrets, don't we?"

Mel tugs at her sleeves. *Does he know?* "I'm just saying it isn't my business who they are as long as they pay up."

"I know," Jeff says. "I get that. So I'm making it mine."

On a good day, Roy believes waiting is a fine art with few masters.

Now and then you hear about others – assassins working for wealthy foreigners, odd-jobbers with the kind of esoteric skills you don't learn by choice. Part-time handy types who do their bit for their neighbours when they have to. And through the Reverend, Roy knows personally a few others: Jan, a canal runner who's in with the Wilbers on the side. Ro – a bobby turned vigilante, who garrottes unsolved case suspects when she isn't making IEDs. Jane Doe, a spark on call – a drone engineer with a sideline in meter hacks and weed farm setups. And even Raj – a retired metalworker who'll convert your replica firearms for a modest fee…

All of these people are masters of waiting. All of them have conquered patience. Yet none of them do it quite like Roy. Lone wolf not because it's simpler, but because it suits him better. A man for whom waiting still means working hard.

Cut to interior. Night time. Roy sitting in the Rose with a woman. Not a date – a job to pass the time. Something to do while he relaxes.

The job was phoned in by the Reverend from a payphone on the bar corner – the fat man's breathing fraying over the line – not long after Roy returned from Sol's workshop. "Domestic client," he tells Roy. "Easy money. Don't you dare fuck it up."

The client gets a spot in the parking sprawl, finds Roy in the corner. As usual he's spotted her from way off, standing next to her dark car. At the bar she orders a straight gin. He guesses she's carrying the world on her shoulders. When she turns, he confirms the heavy look – someone at the end of their tether. It's a look his clients often have. It's the look he wears inside.

She sits. She says, "Are you the man I called?" Her voice is snippy, precise.

Roy smiles. "No. You spoke to my boss."

"He was incredibly rude."

Roy pretends to look shocked. "Surely not. How was your journey?"

She points up ambiguously. "Overseen."

And from there it all blurs into one:

How much when how long will I have to wait will it work though will you get caught will I go to jail will you go to jail how can I trust you the best price on the table what he's done to us it needs to end I'm not scared he doesn't listen no one else no thanks can I buy you a drink though are you sure this is all you're drinking I understand do you have a partner kids a dog a place to call home…

And fifteen minutes later Roy finds himself behind the wheel and outside the first ring of Didsbury's defences. His client in the back seat, swallowing hard. Death sitting patiently alongside him, its heavy limbs around his shoulders.

Roy smiles. The compound's mesh fencing and sharpline fixings catch sweeping torches like dewy spiderwebs at first light. The car's facing toward the guard booth windows. Roy can see his breath. He thinks: *The world goes on like this because the world's always been like this.* He thinks: *It's better now people are more honest, more accepting of their nature.*

He thinks of the Reverend, the cost of failure.

"I don't want him dead," the client says. "You

understand me, don't you? I'm not a murderer. That's not what this is about. I don't want you to be, either."

Roy adjusts the mirror. "They'll riddle us if we move another yard forward," he tells her. "You sure he doesn't leave?"

"Not often, no. I mean he works all the hours God–"

"You told me."

"How do you get in?" she asks. "What about the drones?"

Roy turns round to her. "I'll suss all that, don't fret. My problem – not yours. And there's not much motorway here, anyway. They don't bother with A-roads."

"I suppose not," she says.

"You can get out here if you want."

"I don't know. I don't know if I want to, you know…"

"Watch?"

The client nods. She wipes her eyes and blows her nose.

"I'd say you don't."

"Then how will I know?"

"You'll just know."

"But how?"

Roy unlocks the car doors. "You'll just know."

Dysentery once seemed a distant ailment – a disease that only came in the aftermath of natural disasters; a partner to looting; a black-winged angel of aid camps; a scourge of refugees running borders.

No longer.

Manchester's learned about dysentery the hard way, with serious outbreaks usually spreading from the markets outwards. It's easily cured, at least in theory, but now it's more common than ever, and the right antibiotics so often aren't, it can have an edge.

One of Mel's employees is stricken with it. She hasn't left her plastic wetroom in two days, and couldn't if she wanted to.

So Mel raids the takings and heads into town for help – hoping she has enough to secure medicine from the charity bus that tours the northwest most weeks, and stops in the centre twice on its rounds.

Out there it's lonely and quiet and Mel loves it this way. She leaves Cassie in charge, Jeff on a stool by the inner door. She ponders him, his elusiveness, as she turns from Ancoats down Oldham Street and into the Northern Quarter: a patch of the city once forgotten, rejuvenated, and forgotten again. Its amorphous edges like a mole worth checking.

Right onto Church Street, left onto Tib Street. A yawning multistorey car park echoing her bootfall. Each street maintains its own smell: blocked grids, food stalls, hawkers' wares and composting rubbish left in piles where once civic lawns flourished. The pavements squelch with mulch as Mel skirts Affleck's Palace, smiling at the tilework sign that reads AND ON THE SIXTH DAY, GOD CREATED MANCHESTER. Back when life meant hot meals, salaries, unfiltered tap water, Mel got her ears pierced in there, up on the top floor, and an ill-fitting nose ring installed another time. She and her mates fancied the piercer, a dreadlocked guy with some wacky name – Diesel or Merlin or Rats – who was slightly too old for them and probably knew it. They came every weekend to see him, and he knew that too. What did her friends call her again? *Mosher*. She thumbs her nostril and remembers. Some scars you're proud to keep.

Tib Street soon intersects Market Street, a bank of rainbow panels to the right, a huddle of bent bollards ahead. It opens out, here, at Market Street's top end:

the bleeding stump of the commercial row. The council had given this section to independent traders to try and revive the high street, but now, almost predictably, it's abandoned.

As she reaches the junction, several pigeons blast out from an alley between a red-bricked building and a concrete garage. Mel jumps; watches them tangle and crash through a lap of the square before settling again. The city's birds seem to have a shorter range on them, and they're getting skinnier all the time.

The drugs bus is parked the other side of Market Street's tram platform, its armour relaxed. Two gutted coffee shops stand behind the crowd here, soot marks still rising up their walls. A bank next door offers unboarded apertures, eviscerated systems; its cash machines having been liberated by a mini-digger whose drag marks spread upwards from the holes.

Mel boulders the tram stop and skips down the platform towards the servery, where masked aid workers pass down bags into grasping hands. She elbows into the crowd, the cold replaced with stickiness, damp sleeves. So much coughing and spluttering. And over their heads, twin laser-dots roam: sentries on the top deck looking down for trouble. Mel doesn't like crowds – feels like something's always about to happen, unseen and unknown, just a half-turn away. When she glances right, she isn't reassured: everyone seems to be in profile, their hoods up and noses pointing forward.

Still, the crowd is subdued, voiceless, if not jostling, and Mel overhears some of the medics' care instructions. Their faces may be masked, but there's sympathy in their eyes.

The wind picks up, brings sleet. Mel flips her collar and buries her chin; watches gathering water stream down the bus's armour panels, bracketing bullet holes and blemishes. These liquid shapes hold her gaze as she shuffles slowly forward, each new position, each gap, carefully negotiated with her elbows and weight.

Someone prods her from behind – an older woman, unsmiling, with a gnarled finger pointing to the man leaning out from the bus.

"You're next," the medic says. Mel refocuses.

"Me?"

He nods. "I'm Daryl – I'm with MSF. What are you after, madam?"

The word "madam" takes Mel by surprise. "Was hoping you'll tell me," she says back.

"I'll try. Give me your symptoms – let's see if we can work it out between us."

"It's not me," Mel tells him. "It's my daughter. Pretty sure it's dysentery. Cramping, nausea, bad diarrhoea. She says there's blood in it."

He frowns. "OK, OK, that doesn't sound too good. Let's go from the top. Has your daughter travelled recently?"

"Abroad?"

"Anywhere."

"Not that I know of."

"What about the camps? Has she spent any time in them?"

"Camps?"

"Immigration centres. I don't want you to think I'm being funny here, but our dear leaders don't provide too well for visitors. If things get grotty in there, poor sanitary care for instance, you've got a nice nesting ground for bad stuff. And contamination isn't rare, regrettably."

Mel shakes her head. "She's been at home. Just at home."

"Well that's something," Daryl says, "because it cuts

the risk of amoebiasis. Usually we'd want to do some tests on a sample, but our next visit's actually a fortnight away – we've got to get the bus rearmoured. And I'm guessing you haven't brought a little tub with you." He smiles again. "Clean water's the most important thing for her, to be honest. And again, not to be funny, but do you have access to good stuff?"

Mel nods. "We boil what we can't buy – there's a rainwater butt in the yard."

"Great. Because she needs to stay hydrated. She'll be losing a lot of fluid. That means making her drink more than she's comfortable with, just to be sure. If she's too dehydrated you'll run into bigger problems. Otherwise…" Daryl darts under the counter, reappears with a box, "you'll need to try these." He shakes the box. "This is your garden-variety co-trimoxazole. Should nuke it."

"Thank you."

"You're welcome. Instructions are all inside, OK? Read them twice, please. And tell her to keep washing her hands thoroughly."

"How much do I owe you?"

Daryl scans the box.

"It's fifty, I'm afraid."

Mel pulls a slip of paper from her coat pocket. She scribbles something on it and hands it to him. "Call it a voucher in lieu of payment."

Daryl reads the chit. It takes a moment to click. When it does, he withdraws into the bus. "Not interested," he says.

Mel goes up on her tip toes. "How come? Easy stress-buster."

"Maybe I'm not explaining myself properly," he says. "It's fifty pounds or I can't serve you."

MATT HILL 121

"What if you give that to someone else, then? Like a gift?"

"Seriously?" He points behind her. "Who's next, please?"

"Fine," Mel snaps. She pulls a wad of notes from the opposite pocket and slaps them on the counter.

Daryl takes the money and looks away. "Let's hope your *daughter* finds a way out of your house."

Mel barges into the faceless crowd. Out through the squirm, in the clear, she breaks into a run, her chest tight and throat sore. She bolts over the platform and down the other side, across the rusting tram tracks.

Daryl's judgment reverberates all the way to the shop. Every step carrying it along with her, while her eyes water and his antibiotics rattle in her pocket like shackles. She knows his verdict will carry a terrible sentence: a certainty that will haunt her, slide through her system for days, weeks, even months. And however fast she moves, the wind still bites holes through the damp wool on her back.

Fleeing Didsbury, killing in his veins, Roy finds an open pub and pulls into its car park. The pub's lounge windows are half shuttered, red curtained, and he doesn't catch its name; too distracted by palpitations and torn muscles. The mark's stolen car stinking of body odour and hot guns.

Roy parks and scopes his surroundings; counts automatically, instinctively: five other vehicles, at least twenty-five witnesses, plus the bar staff. He decides to repark the car in a shadow beneath a naked oak. *Concentrate, Roy*.

Roy breathes in, gets out. *Fuck*. Distracted. That's it. He feels distracted. It's not guilt. It's not remorse. It's simple, refined distraction. He locks the door and pockets his gloves. Away from the smells of murder, he can better control himself. Some relief as a kind of dissociation begins to wash over him.

"Sociopathy," he recalls the Reverend saying, "has a steep learning curve."

Is it folly to be here, so close to Didsbury's control gates? Probably. But after a swift half, a settler, he can steal another car and get moving.

Roy goes inside; pays for his beer with pocket change that rattles a rain song in his hand.

The things you do for love –
The things you do for money.

"Shit," he whispers into his glass. At least a concession the job was messy. That it went more wrong than most. He never liked strugglers, fighters, survivor types. They made him operate right at his limits.

Here's what happened:

The mark saw Roy coming, grabbed Roy's revolver and threw his shot. The mark rallied first, and took Roy hard. In the mark's home there was a mini-bar, gold edged, the trappings of wealth, of ostriches with buried heads, and Roy and the mark fell across it. Tooth and nail, clawing to be on top. So much glass shattered. Cuts in strange places. Curiously a photo flopped from its frame nearby: a picture of the mark in medical overalls against a bullet-pocked wall.

The mark was vicious, running on fear. Roy didn't fight hard enough, ended up on the bottom, head filled with the animal musk of the mark's body. His revolver skittled, bounced, spat a single shot. The wall puffed plaster, revealed a gash. Imagine the scene: iron-brown water frothing out onto a shagpile carpet.

Roy wriggled, absorbed several blows, somehow

forced his way free. His face felt lumpen, and something vital was leaking.

The mark still had hold of Roy's leg when Roy reached his revolver. Roy angled, fired, a foot or two away, the noise of his makeshift silencer breaking, and the shot took the man in the side of his neck. It carved out a flap of ham.

The mark tried to scream. He put a hand to his throat. Blood came in hell's rainbows between his fingers –

He looked at Roy, no words, all eyes. There was so much hurt in that look, with one side of his face sopping red and the other turning white. Roy turned away and fired again: shot the mark in the mouth in such a way that the round went in and out of his cheek via the lower jawbone, and the bottom of his face exploded.

Now the mark's screaming was glottal-stopped, bubbled air escaping through pockets of meat. He had no definable lips, just a half-jaw dangling from the hinge on one side, and connective tissue daubing his collar.

In the pub, Roy closes his eyes. Locked back in that moment, his memory-image grows iteratively worse. Sometimes it's hard to kill another human; sometimes so much harder than you think.

So Roy being Roy he shot again. And again. A fifth time, then, so that the mark sagged back on himself, only the strength of his spine to hold him; so that he wobbled there, suspended in the amber of lamplight, rocking over his knees on the thick shagpile, with his face dripping like a hung paintbrush, and the noise from his throat phlegmatic.

Roy threw up in the mark's front room. All over the leatherette sofa. He scrambled backwards like some damaged crab and watched the vomit roll down the fabric in clumps. He distinctly remembers thinking that the nice carpet wasn't all that nice now. He thought that's what the Reverend might say.

The violence was finished. The job was done. And Roy sat and watched his victim, senses glowing with a prehistoric thrill.

His next decisions, he knew, were critical. He knew he had to stage this. Make it look amateur. Make it look opportunistic – a Didsbury burglary gone wrong. He showered, wiped down, bagged his clothes and trashed the place, before setting a small fire in the kitchen bin. Finally, he pocketed a black key from a hook by the door, and drove off in the mark's car.

Roy sips his drink. The next thing was perhaps the most surreal of all:

The gates of Didsbury had opened automatically. The guards actually waved him out.

It's all kicking off when Mel gets back.

Outside the Cat Flap, Cassie and two other women are standing in their nighties screaming at an unkempt man – also half dressed – about something he's paid or not paid.

"You're a bunch of cheeky robbing bastards," the man keeps shouting. He has painful-looking clutch marks on his arms, and both hands outstretched. Mel doesn't recognize him.

Cass is doing her best to separate them all, and locals are starting to come out on the street.

Mel starts with the man. "I'm the owner here," she tells him. "The owner – will you listen to me? Tell me what's going on." She turns to Cass. "Get them inside. *Inside*. And get Jeff out here." *Where the hell is Jeff?*

"Get these slags to tell you," he spits. "I want my money back!"

Mel turns him softly, redirecting his rage. "Listen," she says, "we won't get anywhere with you talking about people like that. You can sling it now, or get your kecks on and talk me through what happened. It'll save you your dignity. But believe me, I won't give you the option again."

The man sniggers, indignant. "Take a lot to sort this lot – especially that gorilla you've got in there."

"Jeff?"

"Jeff, Jim-bob, Jeremiah – need to put a leash on him, I'm telling you."

Mel pinches her nose. A pressure mounting behind her false eye. The man's skin is flushed and bumpy. His nose is crusted off-black where someone's bopped him. "Go on," she says.

"You tell me! I was enjoying the service I frigging *paid for* when he stomps in and starts knocking us about–"

She squeezes his shoulder. "He went for you?"

"Not just me, no – them two as well. Nearly put one of them through the bloody window he did. He's off his head!"

"And you were alone with them."

"Yeah." He looks at the parlour window and growls in frustration. "Filthy fucking–"

Mel squeezes his shoulder. "Less of it. I told you: I don't like that tone."

"Well it's bullshit," he says. "You're lucky I haven't called the council. Worked my arse off for that money!"

Mel holds his stare. He doesn't know which of her eyes to look in. "What next?"

"We all got him down – someone leathered him with a shoe. Threw him in that manky cupboard – the door was right there, right next to the room, and we locked him in."

"And this was out of the blue? No misbehaving?"

"Nothing I hadn't paid for."

Mel looks away and tears a strip off her fingernail. It pulls skin right from the nailbed. "I think it's time to go," she tells him. "How much did you pay?"

"Eighty."

"Well here's twenty of it." Mel throws her last pair of tenners on the road.

The man swears at her and reaches for his tenners on the wet ground. "It's snide as fuck, this. I swear it. What happened to 'the customer's always right'?" He closes his belt, angles to move away. "The customer's always right!" he shouts again.

"Course he is," Mel says back. "Course he is."

Inside, the waiting room's a state – one screen off the wall, scattered. Chipboard stripped from the damp wall it covered. Even some of the window blinds are bent.

Cassie's sitting there, a slender joint on the burn. "He gone?"

Mel nods. The smell of green is dizzying. "What the bloody hell was that all about? You heard what he said?"

Cassie grimaces. "He's not far wrong about it, M... Jeff's been prowling all day. Heard him outside mine before – even caught him leaning into the door when I opened it."

Mel tries to mask the despair of knowing her gut feeling was right. A breath before she speaks again. "Where are the others now?"

"Stropped off home."

Mel shakes her head. "Look at the state of it."

"It's sortable," Cassie says. "Dustpan and brush. But Mel, don't give them a hard time. He was way out of line that punt – too much coke probably... too much swag. And Jeff... you tell me. He's been acting like king of the castle. He bounces up there, opens the door and–"

"And what?"

Suddenly Cassie looks uncertain. "I'd just keep him locked up, if I were you. Get to the bottom of what he's playing at, going after clients like that. No wonder it booted off."

Mel feels pale. "What did he do?"

Cassie doesn't reply.

"Cass."

Cassie sighs. "He went in there with his hands down his pants. The girls said it was like he saw something and decided he wanted a go himself. Like he just couldn't help it."

Mel finds herself leaning on the counter, head swimming.

"If it was me," adds Cassie, two fingers scissoring, "I'd chop it off."

Y

Tomorrow came. They extracted Y before sunset, when purple skies gave into brown, and thin clouds like cracks appeared and ran to the serrated horizon. Several armed makers escorted her across the training lawns and down the mansion's drive. "You're ready, you're ready," they chanted, like an incantation.

They passed rock gardens where the flowers had faded into blue and brown, a thousand sad things left unwatered, and Y noticed that the sprinklers were limp, dribbling, and that even the drinking fountains were off. Everything was losing its colour.

She walked her last walk in this place with bare feet, her training pumps in two hands, her third hand coiled into her chest, taut over the pendant. She thought of her brothers and sisters left behind, with their incubators fixed above, and wondered if they'd leave today, too.

The grass was still tickly, its heat from the day starting to dissipate. She found she could scrunch her toes and pull little clumps from the soil – a final act of petty rebellion. She tried to smile to herself, but a numbness stayed her. Whatever happened in the bursor room had exhausted her. Her shoulders wouldn't rotate properly, and the articulation of her joints was different. In her mind she kept revisiting the space; remembered the anger, the warmth in her hands. Then she felt frustrated: it was all too abstracted – another misremembered dream.

What would she miss? Certainly not the asinine things the makers and their minions said when they woke her. Certainly not these lawns. In fact, she'd miss nothing except perhaps the homeliness of routine. The structured monotony of life here. Now, she knew, it was only her ability to adjust that mattered.

At the same time, she knew she was good at adjusting. She'd become even better at forgetting. By design she'd become a woman of sinew and tough, gristly meat – there was no capacity for floundering. And if she came back here, it would be to do one thing.

Beyond the mansion's gates sat a matt-black vehicle with enormous caterpillar tracks. For a time she stood in the warm breeze of its exhaust vents, until someone behind, another maker in a surgical mask, gestured towards the top hatch. Y climbed it and turned to the mansion, its immaculate lines. In the odd light it was the colour of baby teeth; had the smoothness of bone. She blinked at it. It was him. It was all him, here.

A maker on the ground said, "You've done him proud. Our finest work yet."

And the whole squad saluted her in unison.

Y lowered herself through the hatch, her sore lats taking the strain. Her feet found purchase on something hard, and she found herself in a cramped hold that reeked of disinfectant. She took a seat on a slab bench facing inwards. The surfaces were greasy with oil and condensate. With the engine running, everything squeaked and rattled around her. The disinfectant stung her eyes.

She wasn't alone. Three others sat on the opposite bench, one hooded, two asleep. A troop escort dropped in after her; stood on the footplate beneath the turret. He pushed the gun up its channel and out on its rails. Then he turned and kneeled and cuffed Y to a pipe.

"Wanna watch her if I was you," he told Y, pointing to the hooded traveller opposite. The hooded head rose, flopped again. "Yeah, that one. Spitter."

Y closed her eyes.

"Look at me, girl."

Y looked at her bonds, the pipe.

"I said look at me."

Y defied him again. She stared at the top of the passenger's bowed head, saw patterns in the hood's weave.

"Dickhead," the escort said, and tutted. "Was only gonna say you'll want to keep shuffling. Give you piles that bench will."

Y responded by tensing her muscles.

You could snap him if you wanted to.

The thought jolted her. Intrusive at best. It exploded from nowhere – but she knew in her bones, in her molten insides, that she ought to believe it.

The rattles intensified. Something clanged against the hull, and the transport juddered and rolled away.

The escort stood up. His hips swivelled left and right; swung his gun turret accordingly – the squeak of the mechanism audible even over the engine.

Y closed her eyes and tilted her pelvis. She braced against the seat. When she opened them again, the escort was back down in the hold, sitting on his platform. He was skinning something with a small knife: a red fruit with a sharp smell. "Only a short hop to the Slope," he said, tearing out a segment and eating it. "So listen up."

Y watched a line of juice run from the corner of his mouth.

"Bet they haven't told you about the Slope," he said, chewing wetly. "They never do."

Y looked down. Only that once, in the canteen. She shook her head.

"It's cosmic up close," he told her, eyes blazing. "Everything's this weird colour. But it isn't a place for humans. The Slope isn't tarmackable – you can't wire it, run a staircase down it, make it safe. It won't roll out the red carpet for you. We shouldn't be using it, to be honest. No one should've found it. Beggars belief we even did. And surprise surprise, it's got a million ways to let you know you aren't welcome."

The escort looked young; seemed younger even than her. There was a little rash of hair on his chin.

"Fucked-up climate on there as well," he went on. "Goes widthways forever – they sent parties both directions, and only a few came back. The ones who did say there's creatures beyond. Forests of gore, canopies of skin, failed teeth. Mad stuff like that. And it's always cold, and slippery – this crazy white dust on everything. Ruins your boots, like lime, you know? And the wind, the stories you hear about that wind – it kicks up from nowhere and puts the powder in the air. It'll sand down your suit and flay you to bone if you even look at it the wrong way. And then he'll find a way to collect you. He owns all of it, that way."

Y listened. In her mind's eye, the mansion was receding.

"Then you've got these random, spilled-over slips,"

the escort said. "Anti-holes you can fall in, lose things down. Like your feet. Your legs if you're really unlucky. Or the slips that open up and dump second-world shit on you. Silly bastards on the other side not using the official bridge in here, you know? And what else…" He scratches his head. "Ahh, stormdunes. Ruthless like waves: they'll slide over and smother you. Shred everything they pass, when they're big enough. And there's ash. Your breathing gear has to chew through that stuff when it starts spewing. Man, the Slope's just nasty… a nasty place." The escort smiled. "But needs must," he said. "Otherwise they'd find the mansion, wouldn't they? And that'd be no good for business."

Y started to feel ill.

"You'll be grand, though. Honest. I'd just feel lucky you've got a trolley squad, anyway. Most of you – them, sorry – go boxed up, on sleds." He nodded, as if the comment were simple fact – as casual as a comment on the weather – then shook his head and looked away as if he'd only just remembered he wasn't meant to speak about it. "Most of you, yeah."

And the transport lumbered on.

SEVEN

Roy's four pints down, with a fifth, just poured, foamy on the bar. He taps at his head. Way too drunk to drive now, though somewhere in there he decides he'll try regardless.

The jukebox cranks out vintage Roses, Mondays, Carpets – predictable tunes for a border pub, where the lucky-rich and damned cross paths. Carefree, mad-fer-it Manchester, repurposed and sold back to the bare future through a haze of nostalgia. The barmaid serving them with a watch-yourself glare. She's got one earbud in – techno music leaking – and her fingers sweep over a tablet when she isn't serving.

Roy peers over his pint glass horizon and sees her with cream wings, blinks, and realizes they're just the curtains across the bar.

"Want a drink?"

The barmaid glances up from her tablet. "You say something, mate?"

Roy pushes a note across the bar. "A drink with me."

She looks him up and down. "I don't drink with strangers."

"Course, love," he says, palms out. He turns over his hand and notices blood under his fingernails.

"Love? I ain't your love, you condescending little shit. Keep your drinks and those grubby mitts to yourself."

"So stuck up," Roy slurs. "What about our morale?"

The barmaid slams a short glass on to the bar just an inch from Roy's hand. He jumps.

"Think I haven't heard all that? All your bullshit? Sad-sack old dicks like you playing Billy-big-bollocks 'cos I'm a young bird with something going for myself? 'Cos you think you still run the world from Didsbury?"

Roy hasn't got anything for that.

"Thought so." The barmaid kisses the back of her teeth, goes to serve someone else. Then, over her shoulder, she adds: "Sooner you old twats cop it, the sooner we'll get back on track."

Roy taps the note on the bar. Then he winks into space, slides his eyes towards the door. "You keep that."

The man she's serving nods at Roy. "Had enough, you have."

"Fuck off," Roy says. "White knight." He topples from his stool, heads for the toilet. On the way he spots two men with eyes on him. Wilbers on the prowl – their blank brown uniforms hanging off them.

"Any *labouring* jobs going?" Roy asks as he passes.

The men ignore him. Look right through him.

He stops, turns. "Oi – yeah. Where's your child catcher parked?"

One of the men pouts at him.

Roy grabs his gut, shakes it. "Wouldn't lift me out of here if you tried." Then he opens the toilet door and wobbles to the urinal. From the sounds of it, someone's indulging a bad habit in the cubicle alongside.

Peeing with one hand, Roy leans back and slaps the

wall. "Council!" he shouts. "You're gripped!" The person in the cubicle simply laughs in response.

Back in the bar lounge, the Wilbers have gone. Roy takes his jacket from the stool, flicks the Vs at the man across the bar and heads for the door.

"And don't bother again!" the barmaid shouts after him.

It's raining outside, and a fine grey mist has drawn in. Without thinking, Roy fumbles the keys, gets back in the mark's car. Starts it. He looks up at the roof liner. Then at himself in the rear-view mirror. A swollen cheek, greasy forehead. He sees the mark's exploded face again, the Reverend on the backseat, applauding it all –

And through his beer fog, he remembers now the news that greeted him when he came off that crane gantry: the first responders bundling him into an ambulance. The heat of the fires and the weird-smelling wind. Roy blinks. The cold has drawn tears. So many questions still over there, over those hills. The drone attack and all the birds that followed...

Jesus, he's drunk.

He asks himself then, his reflection: "Where to?" As if he really doesn't think that anywhere else will do.

By now Sol's dialled 999 too many times to count. Each attempt yields the same result: his breath looped through the mic and out through the speaker.

Hollow, he paces the customer room with his overalls done up to the neck. The woman sits in stasis, her sheets damp, the sofa eating her up, the rootball of her double shoulder set forward like she's trying to curl into herself. He watches her and listens to the rattling windows and with every lap understands that his night is sliding towards the inevitable: a call to the last person on Earth he wants to call.

In the gaps between dialling, he asks the woman for information. Names and addresses; parents and friends; doctors, teachers or institutions. Anything.

"Writing it down might help," he says, looking at her ruined lips. "Anything at all. We're going to get hold of someone for you. Just try and tell me something."

But there's nothing. It's like she isn't here at all – her eyes clouded, implacable. He looks helplessly over the dirty marks on her arms and neck where he's touched or held her and finds himself wanting to clean her, erase them from her skin, as if this alone might be enough to help her start anew.

Next he tries an old roadmap; guides her shaking finger to the paper. "Manchester," he says, outlining the city's uneven shape, without considering how she might not think his way; might not possess an engineer's perspective, the deconstructor's curious mind. Then, farther out: "Greater Manchester. Cheshire. Yorkshire. Liverpool over there. And this is the whole of the north west. This is the whole country. And this, this is the continent... You don't remember *any* of this?"

He holds her finger and pleads for her to show him home. For her to see something she recognizes.

"Please," he says.

But there's only blinking. The blankness of catatonia. The smells of oil, solvent, rust. And the sound of Sol's pulse in his ears.

He dials the nines. Failure. He moves around in Spirograph circles, appetiteless, knowing he should try to eat anyway. There's little on offer here, except a jar of gone-off synth-milk that smells like eggs. All he can do for now is pour glasses of water, guide it through the tiny gaps in her lips...

Occasionally, though, her mistiness passes, and she seems more tangible in the room; watches the walls, the clock, with fascination. Sol flits around her, a drifting moth, trying to capture her attention before she slips back into her private void.

It gets to well past midnight. He dials once more. It rings. It rings. It rings.

"Hello caller. What's your emergency?"

"Oh my God," Sol whispers. "Oh, thank Christ."

"Hello? Can I help you?"

"Yes, *no* – holy *shit* I need an ambulance. Old Trafford, workshop off Chester Road – as soon as you've got one ready get it out here and–"

"Sir, you're blurting," the operator interrupts. "I'll need you to calm down for me. Can you do that? I'm here, now. You're going to be fine. Calmly, now, tell me what's happened. This is a triage call. Do you understand what that means?"

Sol goes on: "It's – I've found someone. She's... oh my God. She's been kidnapped or something. I don't know. She can't understand. She doesn't, she can't speak and–"

"OK," the operator says. "OK. Sir, let's breathe. You're hard to follow, and the line's bad. Is she injured?"

"No," Sol says. He looks at her. "I don't know. Her mouth's sealed up–"

"Sutured?"

"No, closed up. Like with *staples*."

"Right," the operator says.

"Right?"

"Sir..."

"Help us!"

"Sir, I'm not sure we can do much for you here. Not like this."

"What?" Sol stares at the patchy floor. "What do you

mean?" Rubber marks from his boots. Flecks of mud and grit on his scuffed toecaps.

"We're only responding to serious injuries tonight. I'd recommend taking her to a walk-in clinic. Your current waiting time's about three or four days. Where did you say you were? Old Trafford? I mean there's a mobile clinic in Ordsall... Can she drink at all?"

Sol looks at her. "I..."

"I know it's not ideal," the operator says. "But if she can take fluids, and you can keep her warm, it's probably your best bet."

"She's got something wrong with her knees," Sol says. "They're *bleeding*."

"Sir..."

"Don't do this to us. Please. Please don't..."

"Sir, you have to understand. We have other callers waiting."

"But she's got *three*–"

The line dies.

Sol hammers the nines once more. Dial tone.

"Fuck!" he shouts. "Fuck it!"

The woman's eyes snap to him. He stares back at her, holding the phone to his head.

"I'm sorry," he says. He goes to her. He takes a hand, and she doesn't protest, and he says, "Help me out. I can't do it on my own."

Her eyes drop. Sol can almost feel her disengage.

Then an idea: what about the note – the circle-monogrammed paper that came with her? He unpockets it: reads and re-reads it. It's so matter-of-fact. Shopping-list banal. It says:

Accessories to follow. Still in transit. Cash in glove box. Any problems, try Knutsford first.

Sol recalls the scene. The Lexus pulling out, the noise

of Irish on the bonnet. The note – was it left for the driver in leathers? Or *by* him? Sol still believes the driver was collecting the Lexus: his unsureness behind the wheel suggested he'd never driven it before. And then the motorbike with its smart pillion passenger – it was too coincidental. Maybe this woman had dropped off the Lexus and swapped places with the man in leathers, making this a link in a chain; the bike a sort of getaway vehicle. Looking at it coldly, it makes sense to Sol that way – if you're hiding something like this, some grim cargo, you'd never leave a car so conspicuous on a street like that. Not without protection, and certainly not for long. The whole area is renowned for thefts. Sol and Irish were part of that. And yet the old man told them he saw decent cars parking there. Did it happen regularly?

Accessories to follow.

Sol holds his neck. For a human? Is that what it means? Something moves around inside him. Pictures coming together. He goes to the car: the cash isn't a lie – there's at least a grand in the glovebox. He flicks through it. Is this, what, a transfer payment?

Now Sol feels way out of his depth. And still the solution could be the call he doesn't want to make, that he keeps putting off. Because if the services can't help, who will?

Sol swears. He's only remembered three numbers his entire life.

Irish's, Miss Wales'.

And Mel's.

He looks at the three-armed woman on the sofa and dials.

"Who's this?" Her greetings were always sharp, clinical.

"It's me. It's Sol."

"It's late," she tells him.

"I'm in trouble."

"Call someone else."

"Please, Melanie. You've got pals in the force."

"The force? Not anymore."

"One of your customers…"

She sighs so dismissively, so disappointedly. Sol imagines her false eye jerking in its socket. Remembers the sweet-smelling fluid secreted from its tearduct when she was happy. "You get yourself into a mess," she says. "You get yourself out of it again."

He finds himself whispering to her, mumbling about the staples, and she goes silent before she tells him to unpick them.

"Start by her cheeks and work towards the middle," she says. "Jaw clamped."

"I don't have the tools."

"You're a mechanic."

It goes on like this. And just as Sol marks shapes on the cold floor, he can hear Mel pacing too.

"She has a name," Mel says. "She must do. You need to find a thread, keep pulling, unravel her." Then some mention of warm clothing and vitamins. She tells Sol to head home before the sun's up. "You'll have to feed her and bathe her. Then you need to let her go. Take her somewhere. Hospital. I don't fucking know. Jesus, why am I still talking to you?"

Finally, inevitably, the conversation veers into a personal wasteland – the tersely guarded emotions left in the wake of their relationship. She tells Sol to hang up on her; that he just isn't her responsibility anymore. He left her, remember – has he forgotten that? "And listen," she says. "I got myself sorted, didn't I? I got out of that bed without your help."

"I know," he says. "I know what you did."

"Then there's no conversation. You can't be ringing me like this."

"But Mel," he says. "She's got three arms."

The line goes quiet.

"Three, Mel."

"I heard you. Tell me that again."

He tells her that again.

"No."

"It's true."

"No, Sol," Mel says. "Oh no. You stupid, *stupid* prick."

Roy hears the lev before he sees it. The distinct whine of the craft's motor slows to a crackle as it matches the car's speed.

He looks at the clock with a sinking feeling. Why didn't he dump the car? He cups his hand and smells his breath. "Bastard," he says.

A cone of light breaks from above, bleaches everything. "*Bastard*." He eases off. No clue where he is.

"When it's safe to move over and stop, please do so." A woman's voice, distorted by the craft's hailer.

Roy continues, plays oblivious. He's got ten seconds max before a second warning. Thirty before the lev's EMP cannon comes out. Roy knows the lev must be close to the roof – its engine wash sends rain whirling into eddies round the wing mirrors.

"Bastard!" He reaches for his revolver, pushes the business end into the roof lining. The broken tube of his homemade silencer a flowered daffodil on its end. He hesitates, holds his breath, tightens his trigger finger.

And stops himself. It'd scuff the lev at best. His luck tonight, the bullet would bounce straight back at him.

Roy slaps the steering wheel. Sobering fast. "Bastard,

bastard, *bastard*," he shouts, and brings the mark's stolen car into the kerb.

The lev pulls ahead and turns one-eighty, airstreams blasting rain from its cockpit shield. It hovers, thoughtful almost, before jerking forwards like a spidery marionette. Nose almost on the roof, the lev pauses again. Roy can see right into the fuselage, the rivets of its armour plating, the channels of its cannon.

"Thanks," the pilot says.

Roy smiles sarcastically.

"Just stay there for me."

The pilot angles the lev's bow-spot straight into the car. Roy covers his eyes as the beam runs its cycle.

"Hands on the wheel, please."

Roy puts his hands on the wheel, leaving the revolver between his thighs.

The lev reverses and settles, keeping the bow-light in Roy's windscreen. The pilot drops the earthing cord and unsaddles herself. For a second she looks behind, and Roy squirrels the revolver under his seat.

Bastard.

The pilot comes to his window, black suit lustrous, her visor sliding to one side. She motions for him to wind down his window. As he does, she reaches into her helmet to move a mouthpiece from her lips. Droplets of rain catch in her lashes.

"You're out late," she says. "This yours?"

"Aye."

"Good nick isn't it?"

He nods.

"Know why I've stopped you?"

Roy shrugs. "Curfew?"

The officer shakes her head. She seems puzzled. "Car's licensed." Silence. She raises her eyebrows.

Roy checks the dash. No warning lights, and his belt feels tight across his chest. "Silly me," he says, mock-cheery. "Forget I pay up front."

The officer flashes another confused expression. "If they make you pay for a curfew licence, the system really is broken."

"Have I got a bulb out?"

"Nope…"

"Then I don't have a clue," he says. "Sorry."

The pilot taps the roof. "To be honest, nothing's actually wrong. Just wanted to check everything's all right. Patrol doesn't just mean enforcement – or at least it doesn't in my eyes. Got to earn some trust somehow. Plus my breathalyzer isn't working properly in this weather anyway. Not that we'd need to–"

Roy can't believe it. If she can smell his breath – and he's pretty sure she can – she's pretending not to notice.

"Late-night supplies run, then? How many do you care for at the moment, doc? If you don't mind my asking."

Care for? Roy goes cold. *Doc?* The lev's lowered beam highlights the flecks of brown under his fingernails. He folds his arms.

"It's…." The sentence collapses. A gust of wind stipples his face with spray.

"Don't worry," the officer says. Her cheeks look a touch redder. "Sensitive stuff, I get that. Just wanted to mention, because, well, I saw your name." She points into her visor. "It all comes up on here. And your… I mean the people you look after… they're just like my sister, and it did her good. It's something to know there's places out there. Places to help out, right? Don't often get chance to say cheers, so I thought I'd at least start somewhere. Let's hope your other sons and daughters turn out as well as she has."

"That's kind," Roy says. He thinks of the mark. He thinks of the client. He thinks of the Reverend saying, "Darling, do this for me: never question who you've just killed."

"What time do the border guys let you back into Didsbury?"

Blink. *Look normal.* "Ah, any time's good. Always coming and going."

"Course. Well don't let me keep you, either. More than happy to see you into town if that's the way you're headed. I don't mean to patronize, but Chorlton's bad for run-ins at the minute."

Roy nods at the lev. "Be tempted if I got to ride that beast."

She smiles. "For that I'd have to arrest you."

"Then I'm alright." He strains for a smile. "Ta very much."

"I'm sure you–" The officer's earpiece blips. "Sorry," she mouths, touching a finger to her ear. She angles her hand over the mic and whispers: "One sec."

Roy can't help earwigging – the only other sound a mild ticking sound from the lev's cooling powerplant.

~ *Shots fired, Didsbury village. LUs optioned for RR. All LUs to respond for location check, over.*

"On it, Ops," the officer says. "LU6 on call." Other units check in, distant ghosts.

~ *I've got you up now, Six. A rattle.* ~ *You on a traffic stop?*

"Copy. Curfew check. I can be there in…" She looks at her wrist. "Three and twenty."

~ *Copy. Likely hot, so weapons live. First respond on scene. Reports one down, sus unknown. House fire.* A pause. ~ *It's a bad one, Six.*

"Copy you. I'll move now."

~ *Copy, Six. I'll clear you with the gate. Stay warm.*

The link blips out. The officer looks at Roy. She can tell he's heard the conversation. "Your neck of the woods."

Roy nods. Roy knows. And any minute the car he's driving is going to be on every authority's screen in the north.

"Sorry again to interrupt your evening. Send my love to those kids, if that's allowed. Hey, what's it they say – when the old men are dead…"

The echo isn't lost on him. Twice in a night –

She turns, points at the lev. "Till then, we'll have to make do."

Roy nods, eyes front. "All the best, officer."

"You too. And doctor…" She mimes swigging from a glass. "Please think about drinking less."

The officer mounts up in her creaseless suit, and the lev takes off. Roy sits there reeling as it fades away. As he watches, a tiny idea sparks, rolls, bursts to life.

He thinks: *Start walking.*

He thinks: *I need my Lexus.*

He pulls out his revolver, unscrews its wasted silencer. He slides out of the mark's car and leaves the door swinging. Sometimes you make mistakes. But you learn from them.

The early hours, rain on the roof, and Sol's still up with the woman in the workshop's customer waiting room. He's taken his time to introduce himself – told her he runs this business, that he didn't expect to find her, and that he wants to help. And when he's finished – when he thinks he's said enough to reassure her – he adds, "Do you get what I'm saying? Nod or shake your head or something. Anything."

The woman makes the slightest sound.

"How about we try the pen and paper again?" He's already drawn a series of hangman dashes, hoping she might be able to fill out her name. He's written out the alphabet, pointing to letters, but the woman has the same reaction to several of them in no particular order. Now the pen's just scratching grooves into the pad. "Let me get another," he says.

In the main workshop, Sol opens a drawer of forgotten things in a cabinet filled with the waste of a failing business – expensively branded stationery, sticky-tape rolls, unreturned tax returns. He scrubs on a receipt with a few pens before he gets a line.

Back in the room, he sketches out a crude shape for her. Eventually it's a house, deliberately childish, with four windows, a door, a winding little path. A chimney releasing an unlikely cloud of smoke. Two figures by a car outside: one without hair, small and stocky. One a bit taller, shaded for clarity.

He holds up the picture and can't help but feel patronizing. And yet she seems to respond. He could swear her irises rotate like focus rings, that her pupils engorge.

He points to the house. "Home, sweet home. This is a car, here, like the ones in this workshop. Not the silver car. And that's you, there, and that's me."

The woman hisses through her nose. Something in her throat clicks. She lifts a hand and snatches the pen and pad. Breathing angrily through her nose, she slashes out the car, tearing the paper, before she scratches bars on to every window, and an over-sized padlock on the front door.

"What?"

The woman tries to speak, frustrates herself, and

continues to scrawl lines, her whole fist around the pen, over and over until the paper blackens and the house disappears and a new structure takes form. A thick, rounded base, with tapering lines that sweep into a rounded top.

"A tower?" he asks. "Is it? Is that a cooling tower?" Then, quieter: "Bloody hell."

Underneath the crosshatched tower, the woman draws a thin caricature of a mouth, an approximation, really, that's filled with a set of tiny nubbins he guesses are teeth. She draws a line through the mouth, writes something beneath and passes the pad back to him.

Sol's eyes feel hot. A burning in his sinuses. A feeling of desperation, immense and glacial, crashes over him. He can barely look at her writing, its neat characters so obscure they could be alien hieroglyphs. "What happened to you?" he asks, voice thick. But when he takes in her expression, he's shocked. For the first time since he found and unmasked her, her sewn-shut lips are straining at the edges. She's trying to smile.

Sol drops the pad. The tower image lands face down. He feels he's staring into something so vast and frightening it's uncoupled him from everything that went before. In truth, he can't be sure the smile isn't malicious. He can't be sure he won't be enmeshed in this cycle of fear and helplessness and disbelief forever. Weighted down by his stomach, with a fizzing, a rancid taste, that persists in his mouth.

What was next on Mel's list again? What did she say? *You stupid, stupid prick.*

Sol attempts to gather himself. "I'm taking you back to mine," he says. "Need to get these things out of your lips. Cold'll only get on your chest if we stay."

He cajoles the woman into standing, feeling her

stiffen. "It'll be warmer at mine," he adds. "Away from all these cold surfaces." He guides her towards the front door, where she makes herself heavier; some expression of reluctance. Sol half-expected this – had already steeled himself. But when the woman sees a car through the darkness – a customer's saloon not far from the roller doors, ready for collection – she switches to active resistance.

The pair of them tangle, five arms wheeling. The woman isn't throwing punches this time, but she's no less strong. In the end, Sol drives his head under her thicker shoulder and marches her outside. She says nothing, a surreal adversary, as her body solidifies in the doorway.

Sol pulls away. "I'm not trying to scare you," he tells her. He wonders if it's the associations she's made with the car's shape – a natural response to the saloon's boot. So instead he leaves her in the side entrance doorway and opens the roller doors, hearing the generator's hum in its enclosure behind the workshop.

"Wait there, you daft beggar," he tells her. "*Wait.*"

The woman glazes, nostrils flaring. She's clearly deliberating whether or not to run.

Sol trusts his judgment and approaches the saloon. He opens the boot and turns to her with two thumbs down. Then he closes the boot and opens the passenger door. Points enthusiastically between her and the seat.

"See? Right? I'm not the bastard who took you."

The woman edges outside, unsure on her legs.

"I'm sorry it's like this," he says. "I'm sorry." He can't stand how he sounds to himself – slow, deliberate, like an obnoxious holidaymaker trying to ask something of a local.

•••

Mel lights a cigarette on her empire's doorstep. She breathes in with the city and out with her youth. She looks out on neon holo-boards and dying brands; towers fading, washed out, as if they struggle to exist in the squall. The sky like wet concrete.

Mel feels she has something to sort. Problems often start like this – phone calls and angry words and cigarettes on the doorstep. It's a pattern she recognizes. She thumbs the edges of her cigarette lighter, the texture of its toothed wheel, and stares out at a city lost in lashing grey.

She drops her fag, scrubs it, heads inside. A couple of the women are sitting cross-legged on cushions in the foyer. On the wall it says THE CAT FLA because the P fell off. Owing to the rain, the smell of smoke clings to her.

"Something on your mind?" Cassie asks.

"Something's going on," another woman says. Mel looks at her – Fatimah.

Mel pushes her fringe across her forehead. "I'd murder a brew."

"No hot water this morning," Fatimah says.

Cassie winces. It's rare and unnerving to see her boss rattled – and it makes her unpredictable. "It's him, isn't it?" she asks.

"Yes," Mel says. "Have you fed him today?"

Cassie nods towards Fatimah.

"Good. 'Cos we might have to kiss and make up. How many days has it been anyway? Losing track of time. You think he's learned his lesson?"

Cassie frowns. "Doubt it. Got a cock, hasn't he?"

Mel blows into her cheeks. "I reckon we give him another chance."

Cassie huffs in surprise. "Yeah?"

Mel senses Cassie's ire. "How many johns we got in?"

"Four or five," Cassie tells her. "Slow-w-w day."

"You two alright to keep an eye on the till for a bit?"

Cassie looks down at herself. Torn crop-top, rib and belly tattoos visible, stockings, shorts. "Let me grab a gown and I'll be down."

"Ta," Mel says. She passes along the mirrored corridor, hears the sound of fake laughter, muffled guests. The store cupboard's halfway. She takes a big deep breath and unlocks it.

Inside, Jeff's wedged between boxes of paper and condoms, antiseptic wipes and plastic-wrapped costumes. Mel kicks his foot until he acknowledges her.

"Wake up."

The big man stirs. Breathe too deep and his odour is overpowering. Plates of untouched food surround him.

"Do you sleep?"

Jeff shakes his head. "More like standby." She hears something rattling.

"I think you understand now that you can't abuse our trust," Mel says. "Never mind manhandling the girls. Or our bloody clients."

Jeff tries to sit up. A joint pops with the movement. Mel notices he isn't wearing sunglasses; that his diamondoid eyes are dulled to pencil lead. "Girls'd rather you rot in here," she tells him. "After what you did. And they don't know half of what I do."

Jeff's eyes seem to glisten. He's listening intently.

"No more of this theatrical shite, either," Mel says. "I know exactly what you are. And I'll happily leave you here full stop."

Jeff shakes his head. He tries to rise again, but no good. He's hogtied; his legs are dead.

"Pull those faces all you want. You've got plenty to learn about bosses like me. In all honesty I don't know why I'm even giving you a chance."

"A chance?"

"How long have I got left of this trial? Till Jason comes knocking?"

Jeff licks his lips. He clears his throat. "Melanie." His voice is slow. "Just under two weeks." His features don't move at all. "Please excuse me. I don't know what happened."

Mel doesn't react. "You know enough. I don't employ animals. And I *really* don't like people who take advantage of my goodwill."

"No," he says. "No."

"If I let you out, could you help me? Can I trust you to redeem yourself?"

"I follow orders, except where such orders conflict–"

"It's a simple frigging question, Jeff."

Jeff doesn't react to his name. "How do I know you haven't recorded any of this?" she asks, angrier now. "That Jason doesn't already know?"

Jeff attempts a reassuring smile. "Recording and playback's an optional extra. I can talk you through the accessories if you like…"

"You'll do what I tell you."

"I said so. It is my pleasure."

"And say I sent you to check up on someone, you could? There isn't a… range… on you? You'd have to pose. Act a bit. Pretend to be a prospect, actually. To know about vehicles."

"Why not? You don't seem to be getting many punters in to see me."

"He's called Solomon." Mel passes him a piece of paper, pointing to the topmost address on it. "He works here. A garage. Maybe try it first – he more or less lives there." She points to a second address. "This is – well, he only sleeps here."

"What would you like me to do?"

Mel's heart skips. She knows the next sentence comes from the margins. From a darker part of her usually restrained. And yet it doesn't stop her.

"I want to scare him," she says.

"Happy to help," Jeff says. So matter-of-factly. A sparkle back in his eyes. "What for?"

Mel shrugs – her own act, but hopefully convincing enough. She's boss here, and Jeff will do well to remember it. "I think he's paid for a new girlfriend," she says. "I want to know who she is, and what he's playing at with her. And I want him to know it's not a good idea."

Y

After they unloaded Y from the half-track, and the troop escort signed her over, Y was ushered into a camp of three-sided concrete tents. For a time she stood alone, shivering in a muddy light that coloured the camp putrid brown. The whole site, she noticed, sat on a rim – its edges stopped abruptly and fell into an ocean of black mist. Back the way she came, she could make out the mansion. It appeared as a featureless lump on the hill, outlined by heavy spotlamps.

She felt disjointed, adrift. The farther she travelled from her cradle, the stronger her memories of her time there became.

Eventually a masked figure approached and led her into the camp. A small tracked robot followed at their heels taking photographs. "Proof of delivery," someone commented. By the entrance to one of the bigger tents, the figure paused. Y looked at the tent's weathered outer skin. These structures had obviously been standing far longer than intended.

"Think your friend's waving."

Y turned. The half-track was pulling away across the terrain, the young escort on his gun platform. "Good luck," he mouthed. It struck her as strange that she was the only one unloaded here. What would happen to the others?

"Let's get you ready," the figure said. Y suspected it was a man, but she couldn't be sure.

The tent was sparsely furnished, with roll mats and sleeping bags arranged top to tail down one wall. A matted floor, presumably to soak up moisture. Several more people in a circle played cards among themselves, all pockets and tabs and gleaming buckles.

"A fine harvest," the figure said. The group considered Y. The figure gestured to her and said, "This is your trolley team. Respect them, and they'll keep you safe." And with that, Y was left with five strangers playing cards by torchlight.

"Pay no notice," the woman closest said, standing up. "I'm Fi, hey. And trust me – you can talk to us however you want." She motioned to the others, and slowly they all rose to their feet.

Another woman piped up. "We've got a lot to get through. Have a seat first, eh?"

"Sit here," Fi said, offering her a cushion. "Don't want a wet bum. Did they feed you OK?"

Y shrugged.

"Maybe some flatbread? We're not meant to. But the gels'll make you feel shitty if you're running on empty."

Y sat down. Fi passed her a plate.

"Dig in," she said.

After their game, the trolley team took Y through their descent plan. They moved her out to a pillbox where many more heavy-suited people milled around. Then they sized up Y's own transfer suit – complete with a visor and comms loop that sat uncomfortably in her ear canal. The woman called Fi said, "Whatever we do, you do too. You need a breather, you say. You need a wazz, then hey, we'll find you some time. Oh, and try to ignore the blokes. They mean well, but they aren't particularly sensitive."

"Only for her protection, Fi," one of the men whispered, chewing with his mouth wide open. "Yet to lose a diamond in the rough."

Y adjusted her outfit while the trolley team went for one last briefing in an adjacent room. This was more of an extension than its own cabin, and its corrugated roof reported the changing weather. Through the window, the pink mountains were absent, and dark clouds rolled past, bringing heavy but fleeting showers whose rain was a corrosive yellow. Y couldn't hear much of the briefing – though she gathered the team were more interested in the benefits of moving her than the conditions outside.

That much was true. For all the danger and exertion and the risks of exposing themselves to cell-mutating dust, the team's rewards were incredible. The volume of their cargo – twice weekly per team, if they were any good – hardly mattered if they did it on time. Handling a Grade One subject, live and kicking, made the risks worthwhile.

For these teams, working the Slope was as addictive as it was lucrative. Every moment down there felt like overtaking a freighter on a blind corner – it was an exhilarating task to transport these rare assets down the face of it and cross them over to the other side.

Soon the six of them waited on hard standing, suited and booted, ready to go. They'd assembled their kit, slipped into gel casings and exo-layers. They'd decided who would take point and rear guard. The lookouts were already taking measurements. And Y, in her protective wrapping, stood between the rank and file, gawking at the insignia on their suits – a symbol of two circles interleaved that looked so much like an illustrated eclipse, or a Venn diagram – which was repeated in gold and pinned like a corsage to her chest plate. The plate pressed down on her sternum, and she vaguely hoped it might break the pendant.

When the dust cleared sufficiently to make the descent, they marched out to the Slope's access plain in single file. The team leader seemed to be arguing with someone – their paymasters clearly expecting their cargo soon. Y took it in: night here was simply a darker shade of mud, and there were no stars. They reached the rim and entered the mist – a miasma drawn from the frontiers of some god's terrible imagination.

Y could sense all of them were nervous and excited. Deep in the line, she went with care. The soil became the glassy powder the escort had told her about; formed a surface that wasn't as unforgiving as ice, but needed almost as much concentration to walk on. It didn't take long for Y's thigh muscles to start aching.

She soon found that whenever the wind picked up, the line hastily changed direction. The six of them crossed the plain like people zig-zagging under sniper fire, and the Slope opened out beneath them.

EIGHT

The woman's stapled mouth makes for an awkward drive.

Sol glances at her when he can, eyes invariably drawn to the knotted shape of her doubled-up shoulder. He imagines what she might be called, his mouth dry, as the car bobbles over the road. He smiles, a tired attempt at comfort, but she doesn't register it.

There's a cavity, a gap in Sol, where the flies of dread are breeding. As they ghost along this road, headlights full beam, his mind incessantly cuts to Mel; shorts out to locked doors, coming home late from the workshop to find a meal cold on the side, covered in wilted kitchen roll. And he thinks, suddenly and ruefully, of the way watching porn made him feel whenever Mel left their house after an argument. That feeling was so much like this. He found he watched it to spite how good they once had it; to explore something anathema to her, to the warm, rusky smell she carried after sleep; her inexorable smartness and dark humour. He watched it while he made a mess of their life – even before their rainy city

seemed to distort and collapse into itself; even before
her skin changed and her bones started to jut. It was all
so base – the figures on his screen were always so flat,
fictional. And yet he did it anyway. To feel *something else*.
To feel not good enough, and then, when he finally left
her, to know it as fact – to remind himself he never was
good enough, and that her addictions had borne this out,
had replaced him. Every time, this unfeeling would swell
and displace his organs.

"Manchester," he says to the woman, gesturing
towards the city. "We used to have a tower there." He
looks over her. Her muscles running like a map. He
thinks: *She's somebody's daughter. Somebody's friend.* "But
they brought it down. God, what a horrible day. It
emptied our sky."

Sol stops the car for a red. He looks at an empty wall
where once an advertising board stood, and he feels he
can remember the image of it – a sea of shimmering
discs – and a sun, shiny-ribboned. Or was it? Suddenly
he isn't sure if it was here or in another landscape from
the past, now superimposed on this one.

"You hungry or what?" he asks her. "I'm starving –
had nothing for tea, have we? Have to see what I've got
in."

Green light. The brightness of the city spreads across
frosted tarmac, flooding the neglected road. From here
to home is basically a two-mile run of churned blacktop,
more potholes than viable surface.

"Can't believe it's nearly morning already," adds Sol.
He nods as if she replies. It's true enough: he'd seared
through the darkest hours on adrenaline alone. In the
mirror, his eyes are red and watery.

The woman puts a hand on the dash and another
on the door, like she's minded to open the window and

inspect the sights: holo-boards and greening concrete; burned-out industrial units; rotting substructures made eerie by the play of shadows; tattered Metrolink lines stripped for the cable inside.

"Wind it down if you want. It'll be cold, though."

They cross another waypoint on Sol's internal map – a near-finished block of flats where the double glazing still wears its tape but the exposed iron pilings of the top floors reach up like the arms of corpses. As they pass, Sol notices something in one of the first floor window spaces. It's only a glint, a near-imperceptible movement, but it catches his eye. A squatter most probably. Maybe a few of them – gangs are common in these derelict new builds. Nonetheless, he slows the car to a crawl.

As he watches, the something becomes a figure, and the figure moves into focus. A mother trying to get her keening baby to sleep.

Sol stops the car. He cranes, can actually see the gummy gap between the baby's lips, the fat cheeks that frame it, the smile lines on its mother's face. The baby is giggling. Sol is desperate to share the moment, but his passenger is oblivious, looking the other way.

Sol smiles up at the woman, and she smiles back – recognition of the hour, but also, somehow, of their respective lives. In that alone there's enough to keep him going. He mouths, "Hello," and thinks: *Good luck*.

Just as the mother and her child move into Sol's peripheral vision, the mother lifts the baby's arm to wave.

"See? It isn't all bad round here." And maybe it stands to reason he loses himself in the moment and decides to nudge the woman – mostly because she's there as well. Because, just for a moment, the dread lifts away.

It's not a clever move.

The woman flattens herself against the door, all three

hands covering her face and head. Confused, Sol misses a pothole. The car drops in on the right side and jolts into the oncoming lane, Sol's driving hand shaken off the wheel. The car bounces on its suspension for a moment, rear end minnowing. Sol wrestles the wheel into the drift before he straightens it up.

"I hardly tapped you!" he shouts.

The woman peers at him between fifteen fingers and thumbs. Her eyes are swimming.

"Wait! I didn't mean to…"

The woman closes her hands tighter around her face, pushes herself into the headrest.

Sol grows angry, first at her, and then with himself, and then with his lot: for Irish jacking the Lexus; for being in the wrong place, the wrong time. He actually wishes above all it wasn't him but someone else with this to bear. A better person might understand her reaction – but Sol's already felt his face change; seen in himself the venom-flash. Now the woman's eyes are set in a nest of interlacing fingers, and briefly their thoughts mesh. For him, a vision: the palms of a thousand hands raised. For her, a desperate man, lost in his circumstances.

How many times have you seen that face before?

Sol struggles for breath, like the car chassis has dropped away. She whimpers through her nose, mucus bubbling through her lips. "I'm sorry," he says, and pulls in, kerbing the wheels. There at the pavement, he gently peels all three hands from her face, feeling her muscles bite, tense against him.

"But I'm not going anywhere," he adds, slowly shaking his head. "I'm not going anywhere." And in the city lights that cast her as a statue and the city road as a pier in an ocean of glass, he can only hope he means it.

●●●

Foot over wet foot.

Something about the rain, the sound of his footsteps, reminds Roy of the first day he killed someone.

That was 2019. A Tuesday six years ago. Back when he had rough hands and lean muscle, and the food never seemed to touch the sides. Before the Reverend.

Roy went on site early every day. Jobs were hard to come by, so you made the effort. The labourers were mostly young: new immigrants working for peanuts, or local lads swaying in their tracksuit pants. The foreman was Harry – an East End man whose job seemed to involve wearing a high-vis vest and stomping about in the mud. Harry had no respect for his boys, received none back. He called them "scrotes" – one of the few northernisms he'd picked up – and liked to rip into Roy for his army surplus cargos, his baldness, his technical fleece.

Harry also called Roy Noodles. "Noodles," he'd say, "have a word with those trousers mate. Lose your skinny arse down a fackin pencil sharpener you would."

Noodles was green on the cranes. He'd spent his twenties and thirties labouring, and now, tipped into his forties with bad tendons, he spent entire shifts up a tower crane next to a sweaty man with a girl's name. That man was Kerry, and that crane was a Titan – a rusty pillar caught in Manchester's throat.

Come rain or shine it was always hot in the Titan cab, and without fail it smelled of suncream and bad feet. Kerry's pits and Kerry's heart-attack food. Roy often wondered how he managed the ladders.

But Kerry was also charming: all monkey-swagger and *alright our kid?* and he looked after Roy like nobody else. His love for words fascinated Roy – Kerry said he was a poet on the side. He said, when he wasn't singing old Man City songs – "Got to remember them, haven't you!" – that he only did this work because it let him think.

Kerry made no effort to hide how much he loved the job. For him, life was all about hooks and cable, steel and load. Home for City reruns on DVD, then back next day to move bricks and mortar and roof for holes. He loved the vibrations singing through the joists. He loved the charts and loads and switches and codes. And he loved the perks. Because it turned out that come noon on every shift, Kerry ate his ham butties on the Titan's concrete counterweight. Dinner with a view, he called it. It put them two hundred feet into space, he told Roy. And on his big grey picnic table above the city, he insisted only the birds could see what you were up to. He'd say to anyone who listened: "You can never tell how shite it's all got when you're up there."

It stayed with Roy, that. He still sees the glossy black letters – TITAN – running away from him down the crane arm. Everything in the glare of 20/20 hindsight. Because on that Tuesday of all the Tuesdays, Kerry took Roy out on the counterweight to have a look for himself.

Roy was shaky out on the structure. The steeplejacks he drank with called it disco leg. His eyes streamed in the wind, and he felt vulnerable until he crawled, got himself flat. Relaxed only when he felt certain he wouldn't be blown off the top.

"Look properly you fanny," Kerry said. "Properly over the edge. Go on."

So Roy shuffled and wormed. He reached the edge and saw the ground.

"Better. Now look out there. Go on lad, just look at it."

Roy turned to him. Kerry stretched out, beaming, his City shirt showing through the gaping buttons of his overalls. He saw Roy's expression. "Football fans are like displaced tribes," Kerry told him. He put a hand where the club badge would be. "We might not get to watch games anymore, but we've got the stuff that matters." He patted his chest. "We keep it all in here."

With that, Kerry checked his watch and stood up. He spread his arms, pretended to be a plane. And he didn't know why, but Roy did too. His legs braced, locking himself against the wind shear. Then Kerry drew out a banana and peeled it. Lobbed the skin, watched it flop away like a lost glove.

Standing on the counterweight again, Roy felt his throat tighten. He could just about see the lashed-up load dangling from the Titan's cables. He imagined the banana skin bouncing off a cabin roof.

"It's a perk, this," Kerry said, in case Roy had already forgotten. "As long as you don't get caught."

A gull floated past, eyeing them. Roy saw Kerry shake his head and take in the kingdom of Manchester and whisper to himself, reverent: "Fuck. Me."

And then for ten minutes they didn't need to speak at all.

Sol's flat is a measly box teetering above a takeaway on the way to Gorton. Most of his row was torched when a neon sign shop on the corner was firebombed, and in the day you can still see the scorch marks, in wet spells smell the brick dust. But where the unsafe buildings were demolished there's now a kind of parking space round the back. A silver lining. And it's here, in the ribs of this terrace carcass, that he leaves the customer's car he's borrowed.

He tells the woman they're home like it's the end of a long journey. He'd hoped they wouldn't see any neighbours, and owing to the time, they don't. He bundles her up the stairs and through his front door.

With a guest, Sol is conscious the flat smells. It does smell; smells the way flats are wont to smell when their tenants are left too long by themselves. Microwave meal trays stacked and sticky by the sink. Bin bags tied with half-arsed knots. Foam boxes and stained paper from the takeaway downstairs. Bluebottles rattling about.

Sol turns on a light. A single bulb swaying from the hall ceiling. Behind them his bedroom, a pile of overalls growing mould by the wash basket. Before him the lounge, an old flat-screen TV, a tatty sofa. Beyond this the kitchenette, and round to the right, a bathroom cancered by damp.

He guides her into the lounge. Just by the window, there's evidence of a hidden talent: an easel and a canvas, on to which Sol has painted the view from his window: skeletal husks in the foreground, a hyper-real ribbon of purple behind. On a narrow shelf stands a framed monochrome picture of a black man in overalls standing next to a Bentley R-type Continental fastback, its coachwork a gleaming carapace.

For once, Sol turns on the heating. He throws loose change in the meter and drapes the cleanest towel he can find over the radiator.

"Get yourself comfy," he says to the woman, pointing to the sofa. "Just got to sort some bits. You can have my bed, if you want."

But when Sol turns again, he finds her taken in by his project wall.

In his younger years – before the rations, the curfew, the riots and the violence – Sol took thousands of pictures, Polaroid prints mostly, which he brought home and overlaid on a corkboard to make composites of bridges and towers and chimneys and overpasses. His super-city soon grew to cover a whole wall – and now, moved from their shared house to this flat, it's taken on the significance of evidence in an investigation room. A hobby that charts Sol's descent into middle age as well as the world that changed around him.

Sol watches, the woman rapt by it, and he by her. He feels strangely embarrassed when she begins to run her three hands across the roads the way a child might run a toy car, past interconnected black gates and mesh fencing, motorways and hidden scrapyards beneath. She strokes the occasional river, canal, even a stranger's head bobbing into shot as an oversized, out-of-focus blob. She finds pylons, substations, stacks. She traces overlapping superstructures, infrastructure splayed out. She explores the musculature of a lost civilization, its concrete cathedrals. She shares in his idea of the country as he'd prefer it: a fallow Britain in which the only thing you can do is *drive*.

He wonders if these structures represent some common language between them. If she's looking for a tower.

Her staples.

You stupid, stupid prick.

"Hey, sit down," he says. "Put your feet up. Need to see what we can do about your mouth." He enters his tiny kitchenette and fills the kettle, before raiding what counts as his bathroom cabinet. He turns out a pair of wire pliers, inexplicably stored here, and a set of nail scissors.

Back in the kitchenette, he takes a pot of salt and boils the kettle to make up a saline solution in a mug. Through the partition, a paper-thin divide between their two worlds colliding, he can see the woman kneeling at the TV, staring at her dull reflection.

"Won't be a minute," Sol tells her.

When the scissor handles burn against the back of his hand – his fingertips too calloused to gauge temperature accurately – he takes the mug through to her. He sits down and pats the sofa next to him; draws an exaggerated smile across his face.

The woman looks at the tools and touches her stitches. She eyes the scissors.

"That's it," he says. "They're coming out. I can't get you to hospital tonight, because it's too far, and we'd be waiting forever. They have all these targets and…"

He can see it doesn't matter.

He points to the lamp behind her. Then he demonstrates how he needs her to arch her neck. "I'll be gentle," he says.

The woman appears to understand. She arches her neck. Sol reaches up and clicks on the lamp. In the slanting light, ropes of muscle step out from her shoulders to her chin. Sol admires them as he might the columns of some ancient fascia. He follows the square of dashes tattooed on her throat, the scar above her Adam's apple. Taken together, these things give him the impression something is missing.

The woman clenches her teeth, and her jaw juts sharply beneath her ears.

Sol flicks excess water from the scissors and leans in to her. It's hard to work out the best angle to come in from – the top, bottom, from the side. Quickly he realizes he won't be able to do this without touching her face, which makes him uncomfortable. He says, "I'm going to have to…" and holds up a hand. The woman burrows into the sofa. "You've got to try and trust me," he tells her. She nods, and with all three of her hands takes his own. She guides it to her face as though it might electrocute her: slowly, tentatively, eyes locked on his. Contact. Palpable shivers as his fingers settle around her chin. He holds her delicately.

"That's it," Sol says, realizing he'd been holding his breath. "And you're in control. You can take it off any time you want."

Sol dips the blades again. She watches the instrument leave the water and move towards her. She keeps one hand firmly against his hand on her chin – uses her others to guide Sol by the wrist of his working hand.

"OK?"

With the scissors just outside her mouth, she lets go of his working hand and returns her arms, slowly, as if underwater, to rest on the sofa.

"OK."

He opens the blades. Twin points, hovering. "I don't know how it's going to feel," he says, perhaps too honestly. Then he slides the blades around the first staple.

"Ready?"

The woman shakes her head. Sol pulls away. She releases the hand on her chin and moves it towards Sol's face. Sol draws a sharp breath before he realizes what she's doing. Gently, she takes his chin in the same way he holds hers, so that now they hold one another's faces in a peculiar embrace; a kind of speechless contract between them. The woman, seemingly satisfied with the arrangement, lets out a long sigh.

"OK." He looks down at her hand. "OK."

Sol closes the scissors again. There – the bite. Apply some pressure. He finds he has to put a lot of force through the scissor handles to even dent the metal. It makes him wince more than it does her. At last, sweat beading on his forehead, the first staple bows, splits, rends apart. It's so quiet in the room that Sol can actually hear the click as a section of her gummed lips parts.

He exhales. She squeezes his chin – a tender gesture he takes as gratitude.

The second staple comes easily, the third like a dream. Four done, and he starts working out the broken pieces with the pliers, teasing out the metal. These offcuts he drops on a saucer.

It astounds Sol that the woman never winces. That while sweat begins to emerge on her top lip and disappears into the holes as he pulls the staples through, she stays so still. By the time he gets to the middle of her lips, some of the holes are ragged, running with something sticky. But even this doesn't seem to bother her: the only sounds the shear and snip of the scissors, Sol's soft nasal whistle. And so he continues, her palm moist on his chin now, and more offcuts, yellow-crusted, meet the saucer. He's working so close to her face he can see the brilliant green strata that run through her eyes.

Another feeling, another response rooted in the terrible intimacy of the scenario, begins to affect him. The longer he works on her staples, the more it makes him twitch, until his hands start to shake. He can tell she knows. Her markedly slow breathing begins to accelerate. He decides to stop and pull back, hands off, and she looks hurt. Her ribs just there. Her pores and fine hairs, the muscle wall of her chest, the tension of the interlinking muscles between. It's all just there if he looks down and across the sheet.

The woman takes his hands. A strange sputtering sound comes from her throat.

"Sorry," Sol says. "I don't know what's wrong with me." He chides himself. He can smell his sweat. And then he tenses the muscles in his legs – his thighs, calves, buttocks – until they all start to cramp.

He wipes his brow and starts again.

"There," he says. Quietly. "That's the last one out."

She wipes her chin with the back of her hand. She looks at him. His eyes are stinging with concentration.

Then the woman bares a set of bright teeth in the frame of a smile, and touches a finger to each one, checking.

"Tell me something," he says, passing her a mug of cold water. "Tell me anything you want."

So she does.

But her language isn't any he recognizes.

This thing Roy remembers: it visits him as a spectre, in bedsits and hotel rooms and rolled-down car seats. And tonight it continues to stalk him on the wet pavements of their city:

It was later on that Tuesday. Not long till clocking off – half an hour, if that. Roy was smoking on the crane's ladder deck while Kerry sat at the sticks, downing some rank energy drink. An eye on the load gauge, an eye on the time.

Below, through the cabin's acrylic glass, its elegant steel weave, the contract labourers were running rings round Harry the foreman. Ahead, the sun was half buried. A siege of dark clouds not far off.

Roy went back in the cabin. Over the radio, he heard the rigger challenge Kerry. "Get that next beam on straight first go," he said, "and I'll send a lolly up with your cabin boy tomorrow."

"Won't frigging see tomorrow at this rate pal," Kerry said back, winking at Roy in the doorway. "But go on then. Let's have it."

Kerry watched the rigger. Roy watched the load. The

rigger's hand was palm up, opening and closing to guide the beams in.

"Harry wants our balls," Kerry told Roy. It was a fair assessment, a site-wide concern: the build was long overdue. It's why Kerry and a few of the others were chewing X10s – diet pills that worked like speed – to pull the overtime.

"They'll run out of money at half mast anyway," the rigger shouted. "We're building ghost houses."

"And yet we're getting paid for it," Kerry said.

Kerry nodded to Roy and rolled his eyes. Roy grunted.

"Get on with it, then," the rigger said. "Bone-idle sods."

Kerry grinned. He mouthed "watch this" and let out the line. Roy's stomach reeled as the load fell free. After what felt like too long, Kerry broke the line, and Roy saw the beams stop suddenly. The working arm shook, sending loud vibrations through the slewing unit behind the cabin. On the ground the rigger had dived into the mud.

"Dickhead!" the rigger shouted. "Prick! I'll have you!" Roy could hear everyone laughing over the radio.

"Sorry lad," Kerry said. "Got put off – you'll wanna hide that cleavage next time."

The rigger stood up.

"Budge then," Kerry said, making a shooing gesture.

Roy smiled, more relieved than anything.

"His problem," Kerry told Roy, meaning the rigger, "is that I've been riding these things forever – and I love 'em down to my gristle."

Roy didn't respond. He watched Kerry land the first beam; lay the second bob-on. Nice and easy, smooth and level. He admired it all; the quiet coordination between Kerry, the rigger and the crew working the ropes. The set done, Kerry swivelled the Titan to the haulier dropoff.

Only there was nobody there to hook up the next load.

"Make it a Twister lolly, eh?" Kerry said into his radio. "And maybe another one for pudding."

The rigger didn't respond. Roy couldn't tell why – he was still down there, still looking up at them.

"Oi!" Kerry shouted. "Gone damp, have you? Come on, nobhead, show us your tits–"

Another voice cut across. "Come down, gents."

It was Harry.

"Boss?"

Through the cabin floor, Roy saw the group of workers growing.

Kerry made a face. Roy was stumped.

"What's up, chief?" Kerry asked. "Bit of rain never hurt anyone."

"Just wind it up for today, and get Noodles off the rig with you."

Kerry tilted his head. He gave Roy a second strange look. The foreman never spoke like this. "Got at least half-hour left in this light. Easy."

"Fuck's sakes," the foreman said, his apprehension now clear. "Just do it, Kerry, right? Look–"

"But…"

"But *nothing* son. Look! Bloody look over there…"

So Kerry and Roy looked. Looked out from their room with a view. From up in the gods. From the best view in the house.

In his mind, Roy still sees it like this now. In the present, he's trying to walk straight down a cold, wet street. But no mistake, he's there: the sight of it like a painting stitched into him. Not a single colour is missing; nothing is lost to the necrosis of time.

Jesus–

And Roy's world changed like this:

The ground seemed to yawn and fracture by the crane pad. Roy stood agog before he realized it wasn't really happening – that it was only shadows.

But then the birds came.

They looked like the tide. The birds cut a big black gash across everything – a wall of them, a dam against the light. It was a spectacle: the biggest formation of birds he'd ever seen. And they were coming full on.

Roy turned solid. It made no sense. It was unnatural, wrong. With it came a dissonance: imagine chewing a mouthful of food while looking into a spider's bursting nest.

The birds didn't deviate, didn't dissipate. They were a plague vision – an amorphous squirm of broken wings and squashed-flat bodies coming into the Manchester basin.

Roy said something, or tried to. It didn't matter much. By then the birds had arrived.

At the front of the bird wall, in looping waves, half-carcasses dropped away, tail-spinning to the ground. Roy watched feathers catch and plume. Birdshit came across the crane like whitewash. He saw pigeons and gulls and geese and swans. Blackbirds and herons and tits and finches. He saw them all, individually outlined in the blur; and even then, he knew it would be indelible. The cabin dimmed, left only the feathers and the noise and the gloom. The ringing in the men's ears intensified to a roar.

The crane started to groan on its basepad. Kerry, panicked but not beyond himself – deathly white but still standing – had the wherewithal to start tracking the hook back into the mast. It was way out on the jib, dragged almost horizontal by the density of creatures passing it, and the noises from the machinery arm were horrible. Roy could smell burning.

Kerry said, quite clearly, "Head down." The bird cloud had thickened, and the sky had completely vanished. Then the first pops rang – *pap pap pap* – as the birds began to hit the windows around them.

Roy ducked and caught his head on the control panel, just as the window cracked and caved. Through his hands, the cabin's cold metal, he felt the whole mast shaking; ringing through his joints and tendons. Then a second cabin window cracked, caved, quickly went, and now there were only guts going sideways with the glass and the muck. Something raked sharply, deeply, across the top of Roy's head. He felt the blood spring up.

On the cabin floor, the radio squealed a tune on a different frequency. Animal sounds. Through the acrylic glass, Roy watched exploding birds seethe between the structure. He couldn't see the ground for feathers and viscera. He couldn't even see Kerry across the cabin, or the Titan's frame through the feathered pall.

A weight slopped onto Roy's head. It was a goose, shattered, its head crushed, eyes pushed together and facing forward. The bird stared up at Roy, he swears it did – and Roy found Kerry again, slumped in a high-vis jacket slicked with blood.

It quietened. Except for a few stragglers, the barrage had passed.

Kerry had his hands over his ears. His knees were pressed but knocking. Roy shouted, "I'll go down! I'll go down, Kerry! I'll get help!"

But it wasn't done yet. When Roy stood he realized the tower hadn't stopped vibrating. He looked out on the tower's face-side moorings thinking he could climb the arm and head down the scaffolding rig. It looked slippy, though. The bird mush was everywhere.

By now Kerry had collapsed into the corner. He looked a state.

Roy shifted. Wobbling. His knowledge of the crane's mechanics was basic, but he knew enough to know that if everything else was shot, the critical pieces were made of hardier stuff. As far as he could tell, even if this birdmeat coated everything, the crane still worked.

Groundside, there was movement and banging. A fire had taken hold of a storage caravan, lighted up the odd contractor running past. Others were trying to clamber up the gantry. Roy couldn't see their faces, of course. Instead he pictured them: parched mouths under the rims of their hard hats. Some corrupt liquid running in the creases of their luminous clothes.

Roy opened the cabin door. He called out, wiping fresh blood from his eyes. The site was ravaged, locust-riven. Deep welts ran from the basepad to the site's orange-ribboned edges. Plastic piping was scattered, mini-diggers turned on their sides. He saw discarded hi-vis vests and boots. Avian remains dripping from doorframes like sodden garlands. The sun was lost –

Again Roy called out for Kerry to wake up. Numb, he got the feeling Kerry was dead. And there was something else, too. A clanging.

Roy looked west. The bird-wave, a colossal V, was rushing away from the city.

He looked down. There. Someone on the ladder.

Roy called down the tube. A yellow helmet bounced towards him, but there were no signs of comprehension. He called out again. "Mate!" His voice kept breaking. "We're up here!"

Sirens blared in the distance. Roy felt sure there

was another noise now, too. He turned – confirmed it to himself. The crane's overload switch had started bleeping – and he could see the meter needles were running circles.

Roy dived back inside. He put his hands on the window frame, cold air in his face, and felt paralyzed by the realization. Through the smoke, he could see a handful of men with their arms and legs tangled round the crane's hook.

Roy stared at it. That scene. Risen horror met fascination and mixed; a pang of revulsion. It was almost funny. Almost slapstick. The man in the middle had somehow – Christ, *somehow* – slipped onto the hook's point. It went in at his belly; up into his chest cavity. And there the man's shirt was open around it; he looked half dressed – disturbed mid-sleep.

Roy understood what they'd done. A cabin burned beneath them; the ground around it blazing, billowing dense black smoke. Hemmed by fire, they'd jumped from the cabin's roof to the dangling crane hook.

Roy felt desperate, felt stuck. In mere minutes, reality had fully unwound.

The hooked man barely moved, his head tilted down towards the cable coming out of him. His boots were melting, dripping, in the heat – one of the memories that would come to bother Roy most. The others clung on around this man, their faces contorted by fear. He gunned the winch and pulled them closer to the mast.

As he did, smoke started to curl from the slewing unit. The whole tower was locking up, juddering. He looked along the arm and saw the vanishing point warping. Roy being Roy had listened to Kerry – knew the arm would buckle, maybe tear, if this carried on. If the tower lost integrity at the base, the crane might even collapse. It was in the training videos. It was in his notes.

Tracking the load towards the mast wasn't working. As the hook moved closer, the jib continued to twist. Roy didn't understand; found it harder and harder to reconcile why the contractors writhed on the hook like bees round a nest. Roy squinted at them, thought he saw the rigger's face among them. And even though he knew these men were screaming, he couldn't hear a thing.

Roy started to lower the men. The crane locked up again. This time the lever stuck. Roy swore, made a fist, smashed it down. The grinding deepened. The motor popped. And in one terrible instant, the lever went slack, and the whole load fell out.

To Sol the woman's language sounds like tutting. At first he thinks she's sucking her tongue against her palate, or against the back of her teeth – but then realizes the sound comes from somewhere deeper, from down in her throat. It seems to accelerate and slow with her breathing: a rolling rhythm with no discernible shape or meter.

Transfixed by her mouth, Sol finds himself shrinking away. "*English*?" he whispers, pathetic.

The woman drones at him; her voice of sticky noises, sore lips locked in goldfish Os.

Sol tries to say more. A lump in the way. He covers his ears, initial relief now wholly displaced. "What do I do?" he says. "Tell me. Tell me something."

The woman takes the mug and drinks what's left of the saline solution.

Sol flings out a hand. "Don't!" he says. "You'll puke." He skitters out to the filter. "There's fresh stuff in here," he calls through. "And no – no, don't touch the holes – we need to get... No, *don't*. They won't get better that way…"

The woman wipes her chin and points to her mouth.

Sol puts a hand on his forehead. Clammy. "Food? Food…"

She nods.

Sol rifles the cupboards for meat cartridges, protein powder. He still hasn't got the stomach for anything, and feels bilious and full as he pulls stuff out – mostly labelless tins traded for smaller jobs, favours. He runs another mug of water, opens a can of peach slices, and goes back to her. She glugs the water in one motion and starts on the peace slices, sore mouth sucking them in, juice everywhere, her eyes ablaze.

"Slow down, slow down," he says. She's beaming, slurping the peach halves straight from the can. "You'll give yourself bloody indigestion," he says. "Or cut yourself. Let me see what else there is."

Kidney beans. Lentils. Another can of peaches. He leans round to her from the cupboard and says: "More of them? And a shower? God, course you'll want a shower. There's a towel warming up by there."

The woman clicks and squawks and quacks. He sits with her while she demolishes another can of peaches.

"Who are you?" he asks. "I told you I'm Sol, right? And you're…"

She turns to him, licking juice from her hands.

Sol prods himself in the chest. "S-O-L. Solomon. Like the king."

The woman clicks twice.

"Can you say it?"

She points to her throat. Under the naked bulb, the dashed tattoo appears raised.

"No, say it. Your name." He's pointing to his heart. "I'm Sol. Now you."

The woman looks pensive, like she's weighing it. The

room is peaceful. A vibrant smell of peach.

Now she pulls a single knee to her front. The sheets ruffle around her. With two hands she frames her face, purses her lips, and she blows, blows, blows – the oval of her mouth expanding out from a tight circle. The sound that follows is breathed, not spoken, not whispered, but formed and inflated with such effort it almost *crawls* from her lips, deformed and suffering.

"*Why.*"

She smiles at him.

Sol begins to cry.

"Why," she rasps again, suddenly pained and confused. "*Why.*"

"Why," he mimics, snotty, voice bunged. And then it clicks. Sol draws the shape in the air with both forefingers. "Y? Like that? The letter?"

The woman nods. "Y…"

"Y."

And even though Sol's instinct is to hug her, to celebrate this tiny event, this understanding, his head is adamant he should run.

In the crane cabin, the smell was burning hair.

Roy was hysterical. He knew what he'd done. The men on the hook had gone. The line was all the way out.

And from the ladder tube came a man with part of his face hanging off.

The man took one look at Roy, striped with blood from his head wound, and Kerry unconscious in the corner, and came straight at Roy, shrieking.

Roy reeled away and dodged the first swing, caught the second full-handed – surprised himself – and pushed back. "It's me," he shouted. "It's me – it's Noodles!"

It didn't penetrate. The man was a frothing dog, and

Roy didn't know why. He came again, and Roy found the reflexes to sidestep him and use the man's momentum to push him towards the door, out onto the gantry. Roy said *stop*, or *wait*, or *sorry* – more likely a garbled mixture of all three – and the man screamed and came once more. There was so little space, and the man's hands went round Roy's neck and squeezed.

Then the pressure eased. Kerry standing behind, pulling at the man by his ears. Roy felt himself freed. He put all his weight through his front foot and shoved.

One thing led to another. Roy hadn't seen how Kerry and the man were knotted. Roy watched as they silently tumbled onto the gantry and vanished – straight down the ladder tube.

Y

After a few klicks down, perhaps when she felt warm enough, the woman in front introduced herself to Y as Karens – their expedition leader.

Karens had a fierce voice, accent unplaceable, and Y was unnerved by the way she kept her face turned against the weather, even despite her armour.

The rest of the trolley team trudged along at Karens' beck and call, chuntering in militarized jargon. Y listened as they encoded and decoded simple observations; struggled to comprehend their clipped phrases, acronyms, status updates. Mainly, though, Y focused on what might've been another squad disappearing and reappearing from microclimates further down the Slope. She wondered if there was another team setting out behind them. And she wondered what waited at the bottom –

Behind Y came a tall photographer, mercenary looking, with shoulders like masonry. He didn't speak much and clearly didn't intend to: the black temper on his face said it all. She hadn't caught his name. Then there were

Babar and Shazad. Glorified thermometers and security, really – stacked-out, fat-necked techies swaddled in wire and light alloy. At the back was Fi, the team's medic, who, as she'd told Y with slow, deliberate gestures, was also tethered to the mansion's silent sentinel: a sort of first-aid pod in geosynchronous orbit. This miniature balloon-launched satellite would keep tabs on Y's vitals from afar. While no one acknowledged its overwatch, its hidden presence was solid and insidious. It told Y exactly how much she was worth.

The group walked. And walked. And walked. And occasionally, they rested. In a circle, they sucked on sweetened oatmeal that stuck to the roofs of their mouths, and chased it down with a silky gel. And then they carried on.

They'd been going downslope for five hours or so when Karens stopped them with a single hand movement. It was testament to their concentration levels that they all saw it.

"Zones," Karens said over the link. The filter was labouring in her mask. Babar stepped out of line, took a defensive stance and scanned their surroundings.

Fi, who'd moved instinctively to Y's side, asked, "What's going on?"

"Something pinging the echobox," Karens said. "I want Shaz to process it before we go on."

Shazad joined Babar and pulled up his sleeve. He started fiddling on his wrist, narrowing down to the signal.

Y swallowed and tasted blood – likely her gums. The suits kept them hydrated, the synthetics wicked the sweat, but nothing kept her mouth from going dry. She thought of the faucet back on the lawns; imagined in her own throat a crimson froth.

Shazad's wrist instrument blipped and spat a slice of waterproofed data. He said something too quiet for his mic to catch, and Karens asked him to repeat himself.

"I said, it's lying flat."

"What is?" Karens asked. "What's lying flat?"

"Corpse," Shazad said indifferently. "About half of one."

Y got the sense the trolley squad were glancing between themselves. Only Fi was staring right at her, and her faceplate had started to steam. Karens motioned downslope, and the squad fell about her, well-rehearsed, so that every angle of sight was covered. Y was suddenly contained by them, a baby elephant folded into the herd. She realized Fi had a hand on her wrist.

"Don't have time for this shit," Babar said, sighting on the edge of the visible Slope.

Karens looked at Y, then down at Fi's glove. "Radio it through, Shaz," she said. "Get them to send a closing team down here. If it's a slip and it's still running we could lose someone easy in this weather. Pull the body's last signal, too – we might have to switch vectors."

Y strained to see down the hill. The ceaseless mist obscured everything beyond ten metres, despite her eyes being well optimized for low visibility. It was the strangest thing to know uncountable miles stretched away in all directions.

"Just get the pod down to scoop it," Babar said. "I want my bonus."

"Karens," Fi said. "You better tell him or I will."

The photographer docked a cold film and started snapping the squad.

Karens nodded and opened a palm towards Y. "Pod's for her, Babar. You know that. And there's still time. We're reporting it." Her look softened. "Now tuck in behind me, young lady."

The squad trekked on down the Slope towards the body, Shazad's echobox drilling faster as they drew near.

Y saw it first. She stopped in shock. The photographer was walking too close and nearly knocked her over.

"Moron," he said.

But Y didn't hear him. She was too busy looking at the body. It was a man lopped in two lengthways – open side cauterized to a glossy black. He looked like refuse; a thing simply tossed away to biodegrade in the silt of the Slope.

"Don't," Fi said.

Y edged closer. The man wore a slick-looking black suit whose burnt edges had curled into his flesh. Whatever had happened here, violence had given over to an abiding neatness.

Next to him was a yellow crate on skids. It was stencilled ORGANS.

"Second this week," Karens said to no one in particular. Y heard her sigh into her mask. "Gate their side must be faulty."

Nobody answered. Y couldn't stop gawping.

"Pass me an M-kit," Karens said. "One of you."

Fi stepped up and unracked a disc from her belt. She passed it to Karens, who flicked it, nonchalantly but accurate, towards the body.

It landed with a soft note, and Y felt a tension swell.

"OK," Karens said. "Inert. Any volunteers for skin checks? We'll need his tag."

Y looked round at all of them.

Shazad registered Y's confusion. "Poor bastard's come through a dodgy slip," he told her. "Always problematic." He pointed at the crate. "And them – they're damaged goods now."

Babar snorted. Fi shot them both a glance.

"Control, it's Karens," the squad leader said. "We've got a body – most of a body – about five hours down."

Static. Something spoken back.

"Inbound, yes," Karens said. "Looks that way. Cloak-suit, full trans-crate."

More static.

"No, it's O-marked."

Inside her gear, Y thought she could feel something moving over her skin. The sensation rose and centred behind the tooth against her sternum. She held a hand there, as if to counter its weight.

"Fi," Karens said. "Can you check his ID? Control's saying the gate filed a bad slip yesterday."

Fi went and knelt by the body. She was looking for dogtags, so had to peel back the edges of the man's suit. Through the gap beneath Fi's armpit, Y saw the man's bruised skin, then an expanse of untouched white.

The photographer took a few shots of the scene.

"Nothing on him," Fi said.

"Fucking great," Karens said. "Must be in the pockets on the missing side. That'll make the paperwork interesting. Shaz, can you upload the co-ords anyway? I'll handle the beacon. They'll want the crate if nothing else."

The big man nodded and played with his gear.

Something bleeped in all their earpieces, and Karens checked her watch again.

"Shit," Fi said suddenly. Then she yelped and twisted awkwardly, her legs tangling.

The group saw Fi fall backwards, land heavily on her pack. "Shit," she said again, and this time fear was in her voice.

The group quickly saw why. A thin line was spreading

across the Slope under her boots, a rupture in the ground that started next to the man's half-body. Silt vibrated either side of it.

"Away!" Karens shouted, her arm out to shield Y. "Fi, for the love of God get back here–"

A rumble cut her off. Fi flopped over, stumbled towards the group. Y was shocked to see Fi's left glove smoking, fingertips of material gone. Fi fell and drove her hand into the Slope's ashen surface like she'd somehow mistaken it for snow. Y couldn't see Fi's eyes, and in the earpiece there was an inhuman gravelly sound – Fi's filter working beyond capacity.

Next came a pop. The man's half-body seemed to jerk, then writhe on the spot.

"Babar, pull her away," Karens screamed. "Jesus. Someone!" Then: "Shaz – how fucking big is it?"

Both men stood wide-eyed, fixed. The air was visibly thickening, and there was a distinct smell in their masks the trolley team knew well – the tang of ozone.

"It's big," Shazad said.

Karens gripped Y by the shoulder and the group paced back from Fi – three, five, ten, fifteen metres. The remains were in spasm now, and Fi was crawling as fast as her elbows and knees could shift her. Several times she seemed overbalanced, close to falling straight on her chin and stuffing her filter unit with silt. Above the whine, Y heard Fi whimpering in her helmet. Her too-fast breathing cut against the mute panic of the others.

From deep brown, the sky turned another colour – greyer, even more opaque – and the Slope was flooded with an eerie light. Then the crate burst open, spilling red bags, coolant blocks and dark liquid.

Y tugged on Karens' arm – pleading with her eyes to help Fi, who was clearly struggling. But Karens simply watched. Finally, Fi's elbows buckled and her chin drooped in exhaustion. Her head, now fully slack, described a terrible arc, and her face went into the silt.

Fi's collapse was too much for Y. In one smooth, assured movement she pushed Karens away and sprinted straight over, protesting voices distant. She dragged Fi up from the silt, faltering slightly under the woman's weight, then leaned deeply into her mass. Slope material fell away from Fi's mouthgrate, from the seals around her visor, and her head hung loose. Y crackled and hissed, and the two of them staggered upwards until they buckled at Karens' feet.

Fi came round spluttering. She looked at Y, who was almost wrapped around her. Y saw that her eyes were brimming hot.

"It's opening!" Karens called out, clamping Y's shoulder and dragging her off. The ground around the dead man tore apart. The air clapped and a deep gouge appeared in the fabric of all things. Through this they saw the inside of a cavernous black space filled with wooden crates, a damp floor. Just as quickly, the vision cut to smeared green, and a huge tree crashed clean through the gap. There was a roar, and a sheaf of leaves and twigs followed. A shower of waxy brown nuts bounced away down the Slope, flickering as they went.

"*Allāhu akbar…*" Babar whispered.

Now the tree, too, seemed to flicker, caught as it was between two worlds, its branches torn in the binary, a duality, pulled with equal force from two opposite poles. And in the middle of this, the dead man's half-body was scooped up, remaining leg and arm seething on its joints, only to be creased and divided with a bloodless snap. Each segment was sent pinwheeling across the Slope in different directions.

The shattered trans-crate hopped in a circle, its red innards splashing on the white.

Y screamed a soundless scream. The others shielded their eyes, reflexively squatting before the frantic tree as it disintegrated in the slip's tangle.

The noise was immeasurable.

"*Allāhu akbar!*" Babar shouted.

"Go," Karens said, pushing on her squad mates' shoulders. "Go!"

So they went, big Babar dragging Fi now, Fi's eyes glazed and her glove still trailing smoke. They left the torn Slope behind, the man there in tatters, the recovery beacon still clipped to Karens' belt, and kept going until they felt sure the violence had petered out.

"Six more hours," Karens told them, dour.

"Never approach a lit firework," the photographer said to Y. He stopped briefly and took more shots upslope. The shutter rang out like a bell over a village in mourning. He caught Y looking. "Pay that man no mind. He knew the risks, as we all do. A slip goes wrong from time to time – it's what happens when you don't fully understand things. And if it's your turn…"

Y felt revulsed by the photographer, the contrast between here and back there, but wanted to know more. Somehow, however, she knew it was all the explanation she was going to get. And Fi – Fi in her shuddering shock, hobbling behind with a raggedy pulse – had exited reality entirely.

NiNE

Sol rolls into work with two stale butties and a sad story. He managed an hour's sleep at best, folded against the wall alongside his occupied bed.

For a time, the sky lightening, he'd watched Y sleep. Seemingly she trusted him enough to relax and return herself to some base state: a mammal with basic needs, organs to nourish. He listened intently to her every breath in terror she'd simply stop or change rhythm, or begin to relate something awful – cropped phrases, dream excerpts, glimpses of a subconscious path to some greater truth he didn't want to confront. From the draught that swept over his skin, he realized Y's feet were exposed to the cold, so he rearranged the sheets. As he did, he wondered if the act made him caring or simply reflected his selfishness. In some way it was enough to convince him he'd earned his sleep.

Y was still snoring when he left. He wrote a note for her, stacked a few more cans, left paper and a pen. *Don't panic*, he wrote on it. *I'll be home soon.*

He didn't write: *Everything must seem normal.*

He didn't write: *Denial is how I survive*.

Back at the workshop, Sol finds Irish dismantling the Lexus, most of its panels stripped away and arranged in neat rows. The lights seem doubly bright. Seeing the car again – its innards, knowing what it brought – makes Sol gag.

"Time you call this?" Irish says.

"No," Sol says, swallowing hard, arm over the Lexus roof. "It's sold, you bastard. Christ's sakes, Pete. We've *sold* it already. It has to go. We have to get rid."

Irish stops working. His breath hanging on the thin air. "Pete? Up yours as well, Solomon. What's the fucken craic here? You seen the clock have you? I come in this morning to a shit-tip – paper, rags, drawers hanging out, insane drawings on the table through there. And here's a kicker for you: we're running on reserves today since some fucker wrecked the gennie and got in the back door."

Sol barely registers the information. "It's sold," he carries on. "The Lexus is sold. You need to rebuild it – it has to go."

"Bollocks it does. You talking about, sold? You turn up acting all banjaxed – and what? We've got two grand in this motor, if we're sensible. At *least* that. And don't you Christ me, man – you gonna tell me what your problem is? Why're you're all wet like that? Look at you, man. Look at the state of you."

Sol can smell Irish's warm, working body – gamey and rich. Lingering cigarette smoke a layer above. The question hangs: tell him about Y? Or attempt to hide her forever?

"We got an order in."

"For this?"

Sol needs to sit down. All his connections feel loose.

"Aye," he says. "And a frigging battle tank." Sweat rolls, a line down his temple. "Modding a car for some runners. Wilbers, maybe. They want fridges in there, God knows what else. I called Miss Wales – got most of the materials on order. Steel. Plating. Same guy bought the Lexus as part of the deal – not a bad price. So just stick it all back together, and give the engine a tickle while you're at it. Then we're done. We're done."

Irish shakes his head. "Just like that? And this buyer of yours – hefty was he? Nagging type? Only you had someone round first thing today as well."

Sol pales. "Who? Not the council…"

Irish barks a laugh. "*Council*? Sweet Mary our Holy Mother on high. We're the last of their bleeding worries. Why d'you spend all that time filing numbers off if that's how you're gonna react? Come on, man. Don't fill your pants on me. When's the last time we got raided? Half this city's on our books!"

"You jacked this," Sol says, tapping the Lexus. "Jacked it. That's plenty of reason to get paranoid."

Irish shakes his head. "You need to chill your beans, man. The guy didn't even sniff at it. He wants you – says he's a friend of hers."

"Whose?"

"Hers. Melanie's. Jeff he's called. Shaking like a shitting dog he was. Jeff with a J. I said you weren't about, but you'd be in later. I goes to him, "You want a brew?" and he looks at me like I've just shot his mam and fed her to the fucken cats. I said I had to nip out for some bits and pieces – that I'd say he called. Then the second I turn my back for a pen, he's gone again. Not even a bye."

"Mel?"

You stupid prick –

"Aye, Mel. What's up with you? Least that's what he

tells me. Seemed no reason to lie. Like I said, he'll call back for a chat."

Sol's head is spinning. He must look ill. He knits his hands – tries to pull the splitting seams together. "Was he on his own?"

"On his own?"

"This Jeff. How did he get here?"

"Jesus, Solomon. He had legs."

"I'll… I'll call her then."

"Colour you've gone at the thought of it, maybe you ought to bury her."

Sol ignores him. "He look handy, this Jeff?"

"*Handy*? What? He was stocky, sure. Though now you mention it, he wore sunglasses. What's with people who wear sunglasses inside? What's that about?"

Sol bites his thumb. Could be anyone, this line of work. Even a pity referral from her. But there's always a but – and if you add Sol's panicked call to Mel into the equation, it can't be coincidental.

Prick –

"Anyway," he says to Irish. "Gonna need you over in Liverpool for this Ferrari."

Irish shakes his head. "You hear what I said about the back door? You know we actually pay to use the spare gennie, don't you? Someone got in here."

"What? The door…"

Someone broke in not long after he and Y left.

"You're going spare for this car, but you don't care about a break-in."

Sol sits down where he is.

"Mate," Irish says. "What's going on? Get yourself up."

"I'll sort it!" Sol snaps. "I'm owed favours. I'll fix it."

Irish looks unsettled now. "Fine. Well I've wedged a

car next to it for now. And we're flipping a coin for the Ferrari."

"It's fine. You go."

"Don't be a fucken lush," Irish tells him. His throat is red – the signal he's getting annoyed. "We don't work like that."

"No," Sol says.

"Heads or harps?"

Sol's guts are turning. Fifty-fifty he gets found out because he left Y alone in his flat while he goes walkabout. Fifty-fifty it all comes down.

He thinks: *You shouldn't be here.*

He thinks: *Why've you left her?*

"Call it then," Irish says, visibly impatient. "Before you start being a pain in my hole proper–"

Sol does his best to hold it together. "Heads."

The coin spins, catches light. Every particle of dust, rust – every speck suspended in the workshop's dead air – seems to glitter.

The slap, the turn, the call:

"Harps!"

And Sol's high is instant, invigorating. He stands up, rushing. "Do us proud," he says, grinning. "And listen: you still got room at home?"

"The shed?"

Sol nods wildly.

"Sure."

"Take it there – work on it there as well."

"I think you need some kip," Irish tells him. "Sort your head out. You honestly want this Ferrari at mine?"

Sol clutches his head. "Makes… makes more sense. Need space for the metal when it comes. Never mind the base rig."

"You mean you want me out your way?"

"Not at all–"

"Time's the pickup?"

"See how you get on today."

"In the truck?"

"No – you'll have to go by train."

"Bollocks I will," Irish spits. *"Train?* Is this the fucken catch?"

"It's getting better," Sol tells him. Another lie. "Armed escorts now. They had it on the news…"

"Better hope the bastard drives then. Or you're paying for my return and a trailer to go with it."

"It runs. They swore on that."

"Fine. But–"

"You're a star," Sol cuts in. He points to the Lexus. "You've just got to sort this."

Irish shakes his head. "You've lost the plot, I swear it."

Sol goes to the entrance and closes the rollers halfway. Maybe. Maybe.

The day drags after that. Sol tries to work. A little groundwork for the conversion project, blueprints on a bank of cold stainless worktops. Working out which bits go where. The machine tools they'll need to hire. He annotates each panel with material lists, thicknesses, dimensions, stacked question marks about welds. The deeper he goes, the more he can forget.

Now and then he looks across the workshop. Odd sounds – unfamiliar shuffling noises – momentarily distract him, but he puts them down to tiredness, the backup generator. For a good few minutes, he watches Irish working methodically through the Lexus parts. He can't bear to think of the break-in, its implications, so he thinks instead of Irish's train journey – of the stories he'll return with, the way he'll tell them. He's dimly aware he owes his partner an apology.

But the unsaid things needle him. Who's he really fooling? Even if he pretends last night didn't happen, Y finds her way in: reminders of her face emerge through the materials of this place, glinting edges, the kerning of every word in the paperwork. A seeping guilt.

He thinks: *Why've you left her?*

Countered by the truthful answer: *Because you hope she'll be gone when you get back.*

Sol stops working. The disparity between today and yesterday is concentrated, overwhelming. How much had changed overnight? It's all muddled up. All spiralling.

Irish finishes up on the Lexus. "It'll be Liverpool first thing," he tells Sol, pulling on his coat. "Unless I get blown up, harvested for organs or shot."

Sol just about manages a goodbye. When the door rolls closed, Y burns into his thoughts with fresh intensity: her knees pulled up under her chin, the stringy spit on her feeding tubes. The sound of her cicada-clicking. The very fact she's over there on his sofa, in his tracksuit perhaps, with a damp-smelling towel nearby in case her stomach can't handle any more tinned stuff.

Why did he think it was reasonable to leave her? To go on like normal?

His responsibilities are washing up like shoes after a shipwreck.

So Sol puts on his jacket, grabs the truck keys. But before he can go back to her, there's someone else he needs to see.

Roy arrives outside Sol's workshop. By now he's soaked through to his bones, and the rain's still falling heavily.

Riding his luck, he hauls himself over a perimeter holo-board – one of the dead units round the side. He kicks and tears a ladder into the plastic mesh that wraps the advert optics, then shins right up it. Hardly subtle, but who cares when you're spurred on by the lunatic singlemindedness you get from a few pints and an impulsive idea.

He drops into the yard. Revolver out. Two steps and a heartbeat and he's blinded by a trespass strobe that backlights the cloud cover like a flak cannon. He falls against the wall. Each time it fires – its filaments pinging – the rain is stilled, petrified by the flash, leaving Roy caught swaying in a field of cold static.

He waits. He watches. He counts.

The lamp dies. Just as he'd hoped, it's blown itself – drawn too much power at once.

Squinting – a neon tear through his vision – he crosses the yard. There's a beware-the-dog sign on the roller doors. Padlocks and sliding bolts layered up.

But then he doesn't intend to get in through the front.

The faint hum of a generator brings Roy round the back: a flaw he'd clocked on his first visit. Close to the generator enclosure, which is bricked onto the workshop, there's a door with rudimentary electronic locks.

Roy grabs the fibre wires lined in from the holo-boards that Sol's tapping for the workshop's power, and yanks their sealant out of the wall. The bundled thread slides easily, thick as his forearm, though he's wary of the cable's live end slipping straight into his hand. After a slight snag, a crack and fizz, the generator dies. Almost immediately, the backup kicks in.

Roy laughs and keeps pulling. Soon enough the live end emerges through the hole, dragging chunks of cavity insulation. He holds it out at full extension, the way you hold a snake, and piles it into the door's mechanism. A sparkle, and abracadabra: the mechanism shorts out. The locks hiss and the door cracks ajar. He sticks his head in.

He looks left to see his Lexus, its glossy outline, boot
lid up –

Looks right –

And hears something coming.

Roy bursts inside. In haste he trips over himself and
bowls headfirst into the side panel of a Transit van. It
gives. Both hands up, balance gone, he slips on the cold-
greased concrete and down towards the inspection pit –
his ankle caught between the pit's edge and the footplate
of the Transit, and the rest of him in torsion, rotating
the other way. A terminal crack – a skull at the point of
impact – and it's done.

Above, a fox flits carefree through the workshop.

Sol takes the work truck, mind's eye fixed on a little blip
moving across his own map of Manchester – the UI from
an old routing app somehow internalized.

As he goes, it's all Mel, a depthless anxiety at seeing
her. He's done so much to subdue her hold, to store
those memories in some shoebox of the soul, pack it into
the corners. But now she's centre stage again. A life he
denies to himself has come crashing into focus.

Through the racing lines of quiet roads, the truck's
rattling bulk against the rain, she floods back, inundates
him. A beach marriage – theirs, more like someone else's
now – at the Gower Peninsula off Swansea. Wind, salty
kisses. Falling into bed together, happy or resentful,
silent or desperate, but together. The possibility of her
death in hospital. Running reds through the city to
be there, a cracked reflection of now. And his earliest
memory of them: a beach with lines of headless fish, his
father's laughter, and Mel's socket, a voided space.

He remembers Mel buttered across a hospital bed.

He remembers the day he left her.

And then another thought, as if revealed only by those that gathered before. As if it were yesterday: Sol floating home unwashed from their first night as lovers, still smelling of them, him and her, Mel still in his hair, crescent nail marks like scars on his wrists. The strange electricity that came with finding one of her hairs trapped in the strap of his watch, and a series of rich images repeating – *clack, clack, clack* – all memory-stills, of the night before and the morning after and their skin in the moonlight through the mottling net curtains, her knickerline, the apex of lace and flesh, and all they did to stave off the grave new world outside. A flashbulb, memories of her eye; their open eyes, no blinking. Bonded lips and wrapped tongues and laughing. Just laughing. Hips and lips and curving spines. And now back to this. Just this. A dial-lit truck cabin, an A-road, and a dissolution of time.

Deeper still, then, into the black: their first time alone in a single bed, possibly her sister's, and while Sol knows he's alone in the truck the recollection is so intense he could be right there now. They can hardly move for the bed squeaking. Their faces so close her eyes have merged, cycloptic, so he can't tell if he's staring into her good eye or her bad eye or a fusion of the two. Her harsh fringe is clipped off her forehead, and she's breathing into his mouth and pulling his hand to her face, his dead fingertips to her dead eye. She's tracing a circle with his forefinger around it, and then she's pushing the pad of his finger onto it. She's making him roll it in the socket –

Gentle, she's saying.

Now she's splaying two of his fingers into a pincer, applying pressure either side till her eye comes loose in his hand. He's tensing, tensing, and she's going, *It's alright*. She's reaching down and taking him and pulling him inside her. She's taking his forefinger, and she's edging it into her soft, leathery socket.

I don't want you frightened of it any more.

He's trying to remove his finger. Trying to swallow. *Mel–*

She's saying, *I love you*, and it's making him come. She's giggling into his shoulder. And all the time, her glass eye is there on the sideboard in its cleaning fluid, and it's watching.

Sol parks the truck. Doublechecks his trader's curfew pass is visible on the windscreen.

He hammers the Cat Flap's door; presumes a camera's on him. That in every private room there's someone buried in selfish pleasure. That she's at the desk, gets up reluctantly, huffing –

Mel comes to the door in a dressing gown she can't be bothered tying thighs all marbled her chest white and blue with blotches her cig half ash and teetering –

The door swings. He forgets to exhale. She's in jeans, a thick woolly jumper.

"Sol?"

Sol reads her expression the way skippers read cloud ahead.

"Melanie…"

She backs off, unsure, hands out. She mumbles something, plainly shaken. She pushes her fringe away from her fake eye.

"Mel," he says. "What's up with you?"

"Just… just wasn't expecting anyone."

"You need to help me."

Mel blinks at him.

"She isn't from here," he tells her. "A man came to the workshop."

Mel puts her hands over her face. "Please, Sol. Please."

"Let me in," he says, and steps into the hallway regardless. Mel backs up to the inner door and pushes it open. Dust and incense. The chipboard palace. "You've decorated."

The video screens blare flesh. Sol with a dead-dog taste in his mouth. Mel closes the door behind them.

"You have to go home," she tells him. "I knew it. I even said to the girls – he's bloody coming back. You know that? I knew. But you can't be here. If any of the girls–"

"If any of the girls what?"

"They respect me."

"What does that mean?"

"Just go."

"She doesn't speak a word of English. And she's got these holes, right–"

Mel puts her face in her hands.

"Mel!"

Another flash of the hospital bed. Life at low tide, draining through the mattress fibres. An old fear that returns as a revelation: *it was always my fault she ended up there.*

"You've got to bloody help me," he says. More desperate this time.

"I said *stop*."

The screens pulsate with morphic shapes. It's like the wood panels are floating.

"I can't let it go," Sol says. "Not this time."

"You're getting yourself in trouble."

"Is that a threat?"

"Where is she?"

"At mine."

"Alone? Oh Jesus, no."

"Why? Why? And who's Jeff?"

Mel stares at him. She goes to speak –

The front bell rings, cuts her off. Mel reels away. A group of young lads fall through the door – goggle-eyed, tripping.

Sol sits down, things spinning. Mel ignores him. She pulls down her mask; starts to take their orders, writing furiously with a pen.

He watches them all. *A beach. A fish. And the insides of her head.*

Sol stands up, sickened.

She doesn't look.

So he leaves her again.

Roy comes round with the sense of being in an unfamiliar bed. Weak light filters through one eye. He's in a pit, concrete lined. Everything hurts. The kind of pain that turns the world purple, the space around you anechoic – so deathly silent the only sound is your rushing blood.

Most of the damage is in his foot. Bad news. He cringes as he massages the delicate jointing, swollen ligaments. A horror-vision of disfigurement – some irrational idea his injury might ossify there and then.

And then a secondary fear. Going undiscovered beneath the Transit van in the inspection pit. Lost or lapsed, like pocket change down a sofa.

When he tries to stand, he realizes he won't put weight down anytime soon. The shock of this fresh pain detaches him, tilt-shifts the view: his foot, still in its shoe, has turned almost sideways. He puts a hand to his face, his forehead dog-nose clammy. Is he concussed? He looks at his foot again. A foot, at any rate – not quite his. It might be dislocated – the tibia's pushing up against the skin to make a convex bowl in his sock. A new corner. He winces, imagines standing and his leg twisting round at the knee. And because he knows damaged biology like few others, he knows it's likely a break.

Now what?

It's hard to know how long he's been out for. It's early morning at a guess, though he knows the sky can sometimes turns yellow regardless of the time. No watch, either – its body is shattered by his side, face burred cocaine-white.

He rifles his pockets, empty, and laughs for his offnet mobile. His revolver.

You could shout, he thinks. *When they get in. They won't like what you've done to their generator, their lock, but at least they'll get you out.*

Except Roy can't hear anything, like he's tuned himself out.

He tries to stand again. With both arms outstretched he can just about touch both walls, shuffle himself along. It's phobic-tight.

A bang. Roy drops. The roller door lifts, and in the gap he sees thick legs, boots. He hears someone swear. He can tell it isn't Sol. Maybe the other guy – Paul? No, *Pete*.

Roy slides upwards, weight on his good foot. He holds his breath. The man flicks on a rack of lights. More swearing. Then a second voice – quiet to the edge of pointless. Roy listens – hears the cadence of questions. Instinct telling him these two aren't colleagues.

The men move closer. Roy hears one of them say, "Not with a *G*. With a *J*."

Then they go silent, as if they've spotted him. Spooked, Roy puts his weight on the wrong foot. It pulses, and the riptide drags him back under. He bites his tongue, slumps to his knees, finds himself too weak to try again. Why doesn't he say something? Why doesn't he shout?

Because these days people kill people for much less than trespassing.

The voices ebb past. "What time's Sol going to be in?" the second man asks.

"I don't know, mate. Anytime really," the first says back, an Irish accent. "You want a brew or anything?"

It's all so tiresome. Just close your eyes and you can sleep, slide, slip –

The Rev'll find you if he really wants to.

Y

The Slope bottomed out like the end of a ski run. Here the dust and mist gave way to a pan of soft ground, clay-like, that was veiny with fissures.

Karens and the squad moved across the last yards, knees and hips aching, postures gone. Y was lost in marching rhythms; noticed only the action of her legs. She had muscle twinge, stomach cramps. She barely knew what carried her.

And still the divided man haunted her. The schism in the air and the tree it gave birth to.

"Stop," Karens said, and they did, with only Fi lagging in response. Y saw a settlement, mirage-like, across the plain. It was a collection of flat, densely packed structures, fabric-sided, and covered with a gleaming material that had the appearance of a single enormous sheet. The sun, rising, gave it a pinkish sheen.

Karens unclipped a cantina, undid her faceplate. She rubbed her eyes and turned to Y. "It's fine – no storms down here," she told her. She held out the drink. "Have a swig."

Y unfastened her own mask. She pulled out her feeding tube and took the cantina. It wasn't water – something sweeter.

"Is that a smile?" the photographer asked, tilting the camera. The shutter snapped.

"Just leave her be," Fi said. While they'd been standing, she'd managed to temporarily patch her damaged glove with insulation tape. She was pale, and her voice was weak.

Karens spoke into her mic from the corner of her mouth. Y couldn't hear this, so she turned and took in the view again – the liquid lustre of the settlement's shell.

"They call it Plastic, the locals," the photographer said. "Kind of place you have to keep checking your pockets."

"Animals," Babar chipped in, "is what he's saying. But that's frontier towns for you."

"They used to grow tomatoes," the photographer said, "under all this. When they first came over, anyway."

Y nodded. The photographer appeared even more imposing on the flat. His shadow was a solid stream of black running away across the pan.

"Then the settlers moved up in the world." The photographer tilted his head back up the Slope. "Left this place a black market. You ever tried a tomato?"

Y shook her head.

"You don't have to say anything to him," Fi said. "Nothing you don't want to."

"Shut up," the photographer told her, putting a finger to his lips. "There's nothing like that smell. Hot tomato plants under plastic–"

"You talk like it was fifty years ago," Babar interrupted. "It's been a few years max."

"I'm just telling her," the photographer went on, "how we broke into another world to start farming."

"Button it, the pair of you," Karens said.

"We haven't even spoken for hours," the photographer snapped. "She looks completely traumatized."

"Then tell her something useful," Babar said.

The photographer dead-eyed Y. "They speak Perune here," he said. "Mangled Portuguese, basically. Good bartering language. Loads of the first crossers were Brazilian labourers – cheap and cheerful."

"I won't tell you again," Karens said. "Her pickup's waiting."

The photographer snorted. "Another one to think about," he whispered to Y. "Why didn't they didn't just build the mansion down here? Why hide it away?"

Y shook her head again.

"Bureaucracy," the photographer said. "That's why. It isn't much good for industry."

And Fi tutted.

Minutes later they reached the settlement proper – a market square. Crowds shuffled round bazaar-like stalls, people wearing either simple cloth or heavy security tech. They were indifferent to her, and she drank in the colour and odd-smelling foods and the sound of alien languages duelling. At the far end of the square was a column of tracked vehicles piled high with extruded profiles and neatly stacked crates. These were stencilled with the word OUT.

From there the squad passed into the capillary-like streets that ran between Plastic's squares. At one point another trolley squad came the other way. Y saw a masked person dressed as she was – twinned circles pinned to their front. She considered, briefly, if they could have been a brother or sister she'd once tried to help sleep.

Down more side streets, past heaving stalls, open

sewers, all of it under the plastic canopy, the settlement's wrapper, this great synthetic sheet that trapped the reek and the sweat and the stickiness, most of which dripped back onto the uncaring crowds below.

Ahead, a heavy mass loomed through the material. Y thought she recognized its shape.

"We're here," Karens said.

And they were. The canopy ended with a run of shanties, and the cramped passageway opened into limitless space.

Y was bewildered. She did recognize the shape. There before them stood the hyperboloid form of an industrial cooling tower, hundreds of feet tall. Dark bricks, patchy repairs, every concrete section of its curve speckled and lined with age.

She'd been here before. She knew this with terrible certainty. She knew it so intimately, so innately, that it couldn't be mere chance.

It was her tower. Faceless and enduring.

As they watched, a narrow-gauge locomotive emerged on a track from the tower's base. The train stopped at a platform, where a fleet of fork trucks began to unload crates from its flatbed cars. In the sidings, hi-vis-jacketed workers were dropping them onto skids much like those Y saw fitted to the ORGANS box up the Slope. The only difference being that these crates were stencilled IN.

Y tugged Fi's arm. Her eyes asked a thousand questions, but Fi shook her head sadly and said simply, "Trans-crates," before pushing her onwards.

As they walked, Y stared up at the tower. Her tower.

"You get to walk in," Karens said from behind. "That's something."

Out of Y's earshot, Babar clapped. "She doesn't like this at all."

Fi shot him a look. "Not her fault," she whispered. "And if I were you I'd be grateful she made it here at all – it's the only reason you're getting fed later."

"Are you smiling again, kid?" Shazad asked Y. "Babar, she thinks you're funny."

But Y wasn't smiling consciously. She wasn't even listening. She was transfixed by the tower, its domination of the landscape. The exhumation of her memories, and its curious erasure, eclipsing, of something about teeth, a man robed in teeth, and a camera lens focusing.

Babar thumped Shazad on the arm. "Freaks me out how she never says anything."

Shazad shrugged. "You didn't see the scar on her throat?"

"Guys," Fi said. "I'm being serious now. A little compassion."

"It's a surgical tattoo," the photographer said, ignoring Fi. "She'll be a grafter, anyway," he added. "Arms aside, look at her back. The size of it."

"A little worker bee," Babar said, scratching his heavy beard.

"Just imagine what she'll do with the extra digits," the photographer said.

Fi was glowing. "Are you seriously doing this?" she asked. "You're really saying this in front of her?"

"Oh don't pretend servitude isn't servitude," the photographer said. "You know what it's about. They cook, they clean, they assemble…"

Babar smiled. "They fu–"

"You're a cretin," Fi snapped, cutting him off. "That what it's about. It's disgusting, behaving like this. You've no clue where they end up, what they have to do. Where they came from."

"No," the photographer said firmly, "it's business –

and it's booming. If you've got a problem with what they end up doing, why are you even here?"

Fi narrowed her eyes. "You try getting a job when you've got a council sanction on your name. You forget there's two kids without their mum over there…"

The photographer shrugged. "Cry me a river, Fiona. It's not your only option. You made your choices, and you can renege on them whenever. You could get your own mods, even. Make yourself a pretty penny. Be just like her. You'd probably enjoy that, playing the victim."

Fi shook her head. "Seriously."

"Seriously what?" The photographer was grinning. "What are you going to do? Shoot me?"

"Fuck off," Fi said, her eyes bulging. "What if she's none of those things? Ask her. Go on – ask her if she can fight. I'd put money on her kicking your fat head off, arsehole."

"She's definitely pedigree," Babar said, nodding. "Her skin's too clear."

"Except *she* isn't a cut of meat," Fi hissed. "You thick bastards."

"Squad!" Karens shouted. "Some decorum, please. She crosses that line safely, and that's all we have to worry about. End of story." The group fell quiet. "Shaz, get me a transit label, please. Basecamp want proof of delivery. And Fi, stand yourself down."

Shazad nodded. "Sorry, K. Where for?"

"Manchester," Karens said.

Shazad whistled. "Lucky girl…"

Alone now, away from the group by metres but separated by so much else, Y blinked away the view. The squad's casual attitude disturbed her. It felt impossible to reconcile their behaviour and what had happened on the Slope. How easily the halved man was dismissed, how routine it all was. It seemed as matter-of-fact, as day-to-day, as strapping on their tactical kit. They'd made the choice to walk away, no question.

And Y was frightened. Of the tower. Of the unknown. Enmeshed in confusion and loss and apprehension – for all that had been taken and all that didn't add up. Her back ached from tensing it so long – not because of the exertion, even, but to counter her near-constant anxiety. Here was the tower. Her tower. This should have been the end. So why did it feel like she was being wrenched away? What could she possibly miss about the mansion?

A hand brushed her hip.

"It's nearly time," Fi said. "Oh, love. I know it's so tough."

Y wished she could say, "No." Because it wasn't tough. It wasn't even an escape. It was a withdrawal – and that was such a lonely journey to make.

At the tower's entrance was a concrete apron marked DROP OFF – the banal language of airports, taxi ranks and leisure centres repurposed to make what was happening seem mundane. A retrofitted stairway curved round the structure like a helter-skelter's slide. From there a guard greeted the squad in Perune, asked for ID. Karens went and met him on the gantry stepway.

The team checked out. As Karens came back, the guard nodded at Y and pulled something from his tactical vest pocket. Y recognized the object as the red fruit the escort ate during their brief journey from the mansion to the Slope's upper camp. She sniffed deeply, wanting to smell it again.

"You," the guard said to her in his strange accent. He held up the fruit. "Want?"

Y shook her head.

"Yes," the guard said. "Well behaved!"

Y shook her head again.

"Bye-bye," he said.

Karens nudged Y's shoulder. "Ignore it." She pointed down the path into the tower's base. It ran alongside the rail tracks, trans-crates stacked up in the sidings. "In here first, though." Karens led Y into a booth where her image was captured by a halo of dazzling red. "And now over there." Y stumbled towards the entrance port with laser-wash in her eyes. A reinforced door irised open to reveal the tower's dark guts.

Industrial gases, metals, must. It was cold, and the echo of their footsteps sounded like machinery. Y looked up through the squad's mingled breath: the tower's insides stretched away to the heavens. Purple light was just about breaking into the topmost quarter. The wiring of mysterious systems dangled from a steel net stretched across the volume.

Dead on, a panel flickered into life. Y's disembodied head rotated on the screen in fine definition; a similar aesthetic to the shapes she'd seen on her incubator's roof. It was strange to look at – Y hadn't seen herself like this before. And then a tone sounded, and to their left a new pathway was illuminated. A door to the right marked CRYO chunked closed and its controls pipped out.

The surface went from wiry carpet to steel mesh, and Y realized the men had stopped back at the screen. Babar, Shazad, the photographer. Karens jostled her arm and pulled her along. "They don't go further," she told Y, and pointed to a partition ahead. "We're up here." Y resisted and turned to them; stumbling, not fully understanding. Fi was at her other side, stony-faced.

"Y," Karens said, her hair blowing around her face.

At the partition, Karens pulled up. "You know, don't

you? This is us."

Y looked over at Fi. The medic's eyes were bloodshot.

"You'll be well looked after," Fi whispered. "Here." She gave Y a woollen hat, pulled from a cargo pocket. "To say thanks – for what you did up there." Y took it. "Manchester's cold," Fi added. "Sometimes." She hesitated, perhaps wanting to say more. But then she stalked off down the corridor.

Karens watched Y as Y watched Fi. Fi went slowly, unsurely.

"My turn now," Karens said, putting a hand on Y's head, rubbing the stubble with her thumb. "It's been a trudge, this one... but you've made our job nice and easy. And you're going on to good things – I'm sure of it."

Y croaked.

Karens gave Y a brief squeeze on the shoulder. "So. See you."

Y looked around; saw Fi join the men, right back along the corridor. Y held up a hand. Shazad and Babar waved awkwardly. The photographer raised his camera one last time. Fi, however, did nothing. She stood offset, face averted, and couldn't seem to move.

Karens reached up and unzipped the partition flap.

"Always follow your guts," she said.

And Y stepped through.

TEN

Frail and hungry, Roy drags himself to the inspection pit's shallow end – the van's rear axle inches from his head. The concrete wet with oil, dank under his hands, and blood pounding in his twisted ankle. Laboriously, he crawls into the unlit workshop. There's no sign of the partners, and a deepening sky cuts abstract shadows from the workshop fittings.

As he's brushing grit from his hands, Roy hears movement behind him. He kneels and waits there a moment, swiping blindly towards the darker corners. The noise abates. "What a shambles," he says to himself, then counts down from ten before he tries to get up.

Wobbling but relieved, he stands on his decent foot. The Lexus' driver-side door is open and close to hand. Roy hops towards it, almost laughing at the scenario, at the fruits of his perseverance.

But as he stoops to get in, the roller doors start to rattle open.

Roy swings. He waits for Sol's surprised voice – prepares himself for the confrontation by reaching for his revolver. It's not there, and its absence throws him.

He squints. No feet planted there in the widening crack...

A sharp sound rings out in the side of his head. Part of him. Internalized. He acknowledges the way it travels through him, like vibrations along a tuning fork.

The workshop tilts.

Roy angles for the Lexus, both hands on the roof sill. A vapour descends. The muscles in his forehead knotting in confusion. He falls against the frame of it – a sudden, hurtling vertigo. Savage pain as he puts down his bad foot.

He registers a large man to his left. The man is breathing heavily, with almost neon-bright discs sitting behind the lenses of his sunglasses. A flash of something again, a plunging edge –

"Solomon," the man says.

"No," Roy manages. A second noise explodes behind his ear. Heavier, more sincere. Roy feels it through his teeth. He holds up his hand, recognizes that it's still empty, but levels it like he's holding the revolver anyway.

"Are you Solomon?" the man asks.

Roy can only shake his head.

"You've taken something," the man tells him, "that isn't yours." The third strike closes everything down. Roy topples on demolished legs. As he does, he remembers a kitchen so vivid he can't believe he isn't there now:

"How did he look?" Kerry's wife asked. "In the end, I mean. When they got him out."

"Peaceful," Roy told her – a lie. In the corner of his vision was a fat man he'd only just met, his sweaty face pressed against the window. "Here," Roy said, and held out Kerry's wedding ring. "They found it when they cleared the site."

Kerry's wife slapped him, flicked the ring on to the lino.

The fat man outside was laughing.

"You didn't deserve to know him," Kerry's wife said.

That was life in those little houses, all ⬤acked up like dominos.

Roy's woken in a few bad places over the years. A few bad states. But he knows this isn't good – he can smell it's wrong before his eyes open and a naked bulb sears in; before he can clear his throat; before his internal compass can calibrate itself.

The
facts
tumble
single
file:

Lying in an unzipped suitbag

Crust heavy in his eyebrow

Pins and needles down one arm

A radiating pain in his head

A kitchen knife in his hand –

Amazed, Roy creases and sits up. Drops the knife and rubs his eyes. Unconsciously he feels for his revolver; only realizes he's searching when he can't find it anywhere.

It's a stranger's place – faint smells of takeaway and brick dust mixed with something metallic. On the nearest wall there's a high contrast collage of roads and buildings, below it a sofa that's seen better days. And then, partially obscured, a kitchenette – elements of beige laminate with chipped edges. In the other direction, a pile of socks, tracksuit bottoms, faded boxers – and a towel drying over a twisted maiden by the window. An easel, tipped over, and a torn canvas. A pile of filthy blue overalls by the door. A framed photo of an old black man standing by what looks like a classic car.

Roy blinks. Nothing adds up. In front of him are his bare feet, the hair of his legs matted. One trouser leg rolled up, and his ankle wrapped with a bag of slush.

Who the–

Roy puts his hand down to pivot, to get a bearing. What does he remember? The workshop. His ankle. The big man with laser eyes. A *pain* –

Roy's hand is wet. He recoils, palm up. The substance is sticky. Light diffuses through it. The floor next him is covered in the stuff, a thick emulsion slowly widening. It looks like setting lava. It looks like blood.

Is it him? Is he cut?

He rolls over.

By the wall is the answer. The man is there, quite still and dead, shirt torn collar to crotch, trousers peeled down, his bread and butter spilling from a ragged hole in his stomach. On one hand the man's fingers are bent too far backwards. His other is down by his crotch, vised around what looks like a thin grey slug. Roy swallows thickly and stares. Apart from the man's cheap white sports socks, which are bizarrely spotless, the man is completely soaked in his own fluids. He looks varnished.

Roy doesn't remember any of this –

Something starts vibrating on the floor by the wall. Roy crawls to it, out of the bag and away from the body. It's a phone – a fully functioning on-net mobile. On its screen, a string of code runs horizontally.

Roy whispers, "What the fuck?"

And, hearing a creak –

Turns and locks eyes with a woman entering the room.

He jumps, and she freezes in the door jamb – throws her hands up in surprise.

Three of them –

Three hands –

The light intensifying –

"You," he says. "Did this?" His voice sounds garbled to him, distant.

The woman seems fixed in time, ribcage high at full inflation, her bones visible through an oversized workshirt. Jogging pants sagging from her hips. She makes a sound like a cat purring.

Roy struggles to his knees, gestures behind. "Did you?"

His mind reels. The garage scene spooling backwards: a cold pit, a man and a spanner. Someone calling him Solomon.

Roy stands up. His ankle joint is sore, but the pain's eased. He points at her and then to the body. "He brought me here?"

She stares at him, expression unreadable. Then, seemingly unable to help herself, she glances down at the bread knife on the floor. Roy understands at once; gleans so much from this smallest of tells. "You wanted it to look like I did it?" He studies the man's body. From this angle he can see livid bruising on the neck – what looks like compression marks at three separate points. The man's eyes have been pushed deep inside his head.

"You did him," Roy says.

The woman edges back into the hall, hiding most of her face with the jamb.

Roy goes towards her. She reacts instantly, flinching at his movement, and wraps herself in her arms. In a flash of self-consciousness, Roy appreciates his own size; realizes his appearance – bald, scarred, bloody – is threatening. She could be half his height.

Roy rubs his forehead, his scabbed eyebrow. "Fuck," he rasps. "I've heard about people like you. But I never saw the handiwork."

He crosses the laminate, bridging infinite space.

"How long?" he asks. "How long have I been like that?"

The woman's backed against the front door now, silent.

Roy pauses, points back in at the body. He looks into the visible triangle of the room beyond – a bedroom. "Hang on," he says. On the floor of the bedroom there's a pair of men's shoes. Not kicked off, but deliberately placed there. Expensive-looking things – polished brogues – that jar in a flat like this.

"Did he? This bastard over here – did he try something? And did you–"

Roy moves closer. No real sense of what to do when he meets her.

Another step. The woman seems to hunker down, using the door to steady herself. She makes an animalistic sound that makes Roy hang half-step.

"Wait," Roy says, but by then the woman has already launched off the door– goes from standing to full speed in barely a metre. He takes her weight fully into his chest. His sweaty hands around gnarled arms as they fall into the partition, twist, and into the lounge. Her tendons are like tree trunks, winter-stripped. Through her shirt's heavy cotton, he can feel the hardness of her blue-vein branches. They tussle on the floor; her so much stronger, weightier than she looked; her with the advantage. "Hang on!" Roy shouts, but she's pinned him anyway. She squeezes his wrists until he slackens, until his forearms are locked up. She keeps her third hand fixed solidly around his jaw. "Whatever he tried," Roy says, his voice with a note of mortal fear, "whatever he did…"

The woman bounces Roy's head off the floor and steps away. She tries to speak but it comes out an angry bark. Then, by the maiden of drying clothes, breathing deeply, she gestures at the door.

"He doesn't live here, does he?" Roy asks, meaning the body. It's rhetorical, really – he knows the answer.

The woman's nostrils flare.

Roy kneels and nods towards the framed picture of the old man with his classic car. Looks at workboots by her feet. The grubby overalls. "Solomon," he says. "It's Solomon's place, isn't it?"

The woman doesn't respond.

"You know who I mean, don't you?"

The woman doesn't respond.

"So who's this?"

The woman rolls up the sleeve on her single arm, her third arm swinging free through a hole torn at the opposite shoulder. Roy can see marks there – heavy welts.

"A pimp?"

The woman doesn't respond.

"But you knew him."

She hisses.

"English?"

She holds a hand over her mouth.

"Jesus," he says. "He came for Solomon and found you."

Nothing.

"Or… no. He came for *you* and liked what he found."

What had the man said in the workshop? *You've taken something*. What had Sol done?

Again the signals betray her. He changes tack.

"Alright then, how's this? Solomon keeps you here… and this one came for you. And after, after you'd done him, did you sort me out? Did you ice my foot?" He holds it out. "Did that stop you feeling bad about trying to bloody frame me?" Pallid daylight reveals burst capillaries in her eye, as if the sclera's been coloured in. And there, when she blinks – he swears there are flecks of luminous green.

"D-d-d," she says, between her clicking. "D-d-d!"

And her lips, her lips are covered in scabs –

Roy surveys the front room. The body's oozing – makes wet sounds and tiny clicks as all the slippery stuff congeals. "Sometimes," he says to the woman, "your luck just runs out."

She patters back into the bedroom. He hears the bedsprings loaded with weight.

Roy eases into the sofa, wheezing, the bag round his foot dripping. It's a new one, this – and not like him to hang around after the fact. He sits there for five minutes trying to process it. It's not the death, or even the implied violence of the man's wounds, but the domesticity of the scene that makes it so unusual. Blur your eyes and here's a man asleep in a lounge. It's only when you look closely that you see the bruise prints each side of his trachea, eyes against the meninges. His accusatory expression.

It wouldn't take much detective work, either way. Breaking and entering, self-defence. For what it's worth, though – and there's something in this – the woman can't look at what she's done. It's othered behaviour to her – evidence of a savagery she can't face down. That's why Roy knows she probably won't move from the bedroom. That she'll sit on the bed's edge wrapped in sheets and slathered in mess, shaking and making alien noises.

He thinks: *It's time to go.*

But something counters the impulse – supersedes his

honed response to countless acts of paid-for violence. After all, he's innocent.

It's not about the body anyway, he realizes. It's her.

He shakes his head. He's heard of them, of course, these modded people, these built-on bodies. You can't run in the circles he does and not hear about the extremes, the excesses. He knows about the trade, a hidden industry. He knows you can get anything you like, if you've got the money. God knows he's seen all that.

He just didn't expect to find it like this. And he certainly didn't expect such a person to tend his injuries.

Roy analyzes his foot. Maybe it wasn't a dislocation after all – it can't have been. And yet he remembers the angle. Its *corner*. He limps back towards the bedroom. The walls getting closer the longer he's in here. He says to her, "No names, right? I'm gonna try and tidy up. Return the favour. Then we can go. Then we'll have to go. You understand that? Your man Solomon's in a world of shit."

Her jaw twinges.

"Aye," he says. "And you hear him coming in, you better make some noise."

Priority one is all the blood. It's soaked the laminate. It's all over the walls, up the curtains. It's flecked over everything. And it's still spreading.

The second job is the body. Where to put him?

He canvasses the flat. The bath will have to do. It'll take a while yet for people to notice the smell, and by then they'd be long gone. And her – he could take her to a hostel, leave her at a clinic entrance. Call it in. Even the Reverend might lend a hand – though these are the kind of details his boss likes to rise above, and it feels like the worst-best option.

"You wanna help me lift him?" he asks. "Bit of a wide load, isn't he."

Nothing.

So Roy knots the man's sleeves across his stomach wound and pulls away the hand around the man's penis to free his wrists. With a little momentum the body slides easily over the wet flooring. It has a strange consistency, the blood – too dark, too shiny. Tacky already. And moving the body seems to have released a ghastly smell, so that now Roy has to gulp his breaths and hold them in.

Roy finds the bathroom light cord. Another bare bulb flickers, sticks, floods the space with desaturating blue. He plugs the bath. Getting the body over the lip proves difficult. Roy has to get right down under it, sprinter-set, and drive up power through the man's doughy chest. He feels the strain all the way down to his toes, wet things touching him, his injured ankle protesting. He pushes until his thighs are molten and the weight shifts. Something – a black placental mass – slops out onto the floor. Preoccupied, Roy doesn't notice it skate away across the tiles like a puck.

The man rattles the whole flat when he lands.

Now Roy hooks the man's legs over, pushes hard to unfold his stiffening figure. Once more those white socks unsettle him. He looks away and runs the taps, hoping to clean the worst; to make the body bleed out faster. He stands back from the spray.

The noise of the water on the man's face is mesmerising. How fragile it all seems. The rising steam carries the overwhelming stench. It reminds him of epoxy resin, a heavy industrial musk.

Another few seconds and the fumes start to intoxicate him – leave him short of breath. Before he's even thought to move for the door, he realizes he's lost perspective, panicking that he's somehow ingesting the man.

A crashing noise rings through the plasterboard. Even in this state, Roy knows it's the front door being kicked open – but he turns too fast and feels his leg flit outwards; the floor too wet with biology. His hands push hopelessly into billowing steam. His knee and hip crack over the tiles, and his head grazes the toilet cistern. From the floor he hears heavy footsteps, an appalling scream, then quiet.

Someone else is in there with them.

Y

Inside her tower, the makers silently stripped Y of her armour and base layers and stood her before a giant incinerator whose mouth they fed with Fi's hat and the rest of her transfer suit. Wearing only the tooth pendant, she watched these things disintegrate; imagined the ashes pulled out through the elaborate ducting that ran into the black maw of the chimney; and understood that Karens had lied.

There was a special area for cleaning and scrubbing. And when they were done with her, these plastic-suited makers with soaped brushes, she watched pink water stream from her feet into scummy grates. By the exit they placed her under a wall-mounted ring to dry: a humming device that for an instant made her fear she was being boiled in her own skin.

In a smaller room – each was smaller than the last, like she was being telescoped into oblivion – they hosed Y with disinfectant and covered her in jelly. She let them paint it on, utterly numb to their rollers; surrounded on all sides by makers in full hazmat suits with buckets.

When they were done, they led her beyond. The next room seemed more like a temporary storage facility – rows of lockers, boxes, trans-crates. The temperature drop was severe, left her holding herself.

When the slime had set hard, a young-eyed maker came in to shave her head. Y listened to the razor's scratch, paralysed by the casing around her. She wasn't sure she'd ever feel anything again. She thought they were stealing the last of her.

Another chamber, brighter than the last. Here, at least, she wasn't alone: there were many other figures – other shorn brothers and sisters, discernible as different only by the tone of their skin. Y stood with them among trans-crates marked OUT, and stared up at the patchwork of filthy masonry that formed the tower walls.

A hailer squawked. "Go," it said. This signalled a conveyor belt, rudimentary and noisy, onto which they shuffled all stiff-legged. Above it hung two massive letters: a Q and an A. Every few metres a sign read: KEEP YOUR LEGS TOGETHER AND HANDS AGAINST YOUR SIDES – FAILURE TO COMPLY MAY RESULT IN LOSS OF LIMBS OR DEATH.

Owing to the casing around her, Y couldn't see how this would happen.

The belt system moved the brothers and sisters along the tower's edge in single file. A production line, to all intents and purposes. Y wanted so much to touch the body in front of her, to stroke its back, take its hand, know it was there; to know this experience was at least shared. She saw their modifications: grafted limbs, altered appendages, and their overworked, obscene muscle. And as the conveyor curved, she saw more severe mods ahead – things the makers had removed to order.

The faceless makers prodded and poked them as they passed.

At last, the conveyor shifted them through a plastic strip-curtain. Y took in the final room, surely the tower's innermost chamber. It was circular, dome-roofed. Y saw makeshift beds, fashioned from every scrap material imaginable. Anything, she realized, to avoid the freezing air sucked down from a hole in the room's roof.

There was only the sound of feet.

Above the masses, all of them stinking, was a platform. Several makers stood up there and directed workers to brothers and sisters in the crowd before them. Hauled on stage, each brother or sister was checked against a tablet screen and led away. Y couldn't see where.

When Y's turn came, she was so dehydrated she found it hard to see. She was pulled up, heard her name, her rank. Someone said, "Manchester," distantly, a bored voice, and pushed the nozzle of a medical device against her wrist. A pop, and Y stumbled into a lucid dream – the chamber walls began to shimmer and glisten and roll.

Wonderfully alone, or so she thought, Y went towards an opening set in the tower's wall. Great tendrils sat around this hole, fat tentacles of plastic and metal, and while there was nothing to actually see through, the hole's murkiness also held a richness – a purer black than any she had known. She felt heavy, robust. And she felt hopelessly drawn to it.

At the hole's threshold, her apprehension lifted. The mansion, the camp, the Slope, the Manor Lord – these places and people were inconsequential. *I am the pure experience*, the hole might have murmured. Y thought of her golden corsage, pinned to her breastplate, and, with unmatched clarity, realized she was now standing in the almond space between its two overlapping circles.

Y stepped in, and slipped.

Inside she was atomized, became a nebula. For that instant, she was truly free between worlds.

ELEVEN

Wreathed in steam, Roy holds the sink and waits for the inevitable. Time stretches: in the bath, the man's body lolls side to side, stringy liquid coming in lines from the mouth. Water brims in the eye sockets, and pieces of reflective material sit in the surface tension – fragments of something isometric. The bath water's dirty grey, and Roy swears it should be pink.

He feels the draught of an open window, the awareness of a stranger sharing his space. He tongues the back of his teeth and tastes metal.

Heavy footfall.

Roy peeks round the doorframe. Down the hallway, the intruder faces away from him: full-face bike helmet, booted, leathers, a mobile flashing in his hand. Focusing, Roy hears the dead man's phone vibrating in the blood. He knows now that the woman is gone; that the bedroom's empty. Only the bedroom curtains move, tethered kites, and the flat's filled with a bitter wind – pale horses rolling in from the Pennines.

Roy steps out of the bathroom. "You the cavalry, then?"

The biker spins. They measure each other. Roy imagines a crack running between them.

The biker tilts his head at the phone in the blood and lifts his visor. His skin's too smooth, his eyes lilac, jeweller-cut. "Where is she?" he asks.

"I'm the wrong guy," Roy tells him.

The biker points at the bathroom. "Jeff?"

Roy nods. "Wasn't me, though."

The biker almost sighs. "Right," he says.

An uneasy calm settles before the men share a mutual nod that says so much. It's recognition of the failures and faults that brought them here; of the roles they've chosen or been squeezed into; and a tacit agreement to the stakes. There's just enough time for a deep breath.

"Nothing personal," the biker says.

Roy nods once. "It never is."

And above the slippery floor of Sol's lounge, their bodies collide, merge, scatter.

Down in the dead man's blood, the men writhe in circles – immovable object and unstoppable force. Hand to hand, knee to knee, rib to rib, scrabbling and striking and spitting. Fraught and animalistic in their struggle.

The biker certainly has reach – lands several shots to Roy's head and neck. Roy has gristle; counters with low blows – kidneys, testes, stomach. They wrangle in the dead man's coagulate; coat themselves in that primal warpaint; stand against each other smeared with grime and fluids that smell so strongly of lubricating oil; and struggle for their balance.

On his feet the biker is taller, keener, more able. He kicks at Roy repeatedly, sends his opponent crashing against walls, through furniture.

But his lack of visibility exposes him, undermines his reach. And as he goes in for a body tackle, the helmet gives Roy an opportunity. He clamps the biker's head under his armpit, bicep in the neck-space, and runs backwards into Sol's feature wall. Here the biker crashes through an image of a bridge under construction, a scaffolding rig in partial collapse, and the plasterboard splits right down the middle.

Face down, dusted in white, the biker finds himself trapped with Roy on his back, sharp knees pinning his arms. Roy grabs the helmet and turns it one-eighty on the biker's head, pulling the mirrored visor down as he does. It reveals his own warped reflection, a beast's face smeared with carmine, the Reverend grinning off his shoulder. There's no honour in this. No clean endings. It's simply Roy at his most honest. His new character in essence. The Reverend's monster, made for Manchester.

Now the biker's face is pressed up against the back of his helmet, and Roy has both hands inside the helmet's front, gripping the chin guard and pulling upwards with such ferocity that he hears the biker's nose crushed against the liner, the tough foam beyond, and a gargling as liquid fills his mouth.

"Nnng," the biker pleads.

Roy pulls harder. He slams the helmet into the floor, feels the biker's neck begin to slacken.

"Nnng–"

But Roy keeps slamming –

Keeps slamming –

No honour at all.

Until the biker stops pleading.

Sure then of the biker's mortality, delirious with relief – with survival – Roy rolls around Sol's flat making guttural noises. At last he enters the empty bedroom.

On the windowsill, diagonal-striped down the glass, he finds the woman's greasy fingerprints.

The prints where she pushed.

And there, down the bottom-most pane, a smear as she left.

He leans out of the window. For a moment there's confusion – he can see nothing, only concrete and scattered tiles and what the landlords try to pass off as grass. They were higher in the building than he realized: four storeys at least.

But when he squints, he can see her. Her three arms splayed like the hands of a stopped clock.

Roy slides away. The victory rush tapers. The water's still dripping in the bathroom. The grey steam moves across the flat ceiling in a knot of squid.

He looks down at his ankle. Swollen knuckles. Slick hands. Aching everything. And knowing – just knowing.

That Solomon's nasty little secret is out.

The rain's been and gone. Heavy green clouds lumbering east. Sol hates what comes next – a grey mulch of newspaper and waste, puddles all over the cracked pavements. It leaves the city centre looking bombed.

Sol comes off the main road on autopilot. Just before his turn for the neon works, he sees a parked motorbike, one wheel bounced up the pavement, and feels his gullet rise. Flashing hazards say it's likely a drugs drop, a payoff, even a takeaway collection. But he can't place why it doesn't feel right.

Turning for his flat, he purposely ignores his mirrors – the same irrationality that stops you looking back down a dark staircase as you climb it. As the ribcage of the demolished buildings opens out, his thoughts fixate on Y, her three arms, and home. Where he should've been so long ago.

Parked in his space is a smart silver Lexus.

Sol stops the truck. He'd know the car even without seeing the Carlisle-marked plate –

He steps out, incredulous. He holds a hand to his brow. "Irish?" His voice echoes.

The Lexus' headlights snap on. Sol rabbits in the full beam. "Irish!" he shouts.

The Lexus roars out of the space and past him – his own dumbfounded face in the glass. Blinded by xenon glare, Sol chases it onto the street. But it's already gone.

Sol swears, loud, and sprints to his flat's ground access door. The cage is open. He staggers inside, bounces up the stairwell. Purple floaters dancing in his vision. A chemical smell hits him on the second floor, grows abject by the fourth. Then he's there at his flat and the door's off its hinges. "Y?" he shouts. "Y?"

No response. No sign. The flies mass in his stomach.

"No," he whispers, and finds his flat upside-down. The strongest stench of blood and shit. Everything overturned, broken. He processes the devastation, each thought butted up against the next…

The unreality of a dead man in biker leathers, his head apparently twisted entirely round on his shoulders.

His feature wall split in two –

Water running, a dirty condensation crawling down the walls –

A strip of shining black that runs from the lounge, down the hall, and into the bathroom –

"Where are you?" he whispers.

He enters his bedroom; trips over a stranger's brogues; sees the window wide open, thin curtains billowing.

He crosses the lounge, stepping through broken glass and wrecked furniture. His upturned easel –

And he shouts her name:

"Y!"

The bathroom light flickers. Sol moves tentatively towards it, every hair on end. She's gone, and he's fighting every impulse to follow. His eyes wide and searching. And yet there's indignation as well as horror. He can't believe this is happening. That someone came here, did this –

That they found him. That they came for her, as he feared they would –

The bathroom door groans.

Sol pushes in –

And cries bloody murder –

At a fat, eyeless man.

Sitting up.

Turning to him.

Quivering in the bath.

Sol slams the door shut. Breathe. *Breathe*. He opens the door again, puppeteered, fleetingly, by some indecent part of him that needs to be sure.

The man in the bathtub shifts. Sol stares in almost total awe. The man's jaw has flopped open and his fingers are inside it, pulling at something sinewy. Sol holds his head, gasps when he realizes. A strange, stinking smoke is emanating from the tub. And between the man's fingers is a mass of wire and circuitry.

The man tries to say something through the gaps. It comes out as a soft electronic tone.

Sol stands there gawping. The flies nearly coming up his throat.

"Who are you?"

The man sniffs at the air.

"Where is she?"

The bloated man drops the wires in his mouth and lurches over the bath's edge. Water slops everywhere. His eyes are hollow but glittering from inside. Coloured wires dangle like slobber from his chin.

The man grips the bathside and pulls himself up. As he rises, Sol sees a wound in his abdomen; more wiring and metal panels showing beneath a layer of bright fat. Sol's caught between disbelief and the despair of knowing it's real.

The man speaks. Deeply, slowly. He says: "Sol-o-mon-n-n?"

Sol slams the door and bolts. He leaps over the dark liquid in his lounge, his nose filled with the tang of wet rust and faecal matter. The door bursts; he spills and slides down the stairwell; dry-retches the flies at the bottom.

Y –

Y –

Y –

What had he just seen? Why had he seen it? There's a fluid guilt, a sense so weighted it makes him feel drunk, and through his pain comes Mel screaming three blunt words – *you stupid prick*. He breaks down in the hallway among the junk mail and the dust. Tears hot and chest burning. He's lost her. Lost Y.

He stands to and slides along the wall. Where to now? The car park. A one-way ticket to somewhere. Europe, maybe. Even one of those dinghies you hear people take to Ireland…

Grasping with this that he can never come back.

Outside the wind shocks him. His bones powdery beneath his skin. Run. Run. *Run*.

Round the block. The car park is a remote, bounded rectangle. Steel bins, takeaway waste. A gate swinging in the breeze.

He pauses and rolls his head. The walls not quite matching up. He finds himself at the work truck, fumbles the door handle. He trips on the step and falls into the cab. He starts the engine but his leg's shaking so much he can't find the biting point, the pedals floppy under his boots.

That *smell*. Sol slaps the steering wheel, frustrated, impotent. When he closes his eyes the man is still waiting in his bath. A flash of Y's mouth with its holes, the staples coming out, twisting, and of their trusting hands on each other's chins. Her little breaths on his hand as he worked.

When he opens his eyes again, there's an orange glow in his mirror, and through the glass he's sure for a moment the bath-man is coming across the yard, his limbs reorganized and bent unnaturally.

Sol screams, a low sound edged with such desperation – for him, for her, the workshop, his home – and understands he'll never escape this smell on his skin, his fingers, bonded to the fibres of his overalls –

He casts out into Manchester's web. No particular direction. No particular way to go. At the nearest lights, he indicates to go left, then right, then left again. The green light comes and goes three times. *I'll find her*, he tells himself.

But how do you find something you never really had?

He sits there too long at the red light. Doesn't move. Daren't breathe –

So that when the Lexus pulls across the truck's nose, he barely reacts at all.

You'd hardly call their coming together romantic, but there's a crushing inevitability to it – a surety pressed in by the weight of Manchester's starless sky.

Roy slides effortlessly from the Lexus, hefty and intent, and hobbles around it – a conspicuous space where he should feel his revolver.

Sol locks the truck cab, reaches down for something hard, anything hard, something to grip.

Roy edges the Lexus, locks on to his quarry.

Sol clocks the movement – the ripple of Roy's divoted head. It's enough. Their eyes meet. The men share a moment of recognition – parsing each other through the glass – before there's a flash of something else: a release, a climax, somewhere in the chaos of two lives crashing, melding, covalent-bonding.

Roy starts to chuckle. Bruised and swollen, he looks demented. "I bloody knew you were a dark horse!"

But Sol isn't laughing.

Roy comes to the window and taps it. "Get out, then."

Sol flares. "That's my car, you robbing bastard–"

Roy roars with laughter. "And your missus up there. Optional extra, was she?"

The question sticks. Sol realizes Roy must've been in his flat.

That Roy must know.

Without thinking, Sol slams his door into Roy, bangs it shut again, throws the truck into reverse. The gears engage; at max revs he swings the wheel and the truck runs up the pavement. Roy yells, hops, rolls his way along the Lexus' flank.

Roy stands dead ahead. Sol jams the truck into first, dumps the clutch. The wheels spin from the torque smashed through them.

Roy stands his ground, and Sol bottles it. Metres out, he swerves into the high kerb. There's a bang and the truck seems to sag before it veers to one side. It just misses the Lexus and mounts the pavement again. The cab bounces back to the road, rumbling as the rear wheels follow.

Sol stops with Roy in his mirrors. He slams the truck into first gear, over-revs, then lets it out.

The truck shudders and stalls.

Before Sol can turn the ignition key, Roy is there at the window. "Serious, man," he says. "You think you've had a bad night. Your neighbours nosey?"

Sol thumps the steering wheel, inadvertently sounding the horn. "Piss off!"

Roy grins. "Been a busy boy though, haven't you? Council's gonna be on you like flies on shit if you don't shift your arse. Never mind who else is on your case. Must want her badly, I'll tell you that. They are some heavy-duty bastards…"

Sol is rabid. "Where is she? Where?"

"Your bird?" Roy points loosely at the flats. "Well, she was up there. Shit, I knew it was your gaff…"

"*Where*?"

"And next news she was down here," Roy says. "But I only did the biker, right? He turns up and she's straight out the window. Makes you wonder. These eyes he had… But your man in the bath? She did for him. Honest to God, I just put him in there for safekeeping. I reckon he tried it on, right, and then she throttled him–"

"Where is she now?"

Roy thumbs at the Lexus over his shoulder. "Back seat."

"Is she hurt?"

Roy shrugs. "I dunno what she is, pal."

Sol pushes open the door; pushes Roy aside. He staggers towards the Lexus, incredulous, ears buzzing.

"Hang on," Roy says.

Sol stops in the road and leans on his knees, gasping.

Roy shakes his head. "She jumped. She jumped out. And all that time she could've just sailed out the front door."

"She was waiting for me," Sol says. "I told her. I said I'd be home."

Roy watches as Sol squats down in the road, head shuddering.

"I had to be sure it was you," Roy tells him. "I had to wait, too." He's frowning in concentration, working it through. "You get why you're a vested interest, don't you? My livelihood depends on delivering the goods. On my subcontractors. But all this complicates stuff. Because they're on to you."

Sol sniffs. A good ten seconds of quiet. "Screw your goods," he says. "We're taking her to hospital." He stands up and nods effusively. "We're taking her to hospital. Now."

"You insured?"

"No."

"Then you don't go down this road. I know about these people – all their extras and that. Expensive shit. And if your biker man called it in, hospital's the first place they're gonna look for someone with fall injuries."

Sol glares at him.

"How much you pay for her?" Roy asks. "You've paid, right? Or is this about debt?"

Sol doesn't reply.

"I'm not judging. My cupboards rattle they're that full of bones. But she's gonna need serious work, man. Something big done. If it isn't too late already."

"Is she breathing?"

"Not really, no."

Sol shakes his head. "I found her," he says, blinking. "In the boot."

"Boot?"

Sol points at the Lexus but averts his gaze. Something repellent, unearthly, about the way the segments of its bodywork convene so perfectly. In turn, Sol knows now that he doesn't want to see Y. He just wants to run. He always wants to run. To keep running –

"Sol?"

"The Lexus."

Roy holds the expanse of his chest. "That explains why they thought I was you, then. Why I got brained in your bloody workshop."

Sol's eyes snap to him. "My workshop?"

"And that fat lad knew what he were doing – he said your name–"

"*You* broke in?"

"I swear to God," Roy says, hands up. "I only wanted what we'd shook on. The car. And your man in the bath… *Shit!* I was pissed – went base over apex down your inspection pit. I must've been sparked out, crawled free after hours, and then that fat bastard did me over. He was asking after her – someone sent him asking after you. Because whoever that bird is, your woman with three fucking *arms*, you shouldn't know her."

Sol closes his eyes. *But only one person knew apart from you.*

Mel? The woman he'd shared a life with was involved in people-running?

Sol can't even begin to believe it. And yet there it is. It doesn't even seem so far a leap from the parlour their settlement money helped to set up.

"Christ," Sol says. "Oh Christ."

"I was out of order going in there," Roy says. "I know that. But I didn't bring the Lexus back here – that must've been your man indoors as well. My guess, he came to your flat, found her, went back out for you. And got me. Must've brought me here in the boot – I was out for the count." Roy pauses. "Don't look at me like that –

like you're gonna start crying again."

"I can't go there," Sol tells him. "I can't go to the workshop. If they know who I am…"

Roy tips his head and shows Sol the fresh marks on his head. The welts and swellings on his face. "Oh, they know," he says. "But like I told you – I'm invested. We're in it together now, you and me. Plus she sorted my foot. I don't forget favours like that, like it or lump it. Call it a pride thing."

"We're taking her to hospital," Sol says. Roy shows a cracked tooth in the corner of his mouth. "You need sugar first. Time to get it straight – get your head straight. Shock's a killer. Can't let you wander off like this, can I? My head's clanging – isn't yours?"

"There'll be somewhere."

"Not before you eat–"

A low rumble interrupts them. Sol and Roy register it, realize in unison that it's coming from the row of flats they left a hundred yards down the road.

Sol looks at his truck, half-mounted on the pavement, and back at Roy, the bulk of him; a man in high contrast. The Lexus dazzling behind. He goes to ask, "What was that?" when the answer comes: the walls and windows of his own flat – now a stranger's, it feels like – open outwards in a storm of black and grey. Brickwork rains down onto the pavement below; the heavy sky a riot of glass and debris. A shockwave blows past, forces on them an uncanny pressure. Then the sign on the takeaway fizzles and winks out.

Roy turns to him. "Here comes trouble."

TWELVE

In the passenger seat, Sol can't bring himself to look round at the woman lying across the bench seat. It's a mixture of things. Even miles down the road, with the burning flat now ten or fifteen minutes behind, he can't seem to order the passage of events; the consequences of his decision to go to work; or the realization that his old life had faltered the moment Irish carjacked the Lexus.

And to look at her, he decides, would be to admit his complicity.

The car is smooth and Roy's quiet, giving Sol space to contemplate the oiliness of the gas that rose from his bathtub, the mechanics of the eyeless man pitching out from it. Along with fire and brick dust, he can still smell Jeff's rustiness. The stench mixed with car seat leather, what's on his hands, what clings to his clothing. What's in the recycled air.

What made the flat go up like that?

Y makes no breathing sounds, no clicking. She's gone. Absent. And that's his fault – his responsibility. It renders him cold and disconnected. His focus rests on a point between the windscreen and the world beyond.

"She isn't gonna bloody bite you," Roy says.

The calmness is menacing. Sol doesn't reply; finds it difficult to deal with Roy's pernicious mateyness. A critical component missing from the man's personality.

"I can't look at her," Sol tells him.

"Talk to me then. Do you no good, playing silent."

But Sol stares outside. They pass a pub, and in its garden Sol sees the indistinct shapes of downed parasols, off-white in colour. A distant glimpse of Mel smoking on her wedding morning, a contemplative cigarette before their day.

"Solomon, don't be a pussy."

"She couldn't speak," Sol says. "Nothing came out right."

"Nah," Roy says. "She couldn't."

"She's called Y," Sol tells him. "I know that."

"Y," mimics Roy. "Like the letter?"

"Yeah."

"Y," says Roy, trying it out. "Y not..."

"What are we going to do?"

"Well, I'm gasping for a brew."

"There's a mobile clinic at Ordsall. We could take her there."

Roy slaps the wheel. "You need to eat. I won't say it again. Blood sugar. You've had a shock. There's a trucker caff near Hyde – we hide this car, park our arses. Tameside General isn't exactly far after that if you're dead set on it, but I still reckon it's shock talking."

Sol holds Roy's gaze.

"Winnie's," Roy tells him. "You must've heard of it." Roy addresses Y on the back seat. "Good, isn't he?" Then back to Sol: "A bloody keeper if you ask me."

Sol holds in a breath until his lungs burn. He knows

about Winnie's: famous because the owner upended a McDonald's sign and stuck it to her terrace. She serves full English breakfasts with ill-gotten meats in her front room at all hours, and you often see whole columns of council pig-rigs, levs and support vehicles parked outside.

"How about it?"

Sol feels restrained, compromised, by Roy's charisma.

"What's that? Say it loud for me."

"*OK*," Sol says. "OK."

"Good lad. Do you right, honest. And we'll sort her after – bury her or whatever. I know a place. It's just shock, just shock… I swear a good brew will see you right."

Bury her.

At last, Sol turns to look at Y.

For a second he stays detached, views her as a stranger once more. She lies there a life apart, once removed. Figurative, even. And as the seconds pass and the road rumbles beneath the car, he's less and less sure of their peculiar closeness. The way she'd held his chin, smiled when the last staple was out, took the pen and shaded in the contours of a black tower in the workshop's waiting room. Drew that grinning mouth. These memories feel implanted, like things that happened to another Sol.

But reality soon follows. A gut shot –

"That face for?" Roy asks, glancing at him.

"Stop the car," Sol says. "Stop the car!"

Roy stops the car.

Sol falls onto the road, freezing tarmac under his palms. He vomits on the kerb, threads of bright acid. He leans his head against the Lexus door, eyes streaming, slime across his top lip, and looks up into the cloud canopy, the abyss of tomorrow. They're somewhere in Manchester. Nowhere in Manchester.

He peers back into the car.

"I'm sorry about Y," Roy says. "I am."

Sol wipes his mouth on his sleeve.

"Honestly."

"She was gentle," Sol says. "I mean that." Looking at her this time he can see where things have gone wrong. Unknown but essential elements jutting through the blanket. Angles where there should be straight lines. Her face half-turned into the leather of the bench seat, and the back of her head a muddle of wires and gunge. Protrusions, labelled things, structures that resemble antennae.

Perhaps the worst thing is that Sol almost expected biomachinery. Y's extra arm had always been a primer.

Roy can tell Sol is trying to say something else. And for all the horror Roy has witnessed, never mind wrought, he looks into Sol's eyes like he's never seen fear like it. Except, perhaps, in his own.

"Come on, sunshine," he says. "Let's get a pint of tea down you."

Winnie's looks like it sounds. On the inside, net curtains sticking to wet glass. Outside, the remodelled *M* dim on its frame.

Roy tells Sol to hop out.

"Aren't you coming?"

Roy frowns. "Can't leave the motor on show. There's a multistorey round the corner – give me five minutes. And if they ask, I like mine milky with one. Vintage brew, that."

Sol nods because he can't ask what he needs to ask: *What about her?*

"Go on," Roy says. Sol's hands are trembling, and he can smell Sol's body odour – the cortisol spike. "Don't pay either – just get them on tick."

"Tick?"

"Set up a tab."

Sol climbs out and closes the door; pretends he doesn't catch a final glimpse of the hybridized woman across the back seat. He puts a hand against the terrace-row wall and glances up the road. Internally, he mashes the view with Mel's body and Y's wires, her stitches and burns. Futility, then: a sureness that whatever happens, all of this will be dust someday, and in time they'll be oil.

As the Lexus drives away, Sol considers running. As if his basest compulsions, denied for a day, have reasserted themselves. He'd do it, too, if his legs didn't feel so heavy, or if he had a clue where to go other than the workshop –

There's Irish's house, maybe, up in the hills. Or down south, to some unchanged village – live a nomad's life on the marshlands.

Sol goes inside. A bell clangs obnoxiously and the patrons stop eating to register him. He apologizes silently and scans for a table.

"Born in a barn, were you?" A woman's standing opposite, hands on hips. Sol realizes he's letting a draught in.

"Sorry," he mumbles, and pulls the door to.

"Don't have to be sorry," the woman says, smiling warmly. "Just more sensitive to the needs of others."

On her striped pinny, embroidered over her heart, it says *Winnie*.

"We'd love to heat half of Manchester," she goes on, "but it's hard enough to keep the kettles going with these sods in charge. Now you look like you're on death's door. Let's get you something warm and wet, eh?"

Winnie's caught Sol off guard. For some reason he

thought the name was convenient – a business built around the gimmick, the repurposed arches, a trophy of the end times. He finds himself nodding. Her jolly straightforwardness is refreshing, though as he crosses the café it only serves to make him sadder – here's a woman who managed to adjust without losing her humanity.

Winnie touches Sol's shoulder. He jumps, reflexes hair-triggered, and she pulls out a chair. "Tea for one?"

"For two, actually. My –" he hesitates "– my friend's just parking up."

The front door bell goes on cue. Roy saunters in and ducks the mechanism, looking round for Sol. Cast against the depth of the room, a backdrop of striped curtains, he looks totemic.

Sol leans, raises a hand. Roy weaves over and sits down without comment. He picks up a serviette – crappy two-ply paper that smells of dry storage – and dabs at the corners of his mouth where a creamy substance comes and goes.

"Two, then?" Winnie asks. She smiles broadly. Again her determined lack of cynicism. Roy and Sol nod. "And a chips and gravy, ta," Roy adds. He motions to Sol. "Owt or nowt?"

Sol shakes his head. Couldn't eat if he tried.

"No *thank you*," Winnie says, and goes to the kitchen hatch.

On the next table, someone coughs loudly. A brawny man in a tatty police blazer. Roy eyeballs him – he's making a whining sound.

"You want a heart-to-heart?" Roy asks. Sol watches him inspect the salt and pepper shakers, then snaffle a lump of sugar. "Nan gave us these for pudding," he says, splitting the lump between his front teeth. He doesn't close his mouth while he chews, making a sound like wet sand. "She was the greatest woman."

Suddenly the whining man moves his chair. Sol jumps. The man gawps back.

Sol doesn't know where to look. Around them, the clatter of cutlery becomes a dirge of industrial feeding. Y's wires creep over the surfaces, her three arms extending outwards from each corner of the room, broken and reset in new directions. Food on plates becomes Y's muscles, her fibrous joints, and a smell of frying mingles with the sickly warmth of a heater haphazardly drilled into the wall –

Winnie approaches with a rattling tray. "Two teas," she says. "For two handsome boys. Your chips are just coming, sweet."

"Cheers," Roy says, and she puts down their steaming mugs.

"No bother. And listen you," she says to Sol, "pay no mind to old Bert here."

"What's up with him?" Roy asks bluntly.

"Oh, says he were kissed by a giant moth or something."

Roy stares at her. Sol doesn't think he heard it right, either.

"Like a mothman," she adds, and rolls her eyes. "I know. So the story goes. But I don't flipping mind, do I? We just make his tea. Oh heck, sorry love – let me get you one of them stirrer things."

Roy puts his tongue in his cheek. Bert carries on whining.

"Mad house," Roy says. "The whole city's gone frigging barmy."

"Where's the Lexus?" Sol asks.

Roy puts a finger to his lips. "Not here."

"Then how did you leave her?"

Roy looks both ways. "Seriously, Solomon. Pack it in."

"Where, though?"

"Back in the boot for now."

Sol starts at this; bangs his knee under the table. Bert stops whining momentarily. "No," Sol says. "No. It's not right–"

"She's gone," Roy whispers. "She doesn't know."

Sol puts his head in his hands.

"Mate…" Roy picks up his mug. "It's shite, but it's happened. Think about your flat – your work. You've gotta look after number one now."

"But–"

"She was just passing through. I mean they're not even real, are they?"

"Roy, that's–"

"That's the march of technology, is what it is. How you can even order girls like that is crazy enough…"

Sol slams the table and stands up, tipping his chair. Everyone turns. "Roy!"

Calmly, Roy settles his mug. The only noise now comes from Bert.

"Don't make a tit of yourself," Roy says. "You're being oversensitive."

"No," Sol says.

Roy's face changes. "Sit down," he hisses. "I won't tell you again."

Winnie's over there with her arms crossed over her pinny. Eyebrows up, smile sliding.

Sol picks up his chair and sits down, cheeks hot. After a moment, the noise swells again.

Roy leans in, speaks slowly: "You've got to understand. She's *gone*. And when we're finished in here, we'll grab a shovel and drive out somewhere nice and quiet and do the decent thing."

But Sol can't handle the thought of it. The chunk of a spade going into northern soil. "No," he says.

"What's your bright idea, then?"

"Hospital."

"Fuck's sakes, man. You think it's legal? That they're regulated or something?" Roy snaps his fingers. "They'll have you in for murder like that. And me."

Sol pulls out Y's delivery note and slides it across the table. "Read it," he says.

Roy flips it over reluctantly, frowning at the circles motif before opening it out. "What's all this about?" he asks. "Accessories to follow? Still in transit?"

"It came with her," Sol tells him. "And I think they bring more like her."

"And Knutsford?"

Sol shrugs.

Roy looks away and refolds the note. His expression's softened. "OK," he says, "I'm gonna just tell you this. You know I said I'd heard of them?"

"Yeah."

"Well when I started out, you heard rumours. Certain investors, on the margins. More cash in people than guns and drugs put together. Throw in customization, and you're laughing. I mean it's no excuse, but you see shit on that side of the fence – the worst of us. You get immune eventually – you learn to keep your nose out." He pauses, looks at Sol as if he doesn't quite believe what he's saying. "But maybe I've met one before."

"Who told you?"

Roy sips his tea. "I dunno. It's only ever been snatches – someone knows someone… But the story's standard enough. They're taken off the streets, the tunnels, orphanages, ring estates, even abroad. Ship the poor buggers away and tell them they owe money for the trouble. The rest you can fill in yourself. Take bits out or jam stuff in – train them up, sell them back."

Sol rubs his eyes. "I can't hack that," he says. "I can't. It knocks me sick."

"Aye. And everyone round here moans about Wilbers."

Sol closes his hands under the table.

Roy smiles thoughtfully. "At least with that lot it's finders, keepers. At least it stays local."

"Then who's running this?"

Roy shrugs. "Deep pockets, though. Cars like that? Never mind the gear you'd need. It's specialized as fuck. A business."

"And your rumours," Sol says, leaning over the table. "You ever heard where they change them?"

Roy takes a breath. "Oh aye, plenty of names bandied about. A few places. But the one I always remember coming up is Sellafield – the power station. Used to knock about with some steeplejacks who took down the Windscale chimneys. They banged on and on about random concrete being poured all over the site. Weird for a decommissioning job – makes you wonder. There's so much money sunk into that place – billions, seriously – you wouldn't be surprised if they were reusing the infrastructure, hiding stuff in plain sight."

"Sellafield," Sol repeats. "Is that Yorkshire way?"

Roy shakes his head. "Cumbria – up the coast."

Something clicks. The Lexus plates. Carlisle –

"Pretty brazen," Roy adds.

"I don't get it, though," Sol says, his voice shaky now. "How can people know but do nothing?"

"Well that's just humans, innit? For starters you wouldn't go near that shithole. Crawling with guns, barriers. Sharpline on every bloody surface. And that's before you mention the radioactivity. The lads I knew got swabbed, tested, every day they left there. Geigers and all that. It's fucking poisonous."

"But…"

"Let me put it another way: there's gulls that sit by the nuclear waste ponds all day. You've got bloody all sorts in these ponds – fuel and cladding… all sorts. Through the miners' strikes they didn't even bother processing it – just lobbed it straight in. Like a stew. And they say if one of these birds shits on your car, your car's pretty much glowing. That's how nasty it is. The workers get a year's dose in a week sometimes. You had fit lads going off sick with lumps and never coming back."

Sol shakes his head.

"Telling you. Fall in one of them, one of the ponds, and you best hope someone puts a boot on your head. That's what I know."

"But that's what I'm on about," Sol says. "If you know about it then the council does too. They'd have drones all over it."

"Depends. You don't bite the hand that feeds you, do you? Production sector's picking up, things are improving elsewhere – with this fix you're getting more labour to clean up the shit no one wants to see. You're getting control back. Why smother that? They're onto a good thing, any way you cut it. They are. And who says they don't benefit as well? Who says they don't get their palms greased? Who says it isn't policy full stop? Not like we've never had sleaze before. Half these council bastards only wanna cling on to their jobs."

Sol shrugs.

Roy points at the window, as if to indicate some imaginary mass of people. "And you don't pull off something like this without someone upstairs knowing," he says. "Amount of nutters you've got running around in the countryside... aren't you better off sending drones out for them? Win back your popular base? Trust me, pal. They're happy leaving them to it."

Sol tries to imagine the logistics. The oiliness of it – such a sludge of corruption and manipulation – makes him dizzy. Where usually he might turn a blind eye, just as you might turn a blind eye to a beggar and subdue that barb of sympathy, Y gives him no choice but to stare it in the face. Feel it, helpless, as the institutionalized horror of it repeats on him.

"Cruel world," Roy says. "Cruel world."

"Yeah."

"There's weirder shit, mind. Remember that thing that blew up a few years back? Up on the moors? You will do. Big nationalist cell – some guy training paramilitaries for a civil war. He throws this convention, right, and supposedly out of it comes this mad equipment that lets you cross universes." Roy leans in and chuckles. "Other dimensions."

Sol frowns.

Roy shrugs. "Maybe it's all out there, Solomon. Ten, fifteen years ago, you'd never believe you could make someone invisible. Lev bikes. Never mind that someone could have an extra arm grafted on. But that's what I heard. What's the thing? A wormhole. And like all the decent kit you get – cloak-suits, plasma gear – it just ends up with the last people you want to have hold of it. Maybe up in Sellafield. Maybe not." Roy stares into space for a moment. "That place in the hills got glassed by drones. You ever see the birds that came across the city afterwards?"

Sol doesn't reply. There's so much to internalize, sift

through. Make sense of. He takes the note from under Roy's mug and reads it again.

"I did," Roy says. "I saw them."

Accessories to follow. Still in transit. Cash in glove box.

"There's something in it for you," Sol tells him. "If you help me."

"Help you what? Mod the vehicle I ordered?"

Sol looks down at his hands. "Find out who she is."

Roy's grin hardens when he realizes Sol isn't joking. He gestures at the note. Sol passes it back, watches Roy reread it. Does something shift in Roy's shoulders? He leans in. "And was there? Cash?"

Sol nods. "Six grand," he lies.

"And you reckon you know where their drop is?"

"One of them, maybe. Old gent up there told us cars were turning up," Sol says. "I mean, it's what we do–"

"We. You keep saying we."

"Me and Irish – Pete."

"And Pete knows as well?"

"No – he's in Liverpool."

Roy blinks. "Mancs grafting in Liverpool? Christ. But someone knows you've got her – had her."

"My ex, yeah. She works in the game. I guess she employed..." Sol's voice falters.

"The web you weave." Roy takes a final swig of tea and points at Sol's mug. "Be going cold that."

Sol pushes it away.

Roy cracks his knuckles and leans back. "And say the news about you hasn't got up the chain yet. Say that biker in your flat didn't dial it in, and the whole racket isn't on your case. Say they're still running drops. What do *I* do?"

"You must have connections."

Roy shakes his head. "Honour among thieves."

"They're already hunting me. The flat's gone, the workshop's a no-go. And we've got all this metal turning up for your job."

Roy tilts his head. "Which is why I said I'm still here. It's manageable risk. It's in my interests to make sure you get a new delivery address sorted."

Sol snorts. That doesn't feel like the only reason at all.

"Alright, listen. We scope your dropoff, and we cut a deal if there's another car. But if you're gonna grasp the nettle, you're doing it my way."

Sol looks past Roy. Sloping shoulders, poor posture, a gamut of razored heads. The glint of equipment in the servery.

"I look after you," Roy continues, "so long as you look after my back pocket."

Sol scratches his head.

"Serious," Roy says. "You know the Reverend, up in Stalybridge? Unpleasant, if you don't stay in the good books. You work for him so you don't have to cross him."

"The armour's for him?"

Roy shakes his head. "Client down south. Rev's just the handler. But there's a week's grace before the guy's gonna expect photos – so I reckon you get your boy Irish on it soon."

"No," Sol says. "We can't involve him."

"Solomon. You don't think he already is? He turns up at the workshop, he'll know about it."

Sol hates how Roy uses his full name to patronize him. But he's right. "He's going home, not back to the workshop," Sol says. "Maybe I can get in touch."

"And then? There's still no way back. Not for you, not for him."

"Not for you, either," Sol says. "I'll find a way."

"Have you listened to me? An outfit as slick as this,

and you think you're gonna... what?"

"Y's missing from somewhere. There'll be lists. At the libraries maybe–"

"She's *forgotten*, man. They're strays for good reason. And libraries? Pull the other one. They've spent them on bombs."

"I owe her," Sol says. "And so do you."

Roy straightens, and Sol wants to slap the act out of him. It went in, though. It touched something. Then Roy says, "Eighty-twenty," with his hand held out. "You get your clues – your little treasure trail – and get yourself killed. Irish Pete works up my armour. And I get my spends."

"You'd be taking the piss at sixty-forty," Sol tells him. "Never mind the damage to my workshop."

Roy sighs. "Look at it sensibly. Just for a second. There's no changing this. That's not how the world works. No bugger's answering the phone. No one's coming out to help. And don't even start me on the drones. You can't even move freely."

"I'm going to do something," Sol tells him. His concentration centres to a dot on Roy's front teeth, flashing between his lips as he talks. "Something."

I'm going now, he'd said to Mel that day. *But I'm not leaving her. I'm not walking away –*

"Be honest with yourself," Roy says. "Why d'you think there's people like me?" He's pointing at his chest.

"People like you."

"I sold what's in here. Six years ago and counting. And I'm still around, aren't I? That's being selfish for you. You'll learn the hard way, caring too much. I promise you'll learn the hard way. Now where the fuck did my chips get to?"

•••

Sloshing with tea, the men enter the multistorey behind Winnie's. It's vacant but for the Lexus, and Roy tuts. "Hold this," he says, passing Sol his jacket. "And keep an eye out."

Sol watches in quiet wonderment as Roy sets about the Lexus with a kind of precise ferocity. He pulls off the registration plates, kicks dents in the doors and bumpers. Then he bounces on the car's bonnet and roof until its profile is completely deformed. "Just in case," Roy says, his lumpen features absurd, and gets in.

Window down for fresh air, Sol listens to the Lexus' tyres squealing on the poured concrete, air buffeting through the opening, the exhaust reverberating around them. "Need to drop in somewhere," Roy tells him. "Before we get rid of this."

Sol is queasy, frail. Beyond the car park he finds himself anticipating a sudden motorbike – every oncoming headlight a fresh twist in his stomach – while trying to ignore that Y's body is in the boot. It seems callous to imagine her as a body at all. That she could be something so inanimate. Was it comfortable in there? The suburbs ghost past – a near-continuous smear of terraces, hand car washes, bookies.

"Where now?" Sol asks.

Roy grins. "Bit of shopping."

For a mile or so the road hugs a train line, itself running parallel with the rear side of a housing development. Sol sees the amassed possessions that, over the years, have been thrown over people's fences: jetsam half-hidden in the wild grasses of the bank: toys, balls, old prams, barbecues, compost, wheels, cassette tapes, oil bottles. It's a reminder that people like to put difficult things where they can't see them – where they might just disappear. Except Sol knows that forgotten things tend to rot, and fester, then get found again.

After Ashton's roundabouts, the vacuum of Stalybridge, they reach a fortified gate between bushes riddled with sharpline. "Stalybridge Celtic," Sol says, pointing to the sign in the brambles. "They were Conference, once."

Roy shrugs. "Wasn't that arsed by footy."

"I think we passed that hospital on the way," Sol says. "Signs for Tameside General."

Roy opens his window and turns to him. "Shut up."

A laser cuts down through cold air. Roy lets on to the approaching guard.

"Gents. Who you here for?"

"The right Reverend," Roy tells him.

The guard's expression is fixed. "He expecting you?"

"Always."

"In you go, then. And behave yourselves."

The three gates open sequentially, and the car heads through.

"What is this place?" Sol asks, gawping at the sprawl. There's so much damp cardboard, plastic barrels strewn about. Some young kids throwing stones at a group of pigeons.

"Emerald City," Roy says. "Basically the opposite of the Vatican."

"It bloody stinks."

Roy grins and wedges the car between two four-by-fours. He cranks the handbrake. "You alright with new people?"

"Fine," Sol says. "But I think I'll stay here with her."

Roy ignores him. "Actually, how are you with psychopaths?"

Sol doesn't know what to say. Instead he asks, "Why are you seeing the Reverend?"

"Because I lost my shooter playing hide and seek in your workshop," Roy tells him. "Listen, if the smell's bothering you that much, breathe deep – it goes away sooner."

Sol shakes his head.

Roy gets out of the Lexus and crouches beside it, hands on the driver's seat, eyes level. "Stop being a mard-arse," he says. "It's networking if nothing else. The Rev seems to think your outfit's the bee's bloody knees. And you could do worse than seeing the place. Might even qualify for a home here, state you're in."

"I don't get you."

"They take runaways, is all."

"Runaways? Like refugees?"

"If you say so. Owner's a shut-in. Wizard, they call him. Fucking lunatic rolls around in his wheelchair reeking of fish, or chills in a bath up in the old business suite. They say he cooks his hair and eats it. But each to their own – if you pay him your dues, keep your head down, you get to call this home. No questions asked." Roy points to the reinforced power lines entering the stadium wall. "Amenities and everything."

Roy savours Sol's puzzled expression and pulls an imaginary zip across his lips. "Yellow brick road's over here," he says. And together they head for the entrance door.

"Password?" the grate asks.

"Milk organ."

Sol blinks.

The door opens. "After you," Roy says.

Sol edges in. A man in nothing but his boxer shorts greets them with gibberish, holding out his arms in shapes from some mysterious sign language. He's covered head to toe in what might be Vaseline.

"Piss off," Roy tells him.

The man totters, unbalanced. Sol skirts him, trying to come off casual.

Roy laughs. "Don't look them in the eyes," he whispers, letting the warning take root. Then, as he pulls Sol through the players' tunnel and into the stadium proper – a grid of shanties crumbling in perfect formation – he says: "See? One of these could be yours."

Sol watches his feet until they reach the Reverend's place.

A young woman opens the door and bows at them.

Roy waves in her face. "Is he in?"

A disoriented look. Then, "Yes, yes." From the back comes the sound of running water. "Come," she says. It's odd, the way she says it. "Sit, sit," she adds, and Sol decides her invite owes more to learned custom than genuine hospitality.

The two men sink awkwardly into a deep leather Winchester. Legs touching. Beside them, an antique clock is ticking itself to death.

"Wife!" the Reverend shouts from the back. His voice echoes.

Sol shifts in the chair, tries to put space between him and Roy.

"Visitors," she replies.

"What?" The man splutters and slops through the shanty. He appears in a towel that reveals his massive slipped gut, indecipherable green tattoos on each tumbling breast. "Royston!" he bellows. "Why didn't you *say*?"

"Evening, Rev," Roy says. Sol thinks his voice is lower, more subdued.

"And who is *this* vision before me?"

"S–" starts Sol.

"–olomon," Roy finishes. "Mechanic on the conversion job."

"Oh, fabulous!" the Reverend booms. His eyebrows twitch madly. "How's the work progressing?"

"It's fine," Sol says. "Fine."

"Bless you. Bless your hands. I'll be sure to let our client know." Then, to Roy: "So that being the case, what's the matter?"

"I've been–"

"Speak up, Royston!"

Roy clears his throat. "I've been a nob and lost something – that's all."

"Lost... what? Should we worry?"

Roy shakes his head.

"What, then, pray tell?"

"My piece."

An awkward pause. "But darling," the Reverend says. "That was a present."

"I know,' Roy says. "I know it was."

The Reverend exhales through his nose. "And what do you want me to do about it?"

Sol realizes Roy is gripping the leather of the seat.

"Just... just wondered if you've got anything going spare," Roy says. "I can't... you know."

Sol tenses, too. Some power exchange is happening here; some latent fear worming out. Why, he can't be sure – the Reverend's overweight, clearly unfit. Eyes so small and close together it's a wonder he can actually see past his nose. Yes, he's brash, but there's something deeper.

"I hate to feel disappointed," the Reverend says, looking at Sol. "It sits heavily in the shoulders, doesn't it?" He turns to his wife. "You'll have to rub it out, won't you?"

"Listen, Rev–"

The Reverend cuts Roy off. "Look at you two. Quite cute, really. Little schoolboys. And does your boyfriend have any thoughts on your forgetfulness?"

Sol stares. It takes a beat to register the Reverend means him.

"Yeah," Sol says. "I mean it's a shame and–"

"A shame," the Reverend cuts in. "Yes. That's about the sum of it. But the Lord teaches us to forgive. So that's what I'll have to do, isn't it? Now, do you break bread, Sol? Do you value that body which was given for our sins?"

"Probably not enough," Sol says. "No."

The Reverend's face twitches. "Come through, then, idiot-boy. Something can be arranged."

The men stand awkwardly.

"Wife – you stay with him. No, no. The black one." He slaps his chair next to her leg.

A lump swells in Sol's throat. He goes to apologize – instinct, maybe. But as he does, he looks between Roy and the Rev, and Roy looks so adrift and vulnerable – his eyes imploring Sol to say nothing more.

"Ought to start going out with spares, you forgetful clot," the Reverend tells him, and a door closes. Sol hears the Reverend's muffled laughter, the dull sounds of drawers and heavy metal clanging.

Sol looks at the Reverend's wife. "You doing OK?"

The woman smiles thinly but doesn't hold eye contact.

He wills her to respond, to say anything. She picks at her sleeves – Sol thinks he can see bruises there, her skin polka-dotted.

"What's your name?" he asks, filled with a cloying sensation.

"Jovin," she says.

"Jovin. And you're alright, aren't you?"

"I am–"

The far door bangs open and Roy shouts up the corridor: "Sol! Three-five-seven or nine mil? Auto pistol? Or a proper hand-cannon?"

"Christ," Sol whispers. He massages his eyes with his fists. Jovin stays still. Hanging on her husband's grace –

Roy comes back into the room, a pistol held high. "*Jawohl!*" he shouts. "*Mein* new sidearm *ist ein classisch!*" He thrusts the gun under Sol's nose, forcing out a laugh. "Reconditioned *Luger!*" Behind him, the Reverend howls with glee.

"We've left her too long," Sol whispers.

The Reverend's laughter crashes. "Her?" he asks, his wide face over Roy's shoulder.

"He's just being soft in the head," Roy says backwards, waving the pistol. "Cheers for this though, man."

The Reverend narrows his eyes and caricatures Jovin's bow. "A pleasure," he says flatly. Then he pushes past to stand before Sol. "I suppose I'll look forward to hearing from a happy client, then. Goodnight and God bless."

Sol glances at Jovin as he stands up. Her face is turned into the wall.

"Come on," Roy says.

As they leave, the Reverend closing the door behind them, Sol catches the face of a business card on the doormat, two overlapping circles on its face.

They're some way down the street when Sol realizes what he's seen. He spins, sprints back, beats the door.

"What the fuck are you doing?" Roy hisses. "Don't!"

Two latches, a chain. The door swings. "What?" the Reverend asks, his face swollen with indignation.

Sol eyeballs the mat again. He has to be sure. He has to know. Is the Reverend a customer? Is he involved, somehow? Or was it simply audacious flyering?

There's nothing there.

"Thought I'd forgotten something," Sol tells him.

The Reverend shakes his head, his bottom lip pushed out dismissively. "No," he says. "You didn't." And he slams the door.

Y

Naked as the day they remade her, Y came through the darkness into the sister-world; emerged down a tunnel that bellowed rank-smelling disinfectant from both sides. Jelly rolled from her skin in butter curls, coagulated in gutters that lined the gangway. She breathed in through her nose: a reek of rotting animals.

At the end of the misting tunnel was a sign reading WATCH YOUR HEAD. Y wasn't tall enough to worry, but ducked anyway. She passed through a plastic strip-curtain into an area cooled by vented walls. Heavy-looking chains hung from the roof. Gears and industrial switches were mounted on mezzanine fixtures. When Y looked around, she saw more piles of trans-crates. There were so many that after a moment she stopped seeing anything else.

Indirectly, she knew this wasn't the same tower she'd entered. Something imperceptible had shifted, and she was aware she'd somehow been disassembled and reassembled with unknowable differences. Molecular shifts had taken place. Atomic, even. The tooth pendant had taken on a different colour – bluer, cleaner, and more abstract.

From nowhere, a bundle of rags was pushed into Y's hands. She glanced up and saw a suited figure sliding away. She looked at her hands. Underwear, top, pants. Y dressed herself there and then, still dripping, clothes dragging over wet limbs. The woollen top irritated her skin.

Away from the strip-curtain, the warehouse revealed itself. The crates were everywhere. There was movement between them – others dressed like her, more suited figures. Y watched a fork truck intersect a line of crates on the conveyor.

She felt lighter. To walk required much less effort – her limbs freer, less defined. Y followed the fork truck as it trundled back through the warehouse. She thought she could hear something clattering inside its loaded crate.

Ahead, a pair of depot gates yawned open. White-out. Y saw a large yard, floodlit and stark.

"Keep moving forward," someone said. Instantly, people were flowing round her. Y almost broke into an amble, carried by the stream of new arrivals. Her feet seemed to hover.

"That's it," the voice said. It was coming from everywhere. Everywhere. "Better," it went on. "You'll be paired up shortly."

And they were. Y found herself marching two by two – her partner a short, sparrow-chested boy with a rattling wheeze. He turned away whenever she looked at him, and sniffed relentlessly into his sleeve.

Y tried to take the boy's hand. She rubbed her little finger against the side of it. He didn't seem to react, though with some repetition his breathing seemed to calm.

By the entrance of the floodlit yard were two women with boxes. Each pair paused by the women, and closer she heard them speaking melodiously: "Headscarves for the girls, blousons for the boys."

"Keep moving!" the omnipresent voice said.

Y and her young partner reached the women. She was given hers without a word – a headscarf shoved into her hands. But as Y took a step forward, meek in her way, the woman caught her arm and lifted the pendant clean from her chest. She had an illuminated patch over one eye that reminded Y of the harridan in the feeding chamber.

"What's your name, princess?" the woman asked.

Y pointed to her throat and rattled.

"Ah. Did he give you this himself?"

Y shook her head.

"Oh," the woman said. "I've never seen one in the flesh. You must be liked. I saw him once you know – I saw him and he waved."

Y swallowed. She didn't want to be liked. She didn't want to be anything to him.

"Don't look so frightened," the woman said. "The scarf'll suit you. Just keep in mind that if you hear a buzzing from the heavens, you put this on. A big noise – *bvooom* – and on it goes. You're a refugee, you understand? It'll help. I know it'll help. They won't bomb refugee convoys. And they certainly won't bomb someone as treasured as you."

Y's new headscarf was already dampening in her hands. Her mods ached. Ahead, she watched the boy take his shirt and murmur something numbly. A sadness was buried right down inside his eyes. What did hers look like? How did she appear to him? A broken vessel, an abandoned space?

Y turned back to the brothers and sisters behind; the pairs being nudged onwards.

"Take care," the woman said, and smiled with such respect that Y went light-headed.

The air outside was bright and cold and stinging. Stepping into it, they were each seared white under the floods. Someone ushering them from the front. In the middle of the yard stood two towers of scrap metal that formed a sort of half-finished archway above. Each pillar had started to lean in, precarious, though still some way off touching. Green lines twinkled down from it, disorientating. Set against the clean steel and piano-gloss finishing of her cradle suite, this new environment collected together grotesque industrial sculptures that terrorized her senses. She walked between mechanical carcasses in the realm of a steel-king deposed. And along with the cold, a persistent sulphur smell repulsed her: left her imagining that an unutterable creature slept here, waiting. The dirt and the dark, the greasy surface underfoot... it was the antithesis of Y's cradle, those immaculate mansion lawns outside. Even the sun, that terrible sun, might be a friend here.

The scrap towers dropped the weirdest shadows across the facility around her. Everywhere she looked she found blackened spires: chimneys, pipes, cable, piles, gantries. Pools of standing water. And so many people in full suits, their faces obscured by elephantine masks. The crowding of it all overcame her, left her stricken with sorrow. It filled her with a perverse homesickness for the mansion, for what she knew of it. Being here, in the court of this alien palace, was worse than remoteness. It was total displacement. And though she clung to herself – her body an anchor – her true memories, those concealed from her, still occupied a stranger who was always a corner away.

The boy next to her was crying now. Clearly the landscape was getting to him, too. Y managed to loop a little finger over his, and together they saw long boxes being loaded with her brothers and sisters.

People had started shouting again when a man in a drab-green suit approached them. He had two black discs for eyes.

"Across the way," the man said, breathing apparatus whistling. "Southbound trucks. But not you," he added, motioning to the boy. "You're transferring north."

Y looked over her shoulder. The tower loomed, its black outline superimposed on the blue. It was still there, and that should've been a relief. But now, she understood, it was no longer hers. Like her routines, she was leaving it behind to carry just one possession forward: a piece of the Manor Lord around her neck. A philosophy in microcosm, a constant reminder. Lest she ever forget.

He watched me. He said he was my father.

THIRTEEN

Not far from the original Lexus drop, not far from the old man's house, Sol and Roy wait in a freshly stolen car. The rain has long since turned to squall; the drains blocked and burbling with urban mucus.

For Sol, the reality of a stakeout is becoming clearer. Waiting time is thinking time, and all he thinks about is time elapsed:

After the Reverend's, in the ruined Lexus, Roy had eventually talked Sol out of the hospital. "Better to act now," he'd said as a closer. "And right now we need a getaway."

But as they'd prowled for options, Sol had other things on his mind.

"Why does he scare you?" he asked Roy.

"Who?" Roy said.

"Back there. I saw it in you. Like a black hole. Could more or less see the strings coming off his fingers."

"Nobody scares me," Roy said.

"Do you worship him?" Sol said. "Is that it?"

Roy laughed flatly. "You best button your mouth."

"You went all meek. What's he got over you?"

Roy shook his head as he drove. "Don't push me, Solomon."

"I'm only asking why you run for him."

"I don't run for him. I work for myself."

Sol sniggered.

Roy stopped the car, clutched Sol's ear. "He sorted me out," he snarled. "There. Alright? That enough? He sorted me out. There was an investigation, a tribunal, and he got me off. He gave me work when no one else would."

Sol grimaced through the pain. But he kept pressing. "How? How did he get you off?"

Roy let go and fell back. Sol rubbed his ear.

"Violence?"

Roy closed his eyes.

"Was it?

"You can't stop him when he gets going."

"But why help you in the first place?"

Roy looked at his hands. "Self-interest? Charity? He doesn't give anything away. I just ran deliveries."

"Until he gave you a gun. Triggerman Roy."

Roy shrugged. "It changed. The market. My opportunities."

"But you never felt the shift."

"No."

"And now here you are. Too far in. Too deep."

He nodded. "Here I am. Are you happy now? Are you done?"

After that, Roy shut off the car and pointed to an '88 Ford Sierra a few cars along, then stole it while Sol watched. Sol found the theft ruthless; winced with each piece of trim Roy tore out. It wasn't just crass – it was feral. And he could've, should've, done it himself –

The Sierra was a shed. Somewhere along the way it'd had a hybrid conversion kit retrofitted, but nothing worked as it should, and the charge console, limp on the dash, reeled a list of critical faults. Sol drove it as hard as he could, lagging behind the Lexus as Roy led him from dead end to dead end, the engine either burning too much fuel, smoking heavily, or stuttering and choking like it was full of rocks. Frankly, Roy's choice of car didn't make sense to Sol – you hardly saw Sierras driving on the road in the early 2000s, never mind 2025, halfway through another thalidomide decade. It spoke of deflection; the need to end a difficult conversation. "Wouldn't you want something more reliable?" Sol asked, as Roy smashed off the ignition barrel. "It's hardly a getaway."

"No," Roy told him. "It's a *blendaway*."

Down a gloomy cul de sac, Roy pulled up and bailed. "Get her out," he said to Sol, and started preparing a bottle and rag he'd magicked from somewhere.

When he opened the boot, Sol caught himself sniffing Y's body. It was automatic, instinctive, and the urge appalled him. His self-loathing soon met relief, however: the liner only smelled of dust and oil, and he understood that he no longer cared that her suspended state made no sense. Though she was injured – damaged – and displayed no sign of life, there was nothing to suggest decomposition either. She looked at rest, asleep, as if she'd simply grown tired of it all. Sol thought: *How could Roy imagine burying her?* To him Y existed in limbo – and it seemed enough to satisfy his internal logic. At last, he'd successfully reordered and reframed the world to accommodate her.

Sol wrapped Y in some dog blankets they found in the Sierra's boot and laid her across its bench seat, securing her legs and waist with two seatbelts. Squeamishly, he tried to push in the spilled wires of her third arm, wet string threaded with metal fibre. It made his nose itch, touching her this way. Her innards. But her expression was tranquil.

Sol thought: *Who was she before?*

As the Lexus burned, Roy said to him: "I never get bored of that noise. *Whoomph!* The sound of not guilty."

Sol tried to see it as an offering. The accursed car dying before him.

Next they went for the recovery truck, found it exactly where they'd left it: humping a pavement near Sol's ruined flat. Incredulous, Sol looked over it; checking, with justified paranoia, for any evidence of tampering – taps, trackers, even explosives – while Roy waited with Y. Sol couldn't believe the truck hadn't been seized, parked as it was so close to the property, and registered in his name. Half-satisfied, he hopped in and powered out of there; found he couldn't look along the road to his flat without his chest tightening.

After this, the men agreed to one last stop.

The workshop.

Luger on show, Roy covered the entrance as Sol went inside. It had the atmosphere of a quickly abandoned village – as if its inhabitants had vanished overnight. Nothing looked abnormal, nothing was disturbed. Sol dashed around, grabbed his address book, notes, the armour project plans. Then, sweating from the pressure, he placed a call through half the world's telephone exchanges to reach Miss Wales, and asked her about the metal drop. "Just to be safe," he told her, "we need a change of address." Then he gave her one – Chinley, Irish's moorside home.

"The hassle you give us," she said to him. "One of these days we'll have to treat you to a 3D printer."

And everything else was in flux –

Sol turned off the electrics. Cut the landline. He emptied the safe. Gathered his favourite tools into a canvas bag. And before he left the workshop, he wrote a note for Irish – a single line in capital scrawl. It read:

P. DON'T COME IN. GO HOME & STAY PUT. I'LL CALL.

As he left the yard, the strobe light dead, he felt a kind of respite. The idea, perhaps, that they were still a foot in front.

But when he saw the perimeter wall, his relief spoiled, became a rancid taste in his mouth. Because there, sprayed in gold, massive on the bricks, were two overlapping circles.

Sol stumbled. Could've choked on his heart.

"I'm sorry, pal," Roy said from the shadows. "Looks like you're in deep, too."

For a time they sit separately: Sol and Y in the Sierra, Roy in the truck.

Sol has the chair reclined, his feet up, his mirrors adjusted so he can see her lying there; a constant pointer to his neglectful nature. He's drawn the twin circle motif on the fogged window a few times now – perhaps some attempt to interrogate its symbolism, or otherwise purge it from his psyche. Looking at it, he's increasingly convinced it's meant to represent two worlds meeting. Lost in the fuzziness of its edges, its shape slowly warping as lines of water run through it, he jumps when Roy opens the passenger door. "I'm sitting with you two," Roy tells him. "Bloody freezing in there."

Seconds out. Minutes down. Hours gone.

"Should've brought sandwiches," Roy says. The comment washes over Sol, who's still obsessing over the things he could've changed. "Even that fake ham shite they make with mushrooms," Roy adds. "Or cartridge drippings. Or a game of Connect fucking Four. Remember that? Always played that on the way to the caravan before our kid went inside."

Sol stirs in his seat. It's late, and getting colder. Dread occupies him, growing fetid.

"You like stories about me, don't you?" Roy asks. "You wanna know why he got banged up? My brother?"

Sol shakes his head.

"Built like a bay bloody window Dean was. Older than me by what, six years? So he must've gone down when I was twelve or thirteen. I said, are you listening, pal?"

Sol grunts.

"Then I'll tell you anyway. Dean liked his birds and loved his knives, right? Mam always said he collected both, though far as I knew he only hung the knives on his wall."

"Roy," Sol says. "Can we just sit here–"

"His birds all had that same look: big hair and panda eyes, always fagging it and all. You'd get in from school and hear them at it, and afterwards Dean would kick my door open and make me smell his fingers. Filthy bastard he was – he'd come out with the worst things and the girls just thought it was piss-funny.

"Then there was Mand. Dean said Mand had been sent to save him. I liked Mand, I really did – she spoke to me like a friend, not a kid, and when she leaned over in a baggy top you could see right down to her bellybutton piercing... you still with me?"

Sol lets condensation roll down his cheek, there but not there at all. He looks at Roy sidelong and dips his head.

"One time," Roy says, "I come home and find them absolutely peppered in the kitchen, tobacco all over the floor. It stunk of weed and I said hi but knew they'd gone west. Then I saw Dean's bow and arrow in his hands. Listen now–"

"I am," Sol tells him.

"So Dean's aiming out the back door at the neighbour's cat on the fence, minding its own. I shout *stop!* and Dean jumps. The arrow bolts and the cat flies off the fence with the arrow straight through its leg." Roy flicks his finger, claps loudly. "*Bang. Fffft.* Just like that, poor little sod. Then Dean gets me to say I did it and I say I will, because it was more or less my fault. I told Mum I'd robbed his bow and arrow off the wall and shot that cat myself.

"But that isn't why Dean went down, Solomon. Thing was, Mandy karked it a week later after a big coke session, on her own in the bath round her old man's place. Coroner calls it bad coke, cut bad, and Dean said the man who sold it to her was a fucker for it – and he knew, since Dean usually scored for them. Not this time, though. This time he wasn't there to check it over."

Sol's staring at Roy.

"Dean wasn't Dean after that, and fair enough to the lad. Would you be? He was on it. And I mean all the time. Pulled double shifts, never spoke, never really ate, nothing – just vanished into the bogs with his keys and a baggie in the top pocket. And then one night he wakes me up, standing there in full camo, balaclava and everything. I go, You nobhead, you scared the shit out of me.

"And Dean just sits down with his head in his hands and says he's sorry. I said, For what? and he looks at me and his eyes are sore and he goes, *She's gone,* again and again. Howling it. And then he took his bow and arrow and went out into the night and found her dealer. He took him up on the moors and shot the guy through both legs, just like that cat. Left him there, crawling about. And that's why he went down."

Sol clears his throat. "I'm sorry."

"Doesn't matter," Roy says. "Lad hung himself a year in. They said he couldn't hack prison. But I knew he couldn't hack missing Mand."

Silence, then. Beneath the covered moon and the hidden stars.

"Your turn," Roy says.

"My turn?"

"Yeah. This ex. Tell me about her."

Sol squirms. "You're alright."

Roy smirks. "OK, the work. You reckon you've ever robbed a car with a girl in it before?"

Sol squints away. Everywhere but the shadow of the car, the ground flickers in greens, oranges. Manchester's night-waves, a fluoro tide. Sol pictures for a moment the Lexus in a scrapyard crusher, the squeal of compressed metal, technical fluids running. The cube spat out at the end –

"I never knew if we did," Sol tells him. "Been lucky. Just have to keep your head down, don't you?"

Roy chuckles. "Course you do. But then…"

Sol looks at Roy. His bald head, the battlescars. His swollen nose, the new scratches and bruises. He speaks before he can think twice. "How come you ended up floating round on the bottom, anyway?"

"Me?" Roy chuckles. "Oh, that's easy-peasy. I just killed a friend."

Sol wakes to coppery frost and a sore neck. Cold air, bright in the fresh sun. It takes a second to reacclimatize to their stakeout at the arse end of town. The car stinks of cigarette smoke, and his lips are papery. His backside's completely numb.

"Morning, soldier," Roy says, knees pulled high either side of the steering wheel.

Sol checks on Y. Still the same peaceable expression. Still asleep.

His dread catches up.

"You slept?"

"Have I fuck," Roy says. He coughs something heavy and spits it out of the car. "Told you. I'm a sniper, me."

Sol croaks. His teeth are furry. "Any luck?"

"Not a peep."

Sol yawns. "I need a slash."

"Bottle down there," Roy tells him. "Or the ginnel behind us. And while I remember – your old missus ever mention you snore like a dog?"

Sol opens his door. "Once upon a time."

"Well, go on then. No one's coming this way any time soon."

Sol picks up Roy's rolling tobacco from the dashboard and flaps the packet in Roy's face. "Habits," he says. "Die hard."

"Just saying. We could be looking elsewhere."

Sol shakes his head. "Can't underestimate convenience. Like you said in Winnie's – you build that many layers into a simple dropoff for a reason: it stops communication with the next crew along. They won't just break the chain like that. And you'd be surprised. When we started robbing, we had six vans out of a courier's yard before they even cottoned on. Even when they did, we managed two more. If it's business, they won't stop for much."

Roy grins. "You sounded just like me then."

Sol leans the door into place.

He stretches on the sparkling pavement, crushes a spray of weeds glistening from the cracks. Both the car and the truck wear a dust of frost, and a thread of web spans the road. He enters the ginnel, sun-soaked, and relieves himself a metre or so along it. His visible breath, bulbous around him, is split into iridescent bars by the light filtering through the mesh fencing.

As he turns back for the road, he thinks: *the sky hasn't been this clear in a long time*.

Then from the corner, he watches a wine-coloured Audi pull into the road.

Sol darts back along the ginnel. The Audi's brakes squeak. Had the driver seen him? Seen Roy through the Sierra's unfrosted windscreen, the panels of condensation on the glass inside?

Suddenly the Audi accelerates, red-lining past the ginnel, and clips an alloy on the corner before braking hard, scrabbling for grip, over-revving, over-steering, and bolting up the next left – a maroon flare that flickers through the fence.

Sol sprints back to find Roy crouching between the Sierra's rear bumper and the truck. Something gleaming in his hands that Sol follows out to the truck's wing mirror and then across the road.

"You pick your moments," Roy says. He looks calm, but there's an excitement being restrained. He's on.

"They see you?

Roy shakes his head. "They see you?"

"I dunno," Sol rasps. "What the hell are you doing?"

"Wait for it."

"What?"

"*Wait*."

Faintly, the sound of an exhaust note carries.

Roy grins. "And you call yourself a grafter. Duck down here."

Sol doesn't understand.

"Down!"

Sol squats as the second exhaust note resolves to the scream of a motorbike. Roy leans, Luger revealed in his belt. Sol's chest is pounding.

"Bastard crossed the top of the road a few times."

"You said there hadn't been a peep!"

"You'd only just woken – I didn't want you freaking out."

Sol can hear the bike closing in. "What's that for?" he asks.

But the answer doesn't come from Roy's mouth. The bald man leaps to his feet and throws his weight against the Sierra's boot. Bewildered, Sol does the same. From there he can deconstruct the scene: Roy's hands pulled behind him, knuckles wrapped in what Sol now understands to be sharpline, pulled out from somewhere, who knows where; the line tautened around the truck's mirror and going up over the road; and the rider reacting too late, rearing back – racing leathers tensing symmetrically across the chest.

"Have it," Roy says, so crisply it rings in Sol's ears.

The impact with the sharpline seems to elasticate the rider from his chest down, flicking him into the air with limbs flailing in insectile panic. The force shears off the truck's mirror and drags Roy skittering into the road, and the sharpline snaps with a crack. Sol watches the rider's head meet tarmac – his remaining momentum dragging him past, body ostensibly liquidized. With an agonizing grinding sound, the motorcycle skids up the pavement, engine gushing.

Only now does Sol realize what Roy's done.

Roy drops the sharpline, hands bloodied, and bears down on the biker with his Luger drawn. "Audi!" he screams back at Sol. "Deal with the Audi!"

Sol twists to the oncoming Audi – low sun creating a sharp enough silhouette to betray the woman driving it.

The Audi stops, uneasily slow, and indecision grips him. The woman gets out and edges towards the scene, mouth slack. He hears her feet turning on the gravel, the clip of her heels.

"Bloody *hell*," Sol whispers, rooted. It's the pillion passenger he and Irish had seen from the old man's front door.

"It's a fucking accident!" Roy shouts, the Luger barrel now jammed under the biker's visor.

Sol's immobility wanes. He looks at the frayed edges of his T-shirt. The broken flies of his overalls. Oil spatter shining. His spindly knees and heavy boots.

"Stay there," he says to the woman.

The woman looks surprised. Her features are indistinct, inappropriate somehow. "My friend," Sol says, "is getting help." He steps closer, touches her shoulder and flicks out his council ID. Now she looks at him, slowly, deliberately. "Sorry," he says again. "I'm from the council. My truck's just over here–"

"What happened?" she asks. She looks undaunted. She moves her handbag to her front and unzips it. "What's the matter?"

Sol tries to smile. "An accident…" he starts, when from behind there's a pop.

He closes his eyes, relaxes his shoulders.

"You're done," the woman says. There's a hardness in her eyes now – a fierce look that streamlines her face, sharpens her jaw.

The scales tip. Smoothly, practised, she slips free a flick-knife and rolls her arm back.

"Ah-ah-ah…"

Sol wheels to find Roy next to him, Luger raised.

"Back it up," he says to her. "And drop that."

The woman's expression collapses.

"Do it. I'll count to three."

The knife clatters.

"And the bag," Roy tells her. "And the fucking *bag*! Good. Now, over there." He uses the gun to direct her. "And don't think I won't do you as well."

"Mate…" Sol says. "Go easy."

"Zip it," Roy snaps. "How often," he says to the woman, "are you coming up here?"

"What?" she chokes, her armour cracked. "I don't know what you think you're doing here, but–"

"Shut your mouth," Roy says. He looks at Sol. Back to her. "Open the Audi boot."

"I *don't think*–"

"I said hush up. Now. Move."

Roy marches the woman to the car. Everything slow, sticky-seeming. The woman glances up at a broken CCTV camera.

"Unlucky," Roy says.

She blips the car. The boot catch releases. "Actually, you open it," Roy tells Sol.

Sol does as he's told. The boot hydraulics hiss. The woman holds her breath.

Inside there's a heavy box, hermetically sealed. A pair of words stacked up on it:

OUT.

ORGANS.

Roy doesn't take his eyes off the woman. She's looking at Sol, and Sol's looking back at her. The air feels charged.

Roy glances over. "What is it?"

Sol says it slowly. "Organs." The word meaningless, fly-away –

Or-gans.

"What?"

"Accessories," Sol whispers. And there's something else: a garment tucked in there, rubbery texture, drab green. "What's that?" he asks.

She shakes her head.

Sol pulls at the fabric. It unfurls weightily – a torso, sleeves, legs. Elasticated cuffs and collar. It's missing a headpiece, a visor perhaps, but it's obviously some sort of protective suit: there's a valve for breathing kit.

"Close the boot and get in the Sierra," Roy tells Sol. "And you," he motions to the woman, "back in the Audi. You're driving."

The woman opens the driver's door.

"Wait," Roy says, coming round the car, Luger level. He gestures to the lifeless rider on the road. "Any more of them?"

The woman smirks cruelly and murmurs something.

"Say what?"

"You'll get yours, little man."

"I'll take that as a no, then."

"Roy…" Sol says.

"Just follow us," Roy tells Sol. "Whatever it takes."

Sol can't believe how fast it's all unravelled. Before he draws breath again the Audi's doors are shut.

Sol reaches up for the car's boot lid, trying to blink away an image of the rider's oozing helmet. As he does, he notices another object – small – nested in a hoop of cable. He leans in, takes it. He closes the boot and turns this object in his hand. It's a square thing with bevelled edges, plastic, with an exposed metal circle at its centre. It reminds him of an old floppy disc. A serial number sits beneath a familiar two-circle motif, embossed. He pockets it and backs away – a million thoughts in orbit starting to fall into the gravity of a dense, lightless truth. If there's a filament that runs through it all – the note, the suit, the circles – it's brightening.

Sol opens the Sierra door to find Y's face impassive, like nothing's happened. Were those her spares in the Audi? Were they *her* accessories? He fumbles the ignition wires, re-shorts the starter. The Audi idles close by; Sol glances out to see the woman's portrait, the end of Roy's Luger wavering. Then the red car moves off towards the sun.

Sol follows, unsure of everything but the life of his precious cargo, her face jiggling in the mirror's image.

It feels like the end of all things. Two cars powering up the M602 from Salford towards the M60 ring road, then east for the M56.

The stolen Sierra squawks through its ratios, often slipping into neutral and making the whole car jolt. To keep up with the Audi, Sol has to weave recklessly through sparse traffic – overladen shippers, lumbering half-tracks, the odd courier trike. He's reluctant to lean forward and look up – isn't sure his heart would tolerate the anxiety induced by a curious drone. Nor does he want to check his mirror, lest he find Y awake and judging.

Soon enough the road signs start counting down to Birmingham. THE SOUTH. Sol wipes his hands on his overalls and tries to remind himself why he's doing this; smothering the temptation to stop and imagine his mind isn't fragmenting; to deny that this has happened to the augmented woman on the back seat. There are no bikes, at least. Only flyovers and road markings and flickering mile counters. Hypnotised by the homogenous roadscape, a grey soup, Sol doubles inwards, imagines his feature wall overlaid like skin on the windscreen. It's so nearly real that Sol feels momentarily trapped in a vacuum between his tortured map and the barren territory. The broken lane lines form continuous boundaries, and his body absorbs the road surface through the footwell, the steering wheel.

Ahead, the Audi brakes sharply and indicates left. A handpainted warning sign is diverting drivers off the motorway through an old police layby. Both cars exit and see the reason: the black flags of militiamen waving from the carriageway further ahead. Sol exhales: they've narrowly avoided a funnel point.

The Samaritan's diversion takes them through what looks like unspoiled countryside to a village fenced away; a zone of life somehow kept how things used to be. While the flowerbeds are empty owing to early winter, and the trees are bare, Sol wonders briefly how easy it might be to make a life here and just pretend.

Back on the motorway proper, the cars pass signs for Knutsford Services. Here the Audi begins to move erratically, slowing and regaining pace, crossing all three lanes. Sol decides the driver is looking for an unmarked exit. He glances in his mirror before slowing off.

Sol blinks.

Is that…

A biker closing fast.

Delirious, Sol flashes his headlights at the Audi; sees Roy's distinctive ears rotate until he's sure he's looking backwards.

The bike draws level with the Sierra, its armoured passenger tapping a submachine gun on the fairings. With a whimper, Sol veers closer to the barrier; some bullied response; clinging to a hope the bike will pass. Airily, even politely, the pillion passenger gives him the thumbs in appreciation, before pointing the gun and firing at the Audi. Peripheral to Sol, the bike seems to flicker.

Sol can see Roy's Luger held to the woman's head – the block-stud of its barrel sight. Then the bike is directly in front of the Sierra, and Sol stares down at raging rubber.

Was Roy ready for this? Had he prepared?

Sol only knows that this is his territory; these roads his language.

He holds the Sierra in gear and plants his foot. With a terrible lurch, he connects with the bike's rear wheel – the shock of its passenger registers, the gun falls – and the bike sloughs right. He watches the wing mirror, anticipating an explosion of parts and bodies against the Armco.

But there's only road.

A single uninterrupted ribbon of barrier –

Dazed, Sol moves left again, convinced he can still hear the sound of munitions whistling, spent casings tinkling on the road. He checks again. *No*. He realizes with a second spasm of horror that the episode was wholly fictive, hallucinatory.

A lack of sleep. A loss of grounding.

You prick.

Cursing himself, Sol notices almost too late that the Audi's now over on the hard shoulder, hazards going. His flashing must've rattled Roy. Disquieted, he moves across.

On the hard shoulder there comes a vibration he knows to be glass under the tyres. Ahead, the Audi weaves in and out of the hatchings until it pulls decisively left into the sloping verge. Its passenger-side window is missing.

Sol stops the Sierra by a three-dashed marker for an exit close by. "Stay there," he shouts to Y, as if she could escape, before legging it away from the car with its engine still running. The Audi's stalled. There's a ragged hole blown out of its passenger door.

"Roy!" A large HGV chunders past, disturbing the air. A moment to hope nobody else will stop to help. By the Audi, Sol skids in the gravel and finds two things at once: the woman slumped over the steering wheel, and Roy giggling to himself.

"Christ," Sol says. "Christ!"

Roy flaps a hand out of the window. The movement reveals his other hand, bloodied, and the Luger pistol clutched against his jacket breast.

"What did you do?"

"She shot me."

"Jesus, Roy. *Christ*. Shot you where?"

Roy holds up his hand. Sol can see straight through it.

"The face on you," Roy laughs. "Only a scratch – chill your boots." He coughs heavily, laughs again. "She's modded, pal. Look at it. Look at that."

Sol peers into the car. The woman's arms are thrown forward as if she was paused mid-tantrum. There's a metal protrusion from her ribs, a dark hole in the fabric of her clothing.

"What is it?"

"Bloody clever is what. How else you gonna defend yourself with this as your livelihood?"

"She shot you? With that?"

"Aye. Heard the bastard coming out. Mental whirring sound. She was quaking, screaming like it was painful. I bent forward in time, but I still had my paddle up."

"And she's–"

"I frigging hope so." Roy taps the Luger against his chest. "Crap driver, anyway."

"You shot her?"

"No – I didn't bloody have to. After this little party trick, she just, I don't know what else to call it, shut down on me. Swear to God. Just turned herself off." Roy snaps his fingers. "Poof."

Sol shakes his head. "I thought it was me flashing at you."

Roy curls his lip. "Nah. She just didn't want us going where I wanted to go."

"Where?"

Roy points up the carriageway. "Next left."

"Services?"

Roy nods, then looks carefully, if dispassionately, at his hand – fascinated by his visible tendons, his inner workings.

Sol opens the door. "Hop out," he says. "You're gonna need that patched pretty quick."

Roy plants his feet, ungainly. "No shit," he says, curling his fingers in around the wound. With his other hand he waistbands the Luger and reaches inside his jacket. Out comes a wad of cash – by some magnitude fatter than the bung Sol found in the Lexus. "This'll see me right," he says, waving the money. "Come to something when a crate of guts is worth more than a person, eh?"

"How much is that?"

"Ten Gs at least. Right here in the glovebox."

Sol shakes his head.

"Get on with it then," Roy says. "Before some do-gooder tries doing us a bloody favour. Or them eyes in the sky come down for a closer look."

"You're leaving her like this?"

"No. But we are."

Sol's throat tightens. "We can't."

"Why? It's your doing."

"I didn't bloody *shoot* her!"

Roy frowns. "You wanted to get your own back, far as I can see. Inspector fucking Clouseau. But – and I've got this sussed – you still don't know how you're gonna pull it all off. My game's simpler. It's do or get done over. And I didn't shoot her, either, so get that straight."

Sol looks away. "You shot that biker back there."

"And I'd do it again tomorrow," Roy says. "Listen: there are two types of person left in this country. Fighters and victims. And I'm not gonna be a victim over ten grand *or* you."

Another HGV passes, air turbulence rocking the car on its bushes. Sol scowls. "She's coming with us."

"Have a word with yourself," Roy says. "And get shoving her car off the road – I'm too crocked to help." He nods at the Sierra, to Y. "Seriously, man. Ask yourself. Is this for her? Or is it for you?" Roy waves the cash in Sol's face. "Because I'm alright with this, me. Get involved with a few more drops like that and I'm a happy bunny indeed."

Sol's disgusted. "What, and sack off the armour project? Let your Reverend down?"

Roy doesn't say anything.

"Thought not. You're a bad liar, Roy. You care. You know you do–"

"Don't be a smartarse, Solomon."

"Tell me what she told you about these services."

"Well what would you say with a gun poking in your face?"

Sol scratches his head.

Roy puts the Luger against Sol's cheek. "You'd say whatever I fucking wanted you to say. Now shut your gob and get this maw wrapped before I go and bleed out on you. I'll fill you in after that."

"What was she called?"

Roy starts tearing a strip from the hem of his shirt. "This one? Sandy."

"Sandy," Sol repeats. "Sandy." And he takes Roy's wrist and starts to bind the hole.

Y

Y couldn't tell how many of her brothers and sisters were travel-sick. Hours on the move had left the trailer floor sopping wet, and the pitch of the container made things worse at the back.

Y was at the back. Around her feet the sawdust had clumped up to expose slippery patches that shifted across the trailer floor like warm spots in a lake. Her hips hurt from standing – femurs ground against dry sockets, pestle and mortar. Her arms, too, ached from bracing against the bodies of her brothers and sisters, who wriggled against each other's sweat-slicked bodies to stay upright.

The air was superheated in there, almost chewy. Thick with sweat and urea. These smells didn't change, but their effects came in waves: Y, swaying, taking shallow breaths, regularly pinched her nose, all she could do to not vomit herself. Several times she clamped so tightly she tasted blood.

Mostly she held her eyes shut, arms tensing against the flow of corners, camber, sudden braking. When she could, she held the trailer's subframe, spare hand spread out on the canvas roll sides – also sopping with moisture – in a vain attempt to cool her system. When she did look around, she saw her brothers mop running sweat from their skin with their blousons. Her sisters were also down to vest tops or less, using what space they had to fan and towel themselves, and each other, with their headscarves. Y used hers to try and comfort the nearest child: a young girl who couldn't seem to stop shaking.

The truck rattled unremittingly. At the front of their trailer, hidden by the seething bodies, collapsed forms, a boy screamed and repeatedly struck his head against the subframe. In a way, if she could disconnect the sound from its source, he gave Y something to fixate on: a rhythm that distracted her from the full bladder she couldn't bring herself to release; from the wetness running between her feet; and from pushing deeper into her infinite memory-mist.

More miles in half-time. Y concentrated on not throwing up. One retch and that'd be it – so she staved it off by remembering how chunks can get caught between your throat and nose. She tried to think of nothing but breathing – the internal sound of the air on her epiglottis; the purr of exhalation across her dry lips. The subtle liquid that rustled in her ears with the trailer's yaw. She tried to comprehend her new lightness. And she counted things – corners, creases in the fabric. The boy's skull beating beating beating on metal –

At last the lorry stopped, and a painful white flooded in. The roller door filled its housing and the silence of the moment struck her: so many of Y's brothers and sisters were broken, past caring.

The man outside had a scarf pulled up to his eyes. He was the driver, at a guess. For the shortest time the man stood and took them in, just as they did him. Left to right, his eyes full of them. Finally he shook his head. Y saw his makeshift bandana ripple as if he'd said something to herself. It might've been a prayer.

Beyond the driver, Y made out more vehicles. A grassy verge to the left. Pewter sky. There was a flat-roofed building surrounded by people in fatigues.

The driver spoke inaudibly and began pulling Y's brothers and sisters from the trailer. He was grabbing whatever he could get hold of, and a round of shrieking followed. The smell of diesel and vomit intensified, a heavy musk. Others joined the driver now, five or six big men at least, and yelled in at them over the racket, unaccountably furious. Y was pushed towards the trailer exit by her brothers and sisters behind. She inhaled, and she waited.

Y did well to stay up as long as she did. When finally she slipped, someone caught her ankles and dragged her backwards through the mess. She twisted, hands grabbing at lumps of sawdust, a kind of human porridge that caught then disintegrated between her fingers. Soon she was over the bumper, on the ground.

Hauled up from the gravel, Y was shepherded into a group standing nearby. She span across them, apologized awkwardly through gesture. She was covered in muck, a breeze chilling her damp skin. The pain didn't matter – unconsciously or not, she'd been conditioned for worse – but she winced as someone leaned down, hand on her thick shoulder, and brushed the muck off her knees.

From the truck trailer she watched a boy with a ballooned forehead tumble to the tarmac face first. He landed between two white lines, and nobody helped him for an uncomfortably long time – the gathering more intrigued than concerned. Then apathy came unstitched as the handlers realized he wasn't moving.

They quickly closed around the boy and dispersed again. On his feet now, he looked haunted. And even from a glance, Y could tell he shared her biomods. The same conditioning. His changes were mostly hidden beneath the blouson, but his gait gave it away. It was the frame; the overdeveloped lats and rolled-forward shoulders.

Y waved, tried to get his attention. He seemed lost. She moved towards him, but as she did a thick arm came down to bar her passage. Oblivious, blood from his forehead curving like parentheses around his gormless features, the boy ambled away.

Y sought other faces she might recognize from the mansion; from the training lawns, from her neighbouring cradles. It was useless, though: their features were smudged, their outlines blurred. All things assimilated, amorphous and beige. Mouths seemed drawn on, smears on canvas. Eyes like black buttons. Everyone's hair so regulation-short. And when she looked forward, above the spectral steam that rose from their wet bodies, between the tallest and the shortest, Y caught glimpses of dark bags hanging from the lighting poles. Rows of black sacks on heavy ropes, binds wrapped around their middles.

The sacks triggered something. It manifested as imprecise dread, and she couldn't fathom the link – it was as if the sacks represented the kind of truth that vanished if you looked straight at it. She cursed. Imagine a scar you've always had but don't remember earning…

She span to the edges – a strip of shale between faded white lines, and the overgrown shrub beyond.

Then someone prodded her sharply in the ribs. "Oi," they said.

Y span, and her attention zeroed to a tall woman holding up a photograph as if to compare.

"Are you Y?"

Y didn't respond.

The woman turned the picture. Y saw an image of herself sleeping, lined in.

"Love," the woman said calmly. "I'm on your team."

Y chirped.

"Long way to come, that," the woman added. She watched Y, considering her, then nodded. "A mission. Must be nice to have some clean air, mind. Suffocating, those trailers. I hope they've looked after you."

Y studied the woman. Her long-sleeved robe couldn't mask a formidable outline. Going by the smoothness of her forehead – its length accentuated by a high ponytail, top-knotted like a hat – Y doubted she was much older than her, though her face held a mass at stark variance from the fatless, razor-boned people around them. Her eyebrows, too, were much thicker than Y was used to seeing. She carried a broadness and a presence – indifference betrayed by sympathetic eyes – that had somehow dimmed the background.

"Quiet mouse aren't you?" the woman said. A fractional softening around her mouth told Y she'd noticed the pendant. The woman cocked her head. "You can say. Did they look after you?"

No response seemed better than lying.

The woman frowned. "Maybe you're cold. Are you cold? Is that it? You look a bit cold."

Y was cold. But she didn't give that away, either.

The woman pretended to look disappointed, and even wagged a finger. But this movement was gentle, too. Then she took Y's hand and pushed what felt like a smooth, heavy stone into her palm. "Grip it," she said. "It'll warm your cockles."

Y clasped. Heat came immediately and spread along her arm.

The woman beamed, gave an exaggerated glance to either side. "Don't show it about," she said, "or they'll all want one."

Y held the stone against her stomach, and the woman seemed pleased.

"I scanned all your reports yesterday," she told Y. "I like a rebel. Just my cup of tea. But you won't make any trouble for me, will you?"

Y shook her head.

"Of course you won't. And as you're probably wondering, this glamorous place we're meeting is called Knutsford Services. A car park, really, and the coffee's terrible. But I promise you're nearly there now. I'm here to get you moved, a quick vehicle swap, another one further along, and then you'll be well on your way." She glanced round and leaned in, conspiratorial. "It's all very long-winded, if you ask me. But they reckon it's the only way to outfox the drones."

Y nodded blankly.

"Manchester's a good city," the woman said. "No fires or floods. No rioting for a good few years, come to that. You might be mistaken for thinking someone's forgiven it." The woman repeated herself slowly. "Man-ches-ter. Had the biggest night there once. Took myself dancing, back in the olden days. Funnily enough, I only remembered as I was coming here to meet you – so thank you for that. And I'm Sandy, OK? San-dy. Like a beach. I'm your chaperone. Like a tour guide. Would you mind popping a spare hand on here?"

The woman held out a thin tablet.

Y, without hesitating, pressed her palm onto it. The surface vibrated softly, snapping her out of a peculiar trance.

"That's lovely," Sandy said. "More nonsense, I know.

But like they say, you don't get paid if you don't prove trade. Now before we head off, a bit of housekeeping. Can I ask you to keep your headscarf on? It's for your safety and ours, and blah, blah, blah."

Y's shaven head tingled. She draped the scarf, cold and damp, over it.

"Suits you," the woman said, and gave her little nod. "Really does. Now let's go. There's a special convoy this way, just for you."

As they walked together, the stone still radiating, Y thought her brothers and sisters were looking at Sandy in reverence. A goddess figure, a black angel, her head haloed by the angle of the gallow-lights above. If Sandy had noticed their appreciation, she didn't show it. After a minute, she said, absently, right into Y's ear, "You've been brave. I know you might be confused. A little afraid. But there's no need now. There's even air-con where you're going."

Y smiled weakly. A little crackle slipped out.

Sandy said, "See the cars over there?"

Y did. Several off-roaders and a pickup set down on its haunches. Privateers squatted in its flatbed, rifles prickling. Above them, the black sacks turned and creaked in the breeze.

"That's yours," Sandy said. "Keep going, if you don't mind, while I fetch some extra signatures from your delivery driver."

Y kept walking until she reached the off-roaders. The row of swaying bags was right above her head.

"Oi!" Sandy shouted after her.

Y turned.

"Headscarf!" Sandy said, and mimed putting it on. "Let's think, please Yasmin. Important stuff, this!"

Y nodded and swivelled back to the nearest off-roader. Then she froze and span. The warming stone dropped to the floor and shattered, soundlessly, into a mandala of delicate pieces. The woman called Sandy was striding away, a funny bobble to her walk. Had she misunderstood? Maybe it was her ears – something wrong with the implants, something playing up. Y watched Sandy with a blooming sadness; again the eerie sensation of floating away. It was an echoed realization: she was too light for this place, this box with cold grey floors, a grey ceiling, ever-stretching grey walls.

By now Sandy had gone inside the rotted pavilion standing at the heart of the services. A ring of barriers had been raised around it. As the privateers in the flatbed looked on, Y tried to rationalize what Sandy had called her. It was the wind. It was the medication. It wasn't a name – it was confirmation bias. And even if were real, even if it had meant something, it still carried no clues to a life she once had – no name could possibly hold such power. She assumed nothing of her past – had only glimpses, vagaries; images of structures, landscapes, abstractions. The rest had been cut away. She was joining up the wrong dots.

And yet.

Y stretched out the headscarf and wound it round her neck. In spite of herself, she replayed what Sandy had said once more. Then, her chest imploding with blunt-force pain, she promised to make herself forget she'd ever heard it.

FOURTEEN

The morning wears down under low cloud scudding fast. A thick grey band moves over, getting heavier, murkier, all the while.

Sol manages to push the Audi fully into the ditch. Though its rear quarter juts out a touch, the incline means you'd have to know exactly where the car is to glimpse it from the carriageway, harder still if you're passing at speed.

In his head, Sol tells himself he'll come back later to move Sandy properly. With dignity. Clean her face; wipe down the spray of dark liquid she's coughed against the windscreen.

Back from the verge, he finds Roy inspecting his injury; winding and rewinding the rag. "It'll fall off if you keep fiddling," Sol says.

Roy smiles at him drowsily.

"I'm done pushing anyway," Sol tells him, "so now you can tell me what she said."

Roy shrugs. "Didn't I already? She didn't know much, and she wasn't in a place to blag. She did pickups, drops

– they do work in chains, like I thought."

"Like you thought? How many?"

"How many what?"

"How many did she move?"

Roy shrugs again.

"Did you tell her about Y?"

"Are you a total bellend, Solomon?"

"Then what about the hazmat suit – you ask about that?"

"Nope." Roy holds up his bad hand. "Is this taking the mick or what? I can't get it tight enough."

"Maybe she didn't know better," Sol says. "And with that thing sticking out of her you'd have to guess…"

"So let's go up there and have a nose about," Roy says, still fiddling. Presently the knot seems to hold. He clenches his fingers over the wrap to test its stretch.

"What's up there?"

Roy nods. "Enough. Sounds like a hub for a right load of miscreants. Stopoff for her, though. She got her time, turned up, left again. Like a courier. But get this: I mention Sellafield and she goes silent and pouts at me. I ask if there's a network – if they pay her a salary – and she cracks up laughing. She worked down south, she said, for some guy or other. Couldn't be doing with northerners like me. And here, well it's the gateway to the north, isn't it? I already knew there were Wilbers working out of here – their runners and that. Packed so full of nasty bastards you'll stay a nobody if you just keep your head down."

Sol thinks: *You'll fit right in.* He says, "And you still believe your fairy tales about this tech?"

Another shrug. "I know people usually tell me the truth when there's a gun in play."

Sol glowers.

"You're driving us," Roy says. "I need a piss too badly."

Sol looks at Sandy's Audi in the ditch and resigns himself to it. They get back in the Sierra without argument. He still feels bilious – adrenaline constantly on and off. Y's peaceful deathmask in his mirror as they head for the turn-off – the shell of a faded green bridge spanning the lanes – and up the sliproad.

Welcome to Knutsford Services.

"Steady it," Roy says. "Nice and steady."

The main car park's mostly bare – lorries by the water pumps and fuel depot, and a cluster of cars and personnel vehicles near the old service station. Its diesel pumps are frontless, their fuel lines crudely delimited to make sure drivers can fill up their tanks as quickly as possible. From behind the main pavilion rises the telltale black smoke of burning rubbish. Tendrils of grill smoke, white, mix in, and through the Sierra's dash blowers comes the unmistakeable stink of tyres melting. Further away, behind all this, a row of long black bags swings from the street furniture. Despite the implications, Sol tries not to dwell on them. Kangaroo courts were common enough during the riot years, but their evidence has always unsettled him to the point of wilful ignorance.

It starts to rain. Roy points out a set of truck trailers with dozens of crates stacked on the ground beside them. "Bet that's how they're moving them," he says. "Look – what's up the side of it – *IN*?"

"Yeah. And the one in the Audi said out."

"Mad," Roy says. "Can't get my head round it."

Sol swallows. Blood from Roy's wound has crept up to his elbow. Things feel fragile, and Sol's shoulders and ribcage are heavy. Are they really moving people around like this? It seems so brazen. "It can't be that many," Sol says. "It can't. Someone'd do something. The drones."

Roy yawns. "I told you. Plenty happens on this backwards island we'll never understand."

The main pavilion is hollowed, ad hoardings empty. On its roof a squad of privateers locked into their sweeps.

"Security?" Sol asks. By this he also means the truck full of privateers looking for all the world like they've staged a coup on a Mardi Gras float. From their chanting – old football songs, at a guess – he'd say they're drinking.

"Keep going," Roy tells him. Sol decides he doesn't seem to mind Sol driving – would sooner have the Luger to hand. But he's clearly on edge.

"Sol," Roy says.

Sol's going too quickly for the car park. Too fast not to get them noticed.

"Sol."

And sure enough, two privateers break away from the main building to intercept them.

"Bastard," Roy whispers.

Sol's too fixated on the men crossing the apron to notice the halo of barriers that's risen up to cordon off the service station. Luckily, Roy has. He touches Sol's forearm to get his attention, then taps his forehead. "Keep driving like that and they'll only shoot the sky once. The rest'll come through that big shiny fod of yours. Leave the chatting to me, and don't do anything daft. Those bollards can stop tanks."

One of the privateers raises a hand.

"Slow off," Roy says.

Sol brakes, his tongue a fat worm. He swallows and wipes his hands down his front.

"Roy–"

"Shut up," Roy hisses, and waves the first privateer to his window. Sol listens to the idling engine, hears every catastrophic failure waiting to happen–

"We're on a drop," Roy tells the privateer.

The privateer snorts, pulls off his helmet. He can't be more than eighteen. Sol looks over his gear: state uniform with patches and tags ripped off. "Pickup only," the man says, a thick accent that doesn't waver from a single flat note. "Drop, no. Here is pickup only. Who do you run for?"

"Can't say," Roy tells him, tapping his nose. "But it's high priority."

The privateer dead-eyes Sol. "And the black friend?"

"Guard and driver. All-round good 'un. English is a bit ropey, mind – fresh off the boat. But you know you need protection round here." Roy winks at the second privateer's rifle.

"You see only his eyes," the man says. "Until he opens the mouth." He laughs at himself, then over at the second privateer. Then he squats to look into the back. "And her?"

Roy sucks his teeth. Sol's confident on how fast Roy can pull the Luger, but he doesn't want him to have to.

"Wait…" Sol whispers.

Roy gets out. Slow, deliberate movement, his injured hand held in one pocket. Sol keeps Y's reflection in sight. He wants to be back there, next to her. A hand on her chin. Hers on his –

Roy asks Sol to unlock the rear door.

Sol carefully extends the lock pin. The privateers circle the Sierra from both directions. They gesture towards the bonnet, and Roy moves there.

The first privateer opens the passenger door. The second stands away, cradling his rifle. In the mirror, Sol follows the movement of the man's camo collar, dreary light playing on his neck stubble. He watches the privateer's hands move over Y. Her blankets coming away like onion peel. Her tracksuit top pulled at, unzipped.

The privateer says something. Sol can't make it out –
possibly another language. He glances out at Roy. Not for
the first time, Roy seems rattled – a look that intensifies
Sol's panic.

Helpless, he watches the young privateer push on Y's
scalp, not far from the churn of her crown. His hand
moves to the back of her neck, where he picks at the
wires in an unpleasant approximation of affection.
Sol fights the impulse to impede him, to distract him.
Anything to stop him interfering with her.

But instead he witnesses Y's eyes flicker –

Focus –

And hold his gaze in the mirror. Her irises seem to
expand and contract.

"Why make her off?" the young privateer says to Roy.
"She's bootlegged?"

Roy looks at Sol. But Roy can't see Y. And Sol can't
breathe, can't speak, can't anything –

"What?" Roy asks. "High calibre, this one. You
interested? Let us through and we'll talk decisions with
someone more important than you."

The young privateer thinks about that. He says, "If I
get to play," and raises his finger towards the pavilion.

"Ta," Roy says. He gets back in the car and, through
one side of his mouth, says, "Move."

Sol edges over the car park markings. The bollards
lower as they draw closer. "Y," he whispers. "Can you
hear me? Can you – oh Christ, Y – can you move?"

Y blinks at him. Her eyes have a dewy quality, and
their colour's changed. At the border of her left iris, a
corona of vivid green leeches into her whites. Her pupils
have contracted to pinheads.

"What you on about?" Roy asks.

Sol puts a hand behind the chair, squeezes her knee. "It's me. It's me, Sol. You remember, don't you? You know me, don't you?"

"Sol?"

"Look at her," Sol manages. "Look at her."

"Bloody nora," Roy says, manic excitement rising in his voice. "Fucking hell. Is she–"

"She's awake, isn't she? I'm not just making it up? Oh shit, Roy. What are we doing?"

"How, though?"

"That guy faffed around with the back of her head. Her eyes came on–"

"Shit," Roy says. "Shit. There's not a bastard switch is there? Jesus, that's insane. Keep up – you've got to keep it up. Look, that guy's directing us through."

"Now what?" Sol whispers.

"She's awake," Roy says. "She really is."

"What do we do? Tell me! Is she in pain?"

"Wait…"

"I'm turning. We're going, right now–"

"No!" Roy snaps. "They're right behind us."

"But she's *awake*," Sol shouts, speeding up. They cut a right angle away from the pavilion. Hearing the Sierra's dodgy exhaust, a nearby crowd divides, like a cell, into two smaller groups.

"No, Sol – *no!*" Roy urges. "We're doing this. Just get past them, past them. You can loop back on yourself. The sliproad's only there."

But Sol is concentrating on the escape at all costs; too frightened, too distracted by Y's laser eyes. He takes them through the gap in the crowd. People in down puffer jackets, others in next to nothing. Huddles of dealers, pushers, wads of cash changing hands. They pass a woman, older, thick fringe, and in her Sol sees Mel for an instant; relives in rapid flashes her long descent to that bed in Salford General; the marks in her arms, the looseness of her back skin when he held her; the spots and sores she endured.

Beyond the Mel-woman, he sees a man and teenaged boy emerge from behind a row of portable toilets.

"Stop the car," a piercing voice says. "In the Ford, stop the car." It's coming through a loudhailer. A woman holding it. She repeats herself, and a breath is sucked from Sol's mouth. The massed crowd stares at the Sierra.

The sky's fully black. The rain's getting heavier.

"Here we go," Roy says. His wrapped hand is held against his face, and the blood's started welling up through the material.

Sol stops the car.

"This vehicle isn't on our list," the woman says. Her English is tart, flawless, but there's a certain lumpiness to her voice, like she needs to clear her throat.

"Stop fretting," Roy says to Sol. "I can feel you shaking."

"Transporting broken assets in an unlisted vehicle," the woman goes on, "is a crime."

Roy undoes his seatbelt and cups his mouth to throw his voice. "We found her," he shouts. "In a skip. She's pretty beaten up, and we thought… We heard of you. A friend of a friend. We thought you'd want a look."

Sol can't tell what Roy is thinking.

The woman steps out of the crowd: tall, white-haired, leather-skinned, and wrapped in a decadent shawl.

Roy gets out of the car.

"I'm Leila," the woman says. She lowers the megaphone in a slow, elegant arc, then raises it to add something: "Not that it matters." Sol gets the impression her megaphone follows the exact same path each time.

"Roy," he shouts back. "And this is Solomon – my detail."

Sol's toes are starting to cramp with the tension. Again he seeks Y in the mirror, again finds her staring. He squeezes her leg; more reassuring for him, he realizes, than for her.

"Let's stop pontificating," Leila says. "What do you want for her?"

Roy leers in at Y as if to estimate her value. He looks at Sol and quickly away again. Nothing can derail the act.

If it's an act at all –

"Including repairs?"

Leila waves a walkie-talkie. "The boy says impact damage, wetware reset, and unlocking. Even before we know what else is wrong, that's a lot of work. Of course you've then got shipping… risk pay… extra to keep things under the table…"

A vague thought pops in Sol's mind: *Strip it all down and put it back together again.*

"Give me a figure," Roy says.

Sol blanches. What did he just say?

Across the car park, through the rain, Leila taps twice at her side. Movement in the crowd – the young privateer at her beck and call. He gives her what looks like a tablet. "Take a stroll," she says to Roy, beckoning. "The chauffeur can stay put."

Sol lowers his window. "Roy, don't."

But Roy struts over, Luger visible in his waistband. An obvious discomfort when he lands his right foot.

Sol enters manual breathing, acutely aware of the surroundings. Despite the rain, it's stuffy in the car, and the window has steamed where his shoulder meets it. He rolls it all the way down.

Leila stands before Roy like an opposing captain

waiting for the toss. As Roy reaches her she holds up the tablet, all smiles. On the tablet is a clear image of a vehicle. Sol would recognize it from a mile off; could translate the vehicle's lines into scale from sight alone. This is the man who could, at least before Far-Eastern manufacturers dominated the market, relay the name and make of every vehicle out there. He'd tell you the *year* of a model from as little as its headlight cluster. And that's why he knows this: on the tablet screen is a picture of the Lexus that he and Irish jacked.

Y's Lexus.

Roy acts bemused. *News spreads fast.* And now he's got his hands up, remonstrative, and hasn't noticed the circle closing around him. Heavy hearts are made of this – Sol knows there'll be too many gaps in his story; that a lie's only good enough if you believe it too.

A bad situation is growing worse. This is the time for Sol to go, but something like misplaced loyalty stays his decision. "Y," he whispers. "Can you run?"

Then the circle around Roy loses its cohesion, or at least its intent. Has he smarmed them? Even Leila's determined appearance has relaxed.

The tablet vanishes. Leila and Roy shake hands. She's still smiling. Not a big smile, exactly, but enough to shift her scalp, open out her face.

A certain weight leaves Sol. He pivots to Y and says, "I think we'll be alright." But Y's gazing beyond him. Sol follows her eyeline to the dangling black sacks. "Don't," he says. "Don't look at that." And the numbness returns. Roy, too, is pointing at something behind the crowd. The row of portable toilets.

"Don't," Sol whispers. "Don't."

Roy sets out. Despite his limp, his gait seems more confident – shoulders held back, chin into the rain. A contented, knowing look Sol's never seen on him before. Something like relief in Roy's motion, as if he's been shorn of some burden.

As he reaches the toilet, Roy stops and holds up a thumb towards the Sierra. Then he mouths something and opens the toilet door.

The crowd watches Roy close the door. But only Sol sees Leila's smile drop. She claps and points, businesslike, and Sol's arms prickle. Instinctively, he twists the dangling ignition wires part way together. Eases the Sierra into first gear.

Two privateers run to Roy's toilet with a heavy-looking bag, one strap each. They wrap the structure with a length of flat-sided cable, effectively locking Roy inside. Sol can see the twined sections of it – the braided cable.

Sol gets out of the Sierra.

By now Roy has realized something's wrong. He's trying to open the door from the inside, but the cable won't budge. He thumps on the toilet's thin polymer walls, bounces off it, rocks it, kicks hard. Stress-lines form in the plastic – lighter sections where the plastic expands. Hearing Roy's desperate shouts, Sol falls back into the Sierra where Y is blinking madly.

The privateers at the toilet remove a lump of arcane-looking equipment from the bag. It looks to Sol like a typewriter. This they separate and clamp to opposite sides of the toilet's shell with a foul sucking noise. Then the privateers sprint away.

Sol can still hear Roy shouting for him – shouting his name, now – and the distress is audible. In response, Sol closes the car door. What else can he do? Powerless, cowardly, he twists his head. The alternative is unbearable.

Roy starts firing his Luger through the plastic,
scattering the crowd. Then there's this single, searing
flash. The toilet twists on its base, as if in seizure. A sound
of rending plastic, crackling, before a final, wrenching
cry – a note that rises sharply, impossibly, then cuts out.
The shooting stops, the cable disappears, and the top
half of the toilet implodes. Sol sits agape. In place of the
toilet's top half hangs a cube of reversed matter; a white
blizzard inside, so brilliant and real it renders its frame as
false. Sol regards the cube in total awe – its edges slurred
by the bleak wind contained within it. As he watches, a
patch of something else becomes clearer, something like
land, another land inside the cube, which is blown with
white granules and pitched steeply. Into the cube, onto
that ramp, fragments from the toilet rise up with a liquid
freedom. And then a glimmer, another flash, and the
suspended cube vanishes to reveal empty space. The top
half of the toilet is now gone, missing in totality. Sucked
in, sucked *through*. It's simply disappeared, winked out –
like a magician's box dropped through a stage trapdoor.

"Roy!" Sol screams. "Roy!"

In his mirror, Y's eyes are dead-set, unyielding.

"Did you see it? Did you see?"

Her face says she did.

"Oh my God. What was it? Like a window! And that
storm inside it–"

Y blinks serenely.

"And it just *disappeared.*"

Y blinks and blinks and blinks.

What's left of the toilet door hinges open. Two thick
ropes – Roy's legs, Sol realizes – with trousers loosened
and falling away from his cauterized waist, tumble to the
tarmac.

Sol retches in his lap, emits a stringy bile, elastic,

that leaves him gasping for air – sucking it down, throat seared.

To the crowd, Roy's legs are a signal. Leila points towards the Sierra with a single finger and the privateers' rifles level. Sol drops his head just in time – a flicker and the side window shatters. There's no pain, only noise and the sensation of sweat cascading from every pore.

Sol scrobbles the starter wires together. Pumps the old Sierra's accelerator till it's growling and lifts his left foot. Bangs, bumps, lumpiness. The engine screams right up to its first rev band. Bullets rattle, closer and closer, and when the windscreen comes in there's something heavy on the other side of it. Sol keeps his face buried in the passenger seat, one hand somehow holding the wheel in line. The weight increases, the steering drags left, and he kicks down on the brake pedal. The weight dissipates.

Sol rises briefly, glass raining from his head and neck and clothes, and finds a man on the bonnet clinging to a protrusion of the Sierra's hybrid kit. Spotting Sol upright, the privateers fire again. Light pours through fresh holes; chunks of plastic debris and chair foam and upholstery pluming. Rain curling in. He must be hit. Somewhere in this squall of deconstructed materials must be his own blood, flesh. The man on the bonnet wriggles – the impact of each round carrying the sound of slapped meat.

The Sierra careens across the car park behind the pavilion, and the firing ceases. Cover. Sol pulls and pushes the car into second, third. Smoke pours through the windscreen frame, and the electric unit whinnies. He can tell the front left tyre's shredded by the way the car dips off its centre line. He needs to over-correct it, holding the steering almost full lock to the right. The man on the bonnet slides straight off, taking a lump of machinery with him.

"Y!" Sol shouts over his shoulder. "Are you hit?"

Nothing.

"Are you hit? Where are you hit?"

They won't make it at this rate. Not with the car limping like this. And as they descend to the sliproad, he imagines the privateers as scrapyard dogs, tearing across the car park.

Sol hits the brakes before the sliproad bend. There's a worrying knocking through his foot, and the car's body rolls up onto its right wheels alone. Some hose, some fitting, cut away. He pumps the brake pedal, and still nothing. He swears, and over the onrushing wind and rain the volume of his voice surprises him. The chevrons narrow as the sliproad merges with the motorway.

Sol knows what's next. A cavalcade in tow. A death-convoy. As they pull away, back towards the city, smoke billowing in against Y and what's left of the rear window, Sol scans the sliproad they escaped down, and the windows of the green bridge that spans the lanes – expecting muzzle-flash to burst from the windows, a volley of shots to ring from every aperture. The lonely road stretches out. The black tarmac expands. The sky yawns wide. And even as the Sierra snakes and shimmies through a long tapering corner and the sliproad and bridge slide from his view, he can't relax – imagines the privateers no longer as dogs but fighters from a carrier, enveloped in noise: one bike, two bikes, three bikes – each emerging to chase after them for eternity.

They pass a column of heavy smoke rising from a ditch on the other side of the road. The penny drops: the Audi. Sol keeps accelerating, keeps going –

Until a searing clarity burns through:

They can self-destruct.

And the realization seals around him:

Jeff self-destructed in his bath, his flat –

Now in the mirror Y's eyes are welded to his – a look of naive fear edged with such bright hope he could navigate by it for all the nights to come. Does she share his thoughts? This nexus of fresh connections? Does she know?

Sol wipes his face on his sleeve. "Just you and me now," he says, only now noticing the torrent of sparks flaring up the car's side. While their gathering speed has stabilized the Sierra's jitters, he assumes the front wheel only has so much left in it; that its steel rim will eventually warp, bend, and crack entirely, perhaps set alight. Or that the stresses on the drivetrain will prove too much, and the axle will seize, and the car will careen off or stop and flip under its own momentum.

You could imagine a hundred different deaths in these open lanes –

But the road stays empty and the sky stays heavy but droneless and all he can process is the stench of the smoke and the cold air and rain blasting through the car.

Manchester's cityscape expands. The Sierra piles in – mile after mile away from Roy; Roy who held up a thumb like he knew what was coming; Roy who was halved; Roy whose death scream has already morphed in Sol's recollection – become more than a blend of fear and surprise. Roy whose disembodied legs are imprinted on his interior space, dancing there on puppet strings held by the grotesque man he called the Reverend...

What kind of autopilot had got them out, got them to here? And Y – untouched, scrutinizing him, adorned with engine smoke – how was she alive?

Inside the walls of his mind, stalking and pushing against his senses, pulling the black curtains aside,

Sol feels something stir: in a woodchip waiting room, somewhere in the city, is a one-eyed woman holding up a headless fish, keening like a fox. *Melanie.*

"That's where you need to go," he says. "Isn't it? Your tower. The teeth."

Y blinks at him.

"I've got my tools," he tells her. "But first we need to hide."

Mel's out of fags and fingernails left to chew. It's early afternoon already, though she couldn't say what day. She's wrapped up in a man's coat – a heavy, grossly oversized thing from the Cat Flap's lost property box. She's been in and out here since morning, withering in the cold and wet and hoping for something to draw back the nerves. False eye itching as the city swims around her. Wondering about Jeff, Sol's dreamlike visit, the woman in his flat. And all the while plenty's been happening on her doorstep: dozens of locals slogging past with bags of rubbish for a protest bonfire on disused land round the corner.

Back when, she'd have complained about her neighbours' noise, their mess. No longer. Now she's actually tempted to join them, join in by adding to the pyre; to bag up and burn the detritus she pulls from her employees' rooms after a shift.

How many years has it been now? All this?

How long have things been going this way?

Mel thumbs a thick scar on her wrist and locks the front door. She thinks: *They can knock tonight.* It's actually tempting to simply close up and pay off the girls with hot meals and what's left in the till – shut up shop for the rest of the day, and then tonight attend the fire; watch it burning till morning or longer, rain or not. She smiles: of all the services you once took for granted but now accepted as gone – the rule of law, medical care, road maintenance, the postal service – it was only really rubbish collections that'd prevailed. This demonstration – an organized protest that if channelled differently, had its emphasis shifted, could do so much to unsettle the council – is happening simply because the rubbish hasn't been collected for a month. How many of her neighbours knew it wasn't the council running collections now but the Wilbers?

It's come to something when you're protesting because the Wilbers aren't doing their jobs properly.

A banging makes her jump. Somebody knocking on the front door.

She checks the time. Possibly one of the regulars, though it's too early for most. She pulls her fringe over her false eye and pads uncertainly to the door.

"Mel!"

She freezes.

"Mel!"

She flattens herself against the hallway wall, watching the front door as if it might reveal some indescribable horror.

"Please, Mel. We need you."

Mel races upstairs, clumsy footsteps betraying her. She can still hear banging on the door, wants to escape its echo. In the farthest room, Mel hops over the bed, unmade, and catches her hip on the open drawer of a subsided dresser. The damp's bad in here. The net curtains are moth-eaten. And a scent: babywipes and antiseptic; latex and dried lubricant. The faintest note of semen. She stands shaking by the window with the net curtain's veil-like shadow masking her face. Looking up, she gets the sense the sun has been scuttled behind the cloud, and that Manchester's ready to swallow it.

"Mel!"

She pushes back the curtain. Streaking wet. So many dead flies on the sill.

Across the road there's an old banger well beyond its last legs; sagging oddly and smoking, its bodywork either perforated or missing. A Ford, possibly. Yes, she recognizes the shape. It'd be strange if Sol's old passions hadn't rubbed off, hadn't crossed the membrane.

Mel moves to get an angle on the pavement. A sharp intake of breath. He's down there, his slender head shining, and in his arms there's a woman. Mel scans her, too: a young but hard-looking face, petite by old-fashioned appraisal, but powerful – dark-skinned, tautly held; the legs of a dancer, a gymnast, an athlete.

And a third arm.

"God no," Mel whispers. She wants to scream, slap herself. And even as she says it she knows Sol has detected her presence somehow; that he's staring up at the window.

Too late.

So Mel goes downstairs and unlocks the door.

"Thank Christ," Sol blurts. The woman's eyes are burning up.

Mel drags him inside by one sleeve and pushes him along the hall, before squeezing past to lean out of the door – checking left, checking right. She scans the dark windows in the squat over the road, weighs up a young boy teetering forward with two bin bags all but covering his face. The faint tang of toxic smoke on the air tells her they've started burning rubbish already.

"Through there," she says, shooing Sol into the waiting room. "Go." And she joins them.

Sol stands motionless with the woman in his arms. "Need to move the car," he tells her. His eyes are red and streaming, and his forehead looks burnt. "We can't keep it there."

"You stink," Mel says. "The pair of you."

"Tell me where I can put her," he says. "A spare bed, mattress. Anything soft."

Mel shakes her head. "Don't do this to me."

"Just a day, a couple of days. A week tops."

"A *week*? They'll know. They'll be here before that."

Sol's jaw muscles contract. "We'll get to that."

"One night," Mel says. "No more." She enters the reception cage and pretends to check the rota. "One night," she mutters again.

"It means the world," Sol says.

Mel nods reluctantly. "Cassie's off, so you can have her room. It'll cost you, though. A night's takings, plus the launderette charge."

"You said she's off."

"Off the rota, yeah. Cassie isn't ever off. Never."

"I'll sleep anywhere – outside if I have to. It's this one I'm bothered about."

Y's eyes shift to Sol's mouth. Mel catches her quizzical expression, isn't sure how best to read it.

"You shouldn't have done this," Mel tells him. He looks old to her, his physique strangely diminished. "Look at the state of you."

"No choice," Sol says. "And I won't be long."

Mel sighs, relents. "First floor, third room on your right. Door's marked three."

"Thanks," Sol says, and leans at her slightly. "Front pocket, just in there – can you grab my keys out? Tools are in the car boot – if you wouldn't mind getting them as well, I'll…" He pauses, as if suddenly conscious of how immense their companionship once was.

Mel sways. She nods unsurely. "Alright," she says. "I can do that."

And now – is he smiling at her?

"Front left, chest pocket," he says. "The big one."

Mel tugs at his pocket flap. It's colder than she expects. The material's greasy, and his smell up close is weird, denatured. She keeps her fingers against the front of the pocket, avoiding studiously his chest wall. With a kind of release she feels the cold keys.

"Leave them out here," he tells her, "and I'll get rid of the car."

Sol carries Y away. Mel listens to him climbing the stairs, Cassie's door creaking open, and the door chain jangling against it.

Up in Cassie's room, Sol lays Y on the bed and folds its thin top sheet over her. "I know," he says. "I know."

He empties his pockets onto the side. Fluff, a powdery receipt, a few pence. Then the strange disc-like item he'd found in Sandy's car. This he places, precise and careful, on the makeup dresser – almost like he's trying to inset a gem.

"What about a change of clothes," he says, and starts rooting in Cassie's chest of drawers for anything that might fit her. In this he presumes Y wants to wear women's clothes, well aware that his attempts at clothing her so far have been inadequate. But it also feels dangerous to decide her identity should be drawn from what really amounts to a differently tailored shape or colour, the simple taper of a garment. If she doesn't understand or care for these things, isn't he imposing a certain system upon her?

He searches regardless, until, by the toys and the bottles, the gels and liquids, the pads and the hair bobbles, he finds a stack of uniformly black T-shirts. He removes the top one – on it a classic Bowie image cracked from washing. It'll do.

Y's spine makes a creasing sound as he shifts her up the bed, props her against the headboard. "You got hollow bones, you, or what?" he says. "Try this one, *Space Oddity*. It'll be more than big enough on you."

She doesn't respond.

"I'll keep them closed," he adds. "Promise." And he sticks to his promise – peeking only to reposition her double-arm in the sleeve hole without popping too many stiches. "There," he says, her head bristling through the neck hole. Then, almost embarrassed: "Can always ask what else is knocking about."

Y releases a croak.

"Try and rest," he tells her, realizing immediately how little that means. He sniffs hard. "Or I'll stick the telly on if you want." Without another thought he puts it on anyway – flicks channels until he finds a picture, and recognizes it, with a terrible heat, as a porn spool.

You stupid prick –

Sol slaps the off button. "Maybe not," he says. The flush has him remove his sweater, and now he can smell himself. "Maybe just try to sleep," he says, unsteady from the stink. Y's shoulders settle into her frame, and he notices her studying herself in the mirrored ceiling. "I'll try too – just a nap. And then I'll be back. You believe me, don't you?"

Something about the way Y is set on the bed – her tendrils of wiring now hidden from sight but stark beneath the shirt, her bald head, doubled arm, the tattoo on her neck – makes her appear both real and unreal. As if Sol could run a finger over her skin, feel a certain warmth, but still find a circle of dust on his fingertip.

He lowers his eyes and leaves the room.

●●●

Mel's pacing when he returns to the reception. Chewing the skin off her thumbs, rubbing her sleeves with obsessive fervour.

"Mel–"

"You've got a nerve," she hisses, shaking an unmarked bottle at him. His toolbag is on the floor by the door.

"You nearly killed us," Sol says.

Mel sits down, takes another swig. "She hurt?"

Sol sits on the bench opposite. "Yes."

"Fuck."

The foyer screens fizz with interference.

"Tell me," he says.

"Tell you what?"

"Who he was."

"Who?"

"Give over, Melanie. The guy you sent."

"No," Mel says. "Sent? No... it wasn't like–"

"Who was he?"

"Oh God, Sol, what did he do? I just needed to know. I couldn't believe you'd bought one–"

"I found her," he says, cutting her off. "No buying."

Mel looks away. "He was only meant to check. I had to know. Why you'd ever need one..."

"Well he brought it all down with him."

A single tear, oddly shaped, runs from Mel's false eye. He knows it'll be painful for her. "Maybe he told them," she says. "I don't know. I don't know!"

"Them?"

She nods. "Jason."

"Who the hell's Jason?"

Mel lets out a sharp sob. "It's just so fucking stupid. I've been so, so stupid."

"No," he says, clawing at his neck. "You're never stupid. Try harder. *Try*. For her – not me."

Mel stands, crosses the foyer and snakes a slender arm under the counter. She returns to him with a ream of rolled paper, wearing a guilty look he knows better than most. "I didn't know what else to do," she tells him, her tone softer, maybe even self-reproachful. "I thought he'd come back. That's what he said. I was going to work it out from there. I wondered if you'd got her from Jason."

Sol unfurls what's clearly meant to be a catalogue – coverless but for an illegible title. The body of it has been mashed together from poor quality photocopies – a lot like the ska-zines he used to read. All those forgotten sounds and colours of his youth, a memory of his dad coming home from the garage, whistling something –

Sol flicks through the catalogue in a masochistic frenzy. It layers up on his heart. Torsos with multiple arms. Extra breasts, openings. Extra anything. Pitiless marketing lines in page-corner flashes; special offers like *Double up for double your money*. Captions talk of modular parts and scarless patches, seamless joints; clinical hygiene and realistic textures. Inbuilt languages, "technique packs". There are swatch samplers you can send off for; skin tone comparison kits; and a whole section, almost a subcatalogue, of wigs. Design-your-own tattoo sets, hints at embeddable weapons, bladed attachments, *household essentials*. The word "appendage" over and over again. He flicks on to find features about near-future developments, a bizarre interview with some well-meaning developer who talks dispassionately about military, ethical and medical applications, as if total unwavering exploitation isn't the bottom line.

As if these people aren't sold as dolls.

By the last page, Sol has come unstuck.

"You use them here?"

Mel looks shocked. "No. None of them – not one."

He places the catalogue under the bench and clasps his hands. "Then what's this about? What is it?"

"A ma... a man came. Jason, right? And Jason left Jeff with me... oh God it just doesn't make any *sense*–"

"You make your money from this place. Tell me what's in it for you."

"Nothing," she says. "Because we only had Jeff in. Like a way to diversify – that's what Jason said. Diversify. A free trial, another income stream. All these frigging *phrases*. But he's like a dog with a bone. He told me they don't sleep, or need it anyway, and the *overheads*, and I figured Jeff could be protection, for the doors. There was this night he did something bad, and we got him in the scary cupboard..."

Sol is blank.

"And you called and I was just sitting there, and I thought, I've got to *see*. It was too much. I couldn't – I couldn't see why you had one to yourself. I couldn't see you like that."

Sol slowly places his head in his hands. Squeezes his scalp. "But why would I tell you? Why didn't you come yourself?"

"Because it's you. It's *you*."

"But we're over."

She swigs from her bottle, splashes it down her top on release. "You think I don't know? Better than anyone?"

"Don't bullshit me. That's all I want."

"I'm not," she says. "The girls, Sol... they can't just go on the streets, out there with the Wilbers, the council. I can't just turf them out, close it all down. Their lives are here. Their network is each other."

"Bollocks to the Wilbers," Sol says. "Bollocks to them."

"I'm just saying. It's a safe place, this. That's how we've made it."

"I saw lorries out there," he says. He splits his fingers, points at his eyes. "Crates and crates, like a production line. This Jeff – he come with organs? Accessories?" He points at the ceiling. "Because she did. Whoever she was meant for – whoever's meant to have her – had organs spare. *Spare organs.*"

Mel looks bleary, unwieldy.

"That's not a life," he says. "Any way you cut it."

Now it's Mel's turn to snap. "And you sit there, don't you, Solomon, lecturing. Who are you to say what living should mean? You think it's always like that? You think the women here don't live? That there's shame in all this? Here's a shitty truth for you, sunshine: it's a *better* life sometimes. The places they come from, the things they've been through…"

Sol shakes his head bitterly. "Go and ask her that," he snarls back. "Go and see if it's a better life. You know how I found her? A pair of pipes stuffed down her throat, sucking white paste through her nose."

"So you're rescuing her, are you? Playing the big hero? Are you gonna rescue the rest of us next?"

"You're getting me all wrong. I'm not comparing choice and pressure. I'm only talking about her. Just her, people like her. And we came here because I know you care."

"But I don't," Mel says. "Not about you. Not enough. You look after your own now."

"Jeff's dead," he says. "So if Jason's due back, you'll need to be ready."

Mel glares at him. Another swig from the bottle, her skin blotching. "Dead," she says.

"Yes."

"Fine," she says.

"Do they know about you and me?"

She shakes her head. "I don't think so."

Sol stands up, crosses the waiting room and takes Mel's bottle. Sips from it. "Then," he says, "that's a start."

Y

Sandy's convoy left the motorway to take a longer route south – something about state security massing at a checkpoint ahead. Y didn't understand much else of the transmission, but the driver turned and said, "Britain today."

Owing to the diversion, Sandy's offroader led the convoy down an undulating country road, sides densely overgrown. Brambles squealed against the vehicle Y travelled in, their berries smearing on the windows. She could smell their sharpness.

Y's driver kept a bracelet of beads wrapped around his indicator stalk, which rattled incessantly. "Too much dithering," the driver said to his cohort, an unkind-looking man with a rifle propped between his legs. "I need my sleep." But the other man said nothing, and Y only saw his face from oblique angles, crops of his features in the driving mirrors. Clearly, idle chatter was off the table.

By a layby, Sandy's vehicle, the lead vehicle, sounded its horn three times. The whole convoy slowed, then stopped. Sandy's driver stepped out and took the opportunity to relieve himself by a tree. His back to her, Y noticed a few grazing animals through holes in the bordering hedgerows of the field beyond him. They were dirty, emaciated things, but they brought to mind the view from the mansion grounds. Like there, the sky here was birdless – a wide smeary grey, threaded with blueish gaps that ran through it like varicose veins. Surprised, Y found herself missing the skies above the mansion.

She was pulled from her reverie by shouting. New orders being barked down from the front and relayed by each driver in the convoy. Her driver got back in, muttering, and said to his silent cohort: "All the same, these bloody bureaucrats."

As they moved away again, Y thought of the water faucet on the mansion lawns, rationed liquid passing her lips.

Before her, and behind them, the transfer vehicles continued to descend through the countryside. Owing to their new orders, however, the gaps between each vehicle had increased by thirty yards. Something had changed back there, and Y thought her driver was tenser. She couldn't have known that this way they would minimize losses if there was an ambush, an IED or drone strike. She wouldn't consider that the vehicles' seatbelts, crumple zones, under-armour or bulletproof glass would only do so much.

Eventually the convoy rejoined the motorway. "But we're stopping again soon," the driver said impassively, and sure enough another service road welcomed them after another few miles.

At the end of this road sat a unique building – a cottage inset between banks of heavy evergreens. As they came into its grounds, away from the road, it became clear that the cottage's traditional walls were cut away to reveal a tinted glass fascia. Inside, visible joists and floors, sepia under the glass, gave the building the appearance of an opened dolls' house. Silhouettes moved between its floors.

Was this Manchester? Y's stomach twinged. Of course it wasn't. She knew that as fact somewhere in there, in some kernel of knowledge, some tiny fortress of her mind the makers hadn't razed.

An armed woman waved them towards a lowered barrier. "Last in, first out," the guard said, mocking. Apparently overthinking the barrier, Y's driver stalled the vehicle and swore loudly. The guard put her hand on the roofline as the driver restarted it. "And if you need a mechanic, you only need to ask nicely."

Here Sandy's convoy broke up: the heavier units rolled closer to the house, while the four-by-fours split off towards the forest. It felt rehearsed, ordinary. By the cottage were privateers on their rounds, and some of the younger children – brothers and sisters – were already out of their seats and stalking across the turf towards the entrance.

At last the minder in the passenger seat turned to speak. His face startled her: his eyes were like Chaplain's, threw intense colour. "You wait, beautiful," he told her. His voice was detached and even, and his eyes were locked to the belt crossing her chest. "They taught you patience, did they? Sandy's taking you from here, so keep it locked. Be a good girl."

Y nodded as politely as she could, squinted as light through the vehicle's sunroof was reflected back from his face as a hundred suns.

"I mean it," the man said. "Invested a lot in you. You've got debts to repay, now. All this transport doesn't come cheap. And if you say, do, or even so much as think about pulling anything on us – anything at all – between now and then, I'll have that pretty little mouth closed up faster than you can blink."

After this he left and slammed the door. Y watched him walk away: a stooping gait, wiry and lithe in comparison to their thick-beamed driver.

Y wanted to get out of the car, now. Being cramped up in here created a yearning in her to do warm-down stretches under the trees, a breeze over her skin. As it was, the driver had left the window down as if she were a dog, and the forest seemed to thicken the longer she looked at it.

Y waited. Y despaired. Had she touched a tree like that before? Climbed one, even? She could imagine holding a hand to the bark and closing her eyes, sensing the tree as it aged in symphony with her, the vibrations of its growth rippling outwards like its rings.

Then something else caught her attention. A gleam in the cottage's glass, temporarily disturbed – like a bird's shadow had crossed it. And a distant noise, a wailing, followed by an enormous crack that jolted the vehicle.

Looking up through the sunroof, Y saw a mirage of two enormous birds, their reflections swimming in the glass of the cottage. As she followed them, she realized they were getting larger. Privateers outside were starting to notice, too – a commotion broke out by the main doors.

"State drones!" someone yelled. And still they came closer, wheeling the cottage like it was carrion.

Sandy appeared in the porch, running from it, hair tumbling from her high ponytail. She was shouting, "Your headscarves! Put on your headscarves!"

Roaring, the first drone hovered above the cottage,

steady and poised. The second drone looped away and disappeared. Frightened, though not exactly sure of what, Y tried all the locks, then slapped on the nearest window until it was smeared with oil from her hands.

There was another crashing noise, a breathless rattle, as the second drone buzzed the group at low altitude. Its sonic boom pounded the vehicle's windows, and so many people, running in streams from the cottage entrance, tripped and went over.

Shielded by the cottage, an anti-aircraft weapon wound up and began to fire.

While everything told her to stay still, to embrace patience, her training, and despite the escort's threat, Y flopped onto her side, drew her knees up to her chest and kicked the off-roader's window with both feet.

The first impact felt like it shattered her knees. The second was more painful, seemed even less effective. And just before the third she saw the drones shimmer again in the house glass.

Sandy reached Y's offroader just as a drone launched its first salvo. Paired missiles spiralled down behind the cottage – presumably meant for the AA battery. The result was horrible – a demonic bloom that seemed to burst then eat itself, leaving only a braid of smoke that hung there, slowly distending.

Sandy was going wild outside. She hammered on the window glass. "Y!" she shouted, "keep it together!" But her words were lost under a steady prattle of small arms fire, and through the sunroof Y saw the drone gain altitude, shrink to a speck. She sat up. It was clear that the dropoff point – this exchange point – had been discovered. So were they her salvation, up there in the sky? Or were they delivering something worse?

Behind Sandy, privateers were running across the

cottage lawns with ash tumbling off them, the air hazy. Something sticky was in their hair and across their shoulders – brownish, a clumpy powder. A man cut through the flow and made his way towards them. It was the driver, Y saw, with his mouth opening and closing mutely. The off-roader's locks sprung and the doors swung open. Sandy barrelled into the back head-first, face paralyzed with confusion. She cupped Y's cheeks and said, words seemingly lodged in her throat, "It's gas – they're using gas!"

Sandy's eyes were childlike, seeking. Her composure had evaporated. Y looked down into the gap between them, at their identical physiques. And there she saw the little tooth hanging from Sandy's neck, displaced from her tight collar, which beneath the madness of war was gently tickling Y's skin.

A little tooth. A manacle –

Y wasn't frightened anymore. Wrath supplanted her. She took Sandy's pendant in her fist and hauled; brought Sandy up and across her body, head crashing against the door. The opposite door was still open, and thanks to her training, a tending towards self-preservation in situations she could control, Y slid feet-first towards it. Released, so close to being free, Y pushed Sandy's feet over and scrambled across the bench seat, tumbling out into long grass. Her escape was rather more convulsive than graceful, and she nicked both shins on the footplate, clattered on all three forearms into the soil. Wheezing, she rocked back and collapsed against the tyre wall, knees aching. The noise above was abominable. The gas haze was spreading. She got up, covered her face and dashed for the treeline. Only as she got there did she find the tooth fragment embedded in her palm.

Sandy gestured madly at the driver to follow their

cargo, and set off in pursuit. She could tell Y was running faster than she ever could – lithe and straight – her hands up and protecting her face from the ash. That speed would be a good thing in any other setting, certainly. She saw Y reach the treeline and scream into her hands just as another sonic boom rang out. Sandy's legs were swept out by the overpressure. She herself cried out, defeated, and down in the dirt, winded, she fought to breathe; her head in her own hands, gasping like a landed fish. Dust billowed over her skin and caught in the fine hairs of her arms.

A grid of green laser passed over. Sandy looked skyward, and knew the hovering drone had dropped its target perimeter, was parsing the terrain.

Sandy also knew what came next. Over the last few years, her various trips had shown her plenty of drones in action on the open motorway. This strike was consistent with the state's modus operandi, not least because the style of attack – sudden and uncompromising – hadn't been altered since the infamous footage the state distributed as a warning, as their proof of concept. That had been the strike drones' first official outing – a raid on an ultra-nationalists' training base in the Pennines. Sandy still remembered the stories: impossible-sounding accounts of thousands of startled birds sweeping into the gape of the valleys and out again through Manchester.

Conversely, Y – who was now in the forest and out of sight – didn't have a clue what was about to happen. Sandy might have sighed in another setting. This poor woman wouldn't know until it was too late. And yet there was a small mercy in that: she'd only really feel pain for the few moments it took for the phosphorous shells to burst and rain their awful jelly; for the globs of it to feast and devastate her nerve endings. So perhaps her sigh was talking more to the waste of all this. Their painstaking process of selection, augmentation, delivery. The cost alone. The Manor Lord's personal approval.

Was it worth it? Was it worth doing all Sandy had done to rebuild her own mind?

Y reappeared among the trees now, going unhindered in the grass. Her three muscular arms were outstretched, hands open. Her shorn head a buttercup yellow. Sandy saw that there was a stream between them, but knew it would offer little relief when the phos came. You can only extinguish phos as long as it's underwater, so when it's in your hair, your choice is simple: burn or drown.

Sandy didn't see much point in getting up. She couldn't outrun the drone. She couldn't outrun her choices.

"Yasmin!" she called. It was emphatically wrong to use the name, but Sandy alone had found this woman, specified her mods, marked out her special dispensations. The boss had been specific on one thing only: that he expected the best possible return on investment. His way of saying, Sandy gleaned, that he wanted the woman who would be Y to do what Sandy couldn't.

But then again, Sandy thought, *we're all replaceable.*

Sandy squinted up at the drone as the grid retracted. Any picosecond now, an inferno was coming –

Only nothing happened. The drone hung a beat longer. Then it soared away.

Sandy exhaled and rose shakily. She pawed the line wrapping her throat where her pendant chain had bitten like a garrotte, and set off for the trees. Y's driver had now intercepted her at the treeline, the off-roader sprawled precariously over the stream. As Sandy came closer, she watched Y's escort – Keating she believed he was called – shepherding her back into the vehicle at gunpoint. By the time Sandy reached them, hair sticking to the sweat of her face, Keating was astride Y on the back seat, and her three arms were trapped beneath her.

"Keating?"

The man swivelled, implants fierce, and Y's knees were bleeding into the fabric. In one hand Keating held high an industrial stapler, fangs exposed. It looked to Sandy so much like a sacrificial dagger.

"Keating!" Sandy shouted. "What are you doing?"

"Fuck off!" the escort hissed. In his other hand there was a small pistol.

"No," Sandy said. "Don't."

"Why?" Keating said. "They think he can't exert himself here? They have to *learn*."

Sandy went forward and took his wrist.

"Not her," she said. "She's too val–"

Keating shot Sandy through the abdomen.

"She's mine," Keating said. And the forest went muffled.

Sandy slid into a silent, painless lake beneath the trees. There, fading in her depths, she listened to Keating's steady breathing as he set about locking Y's mouth.

FIFTEEN

Sol wakes up threshing, sopping wet. Half-light greets him, brings a splinter of moon. Slowly, he wades from the hinterlands of brittle sleep to recognize the room.

We're in the Cat Flap. We're on the run.

For a time, he sits naked on the bed until the dead air leaves him shivering – worried, in some way, that he might otherwise return to the same dreams. Should he check on Y? Probably it's better she rests for now. So instead he turns on the TV to an unlikely-looking threesome. He watches, loosely fascinated, but finds after a few minutes that the video's making him feel ill. It's not because of its content, per se, but the fleshy colour it turns the walls. What signals have been absorbed by all this peeling plaster? It's easy to imagine a substance like asbestos, leeching in.

Sol flicks on from porno to porno to porno, until he finds what appears to be a compilation of headcam war footage. A smoking compound, tracer rounds in the night, harrowed land. The dark sheets around him stripy with salt. Boom – another soldier. Rattle – another. And then the newslines that mass in from the margins: *For the king he/she gave. Next of kin have been informed.* Cut-and-paste headlines on government troops, loyalist militias, terrorists, extremists – words that seem to mingle, melt, and mean increasingly little. Atrocities so common as to be glazed over, now, and relayed with such dilute reasoning. Reporters only ever dipping their toes – or straight up conniving. He thinks: *How come nobody ever asks why?*

Sol looks at the ceiling and regards his body, his face, in the mirror. It's like the rings slake out from his eyes in real time; his torso covered with baggy flesh in liquefaction. "Prick," he tells himself, and swings off the bed. He enters the room's small ensuite – a plastic shower pod – and showers in water so cold it pushes all the air from him.

Tomorrow. *Tomorrow.* Sol keeps thinking about tomorrow. But tomorrow never comes, does it? And he knows he won't sleep again now. Better to crack on, surely. Get things rolling. He goes on wrestling the quandary as he dresses; as he pads down the stairs to the waiting room. No sign of anyone, but there's a lingering odour of damp fires. It's not the Sierra, either – he'd left that too far away. No, this is closer. He goes in Mel's reception cage and picks up the phone.

The dialler clicks. The tone carries.

"Hello?"

"Irish."

"Jesus, Mary and Joseph. Sol? What time is it?"

"Has it turned up?"

"Has what turned up? What's this number you're on?"

"Irish," Sol says. "Is the car there? The gear?"

"Solomon… you seen the clock, man?"

"I'm asking you."

Irish sighs. "Jesus, yes, it's all here. Came in a bin lorry, the clever bastards."

"That's good," Sol says. "They're early. And if I tell you there's a change of plan–"

Irish coughs, asthmatic. "This better be worth my angelic slumber. The heartburn you're causing me."

"I know," Sol says. "I know."

"Well what's going on?"

"Honestly?"

Sol considers telling Irish just enough – that people came looking for the Lexus after all. Nothing more than necessary. Nothing more than believable. Which by extension means nothing of Y, of Roy, or of the things he's seen and done. Assuming the two dead bikers were the same bikers present the morning Irish jacked the Lexus, and that Sandy was the only other person linked to the scene, everyone directly connected is now out of the equation. Only the unseen structures persist. And in any case, Sol's overriding selfishness will force the issue. He might tell himself it's for the better good, but the truth is simpler, more reckless than that: Y is all that matters.

"Honestly," Irish says.

"It's fine," Sol tells him. "There's not enough time."

"Then what's this changed plan?"

"You got a pen?"

"I've always got a pen. Spit it out."

So Sol gives Irish his instructions – poring his way across a mental image to relay its nuances. When he's done, he closes his eyes, holds them shut. A long exhalation through his nose. "You get all that?"

"I got all that. God knows I wish I didn't. But I've got it."

Sol nods, wired now. "You're my favourite," he says.

Irish coughs again. "And you're deeply fucken tapped."

Tools over his shoulder, Sol waits at Y's door. He aches with anticipation, muscles constricting his joints. Is it too early? Would more sleep be worthwhile? Would he do a better job?

He enters Room Three regardless. Inside, Y's awake too – eyes pinned to the mirror above her. Her arms are crossed, pharaonic. The sheets still drawn to Bowie's chin.

"Hiya," he says, sitting at the foot of the bed.

Y blinks.

Sol wants to add some nicety, some attempt at reassurance. The room still as he unfolds a length of tarpaulin from his bag and lays it in the space between the bed and the partition wall. "Sterile," he says to her.

In the wet room, Sol dilutes a quantity of bleach in a mop bucket and leaves several tools in there to soak. Then he splashes his hands and forearms with the dregs of Mel's tiger-striped bottle, and uses one of Cassie's exfoliator brushes to scrub them down.

"Never had to blame my tools," he tells her, kneeling at her side, before giving her a promise he can't be sure to keep.

Sol pulls away her sheet, rolls it deftly into an extra cushion for her head. He cuts off a length of string and divides the tarp into eight – weighting down the string's ends with old spanners.

He smiles a little. "We'll start with your left knee," he says. "The craggy one." Wiring and substructure here spills through a long fissure, a rupture. The wound has exposed visible seams in the skin layer, which he peels away from the kneecap. Beyond this, he's able to access the muscle wall – a second peelable membrane that sits above the motor unit site. There's very little blood.

It's a strange and beautiful thing, the way they've done it, and this alone distracts him from the surrealism of the whole. So many pieces, sealed against translucent pods and beads of biology. Black-edged joins where the connectors meet Y's organic matter. Pure engineering, pure maths: a spotless jigsaw constructed with precision-machined pieces, whittled spindles and micro-cogs. Power drives and strengthened tendons. Pluses and negatives and motor controls.

He thumbs alloys, follows wires. He unscrews the knee unit delicately, carefully. Mapping Y, never less than staggered by her intricacies.

Down on the tarp, Sol starts his first exploded diagram in earnest. After the knee, he removes the artificial sections of Y's fibia and tibia, which are sealed off from her real bone by what appears to be a series of delicate valves and coverings. He extracts wiring looms and support structures, along with a set of clever-looking muscle modules, until Y's left leg resembles a hollow assembly above a blizzard of parts on the tarp.

Sol makes a note of bent fixtures and panels behind the knee. He takes the pencil from his mouth and marks the joins.

Then he starts on her second leg, applying what he's learned from the first. The knee system isn't as badly damaged, but the case is loose around her moving parts, as though violently shaken for too long.

By her ankle, the tight coil of a spring-loaded Achilles tendon, Sol takes a break. He looks up and feels he should ask her for something. Forgiveness, at least. In the mirror, Y watches with an expression impossible to describe – not pain, not fear. Not thankful, nor thankless. Curiosity, compulsion. Wouldn't that be something, to imagine her willing him on?

Sol continues, meticulous and entranced. Time soon ceases to matter or even to be; the whole universe shrunk down, condensed and confined to these four walls and the replications of them above; sensations only the pins and needles of his hands and feet, cut off under his weight; and the only sounds the clink and chink of his tools. His hardened hands maintain their steadiness, and the deconstructed pieces of Y become as gems, pearls from the ocean bed. Her soul counted out in little treasures.

Sol's distantly aware of pain from his own limbs, but he doesn't stop. His tools – only a few proving much use – have become a part of him. As his fingers move around, the calluses burning, he starts to feel a pure form of relief. As if, in doing this, he's reaffirmed to himself that Y isn't an object, not a subject, not a thing. And never – never – a toy. Watching her eyes watch him, he understands that pieces alone can't form a person. And that whether he was created divinely, or was delivered by evolution, his own meat was not entirely pointless – he could have a purpose after all.

Soon he completes her single arm. The elbow structure seems intact, but the wiring, an elegant yarn, is desoldered; the mother unit drifting towards Y's soft tissue like an unmoored craft.

Next he starts on her double-jointed shoulder. The most fiddly section, to his mind, as well as the most sophisticated – even despite the appearance of several cheap fixings. Progressively he unravels a labyrinthine configuration that starts on the opposite side of Y's neck: a series of panels which reveal a missing section of trachea and larynx beneath the tattooed square – though he wouldn't know these names – and in their stead some sort of chip and speaker, wired carefully into the encased biology of her throat. His tools seem magnetized to this setup, and here more than elsewhere he needs to pause to appreciate the marriage of the pieces they left and the parts they added. It's both terrifying and sublime. Then he works outwards towards the doubled joint, removing delicate modules and breaking them down separately, displaying them on the tarp in their own orbits. He reaches the servos of her new shoulder next to the wrapped-up ball of her own, the clavicle apparently strengthened to bear extra weight, and the ligaments replaced with struts of tensile material.

Twinned joint fully derigged, Y's third arm at last comes away in one whole piece, synthetic skin and all. With the city pulsing through the walls, he breaks it down into its major components.

This done, he stands up. His legs are close to buckling.

"Does it hurt?"

Y doesn't blink.

"Promise?"

Y blinks.

"Have I missed anything?"

Y blinks downwards.

Sol motions to her chest. "Here?"

Nothing.

Her stomach?

A murmur from her naked throat.

Sol kneels again. He rolls up her T-shirt and looks across Y's hairless belly until the seams catch the light. From her navel to her lowest rib is a panel. He pushes at the skin. It gives, and he goes inwards, past subdermal screws and plates, until a tiny compartment opens out, and a cylinder, seven or eight inches long, slides free. This he can't break down further. Sense tells him no organ would sit here; that it's not a replacement but an addition. He rolls it over in his hands and finds a faint warning triangle etched into it. He thinks of Jeff and thinks of Sandy and goes cold.

He puts the cylinder to one side. Y's still watching him. "Is it what I think it is?"

Y blinks.

Tight breaths. Tight little breaths.

"And you know how to use it?"

Nothing.

Bastards.

"There's one last bit," Sol tells her. He taps his head and gently rolls her over. Then, using needle-nose pliers and a damp cloth, he removes the accumulated grit and gunge from her nape, her hairline.

What had the young privateer pressed? Sure enough there's another subdermal panel under the lowermost plate of her skull. Here Sol finds a bank of rudimentary I/O switches, each jacked into the boss of her spinal cord. He unscrews the switches carefully, lays them out with the rest. So that now Y is almost completely incomplete; a whole galaxy of parts. Colonies of disparate components, enamelled by indefinite light. Each square of tarp its own distinctive lab culture.

Sol closes his eyes to the fragrance of sweat and oil. Burning there in the darkness, his father's voice: *If it don't work, take it all apart and put it back together again.*

He doesn't take another break before he starts unbending and cleaning and reassembling the pieces of Y. In fact, he only hesitates when he goes to reattach her third arm. She blinks rapidly at him until he grasps why he must continue. For better or worse, it's part of her. Keeping this in pieces implies Y's modified body is something she should be ashamed of – gives her one less thing to reclaim.

With Sol and the woman upstairs, Mel locks and bolts the front door. She can't remember the last time the Cat Flap closed like this, or what might have closed them. She's found a packet of cigarettes, though, which she takes to be a sign, a portent.

Inner door barred, Mel turns off the foyer screens and fans. She tuts at the puddlewater Sol's toolbag has trailed in.

A time check. The girls will start arriving for their shifts any minute. So at the back door, Mel unfolds a plastic chair and sparks up – her feet wedging open the door, and the cold, damp air bringing in the smell of burning rubbish. It's all Mel feels she can do to keep a nightwatch like this, with the clouds lit red above and a paroxysm of jagged thought threatening to burst in her. A haze of smoke expands across her view of abandoned terraces, denuded trees, analogue aerials, chimney pots. Not for the first time tonight, an old habit feels more tangible than the ghosts that usually haunt her from negative space.

Cassie arrives first, as Cassie always does.

"Hi sweet," Mel says, hoping not to scare her.

"M? You doing out here?"

"We're closed tonight."

"How come?"

"Just head home, Cass. I'll pay you all double tomorrow."

"But we've got–"

"Don't hang about. And if you see any others on their way in, tell them the same from me."

Cassie's jaw sets. "It's him again, isn't it? You know I can call heads down here."

"No. It's not him. Just get yourself home. And anyway – this lot round the corner'll be kicking off the second that fire's out. We'll have cordons both ends of the road."

"You seen the size of it? Won't be going out any time soon – they're still chucking stuff on it."

"No," Mel says. A weary sigh. Then: "Please, love. I'll make it up to you when I can."

Cass looks out the gate. The little square yard with its dented tin bins. "Fine," she says.

Mel smiles sadly. "Everything's grand," she says.

"You swear?"

"Yes."

"Well, you take it easy." And Cassie waves and heads back through the gate.

Mel sparks up another cig, resumes her vigil. Thick clumps of ash have started to fall in the yard. Again a temptation gnaws the insides of her arms, accompanied by a taste – bitter – that makes her salivate. There's already a pile of dimps at her feet, and her fake eye is sore, sticking.

Then it's dark. The early hours rolling around. And sooner still the inevitable arrives at the Cat Flap's front door. Mel was dreading this sound: bone on steel, the building ringing with it. She removes her blanket as the thumps come again; eases the back door shut and moves along the corridor towards a certain fate. Down here, at this time, you're so used to hearing laughter, pleasure, and the peace is unnerving. She pauses at the stairs: from Cassie's room comes the faintest report of clinking, dink-dink tinkering. A gentle interaction of precious metal that's almost xylophonic. Is it folly to guess? Silly to presume? She takes the stairs and wonders if she should go in, but a lifetime of distracted looks and bad moods has taught her not to interrupt Sol while he's working.

Knock knock knock. And a voice, stern and crisp: "Open up, Melanie."

From the landing, black damp risen as if to a high tide mark, she looks down at Jase. Suited, booted, immaculate. He's alone, which surprises her. Maybe he doesn't know. Maybe –

Mel goes back downstairs and enters the little kitchen alcove; washes her hands. She stoops down to the washing machine and picks out a pair of sheer stockings.

As she goes to the reception cage, she carefully pushes one of the stockings into the other. Puts the paired stockings down, and opens the shutters remotely. Her little camera flickers on, slaved monitor hissing.

Jase looks into the camera.

"Wondered when you'd show up," Mel says into the output. She puts the stockings in her pocket.

"You going to let me in?"

Mel comes across the waiting room. She unlocks the inner door, unbolts the outer. Deep breath. She opens the door a crack and talks to him through the shutters.

Jase peers through. "Melanie," he says. "Sorry it's so late. Got a few?"

"Might do," Mel says back. "What tripe you flogging now?"

He grins and puts a finger to his cheek. "You look knackered. Rough night?"

She slides the chain. Jase looks coiled, holding something back. She opens the door wide and almost reconsiders.

"I'm fine," she tells him. "I'm fine."

Jase steps into the building, taller than Mel remembers. "Didn't realize you shuttered the doors up here," he says. There's not much between them in the hallway, and the tinted glass dims their skins to a sickly hue.

"Huge bonfire over on the supermarket. I thought there'd be trouble. Usually boots off."

"The bins, is it? Saw a few things smouldering over my way too. But still – been a while since they did a collection."

"Mmm," Mel says.

"So. Let's cut to it. How's our little helper getting on?"

He does know. Mel's sure of it. *He knows Jeff's gone and now he's blagging.* She swallows. "Good." Swallow. "Really well, yeah. He gets on alright with the girls."

"Great news," Jase says. "I'm made up for you."

Change the subject. "You want a brew, something to eat? Come through, yeah – can't see you properly in here. I'll get the kettle on while we chat. Filtered, so it tastes pretty good."

"Go on then."

Jase walks ahead of her. Into the waiting room. She closes the inner door and clocks the outline of his wallet with a lump in her throat – this could be easier than she thought.

Now? Do it now?

"Where's the big man then?"

"Nipped out for us. Milk. A few other essentials…"

"What, like proper milk?"

Mel racks her brains. *Was there any this week?* It's a dance. It's like a dance. "Yes," she says, a little too firmly.

Jase stops where he is. His eyebrows rise a touch. "You've got him doing long days then? Because I think you should–"

"Cold in here, isn't it?" Mel interrupts. "That bloody heater on the blink."

"It's fine, Melanie," Jase says. His voice is getting terser.

"Well–"

"Listen. You need to know when your next delivery's coming."

Mel's heart sinks. She could crumble right there. How did she not see it coming?

She puts a brave face on it. "Our next what? Come through, come through, come on – this foyer's too nippy… Got a much cosier spot for the guests I know."

Jase stops pretending altogether. He turns full on. "How long did you think we'd let you enjoy a free service?"

Mel's trembling. She knows she can't let on. *He knows.* "Come on," she says. "We can talk about it." She shocks herself by touching his arm, rotating him towards the corridor. It seems to take him by surprise, too, and he moves there without resistance, apparently diverted. With his back turned, she crosses over herself, and – there, *yes* – dips into his pocket; two fingers like slivers, pincer-poised. She manages to sneak his wallet straight out.

Breathe. Breathe.

Jase strolls down the corridor oblivious to her theft. Straight ahead. Head reacting to a bang, something dropped upstairs. "I just think we need to have a sit down and a good chat," he says over his shoulder. "Wanted to ask a few things about your ex, too, actually. Head office interested for some reason." He's calm again. The veneer quickly reapplied. "And bend your ear about payment terms, your expectations, whether or not you want to extend your trial, and when we can expect you to start retiring your current stock." He smiles at her. There's a distilled cruelty in his face, but Mel nods and smiles sweetly back. *Play the game.*

They draw level with the store cupboard door.

"It's just by there, Jase," she says to him. "Yep, just round that way."

Now Mel pulls the stocking from her jeans pocket and simultaneously plucks her fake eye from its socket, lower lid, upper lid, an uncomfortable feeling of suction as it comes out unlubricated. *Thwock*. She drops the ball into the combined stockings, weighs it, and halts on her front foot.

Jase hears her shoe squeak and gain traction. He turns to find her hand in rotation – a grey rotor blur at the end of her arm.

Mel doesn't falter. She swings for him; her eyeball glances off his shoulder, connects with his neck. More from astonishment than pain, Jase crashes against the partition wall.

"Bitch," he says.

Mel makes a second attempt. This time the ball connects above his right ear with a deep crunch that resounds in the tightened space. Jase looks like he wants to say something else, something intangible, but Mel cuts him off with a third strike on his cheek. His face swells instantly.

"You can say that again," Mel tells him, breathing heavy.

Jase whimpers, on his backside with a hand out to steady him, the other up and defending his face. Mel reaches across him and opens the storeroom door. The smell of it, of Jeff. Rotten food. She swings the makeshift cosh once more, into his knee this time, and the glass ball halves on impact. Jase screams in pain, clutches his leg, and Mel kicks his shoulder so that he collapses into the cupboard.

She raises her hand. The two halves of her eye jangle in the stocking. Perfect friction. Jase doesn't speak, but crabs backwards from her in retreat.

Mel grabs the door handle, pulls it to. She locks it and pockets the key.

"There," she says to herself. "There's your fucking retirement."

The waiting room is peaceful. Mel sits in a wreath of blue smoke that hangs in the room like a rain cloud seen from a distance. She watches the smoke churn, impossible fluid, while absentmindedly tracking the conjunctiva of her empty socket with a finger. She listens to Jase pounding the cupboard door. He'd tire soon, wouldn't he? She's already turned out his wallet – a credit card, a clip of petty cash – on the floor. On top of the pile, a set of calling cards inscribed with two overlapping circles, wrapped in a list of local addresses. Who are these people? Who are their Jeffs? And who will turn up next?

Sol sleeps at the foot of Cassie's bed like a cat by the fire. In one hand, a multi-tool with attachments splayed. In the other, loosely, his collar, turned up into his chin. He's snoring.

Y stands up on the bed to begin with, angling pressure down through her feet. Her curious weightlessness has persisted. She articulates her knee and hip joints – carefully shifting weight from the ball and arch of one foot to the other.

Now she stretches upwards. All three arms, the stem of a flower in time-lapse, pushed up, hands and fingers straight, splayed, before they blossom into three petals and spread, a satisfying pop sounding off in her doubled shoulder. Each arm feels so new. Even the splits in her skin have resealed themselves.

From this bloomed stance she dives forward to touch

her toes. Her back lengthens, and her stomach muscles engage. It's the best kind of stretch: relief bordering pain. Long lengths of pleasure.

She smiles, then: how liberated she feels to escape that locked-up body, her doppelgänger in the ceiling mirror. The afterimage of the reflection is now stark but dreamlike: her limbs open, Sol discovering the truths of her implants and biomechanics, untangling her pieces as if she were constructed from a series of interconnected lockets. The decorated face of this stranger on her chest, his half-head rolled and manipulated into new shapes depending on Sol's progress. But what strikes her most is the bliss she feels. A reconciliation with herself, almost. As if she accepts now she won't get her old self back – that her old identity is gone – yet recognizes that she alone has forged a new one, shaped it herself. Not under orders, but in spite of them. Not uncaring, but filled with a compassion; a will to resist that the makers could never scrape clean.

Y looks down at Sol. Is friendship right? Is this man a friend? Would she do the same for him? Objectively, she thinks there's an answer: despite the opportunity it presented, she'd responded instinctively to the unconscious Roy's ankle injury without even knowing who he was. The basics of wound treatment, triage, had flooded to her from some hidden reservoir. Whatever the makers had deleted, there'd been no empathy bypass. She felt for him, this man, this damp human, fatty and unmodified, just as she'd felt for the brothers and sisters who couldn't sleep in their cradles.

Oppositely, however, stands the partitioned memory of her response to Jeff's advances. The ferocity, the skin and mechanics of another Y – one who'd crushed Jeff's throat and pushed his glitzy eyes deep inside his head, her bulk against his assumed right to dominate her. Acceptance or not, induced or teased out: barbarity is also part of her, entwined with her. She knows she can mete out lethal force on her terms as well as the makers'. That with these three hands, it's easy enough to take as well as give.

So yes, she'd do the same for Sol.

Down from the bed, she crouches and touches his face – hot, sticky. His yellowy eyes open, adjust, and there her face glistens on the bowls of his irises.

"You're up," he says.

Y nods.

Sol rubs his stubble. "Look at you."

Y smooths down her arms. She demonstrates for him her fresh dexterity, hesitating briefly when his eyes brim over.

He sniffs it up and says, "You don't hurt? You aren't just saying?"

Y shakes her head.

He laughs through the tears. "Even without that thing in you?"

Y looks to the corner of the room. A sports bag with both handles fastened. She crackles.

"You need something warmer on," he tells her. She observes him closely, his body language at variance with his words. He's either completely overawed or coping with an untenable guilt. "Have a good root in these drawers before you catch your death," he adds. Then, looking away: "I'll… I'll just be downstairs with Melanie."

What is Sol frightened by? Does his relationship with the woman complicate something? After he leaves, Y humours him and rummages for a while – finding a second pair of tracksuit bottoms and a hoodie. These she matches with long knitted socks and a pair of low heels that make her walk strangely. She doesn't like the way they stretch her calves.

Clomping out of the room, she stops by the dresser. A thousand other times she might not have; might not have even noticed the object Sol left on its corner, or recognized it as technology from the other side. Her other side. But the object, this little square, metallic circle at its core, is definitely a detail of the sister-world. And as she picks it up, she knows without question what it's for.

A knotty ball of certainty glowing inside, Y holds the square closer. Written down one edge, in glyphs she can read, are two words: BINARY DECODER. Y holds the device to her throat and feels the primordial pull of two opposing magnets desperate – or destined – to meet.

Y follows the sound of Sol's voice along a first-floor corridor she doesn't recall being carried through, paralyzed as she'd been around the rebar running from nape to spinal base. With the throatpiece in place, she relishes a new sensitivity to the environment; calibrates herself to the frequency of passing traffic, animals calling, a rich cocktail of polymer fumes, carbon molecules. Compounds forming or breaking down. She reaches a staircase; takes the stairs in twos, attuned and silent. Perfect noise between her ears, a melody of precision, her head vibrant with sensory mass.

Y lingers in the doorway unnoticed and sees Melanie balled up, legs crossed, trying to occupy as little space as possible on the waiting room bench. Sol's stooped over a washing basket marked LOST PROPERTY.

"Alright to use the phone?" Sol asks Mel.

"Do I have a choice?"

Sol gives her the thumbs-up. He's got the phone to his

ear when he finally notices Y in the doorway. "Oh," he says, and lowers the handset to his chest.

Y steps out of the heels and enters the foyer self-consciously, finding it odd that the woman simply accepts her presence. She's seen that glassy stare before: perhaps the woman's been sedated in some way.

"Sit down then," Mel says to her, patting the bench. "You'll make me feel uncomfortable."

"Found you a fleece and a shell jacket," Sol says, gesturing to a pile of clothing. "More than enough to be going on with anyway. Definitely good enough for a quick shower. And some boots. What size are those–"

Sol stops talking. Mel takes notice.

"What is it?" she says.

"Y?"

Y opens her mouth and emits a low crackle that rises with a shape, a timbre, through an unstable register. As she babbles, crackles, her tongue against her teeth, she finally lets out two definable words: "Good hello."

Sol's mouth hangs open.

"Hel-lo," Y says again. The paired syllables leave her throatbox with a sound of metal scraping metal. "Man Sol."

Mel unwinds from the bench and plants her feet. She's glaring at Sol, willing him to respond.

Y shrugs. "It's me, man Solomon."

The mundanity of the environment serves to amplify Y's voice, and Sol starts to sweat. He tries to say "What?" but it's stifled, trapped. To Y he looks visibly weakened – a loosening of his posture she takes to signal either relief or capitulation.

"Sol," Mel says. "What's wrong?"

Y steps backwards.

Sol clears his throat. "Do it again," he says. Clearer

now. "Say it again."

"Hello," Y repeats, her mouth clicking. This time she looks embarrassed by it: the motorized translation of so many little ones and zeroes, compressed and squirted through the valve of her throat.

"You're talking, Y."

"But Y is not the principal moniker," she says.

It takes effort, Sol realizes. Does it hurt her? Does it chafe? "I don't–"

"There is sorry," Y says.

"Sorry?"

She points at her third arm, more urgent. "There is… theirs are… there are apologies."

"For what?"

"The abode of Sol, your ally – the man Roy."

Sol clutches his forehead. The oddest sensation that gravity's failed. Again the powerful urge to hold her, to make this a celebration of them, and of providence. And yet he's breaking up inside. The noise of the throatpiece is as alien as it's frightening.

"Roy wasn't a friend, not a real friend," Sol says. He holds his nose. "Sometimes you meet people and you try to turn your cheek. Even when they've got an arm round your neck."

"He was our friend," Y says. The throatpiece bobs on her neck. And then she begins to laugh, her whole body convulsing, and the module translates it as a hacking cough.

If it's not painful, it's tickling her, Sol thinks. "I found that thing," he says, touching his Adam's apple. "The thing over your throat. In a car, with a biohazard suit. There was this crate, and a woman. Sandy–"

At the very mention of her name, Y scowls and begins to chirrup angrily. Sol grimaces and steps back – Y's module's shrill at the top end. How insensitive could he be? Of course she and Sandy had met. But does this confirm that the Audi's crate held Y's accessories? Or do more of them have her tattooed, expandable throat?

Y grunts. "Sandy is a betrayer," she says.

"She's gone," Sol tells her, picturing the abject spray on the interior of Sandy's windscreen, the gun barrel poking from her ribs. Y was sleeping then; couldn't have known. But what difference does it make? "I can't do this," he says. And with that he severs the link; turns and crouches down to pick through more clothing. "Maybe these," he mumbles, pushing away scarves and gloves. "All these warm things."

"Sol," Mel says.

"Can I use your phone again?" he asks.

Mel shakes her head. It's not his fault. Where others might consider it rude, even obnoxious, she recognizes the diversion. Sol's scared witless, and now he's disengaged to protect something of himself. That stubborn selfishness prevailing. Anything to avoid what really seems to be happening.

Sol produces a mid-length peacoat, navy, heavily bobbled, that he tries on for himself; pulls tight round his body. He turns and makes a satisfied face as if Y has left the room entirely, or never came in to start with. "Got taste, your forgetful johns," he murmurs.

Y is locked. Patient. Is she being respectful of the situation? Or simply analyzing it? It jolts Mel to realize another woman might comprehend Sol, has invested the time necessary to. And by the way Y gawps at her, it's clear she's noticed the hollow eye socket, too. "*Sol*," Mel whispers, rearranging her fringe to hide the cavity.

He ignores her.

"I think she needs you."

"Who needs me?" Sol asks. "No one needs me. I can't."

Y crosses the room. A broken stride, a distortion or imbalance on one side. She picks up and envelops herself in the fleece he's found. "Good base layer," Mel says. "Sol, I think you should listen."

"You don't understand," Sol says under his breath. "You never understand."

Behind him, Y puts two hands on Sol's shoulders. A third, tentatively, in the small of his back.

Mel inhales.

"A steeple," Y says, letting go and pressing her three hands together into a pyramid. The module's attempts at restraint are lacking, and her words sound more sinister than soft.

Carefully, Sol straightens up. He drops the sweater in his hands. "A steeple?" He twists to her, takes her two hands in one of his.

Carefully she places her third hand on his chin. "No," she says. "A tower."

"A tower."

"My tower," Y says. "Where the circles convene."

Sol blinks at her.

"I must revoke the father's ownership," she says. This time the words are perfect – the module enunciating each one with unnerving precision.

"Your father?"

"Not mine."

"But the person who sent you."

A curt nod. Then, "He sent all. He watches."

"From the tower."

"Yes," Y says.

"I think I know where it is," he says. "Your tower."

Mel exhales. While she doesn't get what they're

talking about, he's come back from some edge, returned to them. Now she's witnessing their fears entangle. A perverse thought pops: *I already had my time with him.*

"I'm sorry for what they've done," Sol says. "I am."

"Why?" Y asks. She taps the throatpiece. "I have a name. I found my name."

"Then tell us," Sol says.

SIXTEEN

In the waiting room of the parlour in Mel's corner of the city, Y repeats the name in ratatat bursts – ejects it from her throat in triplets.

"Yasmin, Yasmin, *Yasmin*. Yasmin, Yasmin, *Yasmin*…"

Regardless of the mechanics – is the binary encoded from *thought*? She doesn't *think* in binary – it thrills and scares her to know she's carried a voice disguised even from her own ears for so long. In one way it completes the picture – nestles alongside her skills, attributes and personality traits as things to apprehend, to slowly tame and use. It also gives her a fresh perspective on who she might have been before the makers remade her, before the Manor Lord chose her, marked her. There are fresh assumptions she feels sure she could verify if time were more malleable: the sound and shape of her mother tongue, a genetic aptitude for physical tasks, a probably genetic tenacity. A familiarity with structures, a knowledge of the semiotics and symbology of these structures. *Towers*. And was there always potential for her to be so nimble, so physically powerful, so controlled? Was that why they selected her? In a strange way, her voice also trickled into the void of her parentage. Were they like her? Had they been contrarians, too?

She's now convinced she lived her first life in this sister-world.

Yasmin. Yasmin. Yasmin.

To hear it now feels no less significant than hearing Sandy say it in that grey car park, beneath those black, swinging bags. And though the throatpiece seems to interpret the binary and sometimes mangle it, it feels like something else she's recovered. A bridge between interior and exterior repaired.

With a voice, she is more human.

And so she repeats her name to Sol and Melanie like a mantra, and tries to think of a sentence, a phrase, some kind of grand statement, an answer to all of Sol's questions. This, though, is too hard. She and Sol like two old friends, reunited, who have so much to say, to fill in, they barely know where to start.

Thank you?

Good luck?

The Manor Lord is always watching, and now I must shut his eyes?

Perhaps the thing she most wants to say is *I'll take care of you* – knowing how she can. The thing is, it's too important, and she's frightened of how the throatpiece might translate it.

Sol's made his mind up. If they're going to do this – if he and Yasmin are going back to her tower together – he first needs to confirm something for himself.

"I need to get online," he goes to Mel, the three of them inert, exhausted, in the Cat Flap's kitchen. Sitting like relatives waiting for the worst news. "Ten minutes at most."

Mel isn't sure. "I wouldn't know where to start," she tells him. "Though I heard it's being opened up to the public again."

"How secure's your line?" Sol asks. He sips a mug of rainwater poured straight from the butt outside.

"The phone line?"

"Yeah."

"It's just a phone."

Sol purses his lips.

"Am I missing something?"

"I just need to ring someone."

"Why?"

He doesn't want to explain that he doesn't know who's complicit in this, that he'd rather be safer than sorry. That they'll catch up with him eventually. "I just do."

"And what about Yasmin?"

Her full name still sounds so novel. Sol hasn't said it enough to normalize it; to copy over the previous version. He likes it, certainly – loves what it means for the woman he's called Y for what seems so long now. But it isn't quite hers yet.

Yasmin bares her teeth at them.

"I want you to stay here," he tells them, wavering on the last word. There's a firmness in his voice – a clear resolve. He kneads his hands in front of him. "And try and find Yasmin some decent boots."

Neither woman responds. It's not difficult to feel like he's palming Yasmin off on Mel, or that she's unwelcome to go with him. Maybe that's the truth of it. He reflects on the ways Roy's influence might've taken root – if he's learned something other than how to fear the man's assertiveness. Thinking about Roy also makes him feel resentful: Roy would know exactly how to get online without any fuss. He'd know someone. Course he'd know someone.

"That OK?" he asks.

"Yes," Yasmin says, and the tone's softer. With his engineering hat on, Sol guesses she's starting to understand the throatpiece's parameters; that she can temper, recalibrate the muscles that feed sound into it. Modified as she is, that seems plausible enough.

Beyond the basics, though, they still haven't found a way to maintain a conversation.

"Keep it all shut," Sol says, as if that wasn't obvious.

"We'll make do," Mel says. "But there's something else."

"What?"

Yasmin places her three hands on the table in front of her. She cranes her neck, waiting for Mel to carry on.

"Nothing, actually," she says, picturing Jase. "I'm just thinking out loud. You can go out the back way."

Sol settles his mug. Mel with an expression dredged from a landfilled past. She's lying, and he can't dig in. "Then look after each other," he says, and moves for the door.

"That's what we do," Mel says behind him. "That's how it works here."

Beyond the Cat Flap, Sol turns past the supermarket car park, where an enormous debris pile still burns, into a row of razed terraces. He's reminded what a sad bit of the city this is, heart pounding as he remembers Mel confirming what she planned to do with her half of the money. Telling him about the friends she'd made on the street. "We've got to make our own way now," she'd told him gleefully, as if the Cat Flap's cheap ground rent was the only reason to put up with its adjoining decay. Strangely it made him ashamed – not of her, nor of her choices, but of himself. He wishes he'd told her once how proud he was of her recovery, of what she achieved. More than that, he wishes he had the consent to even have an opinion on her life.

Sol walks on. The destitution is astonishing: swathes of ruins; barren tree roots spidering from churned earth; a homogeneity to the housing foundations that evoke the battlements of a castle parapet nearly buried. Alien moonscape, monochromatic dream. And he's glad that all the discarded shoes he passes, many of them children's shoes, tied by the laces, remain inscrutable.

This lunar slew ends at a sort of inner-city border: a block of tall, still-standing buildings that leer down at his approach. At these bounds of inner Manchester – Ancoats the threshold – he finds a windowless phonebox with a rotten floor and a hot toilet smell. He wedges the door and throws in a few coins. Then he dials right into the order chain – his call bounced from link to link until a Swansea accent pipes through.

"Who's this?"

"It's me. Mr Manchester."

Silence. Then, "You're not at home, are you?"

"No home to go to."

Miss Wales chuckles. "You graft too hard, you do."

Sol's more comforted by her voice than he wants to admit.

"Wanting updates on the shipment, are you?"

"No no, that all came."

"Just checking. What is it, then?"

Sol sucks air through his teeth. When did he last clean them? "I need a favour."

Another pause. "Favours? Haven't done favours in *years*."

Sol doesn't say anything.

"Go on then…"

"I need to get online. Securely, though. I know it's easy enough if you ask the right people. But I can't have interference, monitoring, nothing. No one can know what I'm looking at. Not anyone. Not even the people I'm borrowing the connection from."

"And what *are* you looking at?"

Sol settles his head on the phonebox frame. "Just… travel plans. I'm making travel plans. Serious, though – anything you can do…" Hearing a note of desperation creeping in, he cuts himself short.

Miss Wales' pen goes click click click. "You know," she says, "I'm sure we've got a connector holed up near you." Paper shuffling. "I'm sure we do. Let me just check my doo-dah." Sol hears her half-covering the phone, muffled shouting to someone else. How many of them work there? A rustling, and she's back. "I'm always bloody right, aren't I? Brian he's called. Brian. Cute, that, isn't it? Brian. I think he does server hosting for us. Good, innit, this proxy business."

"Brian," Sol says.

"He's your best bet. Unless you feel like going cross-country. We do run our own stations further south – a few guys closer to us in Bristol, Merthyr. Obviously wouldn't recommend London unless you want ructions…"

"Brian," Sol repeats. "Brian's fine."

Miss Wales stops tapping the pen. "You know, if it's a quick fix, you should just knock on doors. Won't take too long to find someone handy – you'd be surprised how many'll get round it. All them little ones weened on code…"

"Maybe."

"If you're really paranoid, though, it's tunnels or bust. Tunnels or bust."

Sol closes his eyes. There's always a compromise. He looks ahead. In the distance, a patrol lev whines across the sky, engines crackling. It weaves its way through the crowded towers of the central block with a flock of pigeons keeping pace, attendant, like the pilot fish that nurse sharks. Every few seconds the bird cloud morphs, reimagines itself. Something about the movement makes him wonder how easy it'd be for him and Yasmin to hop the city entirely. The coast further north, maybe. A North Sea wind.

"I think I'll stick to who I trust," he says.

Miss Wales laughs. "You're very flattering."

"How soon can I see him?"

"Brian? Can get it teed up for tonight, if you like."

Sol shakes his head. "Probably too soon. Need wheels first."

"Tomorrow? Day after? Bear in mind he'll have you jumping through hoops. Nobody my end likes taking risks, so it'll be on my word he agrees to meet you."

In the phonebox, the air stops moving, as if the massed particles around him have become a superconductor for some coming malignancy. "Tomorrow then," Sol says, gambling on Irish. He wipes his forehead with the back of his arm. Knife slashes on the glass. It's started raining again.

How do you say goodbye to someone you've already left? Do you sneak out? Do you leave, casually, with a kind of breezy farewell that suggests you might see them again soon? Or do you repeat the whole sorry process – retreading the emotions of it, that rawness, looping up the present moment with a fixed point, a rupture of the past, in the way you might create wormholes by folding the universe itself?

Sol stands with Mel and Yasmin in the Cat Flap's waiting room, wondering how best to let go. Mel appears lost in herself, navigating her own labyrinth. Sol can see it in her single eye's movements – slowly down and up, briefly to either side, like an animal doublechecking its surroundings. A rueful glance at her watch, then back at Sol. Finally, a look of veneration for Yasmin, before she starts the sequence again.

It keeps occurring to Sol that an outsider – a punter – might peer through the boarded windows and mistake them for a family. Maybe they'd be preparing to go on holiday, waiting on their airport transfer. God, it'd been so long since a morning like that. You get calluses on those memories; the fixtures of their old normality rubbing up against the casual horrors of the new –

"When we are ready?" Yasmin asks, syntax just out. Sol smiles: it's like she understands how this scene would appear to a stranger, too. She's all layered up, the sports bag containing the cylinder by her feet. And she keeps stretching her legs – apparently to check they're still working as they did ten minutes ago.

"He won't be long now," Sol tells her, hoping it isn't a lie. He's in the big peacoat, getting warm inside it. He imagines their next movements, and runs through Miss Wales' instructions for contacting Brian. And then he goes back to how he'll leave her this time.

Mel clears her throat. She hovers on something, then dismisses it. Another moment passes, and she speaks anyway. "Do you trust him?" she asks Yasmin, apropos of everything that's ever happened since they met on that frothy beach and poked dying fish as their parents ignored them on the dunes.

Yasmin doesn't answer directly. Instead she wraps a hand around her chin.

"Do *you* trust *me*?" Sol asks Mel.

Mel shrugs. "Would you?"

Sol shrugs back. In some small way, he knows this is the answer: that this is how they leave it. Not with a speech or an apology, not with tears or mumbled regrets, but with an exchange of indifferent, tired pleasantries, and the conviction that things never stopped changing.

At last a V8 purr pulls Sol out of the Cat Flap and into the road. Fresh air balms the cuts in his fingers, chills the sweat on his palms. "Stay in there," he calls inside.

The Ferrari: a gothic wedge with comically flared arches. Its prancing horse on a yellow badge just ahead of its front alloys. Irish winds down the passenger window and leans across. "Travelling light, fat boy?"

Sol grins a full rack of teeth. "It's a frigging Mondial," he says. "And it isn't red."

Irish climbs out of the car and throws Sol the keys. "Mondial T. Different beast. And anyway – red's what the wankers go for."

"Think I expected a 360," Sol says, shaking his partner's cold hand. "Or maybe a Rossa. What you dream about when you're a nipper."

The corners of Irish's mouth curl downwards. "Same chassis as your 360," he replies, and starts listing on his fingers: "Power-assisted steering. Mid-engined, tasty whine at the top end, not too throaty. And look at it, Solomon, heavens be: just look at it. It's a fucken ninja. Steel body, box section space frame… moan all you want, but given your nasty timelines the welding was a dream. Even replaced your engine cover. Went with new springs and dampers, stronger sus-arms and a set of big old pots. Otherwise it'd go like a fucken blancmange round every corner."

Irish circles the thing, clearly proud of his work. When he comes back, Sol can't help but drape an arm round his shoulder.

"Been a week," Sol says.

Irish wriggles away. "Get on with yourself. You drag me out here to this whorehouse and now you want a cuddle as well?"

"I mean I appreciate it, Pete. It's..."

"Who's *Pete?* You keep doing that! What's with all the small talk?"

Sol laughs nervously. Perhaps their appreciation of the Ferrari is all that's left to bind them – or distract them from a glaring rift. The pair of them stand there, stomachs unsettled, half admiring the car. No mistake: it looks battle-ready. Sol knows the average drone system wouldn't tell it's been modded, and it excites him to know its hidden features are designed with his whims in mind. A bloodlusty vision, then: the car colliding with Roy's murderers –

"Is it heavy?" Sol asks, grasping.

Irish nods. "Course. More than a few horses got away, but it still goes like shit off a shovel. Inch-thick box for your legs. All the doors are lined. The chassis is dripping with it. Radiator's drilled out and replaced. Blast film for all the windows. Steel-sheeted the rear. It's a tank. It'll drink a lot of juice, mind..."

Sol steps forward, runs a finger over the paintwork, then under the arches. He stands up and sniffs his fingers. "It's rusty."

Irish rolls his eyes. "It came out of a canal, Solomon. It'll be damp as ballbags for a long while yet. But mechanically, it's sound – and you wouldn't wanna get in its way."

Sol smiles.

"Well? You telling me what the bejesus you're playing at?"

"I wouldn't know where to start."

"It's not you and her, is it? You running away again?"

"No, not really."

"Ach, your cryptic bollocks. How long's it gonna be?"

"Not much longer."

"And work?"

Sol suppresses a wince. Do the ends justify the means? He knows the workshop is unsafe, even without the bikers, or Jeff. Mel's contact Jase, the card on the Reverend's mat, the boxes and Leila's mob at Knutsford Services – all these stack up to a bigger threat, something monstrous, larger than he can comprehend. But at the same time he knows Irish can't stay away forever. He has little choice but to assume Irish's absence gives him an alibi. A perverse sense it's only *him* being hunted. "Do what you can," he says, with the feeling of a cold finger stretching up his throat. *Because Yasmin's my priority.* "Any cash is yours. Whatever comes in till I'm back – and I mean all of it, plus what we're owed. Pay some bagheads to graft if you need to. That bastard Transit's still up on the ramp…"

Irish gazes at him, mystified. It's rare for Sol to see him this way: expectant, stricken by concern.

"You'll find a note from me there," Sol tells him. "Just ignore it. And if anyone comes asking for me – anyone at all, asking for my name, where I am, or about the project, you tell them they're knocking on the wrong door. The handler didn't cough up, so they should take their shit to him, this Reverend. Out in Stalybridge."

"The Reverend? That guy in Emerald City?"

"You know him?"

"Half the fucken city knows him, Solomon. He's an animal. How've you got us involved with him? Is this her as well?" He points to the front door. "I swear she's bad news."

Sol bites his lip. He wants to say, *I think the Reverend buys trafficked women.* Instead he follows the Ferrari's lines to vanishing point; its paintwork catching the light in such unpredictable ways.

"I'll get off then, should I?"

"I didn't mean—"

"You've gone weird," Irish says. "Cold. It's fucken sketchy, all this."

Sol turns and scoops his partner's hand. He pulls it, pulls Irish into his peacoat. He says, breathy in the man's ear, "Thank you, brother."

Irish pulls back, confused. He shakes his head and steps away, angled as if to sprint off.

Sol doesn't say anything else. He knows it'll be the longest walk.

The departing Ferrari skates a near-lagoon of black standing water, appearing to carve out a bow wave from the tarmac itself. Mel watches the water resettle and the car's circular sidelights defocus to cooling hob-rings, its outline bleeding into the night.

For some reason, caught alone there at this hour, she prays for an inversion: for Manchester to run hot, tropical – its fine rain turned to steam. In this humid republic, lampposts swinging with dead bulbs become verdant palm trees; pigeons become parrots; and the sharpline thickets and bird-spikes morph into exotic plants. And then from pothole puddles rise fresh mosquitoes like vapour, fluid under Mel's command. These she'd send after Sol and Yasmin, away across old Albion's leylines, the city's hidden tracks and tunnels and channels, to surround their car and shield it from harm.

Mel shivers. In with a cigarette and out from the heart. The Ferrari indicates and dips off towards the motorway. Mel drops her cigarette, listens to its hissing death. She pulls away the strands of hair that have blown across her socket. She'd better find her spare.

Back inside, though, Mel is preoccupied by change. Her idea is simple: she sits in the reception cage, flattens the menu and scratches every price from it. She'll make the Cat Flap a collective – let the girls decide their rates. She loads a new film tape into the monitor bank with a heavy gut. She switches on the front door cameras. Smiles at herself. Jase there in the cupboard can bang the doors and walls all he wants, because she's got things to do.

She watches the camera feed for a time. Adjusts the focus. She'd made a mistake with Jeff, pushed into a decision that didn't bear scrutiny, and put imagined profit before their safety. It was a misjudgment, and it wouldn't happen again. She and the women would make this work – will make their living how they like, serving the punters they know, many they trust – because that's their choice, and this their space. She's come too far to compromise. The alternative – stolen people, Jase's half-people, the girls going back on the streets – is intolerable. And why should she run from the only city she knows?

On the Princess Road, damp overalls hugged by the bucket seat, Sol tweaks the Ferrari's throttle. The Mondial is undeterred, unscarred, by its near-drowning, even if filthy water still sloshes around in

the instrument binnacles. The road's poor surface is
forgiving at least: normally you'd expect a harsher
ride owing to low-profile tyres, especially with the
weighted suspension, but Irish has even thought to
mod the bushes so there's a more generous wallow
in the arches. Enough roll for decent feedback, if you
don't take the corners too fast. This he learns as they
leave a roundabout: Yasmin tipping against him with
all her shoulder mass.

More than straight, Princess Road is long – running
all the way out to the M60. Their journey there is
soundtracked by the sweetness of fourth gear, the hiss
and whine of the engine bulk, rear-mid, right by their
legs. A sense of velocity enhanced by their closeness
to the ground, and the low slung seats that have them
almost reclining.

Traffic lights. Bleak terraces ranged left. Naked football
pitches right. Sol downshifts, the gearknob a cold ball in
his fist. A chance to doublecheck Miss Wales' directions
scrawled on the back of it. From here they pass under
the Hulme Arch, headlights picking out the cables
fanning out from its bowed beams. Unseen debris rattles
the undercarriage – all the road markings are missing
here, and the potholes are more like craters.

Cabin-wise, the Mondial has subverted Sol's
expectations. He expected sharper edges, rough welds,
but Irish has been fastidious, and the extra steel is
perfectly applied. It looks like a Ferrari. It feels and
sounds like a Ferrari. It just about drives like one.

Finally Sol speaks. "Was it out or in?" he asks. "I keep
forgetting what he said. Roy – about the crates."

Yasmin points out of the window. "Out?" She points
at Sol. "No, in," she says. She giggles gently.

"In," Sol says.

Yasmin nods.

"You know your left and your right, don't you?"

Yasmin holds up three hands to him. "Left, median, right," she says, and laughs fully.

"We're stopping for petrol in a minute," he tells her. "And we're going to meet someone."

Yasmin stills.

"Fluids," Yasmin says, then looks frustrated with herself. "No. Buy bottled water."

The petrol station is more a bank of graffitied shutters, spilled oil, scarred with overuse. The attendant-cum-guard lets on – plainly can't believe what he's seeing. He lowers his shotgun as the Mondial pulls across the forecourt, and doesn't say a word when Sol pays at the grate – forty pounds and a penny. An extra fiver as a warning: keep your mouth shut. A few pieces of shrapnel dropped in a charity pot for some unknown war, some other lost cause.

"You hiding from?" Sol asks Yasmin as he gets back in the Ferrari. She's got a sleeve over her mouth, nibbling loose thread off it. After a few seconds, he realizes why – petrol fumes.

"Old cars," he says. "I quite like it." He rolls down his window, then leans across to do hers. "Let's sling it over there, shall we. And here – shove these bottles in the bag."

They park up. They wait. Just enough time to ponder what could've been if he and Irish had taken the cheap hatchback instead of the Lexus. Had he chosen to stay legit, honour his father's work ethic.

A car pulls across the forecourt at almost exactly the time Miss Wales said it would. A nondescript saloon. Navy or purple, Sol can't tell. It turns and reverses up to the Ferrari so both drivers' windows sit adjacent.

Sol wipes his forehead. He says to Yasmin: "Keep your extras hidden."

Committed now –

The saloon's driver opens their window. An older man, late-fifties-ish, on first glance reminiscent to Sol of a stereotypical farmer: lank hair scraped over a balding pate, crusty with an obvious skin complaint. Ruddy nose, heavy brow, a weary expression. He's wearing a tightly wound scarf that appears more practical than fashion conscious, and Sol can't be sure it doesn't stick damply to the man's neck when he inhales.

"Brian?"

Beside him Yasmin has crushed herself into the seat.

"Don't bloody say it out loud," the man says. Sol can detect something on his breath – a marine scent, a seafront. It pervades the Ferrari. "They're listening," the man adds.

Sol might be in Roy's world now, but there's plenty left to learn.

"Right," Sol says. "So do we follow you from here?"

"Follow? No. You got the stuff, have you?"

Sol tries to pass the bung through the window. The wad of cash from Sandy's Audi.

Brian glares at him. "For God's sakes," he says. "Not here you numpty – put it away. Just answer. Have you. Got. The stuff?"

"Stuff? Cash? That's… it's all here."

Brian doesn't immediately react, and Sol notices the lingering smell has turned to rotten fish.

"We were raided this morning," Brian tells him. "We're waiting for the all-clear."

Fear pools in Sol's legs. Something nagging. "I'm lost. What do you mean?"

"I mean the council raided one of our tenants."

"Tenants," Sol says. "And what... what do you want me to do?"

"Wait. That's what I'm saying. Just hold your bloody horses – I have to take care."

"But–"

"Shh will you! You not clocked him over there?"

Sol hadn't, no. A burly man leaning against the petrol pump, staring at the Ferrari in partial disbelief. Sol bows his head: again his lack of awareness has undermined the act.

"And they told me you were an old hand," Brian snorts.

"I'm not used to–"

Brian puts a finger to his lips.

All paid up, the burly man gets back in his car, and no sooner than he's navigated the off-ramp, Brian opens his door. The gap reveals to Sol a blanket covering both of Brian's legs, which seem clumsily positioned, too close together, and a steering wheel adapted with driving aids. He's taller than Sol assumed, with a tattoo of dappled scales running in spirals from his stringy bicep to the back of his hand. From the passenger seat he retrieves two walking sticks and manoeuvres himself to get out of the car. Sol watches, fascinated, as Brian extends like a tripod onto his sticks and bundled feet. Then he goes like this to the boot of his car.

"Take this," Brian says, passing a carrier bag through Sol's window. Sol recognizes what's inside as a tablet of some sort – weighty, wrapped in a matt case. "It's disposable," Brian goes on, "so when you're done, stick it under your front wheel. No hard drive, no signature, and the case is fingerprint-resistant. Crypto-keys are automatic, so you'll connect by proxy the second you switch on. It'll be slow, unfortunately."

"Connect to what, though?"

"The frigging satellite," Brian says, throwing his head back.

"Satellite?"

"An old Soviet weather sat. How can you not even... Never mind. It does the jòb. We bounce info up... the sat bounces info down. All runs off our remote servers."

"OK," Sol says. "Great."

"Great? *Great?* Do I need to show you how to turn it on as well?"

"It's fine."

"Good," Brian says, and snatches the bung from Sol's resting hand. "You never met me, alright? Never seen me, spoke to me, nowt. And I'm talking about you *and* her in there. Bunch of fucking luddites."

"Wait," Sol says.

"What's up with you now?"

"You're from Emerald City."

Brian's face remains clear, but the smell of fish intensifies.

"Call you the Wizard, don't they?"

Brian rubs his head. Grains of abraded skin float free.

"And there's someone with you in there, in Emerald City. The Reverend."

Brian switches off his engine. His mouth's constricted. "What about him?"

"He buys people." How unreal it sounds. "Wives. He buys wives."

Brian goes to speak but falters. "People can be difficult," he says. "It's a big world. A big, cloudy world. You've got to live and let live."

"Against their will," Sol says. "And I think–"

Brian cuts him off with a groan, the façade fully gone. "You know something I bloody don't, do you?

You with the council?"

"What? Me?"

Brian exhales. Then, more angrily: "I knew she was nervy about you. I knew it. And you feigning indifference – the Reverend, that silly shit's why we just had a whole bloody lev squadron blowing holes in our front door. Grassed on by one of his regular gophers, he was. Taken a few others down with him, and all – some bigwig from London. Havelake, Haveland... Havelock? False imprisonment, people smuggling."

Sol reels. Brian's words boom at him. Tipped off? Regular gopher? *Roy?* His vision falters. *Roy grassed on the Reverend?* And then a logical stride: Roy knew more about the Reverend than he ever let on. And Roy knew more about the Reverend's client.

Sol's nervous system goes haywire.

But when? Sol had been with him since...

In the car. With Sandy.

What else had Sandy told him?

That arrogant walk to the portable toilet. That thumbs-up. Roy knew. He *knew*.

Brian restarts his car. "This is why I stay behind the curtain," he says. "Like a bloody soap opera." Then he pulls away – the smell of seaside in his wake.

Sol looks at his hands. His veins. His coordination failing.

"Manners," Yasmin says. She's trying not to laugh at something, and in the Mondial's cabin he sees how well her scabbed lips are improving. "He was incomplete," she adds, nodding firmly. "The Wizard. A semi-man."

Plenty happens on this backwards island we'll never understand.

"Small world, though," Sol says. "You might've been right about Roy."

He opens the tablet lid. A message reads: LINK IN 52 SECONDS, and the timer ticks down. Together they watch the screen, its glow flooding the car with weld-spark blue.

They say your muscles can remember. Sol finds it amazing what aging lets you forget. After so long, typing on a touchscreen feels like experimenting with some exotic hobby – there's a resignation that years of mastery lie ahead. For most people that's probably part of the fun, but for Sol, pecking at the screen with a single wavering forefinger, it's a perfect definition of frustrating. Without office experience, he was never great to begin with – preferring to write with that solid all-caps scrawl of the trader – but this precious time beneath the hijacked satellite make his efforts all the more desperate.

The tablet browser runs slowly, wheel chugging away in its centre. The connection is fleeting, in and out. He's already searched for his own name and related keywords – fire, business, flat, warrant, council. No meaningful results: just random stitched-together stories from disparate paragraphs, and an archived picture of his father on an old business directory, standing in front of his Bentley.

He turns to Yasmin and asks: "What first?" as if he hasn't already sat there looking for anything that might incriminate him.

"Tower," she says. "The tower first."

Sol grimaces.

"Go," she says, more insistent.

So Sol types *COOLING TOWER SEL* then backspaces to *COOLING TOWER* alone. Search. The page loads, white, to grey, rendering frames of content. A gallery of over-familiar shapes streams in. Seeing them, Yasmin releases an almost orgasmic noise. "Our crossing," she says. "He is there."

"Right," Sol says. Then he types SELLAFIELD.

The pictures load. Black and white, many of them – artistic shots, too. He'd be the last person to deny the anonymous allure of Sellafield, or of facilities like it. How was this tangle of process line and cables and scaffolding so crucial to the running of a country, yet so foreign, forbidding, to everyone but its workers? With its stark perimeter, barbed wire, sharpline fortifications, it carried an obvious foreboding: a concrete temple erected to commemorate man's triumph over physics, then bulwarked against the world.

The thought of getting inside excites Sol in the same way the Ferrari does.

It also excites Yasmin. "The tower," she says, pointing to the second in a run of four. Then to its base. "Entry here."

Sol scrolls down. At least a dozen of the images would make – would've made – a fine addition to his Polaroid collage. A centrepiece, even. But while there are four cooling towers in most of the images, there are no cooling towers evident in any newer shots – even in photographs taken from comparable angles. In most of these, even the two fearsome Windscale piles reactors have gone. And when he sorts the results by date, it's clear only the massive golf ball structure of the gas-cooled reactor still stands. Sol swears, confused, and refines his search to text on SELLAFIELD COOLING TOWERS. Fresh results strain through.

At random, he taps for a page whose description tag sounds relevant. Poorly formatted, almost illegible, the text loads up – describes the demolition of all four Calder Hall cooling towers in 2007.

His heart sinks.

"Yasmin," he says. "There aren't... They aren't there anymore. Your tower can't have been here."

"No," she urges. "I *passaged*."

"But towers like the one you drew don't exist at Sellafield, not anymore. They haven't for years." He's devastated. He thinks of Roy, the rumours he shared at Winnie's, and what happened at Knutsford Services. A hopelessness rises to engulf him.

"Go," she says. "Continue."

He flips the tablet. "There's nothing there, Yasmin. They pulled them down. I'm sorry – they're all gone. Says it plain as day: those towers were demolished nearly twenty years ago."

"No!" Yasmin shrieks. "You have to keep!" Her breathing has quickened; sounds like an angry creature rattling around in her chest cavity. She grabs the tablet and thrusts it in his face. "I see this and I know inside." She taps her breast. "You trust it. You trust me. He is still there. Watching."

"Yasmin... we can't just–"

She slaps the dashboard with all three hands. "Yes! We will!"

Sol bows his head and tabs back. Maybe another will dig something out, prove it wrong. With terms like what, though? His mind wheels. Sandy's car? The Lexus' registration number – RA, *Carlisle*. The boot and the organs crate.

Inspired, he tries SELLAFIELD ORGANS. Even the words together look outlandish. He feels Yasmin's breath on his forearm, fast and gentle.

The buffering wheel spins and results begin to filter through. Not just any results, either. Dozens of articles and book extracts and opinion pieces, masted below the old names of long-deceased publishers and newspapers. Sol flicks and engages: gaping at the scraps in silence. The tablet in his hands reveals a jumble of missing body parts scandals, unlawful tests on workers, radiation experimentation, disaster reportage. All of these things at one site. All these things at Sellafield.

He reads what he can of the first articles, heart racing. And this is only the front page – only the surface. What he consumes joins a widening slurry: while there's nothing that explicitly mentions the transportation of people, there's plenty to suggest their exploitation. And it's been an open secret for what must be years.

He drops the tablet between his legs.

"Yasmin."

"Trust," she says.

He picks up the tablet, reopens the browser. Some decisions can't be unmade. And there, broiling in his peacoat, Sol taps out one final search term.

SELLAFIELD MAP.

Y

Y woke on her side in a cramped space. An onyx chamber, polished and vast. There were green waveforms in the pitch.

Her face was hot and slimy, and she couldn't open or breathe through her mouth. She strained. No telling which way was up, which way was down. A rotten sum brought a distressing answer: something was tight around her head.

Escape mechanics fired. But quickly she remembered her arms were trussed up behind her back, and her legs were bound and stinging at the knees. When she tried to scream, wincing, eyes stinging, there was only the taste of a soft, bitter material in her mouth. And the pain of the staples cut in with a tearing sensation. Her jaw, too, was secured, the muscles in her chin allowing mere fractions of give before cramping up. She wrenched every ragged breath through her nose, retching on the moisture this pulled into her body. Her chest heaved – a purity to the terror she was drowning slowly.

Y kicked out. The pain in her knees was disgusting.

She wriggled and rolled, found herself maggoting over and over, blind and flailing, before she wedged herself across the space at an oblique angle. Again she was deluged with abstract pain. But now there was something cold, a curved panel, pressed up against her face, and its physicality gave her purchase.

Y turned over. She needed to calm down. Struggling made things worse – experience told her that. And she was starting to trust that voice. The air would last longer if she regulated her breathing…

Y exhaled and tensed all her muscles. Every sinew stressed. Y released, let it out until there was only her mind, a mess of foam on the wavecrest, and the pain ebbed.

She remembered this: a tooth lodged in her palm. An angry man with his fist held high. Deep stinging behind her knees. And the woman – Sandy, Sandy like her, chosen just like her – screaming beside them. A loud shot. The first bite of the stapler against her teeth. And then, emptiness. Nothing else before this.

She kept still until she was satisfied with her recollection of events. She understood, weakly, that she had been taken from Sandy's care. All the while, her ears were full of the sea. Her pulse. And there was another noise, ambient, further out. She recognized it as road drone.

Y was in transit again.

Eventually the vehicle came to rest. The sound from the tyres had changed from a soft burr to a noisy rattle – something granular kicked up and speckling the insides of the arch she'd stiffened herself against. A door slammed.

The boot opened. The quality of light didn't change. Y was lifted out and carried across a loud surface, where another door was unlatched. Y found herself seated in a chair, deprived of all but the sensation of its fabric. Her knees were so tender.

"Do you know where you are?" a man asked. It was the driver's escort. The one Sandy called Keating. The one who'd closed her up. "Nod for me."

Y shook her head.

"Do you want to see?"

Y shook her head.

"Oh, you do. You'll have to promise you'll behave. I know what you things are capable of."

Y shook her head.

"We'll be happy here," Keating said. "You and me. We can keep each other company. I'll even take you fishing."

Y shook her head.

"Do you mean to keep saying no? You've learned what happens when you disobey me."

Y nodded.

He breathed deeply through his nose. Then he said, "That's no good. Look where you are."

Keating unwrapped Y's head. It was like popping a blister. A warmth settled over her face. Her chin was wet with fluids, and her lips felt peeled.

Y looked out of a window. A seafront and the ocean; a beach of shingle and white sand mixed. Closer, tufts of overgrown turf. It was like a picture. It brought a nostalgia so alive she winced.

Out there, on the rim, she made out the outline of cargo liners against the night, lumbering sea-castles four or five in number. They swung spotlights round their bow and aft sections to deter would-be pirates or activists in dinghies.

"Shoot to kill," Keating said behind her. "But they still have a go. Got to admire that, haven't you? To go out there and try anyway."

He came to Y's side. "Always wanted to live by the sea, I did." Round to her front. "I think I did, anyway." Y straightened – she already knew it was the man who'd stapled her, but confirmation made her stomach turn. He lit a camping stove that illuminated four walls of unpainted brick. He brought it to her feet.

"Do you like it?" Keating asked. He yawned innocently and pointed out to sea. "Old friend's place. He bought here because it wasn't the south coast. Died in the last troubles, bless him, but I'd been taken over to the mansion by then. When I returned I could only evoke that single place, burning there, a singular flame in me. And I found it, eventually. Took out his old rib and placed a wreath out there on the water, and watched it as my memories came back. I could be wrong – I could well be – but as I rowed to shore I thought I saw dolphins leaping over it."

Y didn't move or speak or twitch. Her feet were secured so she couldn't put them on the floor.

Keating tapped her on the temple. "Your memories will come back, too. Eventually. Little buds of a life before, which sprout and pierce the cortex. Don't you think that's wonderful?"

Y shook her head.

"I think you'll learn your place quickly," Keating said. "What with all your gifts. They wanted you all to themselves, but when those drones arrived... I only want to look after you. In time we might even take out those fastenings."

Y turned to him and burbled.

Keating pulled a sympathetic smile. "You don't believe me. Fine. That's why we'll keep you like this – who's to say what you'll try? Eventually we'll compromise. You'll call me Keating, and I'll call you Jane. There's a place here for people like us. Because I've been waiting for someone like you. Someone like me."

The sun was sinking into the sea, and the ocean liners were increasingly toy-like. She wondered if she could fit them all in one hand.

"I was made like you," Keating told her. "That's why it makes sense us being together, away from them. But did you ever work out why? Why they took us there at all? I did."

The horizon was so even.

"The slips don't just go across. They go forward – a fixed link. And when the first settlers went through, they found new technology, new materials, new ways. No wonder they colonized it. It only needed a visionary to civilize it." Keating came close and lifted the pendant from Y's neck. "He'll miss you, won't he? He'll be jealous of me."

A phone rang in another room.

"Excuse me," Keating said.

The man went away. The ringing stopped. Y listened.

"Had no choice, did I?" Keating said. "No, it's not like – no. What do you mean, paid for? I've paid enough with my service..." And then quiet, the hiss of the stove, the lapping sea. Suddenly there was a thump, as if Keating had struck something. Dust drifted across the room. "Tell him to fuck himself, then," he said. He was irate. "You and them sideways. You won't find us in a million years."

Keating paced back into the room, still talking. Caught in the window's reflection. With the evening approaching, Y's ocular implants had kicked in, but it was a challenge to catch the words without seeing his lips move.

"It's not like you don't have any more of them to

hand," he told the caller. And he sat down on a chair behind Y. The voice coming down the phone was quiet, measured.

When Keating next went to speak, his voice broke. "Please. If I'd known that, I'd never have…"

Y knew he was looking at the back of her head now. His eyes coruscating.

Keating had started to grovel. "I get it," he said. "And if I arrange this, there'll be no repercussions? I can wrap her for you… I can prepare her for delivery. Let's call it a… transgression."

Something outside caught Y's attention. She blinked. The sunset was a wedge of red, and the liners had crossed the horizon.

There – another movement.

Again. A blur this time.

Keating's conversation faded out. Y focused with a surge of hope. Her arms riffled with goosebumps.

She knew it. Someone was in the garden. A person moving across the lawn between the house and the beach. In and out of visibility, using the bushes for cover as they approached the window.

Y swivelled to Keating and back to the garden. The figure vanished one last time –

Y jumped in her binds. Her vision fizzed with grain. The figure was right there, right outside. Bushy eyebrows. A woman. A medical swatch plastered on her belly. She spoke into a black strip on her cheek, then snapped back out of sight.

It was Sandy.

Still Keating bleated on, pleading down the phone with a pathetic whine.

Twitching, Y waited. She was wide-eyed, rattling involuntarily.

Keating dropped the phone. The line had died.

And Y heard the faintest noise: a sinewave song.

Keating came round her. Y looked at him. Keating sneered.

And the whole window came in. Glass showered Y – all of its turning edges lit up.

Keating darted away from the cloaked hunter. By Y's feet, the camping stove tipped over, redirecting the heat, then went through the room in a crescent. The gas ring puttered and the stove connected, spat flames to the ceiling. Keating went for the door, but it slammed closed. Keating came back to Y as if to ask for help, and his arm was twisted up behind his body. The force put him on tiptoes. He yelped, lashed out with his other hand. He was fighting himself – tumbled about the room in some deranged dance.

Sandy phased in, coated with an oily substance. "Did you think you'd topped me with your peashooter?" she said. Her hand went once, twice, against Keating's neck, palm magnesium-bright, and Keating didn't have a chance to reply.

Sandy was at Y's side before Keating collapsed. She spoke breathlessly: "Never trust anyone with the eyes – they're only after one thing." She cackled a little. "Shame their firmware doesn't handle cloak-suits."

Y bowed her head.

"What a detour," Sandy went on. She severed Y's restraints, took Y off the chair. Y's knees wouldn't support her, and she fell to the floor.

"I told him," Sandy said. "I did tell him."

Y massaged her knees, staring vacantly. Keating's body seemed awkward, and his leg was twitching. She wanted to be glad. She wanted to be grateful. But she wasn't. He wasn't the Manor Lord.

Y swallowed and reached for Sandy's sleeve. Sandy didn't resist. Y opened Sandy's hand and took the blade out of it.

"Now don't you get any ideas," Sandy said.

Y shook her head. She weighed the blade. She brought its chrome edge to her neck and started sawing at the pendant chain.

"Don't you want that?" Sandy asked. "Aren't you proud?"

It was difficult to cut, but Keating's silence spurred Y on.

"Oh, little stray. It's a necklace. And the staples – they can be taken care of. You'll heal so quickly."

The chain broke with a chime. Y dropped the blade and took the tooth and severed chain and dragged herself towards Keating's body. There, on him, using his limbs like rungs, she took his bloody nose and forced his head back to widen the slit in his neck. Inside, she learned, Keating was mostly human. Only the length of visible tongue was foreign: a titanium snake.

"It won't free you," Sandy said. She sounded impatient. "It won't change this."

Y didn't care. She pushed the tooth and chain into the gaping meat and pulled it closed again.

Sandy tutted. "That's revolting."

As Y slid away, she realized Sandy was over her, pulling a bunch of thick plastic ties from a pouch on her hip. Along with these, she produced a pair of telescoping tubes that hung flaccid from her fingers. "Don't make that face," Sandy said. "I'd obviously prefer not to."

Y crabbed backwards.

"You might forgive me eventually," Sandy went on. "It's not like I'm a sadist. It's just time for work. My retirement's riding on you."

Y met the wall, slithered up it.

Sandy had a roll of clingfilm, a roll of tape. A number of cable ties. She held them all out. "You'll understand when you have to do this," she said. "Because eventually you will." She gestured at Keating's body. "They can't know about these complications. The supply chain stays intact. The process stays the same. That attention to detail is how our father prevails. And obsolescence – well, it's part of the cycle."

Y thrashed as Sandy came to secure her limbs. Her hands tore at Sandy's hair, her cloak-suit, but to no avail. Sandy was stronger.

"Don't," Sandy said calmly, as she then brought the tubes to Y's nose and pushed them too far in. Choking, struggling to breathe – or refusing completely – Y closed her watering eyes and heard Sandy say, "Suppose you ordered an ornate vase only for it to arrive without protection. Would you be pleased?"

Y tried to expel the tubes. Tried and tried and failed.

Sandy held up the masking tape, its end fluttering. "This is the last of it. Don't fight me, little rebel." And she began to wrap Y's head. "Mr Havelock has his preferences. It'd be a shame to need a refund, to return the goods, given how much he's already invested in you… never mind how much he's keen to see me get some rest when you're ready."

Over Sandy's shoulder, naked but for her sheath of clingfilm, Y was carried outside. She had no way to see the smart silver car waiting on the shale by Keating's off-roader. Its registration plate that started RA. Its badging that read LEXUS.

"You'll be happy in the end," Sandy told her. And she popped the boot.

SEVENTEEN

The road north isn't as quiet as Sol predicted – and the car's low height means other vehicles' dipped beams still dazzle. They skirt stark land. Sepulchral windfarms. Under bridges, up entrance ramps. Fortress towns flashing past. Cathedrals of concrete beneath motorway overpasses. Into the M61's funnelled mouth, and a night-time carriageway criss-crossed in light, a zoetrope flickering through the Armco supports. Whenever he can, Sol plants his foot and sends the Ferrari snarling to eighty, ninety – its sleek shadow repeatedly smashed against bright blue signs.

Eventually they join the M6 towards the Lake District proper, passing Preston, Lancaster, before a left onto the A590 trunk road, a wind-bitten dual carriageway with jungle verges. Neglected farmland sprawls either side, dark bodies of water spreading away to silhouetted hills tacked with pylons. What little the headlights show him is so overgrown that with some imagination you could imagine the Ferrari as a machete lunging through. A black line on bare canvas, cruising like a bird between the eternal moors of the place.

"Morecambe Bay's somewhere down there," he tells Yasmin, pointing left. His voice hoarse because they haven't spoken much. He has the coat's collar up round his face; the window cracked and howling. "Have you ever seen the sea?"

"The sea," Yasmin says. "I have."

"Went down there all the time, my dad and me. He drove this great big Bentley – restored it himself. It was one of my father's favourite things in the world, driving that car with me sitting with him. I was too young for decent conversation, though. Whenever he took me out, I'd count the shadows of posts across the motorway, or pretend the car was flying between bridges. Wasn't anything else to do – he didn't believe in radio since it stopped him hearing the engine. One time, there was such amazing sunshine on the hills, and he turned to me and said, 'Oh, my boy, just look at that,' and took my hand, like this." Sol takes one of Yasmin's hands and squeezes. "He has it like this, right, and he goes, 'It's like we're driving towards God, Solomon!' And I was so scared, shit-scared, because I didn't know if he meant we were going to crash into the lorry in front, or whether I'd been a good enough boy to get into heaven."

By Greenodd, on a smaller road, single carriageway, the clock is creeping towards dawn. Everything narrowing down as shadows slide in the darkness – trees and road signage stretched and sharpened as Sol and Yasmin pass woodland and dead villages.

"Don't you get nervous?" he asks her. The closer they get, the drier his mouth becomes. A twinge in his bladder. "No?"

Yasmin shakes her head. "No," she says.

Sol takes this to mean something else. Maybe she misheard the question. Or maybe it's more like *not anymore.*

At points the road seems impossibly narrow, forcing him to drop down; engine-brake to a crawl. The car feels heavier when it's slow – a cruiser coming in to port, carrying with it a grim inevitability, an extra bulk that's hard to quantify. And closer still, they thread through a series of roundabouts, pass torchlit cabins. A difference in atmospheric pressure.

"What do you remember?" Sol asks Yasmin through the V in his collar. "From before, I mean." She looks over at him, gives him enough time to redden; enough time to wonder if it's too much, a question like this – like asking a soldier returning from war if they've ever shot someone.

Finally she shakes her head. Sol thinks of amnesia and brain damage and strokes.

"Not even your parents?" he adds. "Or where they took you from?"

"It is so empty," she tells him. She pokes herself in the head. "A crack here where nothing grows." She pauses. "Diminutive... memory-images. It's..."

There's a whirring sound. She crackles but the throatpiece doesn't find anything to translate. Sol's reminded that the device is only an accessory, an add-on, an optional extra. Would she have to wear it wherever Sandy's contact took her? Would she have to talk in it? Work in it?

"Barren," Yasmin finishes.

Sol swallows heavily. Her translations seem to oscillate between nonsense and a kind of algorithmic poetry.

"It's hard for me to imagine," he says. And it is hard, because how does a person close such a gap, or begin to confront the idea you must rebuild yourself from scratch? How do you accept that a version of you has vanished, and with it all your vested years – family bonds, friendships, lovers, tastes? He can't begin to imagine the trauma of it – being torn from somewhere, only to wake up and remember nothing. And yet, equally, he knows that people do have the capacity to rebuild, remould, rework themselves. Don't we do it all the time? Mel certainly has. And, in a sense, Sol has too. They all had to adapt when things collapsed.

When he looks at it this way, there's only admiration for this woman beside him.

"What's the first thing you remember as Y?"

"Wakefulness," she says quickly, as though she'd predicted the question. "Masked creatures of the house," she adds. "Alterations. Physical exertion. We were the children of the tower. They made me solitary. He made it so."

Sol closes his window. "Did he hurt you?"

"Nothing to hurt," she tells him, tapping her head again. "They took away the things that cause hurt. He made us all…" She flexes her body under the shell jacket. She puts a finger to her breastbone. "He made us like this."

At last Sellafield comes into view on their left side. Rows of jutting things, cut from the navy sky in such a way as to seem materially absent. Clusters of simplistic buildings inside the perimeter have a strange density to them, like their stained walls have soaked up a nation's dread and somehow banked it. The golf ball-shaped reactor is far bigger than Sol imagined it would be. And set farther back from the road is another structure he didn't expect, but knows he must confront.

It's unambiguous. A singular, dark, hyperboloid mass. A cooling tower.

Sol goes from surprised to aghast. His throat full with it. From the pictures he'd seen, he knows – *knows* – that this is one of the Calder Hall quadruplets: towers erased from records since 2007 – but apparently living on.

"Trust," Yasmin says. "You trust me."

Shaking with adrenaline, Sol ignores the warning markings, the arrows, drives on with the lights turned off. They end up doing a full pass of the site, colossal in breadth, then turn the car to retrace their route; this time spotting what looks like a battery of anti-aircraft cannon – four-pronged systems on swivel mounts. He sees a fleet of HGVs. Sentries, armed, torches ranging. And the fencing – what must be miles and miles of it.

"It's impossible," he says.

"Yes," Yasmin says. Her eyes are lambent, almost as if someone is watching late-night TV inside her.

Sol stops the car. "Maybe we should wait. See if anything comes in or out."

"In or out," she says.

But the minutes slip by and nothing much changes.

"And you came through the tower itself?" he asks, like they hadn't stopped talking. His eyes are wide, scanning for possible entry points, weaknesses.

"Yes. Inside. In, out."

Sol reaches behind his seat for the sports bag containing the water bottles, an extra pair of jeans to wear under his overalls, the cylinder he excised from her abdomen. At the bottom of it, shedding dust, there's a house brick.

"Can you run?"

Yasmin goes to open the door. "Run?"

"Hang on, wait," Sol says. "Not here. They'll have

heard us coming even if they didn't pay it any mind. We have to leave it a while. Camp out."

Yasmin looks at him confusedly.

"Should've bought bloody cloak-suits. Done this properly—"

"False," Yasmin interrupts. She straightens and lets the seatbelt roll across her. He wonders if he's made her angry. "No see-through qualities," she adds. Then, "We cross the tower before the sun. You should have brought protection."

Sol holds her gaze. Protection? What, a gun? He isn't Roy. But all the same, the comment rattles him. They'd definitely been hasty to act, and they were ill-prepared for this amount of security. Then he thinks: *This car's our protection.*

"You remember what I told you about the car? The armour?"

Yasmin nods.

"And you're warm enough?"

She pulls at the fleece collar under her shell jacket. "Thermal," she says.

"You swear it? Because I'm bloody boiling in this coat, me."

"Trust," she says. "You must have strata."

Sol frowns, then realizes what she means.

"We'll need a bigger run-up," he says. "Christ. I can't remember the last time I ran anywhere."

Sol edges the modified Ferrari to a point closer to the tower, pointing its bonnet towards the fence. He takes in the tower's formwork, its supremacy in the skyline. How he wishes he'd brought his Polaroid camera. He visualizes how bulbous the tower would seem through the viewfinder. Yasmin, too, is rapt by it. It's getting easier and easier to comprehend the impression it's made on her psyche.

The longer you look, the more you see. In the tower's shadow, Sol scopes a pile of crates identical to those stacked by the trucks at Knutsford services. Many have IN stencilled on their sides – further confirmation of the tower's purpose, if it were needed. He swallows. Are they really doing this? He opens the car door with care, smelling grass, burnt ozone. He creeps out across the slippery verge, knowing that if he stops to think, it'll be over. If it isn't already. In truth the only thing he can rely on is the assumption that two people wouldn't dare to infiltrate what's fundamentally a military installation. Let alone somewhere with such a litany of disasters to its name.

"I know I said about them hearing us, but if we don't go now..." Staring into the breach, Sol can't admit to even considering second thoughts. He kneels by the car and sets to work in the footwell. With parcel tape and his teeth, he rigs the accelerator with the brick. It's crude, but his logic is sound: this is how he and Irish used to dispose of their stripped cars in the Bridgewater Canal.

Nearby, eyes on the perimeter, Yasmin lies flat on her belly.

Sol climbs into the back of the car and pulls out the length of hosepipe he instructed Irish to leave under the driving seat. Never an enjoyable task, but needs must. He feeds the tube into the fuel tank and sucks its end until the siphon takes. With the first surge he spits out the tube, gasping, and splashes fuel into the car, over the driver's seat, the back seats, its body. Then he turns the car's ignition, rams the Ferrari into second, and rolls away.

Sol winds himself on landing and lies wheezing as the Ferrari accelerates, straight and true, pulling, still pulling, through its modified torque band, engine piercing in the night-quiet. It's heading for a section of the fencing that runs close to a cluster of outbuildings, driver's door held back like a damaged wing.

Y crawls to him with the sports bag across her shoulder.

Sentry torches swing to the car. Bewilderment, before angry flowers burst into the night – metal on metal on metal – and the Mondial ploughs onwards.

A generator sound. An alarm. The perimeter floodlights surge. Gunfire tears paint from the car's body, but too late: the Mondial is inexorable, its trajectory guaranteed by speed and weight, simple physics. On the fringes, Sol and Yasmin perceive a rush of air and a *whump* as the petrol catches. It must be doing fifty when it punctures the fence. Another flash, a vicious crunch, and then the car is embedded and burning in a store building's side. The shockwave rattles trailer buckles even beyond the outbuildings.

In the glow of the fire, Sol and Yasmin see the tattered hole in the fence. Sentries scatter from their posts. A dull crump as something in the Ferrari explodes, and a liquid fire spurts up.

"Now," Sol whispers. He'd intended for them to wait, for them to take advantage later. But the thick smoke pouring from the store building provides ideal cover.

In any case, Yasmin didn't need telling. As they flit across the road towards the fence, it's clear she's doing all the dragging.

Reduced to visual prompts by the siren, Sol and Yasmin hug the buildings, lacing between each other as well as the brickwork – over low walls, shallow gullies, and into the tower's expansive shadow. Here they stop for breath between crates – Sol gesturing to a loading ramp attached to a storage bay; each acknowledging that the tower's entrance is locked down. Going first, Sol finds several rows of crates sitting on fork truck pallets. It's organized, scrupulous. And otherwise deserted.

Yasmin follows inside. Scattered voices and footsteps from somewhere indistinct – more sentries running to the crash scene with comms blazing.

Wordless, Sol and Yasmin move deeper and deeper into the unit.

"More crates," Sol breathes.

So many crates.

Without warning, Yasmin goes at one, brute force applied to wrench its stapled lid half-off, her face straining until the whole piece creaks and gives. Sol goes over and looks inside to find a second box with an obsidian-like finish, a basic instrument panel. This flashes a temperature in crude red digits: -40c. Its metal feels impossibly smooth, like the finish of a vault. Y slaps it in frustration.

"Try another," Sol urges, understanding now what she wants them to do. He alternates his focus between her and the gap where a sentry might appear. A static conveyor line behind them. "Just make sure it's enough for both of us."

Y tries the next crate along. The same story under its stapled lid. Another. And another. The more crates she opens, the more Sol thinks this might be the worst idea in a whole series of them. He listens to the distorted shouting near the crash site. A mixture of panic and disbelief. This alone feels satisfying – but he can't help but expect the sentries' torches to swing back this way and pick out his face.

"This!" Yasmin shouts, pointing down the conveyor line.

Sol doesn't need persuading. They charge along

it, deeper and deeper, until they enter a red-lit space with a rubberized floor. A strange odour meets them – it imprints on Sol the idea of an abattoir, the stink of frightened animals. Between dark corners, the far wall's covered in wires and box units similar in size and shape to the device that wrapped Roy's toilet. The thicker cables create a square on the brick.

"They cross here?" he asks.

Yasmin shrugs. "Not me," she says.

Sol looks about, fascinated by the grim efficiency of the place. Trays marked IN on the walls, and a store of trolleys and pallets labelled similarly. A crate of bandages and supplies tipped out and left to soak up what's on the floor. Propped-up panels from broken crates–

"In," Sol says. Trying to see what's missing, trying to understand. Again he looks to the equipment arranged on the wall. Is this an auxiliary transfer space? It'd be ridiculous if it didn't smell so tangible. And anyway, the science is irrelevant: he's already seen Roy's top half vanish, had his glimpse of extraterrestrial space. Maybe it's odd that he's never tried to deny the vision to himself. Maybe it was too pure, too convincing–

"You came through the tower?"

Yasmin's throat thrums. "Yes."

OUT.

"And that thing over there," he says, pointing. "Rigged on the wall. It's like the kit we saw at Knutsford. Like they had round the portaloo."

Yasmin nods and skips past him to a set of weathered crates whose lids aren't fully sealed. She prises one open. "In," she says, and points inside.

"Go on then," Sol says.

And that is pretty much that.

●●●

In the dark of the trans-crate, their arms and legs tangled and buttocks numb, Sol and Yasmin try to breathe slowly. As they do, the crate around them creaks gently, like an old ship. The air is thin and hot, and they share water and open a cereal bar he found secreted in his overalls. It's stale – probably months past its use-by date – and coated in a bitter synthetic chocolate.

"Energy," Yasmin's artificial voice grates – intimately close, sinister in the dark. The cereal bar leaves a fine dust when it's broken, and the two of them feel it powder their faces, sticking to their sweat. "After you," Sol says, handing her a piece. But they bite down simultaneously, chew dryly.

Occasionally, voices carry down from ducting above, and at one point a set of heavy boots rings in the room itself. On the whole it seems quieter: the radio chatter has died down, and the most immediate danger with it. Sol reckons they've been in the crate an hour, possibly more, and is sure he can hear tracked vehicles moving in to clear things. They listen with hearts slowing and quickening by turns; wallow in the scent of must and rough timber; savour the gooey debris in their teeth.

"Too many limbs in here," Sol tells her. His coccyx feels like it's being ground into a nub.

Yasmin taps him in three places at once.

"It's you," he whispers. "You're a bloody limb party."

After another half an hour, they find themselves shuffling to find comfortable spots, silently consulting each other on their positions. Wool and skin and breath mingling. Whenever they hear a noise, they stop mid-movement – teenagers fumbling on a narrow bed.

Eventually there comes a more consistent sound. Another generator, Sol decides –a unit running diesel with bad additives. Listening to the rhythm of it, its chains and sprockets, he realizes crates are being transferred along the conveyor belt into their room.

"They're starting up again," he whispers.

Next news, their own crate starts to move. A sudden lurch, a scraping – though Yasmin seemed to be expecting it, and immediately clamps Sol's mouth. Sol wedges his elbows in the crate corners, body rigid.

Outside there's shouting. Voices that resolve as another language entirely. Their crate shifts across the space and is dropped without ceremony onto another creaking structure – a pallet, Sol guesses – before it's dragged along the floor.

It stops, and someone taps the box. This precedes a bang – a washing sound, pebbles in water, and a flash that penetrates the crate's joints.

Sol thinks: *We're palletized freight.*

The loudest voice guides the passage of their crate, with at least one or two others making alarmed pleas about something. A problem? Is their crate an anomaly?

Next comes a terrifying drone that rises in frequency and intensity until it's just white noise. The crate handlers, yelling across the space to actually hear each other, fade to irrelevancy.

Gradually, the noise reaches a climax. A sizzle at the extremities of the spectrum, and Yasmin and Sol cover their ears. Then a wash of static electricity, crackling, every hair on their bodies prickling, and for the briefest of moments, Sol and Y can see actually see each other's faces lit from *inside* the crate; some bizarre reversal of natural law, like a cartoon electrification that reveals the unlucky character's skeleton.

The white noise drops.

A quieter man speaks. An imperious tone. "Slip three... is... *on*," he says.

Sol thinks: *Three*.

Sol thinks: *There's more than one crossing point*.

And Sol's father whispers in his ear: *That's just the economies of scale, son*.

Then Sol finds himself floating, limbless, torso apparently separated out. Yasmin's hands seize his ankles, tighten, and finally let go. "Is that it?" Sol asks. It all seems so straightforward.

"No!" he hears another worker shout. A moment to register the voice isn't answering his question. Flustered, the worker continues: "Turn it off. *Turn it off!* That's not Plastic you're sending it to! That's not the right place!"

"Stop fussing," the calmer worker replies. "They're used – they're all empty. They'll only get dumped or burned."

"But you'll have trolley teams tripping on wreckage for weeks–"

The voices wane. Sol doesn't have any more capacity for worry. In its place he feels himself shuddering. There and not. Here and not.

Nowhere and nothing…

Through the slip, Sol and Yasmin are liminal. The transcrate is around them and then is gone; its particles and atoms fragmenting, rebonding, meshing; creating new structures – unfurling arrangements of wood and plastic, ink and alloy. Their bodies, too, are torn to pieces and remade inside their fabrics again, existing as streams of particles on some separate plane, yet still intact, functional on another. With sublime objectivity, this separation of self, comes the shock of seeing your insides in linear time, speeded up preposterously so that only machines might capture your passage, your

contrail: organs filtered through a childhood X-ray, a
CT scan, a mammogram, a trace test, wavelengths from
across the light spectrum or beyond. You are as your
creator(s) made you, or not. As the maker(s) remade
you, or not. And inside that box, neither here nor there,
as you transcend the slip to the sister-world, arrive
comets and hard diamond points, nanoscopic drill-tips
boring into your vision, ventilating your perspective.
And as you marvel, as you gape, new elements scorch
through these tunnels into thin flesh, make mauve
rivers of your capillaries, illuminating floaters before
recreating them as whole new suns, fired by universal
truths. And these fresh galaxies, unexplored, annihilate
your thoughts and fears and concepts of all but the
twinkle of your self and both the vastness and the
minuscularity of you; a speck in the borderline, a spark
in the borderlands. And you realize: this slip is a no-
man's land. It's the space between. It's the line between
your interior and the physical world, distending,
bending back to meet itself.

Somewhere in there, in all of this, their cosmic
tangling, the two of them, a woman called Yasmin and a
man called Sol, find each other and plug themselves into
a shared connection, a fresh being. They feel this change
their journey, even as they can't see one another, only
the blurred starfield around them, the infinity of the
cosmos extending away. But they can feel each other.
And in that immortal grip is a rubbery birth-sac of bones.
A many-tentacled hydra. A slop of something. Polyps
and gristle. A chowder of crucial tissue. A damp powder,
forgotten then refound. It's warm there in that space,
so tender and amniotic, and their nerve endings shiver
with the closeness.

Soon the diamond points harden. The galaxy visions

soften, spiral right back to a singular orb, balancing in the gloom. Serenity, wonder, as tangible objects drift past. Panels? *Those are crate panels.* And then the black. A stiff wind in the face. That stench again – the spoiled meat.

Sol blinks. Before him, Yasmin's eyes bright green to balance the dark. He wants to sneeze. "Yes?" he says, but he doesn't know why.

Yasmin drops Sol's hand. There's a fine coating of something on the crate floor, slat-lit where the crate's joins have expanded. It looks like frost, except it has the flyaway quality of dust or glass powder.

Does it change you the same way, this jump? Were those slats in the crate there before? Or were they all, as in Sol's revelations, put back together differently? He certainly feels heavier, and there's a sense he's still moving.

"You've done that before?" he asks Yasmin. A sort of relief floods his system – the curious certainty they've lost something.

But where's this now? And why is he so accepting of it?

Yasmin taps him and puts a finger in the box's strange powder frost. She quickly writes OUT.

"I feel mashed," he tells her.

Yasmin nods.

"Then say something," he says. "Why aren't you saying anything?"

Yasmin comes closer to him. She points to her naked throat. Sol could count every dash of her tattoo.

Sol clutches her shoulders. "How?" he cries, searching for the throatpiece on the crate floor. "How?"

Yasmin stays him with all three hands, holds his chin up to hers and touches them together. She shushes him.

She spreads out the dust. Then she draws something else.

Sol follows her finger as it goes.

The stroke of an I. The turns of an N.

EIGHTEEN

Trekking upslope, metres ahead, Yasmin realizes it'd be easy to leave the man Sol here in the scree. Why not let the Slope's winds clean him down to his bones, and then, later, to dust? A savage end to meet in his world, certainly. But a kind of mercy here in hers.

Yasmin assumes they'd arrived around halfway up the Slope. That for whatever reason, the slip had malfunctioned and jettisoned them far north of Plastic, just as it had the bisected man she and Karens' trolley team had discovered. The difference being, through some dint of luck, that she and Sol had survived their entry; clambered from the trans-crate intact and started moving, driven onwards by Yasmin's tenacity alone. She'd been surprised that fifteen fingers pointing up the Slope was enough to convince him. Astounded, too, that the muddy skies lurking in her mind were in fact much cleaner – that the black mists were considerably whiter.

So is it relief or hysteria she feels to be here? Or just the simple force of will that motivates her? Some bond, forged in her first journey, has made the Slope familiar, reassuring beneath her feet, regardless of its enormity, its apathy to life. And as they hike its face, tendons starting to pinch, Yasmin doesn't worry about making it, but fantasizes about the entrance she'll make at the top. A daydream: strolling into the mansion's atrium and chaining herself to its bone bannisters; dragging it backwards, the whole house and its Manor Lord, into the Slope's shifting dunes; and watching the wind excoriate its brick, cladding, its roof. Witnessing the mansion walls' smoothness eroded; its sterile insides split open and peeled; its cradles flayed with unrelenting pressure. Until all that remains are her brothers and sisters, safe in trolley team suits, running free down the Slope to Plastic's black market, where, emancipated, they hear the ruffling and snapping of the tarp that covers everything, then make their own journeys onward.

Or is it just vengeance? Yasmin isn't sure you can avenge nothing. In reality, she's still fighting for a collection of vague memories. The remote glimpses from another woman's past.

"Wait," Sol pleads. "Please. Just a minute."

Yasmin stops for him. He's struggling badly with the angle of ascent, and already staggering. Just as she enjoyed a new lightness in his world, he carries the burden of extra weight in hers – and she should have known. She yanks the bag off his shoulder and brings him into her; to share what she can of her warmth. A sort of affection. She has him drink some water, pours a little on his head. She knows, however, that they can't rest for long, that this can't keep happening, and nods encouragement. They continue.

Sporadically the couple chances on the scraps of previous expeditions – at one scene a pile of ragged screed, torn sections of the black, waxy material that

Karens' trolley squad wore. There are other redundant materials too, and Yasmin recognizes at least some of it as elastic cloak-suit fabric. It's lightweight, so she drapes a section of it round Sol's shoulders in an attempt to insulate him.

Drink more water.

The airstream often switches and brings a nettling wind directly downSlope. The further they travel, the harder this wind makes it to move, and with increasing frequency Yasmin has to abandon her footing, her rhythm, to help Sol find his. Extremities fading, they stop and start, dodge and tack, until he begins to falter in earnest, feet dragging clumps from the Slope's pallid face, his shadow stretched behind as a leash.

The first time he stumbles, she's there to catch him. He goes to his knees, one foot flat, the other turned beneath his backside. With a flashback of Fi falling face-first, she promises to stop it happening again. Sol bows against the wind and roars, guttural, standing again. His hands are bleeding where he's steadied himself, and the dust's opened microcuts in his cheeks.

Yasmin turns up his collar, wraps more of the cloaking material around his face.

Drink more water.

The second time he falls harder. A desperate bark, his mouth a rectangle of pain, tongue white with dehydration. Sol submerges his hands in the surface silt, but his forearms collapse under his weight, exhausted beyond the point of failure. He'll not get up this time, she thinks, and kneels to his side, crackles into his exposed ear. Sol stirs. "I can't," he tells her. "I can't."

Yasmin tugs the cloaking material on his back.

"Too heavy," he says. "I can't carry myself. Why don't you get on with it. Just bin me off. I don't care–"

Yasmin places her second and third hands on his shoulders. She grips him, leans backwards, gets him into a sitting position, his feet and legs lotus-like. His cuts are starting to weep.

Yasmin croaks an imperative. She gestures skywards and down at his feet. Sol pitches to his knees. She rearranges the sheet of cloaking material about his chest and pulls up the peacoat's hood with her third hand.

"Cheers," he manages.

Yasmin nods, imploring, and points upSlope. Down at her feet, alternating. Left, right. Left. Right. Sol pushes off his knees, and the heaviness slides back to his feet. Within a few yards his thighs are boiling with acid. Yasmin pushes against his lower back as he slogs on, twisting her own feet twice in succession because she isn't following the terrain.

"Keep going," Sol says. "Keep going."

To reply with nothing comprehensible racks Yasmin's heart. Another compulsion to leave him in these winds. It'd be a delirious way to go, crawling into the Slope's edifice. Total white-out—

Sol trips again. Yasmin catches him this time. She measures him, and her muscles catch and stay themselves. She trembles under his weight. It's no use –

"I only let you down," Sol says.

Lithely she props him with her third arm and darts beneath him so her back and shoulders support his stomach and ribcage. His arms flop over her shoulders like unreeled hoses, his depleted body jigsawed into the receiving contours of hers.

One, two, I'll break you.

She pushes his dead weight right through her tri-planted hands. Up through her centre of gravity towards a new one; pivoting till she's worked out the sweet spot between Sol's bulk and her own.

Three, four, you're good for more.

Hunched, set against the Slope, Yasmin places one foot into the scarp face, digging in her toes. She builds up to the next movement – a balancing act controlled by her core. Slowly, she brings her other foot to bear. Digs in. Breathes out. Her stomach muscles ripple.

One, two.

Yasmin starts to build momentum, little increments of speed as she grows confident in her power, her balance. And then, gritted, grimly, she begins to carry Sol upSlope, all three arms stabilizing the man distributed across her spine. From a distance they must resemble some clockwork creature, metronomic in its steps; a machine that marches surely into the granular wind, its double head set low in makeshift scarves, with sails of dark material whipping off it.

Impossibly it goes on like this. An hour. Two hours. Miles. There's no way to gauge it. No other trolley squads coming down or up. No more detritus, bodies or otherwise.

Sol stirs here and there, tapping softly on Yasmin's shoulder as if in appreciation, but he can't seem to find any words to relieve her of the drudgery; the arduous shovelling of her boot toes into the diagonal; the constant rocking motion he creates; and the decoloured world – unyielding white, bleaching to such an extent she finds it hard to know if she's even the right way up.

Internally, Yasmin's focus has shifted to making little journeys. Great voyages from metre to metre. She climbs the Slope steadily and methodically and purposefully, taking short, even strides to preserve her energy and maintain pace. Left over right over left. One. Two. Three. Four. She inhales with each footfall, exhales for the length it takes to land two more. Thinking in threes over fours – left, out, right, out, left, in, right, out – until the syncopation is naturalized and her mind floats ahead, fixates on forcing away the burn, correcting her slanting shoulders, ignoring the cramp in her feet.

What was that?

Over there?

She alters course towards it. A half-melted cube of luminous green plastic. From it, a dark-haired arm extends outwards, flensed down to the bone on one side. In its hand, a pistol, a Luger, held in a death grip.

She glances up at Sol, passenger and cargo. He's unconscious, hasn't seen it. *Protection*, she thinks, lowering him, herself, to carefully unclasp the gun. *Protection*.

Now she must get there. The unlikely sight of these remains a reminder they both do. And yet with an unknown distance still to go, the Slope twisting round an outcropped ridge – a topographic quirk – Yasmin begins to hallucinate the transit camp beneath the mansion ridge, green-edged; its concrete outbuildings; a wick-hot glow from bioluminescent pots; and a barracks full of trolley operatives. They welcome her, bathe her body in flower essences, feed her polished fruits, delicately sliced fish and meats, before letting her sleep on a film of warm air in a sterile chamber, free of coldness and teeth and of men with glinting eyes. Free of these things but gainful of another: a recording of a voice, maternal or paternal, deep or soft – anyone's voice but the Manor Lord's, or the man Keating's – and this voice extols her name over and over: *Yasmin, Yasmin, Yasmin*.

The razor outcrop vanishes. All things left behind out here. Yasmin notices the scree starting to level; the incline of it tapering. Sol's still unconscious, a frozen string of mucus attaching him to Y's twin shoulder-mount.

One, two.

And on she climbs through the pale hellscape with Sol on her back. This man who knows as much or as little as her; who knows in himself what she's suffered, and how she intends to conquer it. Until the silty surface gives way to ground that's harder, rougher, and Yasmin's boots start to roll on clumps of rock; lift clods of soil; slip on hardy vegetation.

She stops and croaks back at Sol, and the wind doesn't take the sound. The man stirs, muffled in her shoulder, and stretches his legs against the stirrups of her crooked arms.

"Where?" he manages.

Yasmin sets him down. Collapses into the earth. For a little while at least, they lie in the scent of disturbed soil, blinking at uninterrupted sky.

Yasmin stretches and massages her muscles. Sol sips drinking water with gloves wrapped around his boots, head bowed, uncertainty displacing fear, some feeling creeping back into his fingers and toes. She closes her eyes –

No.

Yasmin crackles again, points across the escarpment. Sol shrugs. Yasmin points again, this time with an agitated noise.

Now Sol sees.

A narrow causeway, and at its end a concrete tent. Sol laughs deliriously. How ordinary. A tent. And beyond it, on a ridge further above, are the silhouettes of more.

"Sleep?" he asks her. "Is that what you mean? Is it safe?"

Yasmin nods.

He tries to smile but his lips are cracked, and it clearly pains him. "Think I can walk this bit?"

Yasmin nods.

"Thank you," he says. "For what you did."

A half-shrug as though she's tentative to admit she did anything. Or was it a guilt that she'd considered leaving him down there full stop?

In any case she stands up. Despite crippling exhaustion, she helps Sol do the same. Limping, each the other's crutch, they advance for the hut.

The hut door's open. The hut's empty. A wooden cot in the corner. A wicker chair.

Sleep-deprived, Slopeblind, Sol falls in and melts on a cool, matted floor, patently designed to soak up bootwater. Yasmin follows him in, setting down the bag. She's more guarded – a reflex flaring, alertness kicking in. But the space is anodyne.

Yasmin swigs from a bottle of water. She looks down on him and considers all things for a time, her heft against the in-swinging door, and her heart still brisk.

They're here.

I'm back.

She unfastens her boots and begins to peel off her layers, each progressively damper.

For a while at least, she wants to simply be.

Will it ever go dark up there in the concrete tent? Yasmin waits on brown skies, purple hues, but through a single frosting window on the far wall, the sun hangs, simmering, a moulding orange. She follows the Slope's curving edifice, coast-like, towards the horizon, where a peninsula juts into an ocean of space. In the out-sweeping curve of this, overhangs cast weird shadows across the Slope's powder. It's definitely less harsh up here, despite the exposed tops, though the wind still buzzes the windows and keeps her awake. She wonders if animals roam nearby. If a bursor might wander into view from the forbidden wilderness, the edgelands Chaplain once told her about.

The man Sol is snoring. Several times Yasmin hears him gasp a name, followed by what sounds like a plea.

Such a journey they'd made together. Alpha returned to Omega. She reflects on their silent pact – an understanding, a common humanity. Little wonder their plan hardly seems a plan at all, rather a feeling they've acted on. As if it were naturally occurring – each the other's active ingredient.

For Sol it was also a choice, of course. A choice, you could argue, to do something more than simply exist – or anyway make amends for something, however self-interested it was. But then only Yasmin knows the scale and the depth of the mansion's machinations, the Manor Lord's interminable pursuits. For her, as for the man who'd claimed her, it's about control. And while she's swimming back to the surface without knowing exactly what will happen after that first desperate breath, she knows all the same what she'll say when the surface resettles: "I will not serve you."

You're going home.

Yasmin wakes with a jolt. She curses in her way. The blood-sun has arced its way down to the east, hazy behind driven Slope dust. She tips forward – how long was she asleep? – and clutches her stomach. It's still habit to reach for the connective pads; to pull away the wires and regulators and remove the drip needle.

But there's something else. Something had roused her. A bleeping that's slowing. Slowing.

And she knows the sound.

Yasmin skitters across the tent, shakes Sol. He snaps awake, terrified. Close to his face, she jabs fingers in her ears, seals her third hand over her mouth.

"What?" he asks, bleary. "What is it?"

Yasmin scolds him without saying a word.

Sol's eyes widen.

"They know we're here?"

Yasmin shakes her head.

Panicked, a woolly mouth: "No?"

Yasmin tenses in frustration. She moves away from Sol and signals for him to watch her. Then she sweeps a flat hand across the matting.

Sol coughs. "Drones?"

Yasmin repeats the action with a sucking noise.

"A sweep?"

Yasmin clicks and hops towards the door. Sol massages his ankles under the tongues of his boots and unzips his peacoat. He's surprised to not see steam.

"Is… is it getting closer?" he asks, rubbing his eyes. Dried blood comes off his skin like dandruff. "Yasmin…"

The bleeping stops.

Yasmin reapplies her weight to the tent's door. Carefully, Sol joins her, convinced for a moment that there's a Luger pistol in her hand. He closes his eyes; listens to feet and equipment moving around the tent. A group fanning out to encircle them.

"Hold," he hears.

Now they're banging on the walls. Sol sinks into the floor. Across the tent, the window darkens.

Enclosed.

Any second. Any moment now…

Finally someone speaks. Muted. The scraping feet of someone waiting impatiently. "Here," they say. A man's voice: deep, discordant: bit-crushed by its relay.

"And here," somebody else says. A woman, and no less unsettling.

They've tracked our prints.

"Let us in, let us in," the man says. "Or we'll blow your house down."

Yasmin reaches for Sol's hand, holds it steadfast in two of her own. With her third she digs the Luger tightly into her side, and he can't stop looking at it.

"Grab the charges," the man outside says.

The shadow on the rear window withdraws as a monumental figure bends down to peer inside. Their face is obscured, but Yasmin recognizes trolley team garb. To Sol they look future-military – tactical in extremis. Whoever it is standing on powered stilts.

The operative slides off their cowl, and Yasmin gasps.

Fi.

The woman recoils simultaneously, apparently overloaded with information. A young woman she recognizes beside a middle-aged man she doesn't. The young woman with a vintage sidearm. Each of them exhibiting the body language of prey.

Sensing her fluster, Fi's suit flashes proximity lasers, parses escape vectors. She thinks: *This is a serious fucking breach.* Then, against all protocol, she yells into her mic: "Don't blow it! Don't blow the door! It's empty. It's *empty*!"

Sol squeezes Yasmin. But she's all in –

"Then who locked it?" the team leader shouts back. "Are you *positive*, Fiona?"

"It's clear," Fi shouts.

"I told them this box needed a service," the man mutters. "Pinging concrete for shits and giggles."

"What's going on?" Sol hisses. "Who's that…"

But Yasmin is riveted to Fi, as if blinking might expose

the operative as an apparition.

Fi tilts her head. *Come here*. Yasmin glides over and places her hands on the glass. Fi leans closer.

"You've lost your hat," Fi says. A melancholy in her voice. Then, more distantly, "You can't be here."

Sol blunders across the matting. Headrush. Dark blotches. "You know her?" he asks. It sounds so trite, so useless.

The operative's breath frosts on the glass. She ignores him. Such an odd face she's pulling.

Sol is cut out; left to observe. He fingers the crusting scabs of his cuts, the plates of dead skin round his mouth.

"Please don't stay here," Fi says. "Whatever you're doing, they'll–"

A device cheeps on Fi's body. She swats at her chest plate, a practised response. Angled into the sun, her buckles flash. "Yes, I'm coming," she says. A harmonic in the "yes" glides across the glass. She frowns.

Yasmin pulls her hands away from the window, leaving three oily prints.

Fi holds up a fingerless glove. "Now we're even," she says. "Now we're square."

It's Yasmin's turn to sleep. On waking they'll leave – motions agreed through their personal semaphore; Sol filled with an irrepressible dread at the idea of what might be ahead.

He holds out Roy's Luger as if aiming for a distant target, then lies it flat on his palm. It's missing its magazine, he believes, hardly the protection Yasmin envisaged. Yet to him it's a talisman nonetheless. Where had she found it?

Aim again. Sweep the tent. The structure's three conjoined walls are aerated like sea sponge, and remind

Sol of the pegwall panelling back in the workshop – the system they, or he, imposed for racking tools. The workshop feels a long way away now, but like his job, the pegboard meant something: a shrine to control in a society collapsing. A distraction from a relationship failing at home. It was reassuring, actually, that even here, even at such extremes, he could seek and find order. It calms him. It rallies him. This might be the ideal place to rehang his photo collage, create a new vista – a triptych. Because, he realizes, a certain kind of security comes with imposing yourself on an alien space.

Roy, though. Roy's end. Sol reflects on all the ways Roy was free, and feels a kind of envy. Sol's spaces were the workshop and the rooms between four walls of a pokey flat. The cars that ran him between. Cells, in hindsight. Roy, though – Roy lived rootless, free on the road.

Aim it. Aim it again.

If they wait here, will the squad return? Almost definitely. He still can't work out why the woman outside had spared them. Something mutual – some contact, some connection; God knows Yasmin has a presence, a certain way of unpicking you. Is it weird to assume the woman was involved in Yasmin's trafficking? He thinks about the logistics of it, the chances of that, and ends up spiralling. Yasmin knew the camp was at the top of the mountain they climbed. She understands this terrain. And this is the other conundrum: she also told him she exited through the tower. How had they skipped it? *Where* is the tower, if not at the bottom of the mountain?

What had the workers shouted back in Sellafield? It's half-remembered now, a gauze applied. There'd been such strain in the workers' voices that something wasn't right. That the crates were empties.

Sol thinks: *Heads or harps.*

There had to be two sides to each coin. So where was the other side of Sellafield?

That isn't Plastic! You'll have trolley teams tripping on wreckage for weeks…

Did they really move people up and down this cruel slope? And if they don't make it, what will the future make of their remains? Sol and Yasmin, their rags disintegrated around them; the leather of his boots, the heavy cotton of his peacoat. This concrete tent a tomb, their burial chamber, or mistaken for a staging pod, used for unknown travel by unknown means. Or then again part of some ancient lift system, like a cable car station, whose other workings – pulleys and cables and joists – were lost.

Now Sol sees their spooning figures as pressed flowers under the Slope. Archaeologists dusting down Yasmin's biomods with soft brushes before excavating and reassembling her for a museum case. Would Sol sink further than her, being heavier? That seems fitting enough – seems fair. She would be so fascinating. A marvel of science…

And yet reducing her to raw mechanics isn't fair at all. There'd be nothing left of her personality. Her doggedness. Her funny sort of humour, come to that. And Sol would be better off as nothing – leaving brittle bones yet no trace of pride or selfishness – no clues about his amateur artistry, his past, his time with Mel and his life without her…

The wind picks up. Sol looks at the door. Nervy movements. Steady your hands. *Aim again.*

Not wind, in fact, but a sudden, distant rumble.

Yasmin sleeps on as dust bobbles up in the floor's gaps, as an engine vibrates the walls. It sounds like a half-track. The sound of riots –

Sol wipes his nose, sips more water. His body in ribbons. He weighs his back against the door and wills her awake. Yet the ponderous vehicle passes without disturbing her. Just as she was in standby, she's almost unnaturally still – a *skilful* sleeper.

"You kip on," he says out loud, then shakes his head. His father's voice: *You're losing it, boy.* His stomach's watery, and he puts a hand to it. "OK," he says. "No." Then to Yasmin, unable to tell if he's really kneeling down to her on one knee or having a premonition.

"Sleepyhead," he says. "Wake up."

Yasmin's pupils pop with green-optic flash. "Hi, bright eyes." She's up in one balletic movement, fists raised in defence. "It's me," Sol tells her. "Only me."

Yasmin pulls a parody of a smile.

"Still know the way?"

The tent darkens. Through the rear window, a single cloud, edged in purple, has moved over the sun.

From the concrete tent they run arm-in-arm over fractured terrain, powder squeaking under their boots.

Ahead, the vehicle that passed churns its way up the hill, and the two of them follow between its tracks. Yasmin seems almost content to move this way, despite Sol's nerviness, their obvious silhouettes against the white background. Frankly she's past caring – enjoying the kind of confidence that generally manifests in hubris. But hubris is only really hubris if you choose to feel ashamed. While her makers had obviously tried to install that sense in her – make shame her default setting, even – it hasn't worked. And now comes her reckoning.

"Security," Sol says, meaning the half-track. "Must be a patrol."

Yasmin doesn't let on. The trail leads upwards in switchbacks towards the ridge, topping out by the main camp.

"Do we keep following it?" Sol asks. "Does it take us where you want to go?"

Yasmin ignores him again. She's willing the house to come into view; eager for it to appear, to invigorate her. And anyway: the vehicle looks exactly like the half-track that brought her from the mansion to the camp. She's angry that Sol can't understand this – that naturally they should follow it.

Then the half-track halts. A snap, a dropped gear. Something grinding. The engine cuts out, and Sol's guts drop. "Over there," he urges, grabbing Yasmin by her doubled shoulder and hurrying to the steep escarpment that falls away from the trail to open Slope. They leap over the bank and press themselves into rubble on the other side.

"Did they clock us?"

Yasmin crawls up to the edge to canvas. She hisses and points to an area next to the vehicle. *No.* Sol joins her, squinting; follows her finger to an outhouse just off to its right. Then a hatch in the half-track opens, and two operatives climb out.

"What are they doing?"

Moments later, the operatives start pulling blank boxes and crates from the outhouse door and loading them on to the half-track.

"Supplies," Sol whispers. "A store. Must be for the camp."

Yasmin nods.

"We could take them," he adds, and his nonchalance shocks him. It illustrates a kind of alteration; things he's willing to do that only a week ago he'd baulk at. Is it

Roy's gun? Or did the changes in him gestate, enter mitosis, when Irish jumped across that Lexus bonnet?

"The house you told me about," Sol says. "You said you woke alone in a house."

Yasmin nods.

"That's where we're going, isn't it? That's where he is."

Yasmin points up the ridge.

Sol nods. "When these two have gone, let's see what's in that store."

They could be in a crater. They could be lost in a gas giant's sweep.

Sol hitches the sports bag up his shoulder as they reach the store. Another unsophisticated structure, flat-roofed, whose uncoated cinderblock walls teem with conveyor entrances and service hatches. Yasmin tugs at Sol's sleeve and gestures to the ridge. There's an armed patrol moving around the perimeter.

"Don't worry," Sol says. "They can't see us."

Sol and Yasmin pop the door. Striplights, a suspended ceiling. Mezzanine storage. A cursory check: no humans, no surveillance. The supply boxes are unnervingly neat – stacked, tagged, palleted – and their heads track across the space, lingering on the far corner. IN crates. Yasmin crackles. A staging post on the road to transfiguration –

The storeroom's hard walls give Sol a false sense of security. He starts leafing through a supply crate. Below foam packing material he finds dry foods, powder sachets, drip bags. Nothing especially strange. The glyphs, however – the sister-world's language – seem more prevalent than they had in Sellafield's storage area. He thinks: *For internal use only*, and inspects a packing slip – a little piece of plastic-coated fabric covered in

iconography. On it, a vertical string of icons marks
out what he presumes are stops on the route. He can't
read the words, but they correspond in part to his
theory about the base of the mountain – the place the
Sellafield workers called Plastic. The bottom-most icon
is a cooling tower, while the middle icon – crossed out
– is a tepee. The topmost icon shows a house with a tick
next to it.

Tower. Camp. House.

Sol opens more crates, analyzes more packing slips.

Finds more ticks.

"This stuff's going up to your house," he tells her.
"Christ. All of it." Eerie light falls through ventilation
slats in the gable end, casting barred patterns on the
crates. "See for yourself. It's all going that way."

Yasmin's more intrigued by the trans-crates, however.
Sol can tell by her breathing that she's agitated. From the
corner she too holds up a packing slip, laminated and
fastened to one of the lids.

Sol nods assent. He gets it. If these crates are going to
the house, they can stow away again. Or is it too easy? A
grafter knows all about diminishing returns –

Yasmin pries at the corners of the crates, straining
against the heavy staples. Sol imagines her arms, sinewy
as a labourer's, working beneath her fleece top and shell
jacket. The twin beams of her clavicle stepped out with
the strain. He doesn't see her pause; can't relive in her
mind the flash of Keating's staple gun.

Exactly the kind of staple gun she's spotted down on
the floor.

She heaves open the trans-crate and points inside.

"Empty?" He crosses the space, checks the packing
slip. A small, innocuous-looking box inside. "It'll do,"
he says. He flips the packing slip. "And look here – the

house icon, see? Another like this and we'll have one each."

Yasmin weighs the benefits of extra space versus the risks of separation. She scoops up the staple gun and passes it to him.

"It'll be a luxury," he tells her, fake-smiling in a way that says he needs to convince himself first. "First class."

Yasmin wrenches open three more crates; grimaces at the hermetically sealed boxes inside them. Realistically, there'd only be room for one in these crates anyway.

A motorized growl on the wind. Sol swears and looks at his wrist. Ascribing meaning to random patterns. How often do the half-tracks come past? How long have they been in here?

"Yes, go," Sol says, pressing her towards the first empty crate. "I'll close you up." They round on it, and she springs inside. "If and when we start moving, tap your panels. I'll knock back."

She looks at him expectantly, eyes pixelating at their edges.

The growl is getting louder. She shoos him, three hands flapping.

"Remember to knock," he says, and secures the lid. Enough staples to secure its corners. "Keep knocking!" he shouts, before he drops the sports bag and Luger into his own crate. Mindful of splinters, he hopes the damage won't warrant inspection. He fires more staples into each corner from inside, at least enough to make the lid look secure.

It's colder in the crate than he expected, and his heart is hammering. Alone with his breath and Roy's gun and the bag, the scale and depth of things threaten to overwhelm him. He could hyperventilate just thinking about it: a system so sophisticated, so efficient, that it must be almost easy to work within. So successful it almost carries a legitimacy – workers calling it "logistics", or "shipping". So finely tuned that coming generations could probably maintain it with ease. And so entrenched that any given worker – supplies driver, brochure designer, escort, crate mover, leafleter – might not even recognize their complicity. You play your part without ever really having to think about what happens at the next level down. A perfect machine, silent and infallible and productive.

Testing his space, Sol stretches out and loses somehow his notion of the crate's dimensions, as if it's grown bigger since he got inside. But something disrupts his exploration; something against his hands. It's cold, smooth in texture, and he slaps it, drawing a slight reverberation. Hollow, definitely, but thick-shelled. How had he not seen it?

In the dark he runs his hands over the object. The approaching half-track filling his ears. The object in Sol's crate is maybe a foot tall, ovoid in shape. At its base there's a powerpack with adducted fans that whir soundlessly, regulating something, and a bitter coldness emanates from them. He paws around the egg and finds a flatter segment on its front, a fascia with its own panel, and by the top, its narrowest point, a different material – even colder to the touch, and slippery. Glass.

He shuffles closer. Pitched onto his knees in the darkness. He stares into the egg for a time, as the half-track draws close and stops. The next pickup. Definitely the next pickup. The engine turning over, and the store door swinging –

Then, as Sol's eyes adjust, the carrier reveals its cargo: a faint blue outline visible through the egg's glass fascia. The curvature of a delicate nose, nostrils. A tiny philtrum widening out, a crown on the top lip. The littlest eyelashes splayed over fatty cheeks.

Sol stifles his own cry: a shout he has to smash at the root. His mouth blocked with it, head pounding, eyes scorched closed. The sound released as pressurized air. Filled with such hatred, he goes to punch the crate wall but remembers just in time –

Sol is desolate, frightened. He's never felt more disillusioned. And that's when the workers start to move his trans-crate. When they slide it along the store floor, up on their moaning hydraulic lift, and into the half-track proper.

He curls up, trembling as the air chills and more crates are packed in around him. Two either side, shells scraping. He sobs then in a womb of silence and leeching cold, while Roy's empty Luger seems to crystallize in his hand. Another crate slots in above, and things go completely black. He wonders, hopelessly wonders, if that's Yasmin up there. Another cube in the puzzle.

Three times he tightens his fists and presses knuckles into the panels, and three times he stops himself. He can't knock yet. Can't risk it. So he waits with nothing to distract himself from the metal egg, the infant, a yolk in its chamber, the gnawing fan. A stowaway with a life stolen away.

Sol can't see anything, but knows his exhaled breath is denser, close to solid. Desperate for warmth, he tugs his socks over his jeans, pulls up his hands inside the peacoat's sleeves, retightens the collar around his chin. The infant's freezer unit works harder still, pumping its polar air against his ankles, his knees, his neck. He searches for the water – finds the bottle rattling, contents half-frozen, and tries to warm it under his armpit. Should he knock now? Should he risk it? The sound of the fan is all the company he has. But he holds off, keeps holding off –

He wipes his face and shivers violently. Lungs rattling. He could swear his tears have started freezing on his cheeks.

And then, at last, he knocks for Yasmin.

He knocks.

He knocks.

He knocks–

NINETEEN

Movement. The half-track on its way. In blankets of humidity, Yasmin taps out rhythms: knock, knock-knock, knock-knock-knock. Sometimes with two fists and sometimes with one.

Sol doesn't reply. Or if he does, she can't hear him.

Rationally, Yasmin knows it won't take long to reach the mansion – but the half-track has a pendulous motion, a top-heaviness in every bend, and it makes her feel ill.

Distractions are scant. Still nothing from Sol. And so in preparation she maps and remaps her cables, her cradle. The rows and rows. The training suites – the target ranges, the food classes. The shifting walls of the entrance hall. The water fountains outside. The bursor room – a scene playing out behind a screen of memory like shadow puppetry.

Tense.

Tense up.

Knock on the walls.

Yasmin pictures Chaplain's compound eyes – the optics of her makers and drillers, blinking. Melanie's empty socket, its leathery pit. The third-eyed harridan from the feeding vault.

Disgusting little creature–

One by one, Yasmin rubs them out. One by one. Until a lone figure remains, crimson in his robe –

When the half-track stops, Yasmin coils.

Her crate is loaded onto another rack, another conveyor in another processing facility. Over its clattering mechanisms, another man shouting. It sounds like "Oh!" Then, "Oh shit, oh shit, oh *no*–"

Sol? Was it Sol?

The belt stops. The line judders, discharging a wave of vibrations that pass along the line and beneath Yasmin's crate.

"Bronze," the man says, tenor grim. Then, surer of himself: "Bronze!"

A radio crackles.

~ *This is Bronze. What are you doing?*

"You need to get down here."

~ *No. Next delivery's in thirty minutes. Shape up – you're down on all targets today–*

"There's something. There's something in here."

~ *Infant crate?*

"It's not alone."

~ *Alone? What's not? Come again?*

"Frozen."

A quiet.

~ *Stop the belt. I'm coming. If this gets out, we'll–*

"Wait. Wait. There's something else."

~ *That's twice you've interrupted me now. Just hold the belt. I'm coming.*

Yasmin explodes from her crate, lid disintegrating around her shoulders. The staffer turns, startled, and Yasmin barely notices the warehouse at all. She's

surrounded on all sides by hundreds and hundreds of
trans-crates, some dismantled, many stacked into half-
pyramids, all of them racked and tagged. A city.

The staffer can't bring a word to bear.

Yasmin sprints along the belt, hurdling crates, to meet
him. A blaze of fists and teeth, saturated – each motion
sending spray from her skin. Nothing else escapes
the staffer's mouth, though there's a kind of jumbled,
appraising look in his eyes, and with it, Yasmin realizes
she's spun his skull too far. She looks at her hands and
the line is silent and the crate city groans and her ears
are roaring.

It had felt automatic.

Sol is foetal in his trans-crate. He looks serene there
beneath a vernix-like frost, face relaxed, with a strand
of frozen fluid leaving his mouth, gummed against his
peacoat collar, and the Luger held to his head like a
cushion. His jeans tucked into his socks. The staple gun
clutched in his other hand, cradled in his breast.

Yasmin heaves him up by his shoulders, the back
of her third hand burning with cold against his cheek.
There's a wrinkling sound as his coat comes away from
the crate floor, and she brings him into her body as a
solid sculpture, his iced face turned into her neck. Here
she holds him with her coat unzipped and top pulled
open to the sternum so she can press her hot skin against
his. She holds him there on the emergency-stopped
conveyor belt, shivering, repeating his name in a river
of code, over and over until his skin is revealed fully by
her thaw and her fleece is saturated with meltwater. The
conveyor, now clean in this patch, drips silently. Sol's
body slackens, slumps, falling deeper into her. With two
arms wound tightly around him and her third stroking
his forehead, she rocks him and rocks him until his

mouth hangs open again, and the dark frozen liquid
runs away down her stomach. But even now there's no
breath across her skin.

A loud siren tears through the warehouse.

Yasmin holds up Sol's face and touches her forehead
to his – wishing more than anything that she could
disassemble and reassemble him as he had her: find his
own little I/O toggle, rekindle his heart–

Yasmin rears back. She opens her throat. The howl
briefly supersedes the alarm, resounds through the
whole space. She lowers Sol back into his own crate, a
casket, and reaches for the bag, the device, the staple
gun. She heaves back the lid and staples it shut.

Now she hops off the line and crouches to the staffer.
Without blinking, she bolts a single staple through his
lips. A concession to what they've made her; a guarantee
they'll know who came here.

The rest is instinctive:

Yasmin pelts from the warehouse floor to a central
stair gantry, mesh and steel, and takes the stairs with
such power they bow under her weight. At the top is
a barred door marked PERSONNEL EXIT. She misses
a chance to see the warehouse hive in its entirety; the
strange brutalist beauty of its twined and ribboned belts,
the quiet systems that attend them. But it doesn't matter.
She barrels through this door bag-first, and on through
the corridors hedged with spiral wires and ducting,
lined top and bottom with pipes and transformers and
stamped metal flooring. She takes more railed gangways,
rigging torn from future battleships. She reaches the next
stairway, encased in a shaft of smooth concrete. The rail
of it winding round the central column·like a parasitic
root, extending all the way up to hell above.

At the top of the column, legs ragged, she finds

lockers, shower rooms, an open-plan changing room. A worker cleaning himself in a tiled quarter, overalls and boots stacked neatly on a bench. Stopping here only to examine the doors – TOILET BLOCK, WAREHOUSE ENTRANCE, CELLAR ACCESS, EMERGENCY EXIT – Yasmin continues, taking the latter with her doubled shoulder, and enters a new corridor, gilded and veneered. From behind comes a wash of strange music, discordant notes. She accelerates to full speed again, feet like rain on glass, arms pistoning, the bag bouncing off her back.

Two makers stand in full view of her. Yasmin arrives with such pace they don't even notice till they're on the ground, their delicate masks adrift. She continues without pause, the impact hardly registering.

More doors. More choices. HOUSE ATRIUM. CRADLE SUITE ONE. She takes the door on the right, explodes into a room of brothers and sisters, lined in, sleep-induced, and feeding.

Yasmin's course takes her to the suite's central console – the tentacled boss of it. Here she stops, gathering what she can of her breath. Her ribcage hurts, too big for her skin.

"Target!"

The suite crackles. A barrage of inch-long darts spin past and embed themselves in the hardware, fracturing hard plastic. A squad at arms. Without hesitation Yasmin bunches as many wires as her three hands will hold and pulls until the unit's superficial fittings break away and many of the wires are instantly stripped from their brackets. She keeps pulling. Keeps pulling. A new volley – another barrage. This time Yasmin feels a dart lodge in her back – a sparkle of pain, then a numbing. It waggles there a moment, kinetic energy transferring. Again she tugs at the gathered wiring, rotating her wrists to wrap each cluster over her hands, and reapplies the force. The wires snap, slide free, sparking off. An alarm wails. The squad's closing her down. And now in the commotion her brothers and sisters have begun to wake and stand. Yasmin turns to see the nearest of her attackers trip over a spun-round cradle arm. He sprawls face-first, arms bent up behind his torso, and the slap of his landing carries.

Yasmin screams in binary: "Malfunction with me!"

At the far side, another dart cluster fizzes overhead. She kicks open the door marked CRADLE SUITE THREE and goes again for its heart. Here the alarm has already roused the sleepers, many of whom are out of their cradles, holding their ears, with feeding and monitor lines still attached. When they see Yasmin coming, her three arms powering, they simply stand aside, too confused or shocked to comprehend. But when they see the squad following, they react with fright – clambering over their cradles, jumping away, their distress surging.

The second core. This time Yasmin's had practice. She tears into the panels to get more purchase; drags more wires free and rips them from their fittings. Her hands are bleeding – several fingers clawing up owing to damaged tendons. But it doesn't matter. It won't matter...

When she turns, she can no longer see the chasing squad for carnage: the suite detonating. All of her brothers and sisters are running towards the exits, or simply at each other, or towards the oncoming makers. Collision after collision – bodies cartwheeling, bouncing. And then something else: a small but swelling group of brothers and sisters have started tearing at the suite's structures themselves. Pulling away extrusions and cradle limbs to arm themselves, to attack other cradles, to defile their comfortable prison.

While the shooting seems to have abated, the dart in

her back has delivered its complete load. It leaves her stooped in gait, slower to react. She pulls it free, feels a warmth roll down under her fleece into the crack of her buttocks. Yasmin opens her mouth, releases another cry, in part a command. Her brothers and sisters echo her. Their response is cathartic. But her back is throbbing now, a screen descending – and she knows in her marrow she won't have long.

CRADLE SUITE FIVE. Already emergent. Her brothers and sisters have seen or heard or intuited what's happening in the suites beyond theirs; have already shed their lines. Yasmin calls it on the hoof – she doesn't need to stop here, doesn't need to do any more. And so she powers through the crowd to the far side. Between blinks, her eyes streaming in the onrushing air, she realizes that five-strong packs of her brothers and sisters are turning on their drillers, the harridans, the makers.

And then she stops. Just stops. Yasmin with her shoulder bag. Yasmin in her prime. Because the number of the suite clicks in, like a lock's last digit rotating into place. A gliss of recognition. This is Yasmin's old suite, the birthplace of Y, and so the corridor adjacent must run to the atrium, out to the drilling lawns.

And to the grand stairway that sweeps up from the mansion entrance. A final Slope, ready for ascension.

Jase is still on the floor when Mel opens the store cupboard. She finds him humiliated, self-nursing – all the sharpened edges blunted. His head has ballooned.

"Melanie…" he starts.

"No more words, Jason," Mel says. "No more smarming."

"You won't–"

She holds up his wallet. "I already have."

Jase scowls – an attempt to focus, to apprehend. An aspect of seeking.

"What's your PIN?" she asks.

"My PIN?"

With her other hand, she holds up the doubled stockings, the glass-ball halves rubbing against each other. "Need me to jog your memory?"

"You've lost it."

"No," she says. "But I do have some chores. How's about when I'm done, we see if it's come back to you?"

"You can't just lock me in here."

"Well, see, that depends on your perspective. You remember one of the first things you said to me?"

Cautious, he shakes his head.

"I just want your business, you said."

"Did I?"

Mel backs into the hall. "You did," she says, and closes the door to a crack. But now, Jase, you're *part* of my business."

Mel needs four binbags to carry Sol's mess from Cassie's room. Balled-up tarpaulin, sheets, pillowcases and hand towels, rolls and rolls of tissue, small bins full of crusted flannels, slivers of plastic, strange metal fastenings, a moist Bowie T-shirt. She attacks the task with urgency, tumbling slack cotton over her arms with the efficiency of an industrial bailer. Muttering at the state of it. Hairs and skin and stains. A muddled smell of baby oil and rubbing alcohol.

She piles it all on the landing by the stairs as she flits in and out of the room, methodical and sad all at once, stripping Cassie's bed back to its yellowed mattress; shaking out dead flies; revealing naked fabric the colour of sun-blasted bones. The room quickly becomes a poor facsimile of itself: sterilized, made absent of material colour.

The trinkets she doesn't touch. A vanity mirror draped in plastic jewellery, hair bobbles, miscellaneous lids for unseen products. A cupboard filled with cheap fantasies on wire hangers. Photos of foreign lands, floral prints, fractal designs. She picks up one of their frames and realizes Cassie's kept the stock display photography inside it, complete with tiny crop measurements, corporate watermark and all. The picture itself is a beach scene, a model holding up another model, both grinning at their false paradise, the sky a paradigmatic blue. Mel turns the photo frame over. Into the reverse, Cassie's scratched *2027*. Mel wells up, her fake eye throbbing. Was it Cassie's dream, ambition? Inspiration for an alternate future?

Mel comes to the window, eye scanning the back yard, black-seamed, and the terraces it borders. The wasteland beyond. She wonders if, given that Sol and her never legally divorced, she'd count as a widow soon. Or if she, on this path to some fate unknown, will make him a widower. What's her own dream?

She takes the binbags outside in two hands, straining through the gate onto common land. Round the corner, what's left of the bonfire: a pyre of blackened metal frames, many resmelted and tangled into new profiles. There's no one about, the crowd long since dispersed. She goes over in her slippers, the four bags spinning smoothly by her sides.

The bonfire's still smoking in places. Even now it carries a harsh smell, easy to taste. Mel steps towards the biggest of these plumes and uses a bag to shift the ash. Flickers of yellow, green, lick out from the grey. A scrap near the surface catches, goes up; she watches a circle of flames rear up to feed on it.

Mel throws on the binbags. One at a time. They begin to melt immediately, splitting to reveal their fouled innards. The sheets and tarp turn black as they shrivel –lighter fibres rising, tendril-like, to escape on the heat, before being sucked back down and annihilated. How hot the bonfire must've been.

Is it relieving to watch the sheets burn? Therapeutic might be a better word. And there in front of it, the heat on her legs, Mel levels out.

What now? In this new order? She has faith in the women's self-confidence, their entrepreneurial brains forever surprising her. She knows also they share a sisterhood, knotty ties forged over a half decade not by circumstances, but by choice. They are each the other's safety net, and so she knows they'll adapt easily to more responsibility, the chance to decide more for themselves.

That said, most of the women have worked this way for much longer than Mel, and some might wish to go on elsewhere. She hopes that won't mean the streets, as this would be a failure on her part, a contradiction of what she wants the Cat Flap to represent. But she can't take things for granted; can't deny anyone their preferences. Briefly she even considers if she might go herself – retire, hand ownership straight to Cassie, or a few more of them. It's attractive, this, or would be if she hadn't fought tooth and nail to be here, to be *something*, a consolidation of previous selves, driven and fortified by her own resolve, her sheer bloody-mindedness. To hell with anyone who tries to wrest that from her; anyone who judges and scoffs; who tells her what she should be or what she shouldn't. To hell with anyone who crosses her. And so as Mel watches the pyre, wiping her nose with her sleeve to find the wool has already accreted its smell, she can't help smiling to herself.

Mind you, there's Jase to think about. How much would he, in his new role as their captive creditor, boost the parlour's income? Enough in the short-term to keep their overheads covered? A rough calculation makes her wince. Most of their punters are humble, respectful, even friends with the girls. But if you aren't, there's room for you and bastards like you in that cupboard with him. She laughs again – possibly at the extremes of her imagination. She'd need a better way to get at his accounts, of course, and some more effective ways to extort him. How far will she go? Starvation? Sleep deprivation? Out-and-out torture? Maybe it's more frightening that nothing feels beyond her.

Cremation finished, all evidence of Sol and Yasmin destroyed, Mel strolls back to the Cat Flap. Back to her duties. A game of numbers. In some small way it makes her want to whistle. Mel will still be there when the walls finally come down. Mel will always remain: the captain of her ship, able to dump the ballast whenever she needs to. She thinks of Sol, and she smiles again. Anything's possible, really. And all she'd have to keep in mind is this: whatever the tile mosaic says on the wall of Affleck's Palace, Manchester wasn't built in a day.

TWENTY

Yasmin rages through the mansion's corridors like a spinning platelet. Her back is torrid with heat, flesh dripping around her hips and flanks. In the atrium, she looks out through broken doors. Dozens of her brothers and sisters stream down the lawns, many still trailing wires.

She turns for the lobby, enters the throat of it. The carpeted stairs, velveted to the point of looking polished, evoke a leftover image of some lost playground, a red slide, a piece of which lives on inside her, a statue, context elided. One more thing clinging to her subconscious, despite the makers' best efforts.

Yasmin climbs the stairs with a certain grace gone. Her legs are bandy, tremulous, and the blackness is swarming like a vignette. The top stair appears so far away. Another summit. Then it's suddenly in the past, withdrawing, and the landing spreads two ways. She gambles on right, assuming that the upper levels follow the anticlockwise flow of the floors below. She follows the path, sluggish yet steadfast, past wall-hung paintings of ancient cities, unknowable monuments. As the corridor constricts, the pictures on its walls become of one thing only: the tower. Floating, she recognizes its form, its stark outline, as the tower from the Plastic side – not Sellafield's hostile twin. A recollection of Sol's feature wall, a feeling he would have liked these portraits. Ahead, the corridor curves back on itself, moving up to another level. She follows the carpet, thick and lustrous, and violent shapes seep from the skirtings to chase her.

Before too long she meets a door of solid brass, engraved with tiny figures, nymph-like, prancing across a body of water. Focusing, concentration increasingly taxing, Yasmin watches oversized lilypads spread and swallow them. Illusion or not, the image steels her. Three hands splayed, bag strapped across her single-jointed shoulder, she pushes in.

The chamber is circular, wide-bellied. Its roof tapers to a hole from which a thin shaft of natural light streams down. The beam illuminates the baroque sculpture of a hardwood throne studded with teeth in various shades. Yasmin observes their arrangement, their linkage across the back of it. In turn, the throne is set beneath a desk at least four metres wide. On this desk, the beam creates a bright, sharp-edged circle.

On the desk itself is an array of minute monitors – dozens of them relaying footage apparently shot in the first person. A cursory sweep reveals sexuality, scenery, hints at violence, then roadway, city, rich forest.

Supporting the screens is a trellis of bone. Yasmin counts tripled rows of polished ivory, more inset teeth coated and sparkling. Many of the bones are painted, giving them the appearance of coral. Only the darker areas, the pocks, reveal the wear of use, give hints to their donators' ages. In this setting, this factory, the trellis is a dark visual gag: its designer having remodelled skeletons and fused them with technology.

Yasmin takes a step forward. Juddering senses. She hears a sound. *That* sound. A delicate tinkling of teeth.

"You came home," the Manor Lord says, emerging from behind the desk.

Yasmin swallows.

He ambles round the monitor bank, the lightbeam and the room's contrast enhancing his odd, puckered features.

"I rewound and watched what I could," he says. He points to a black square in the monitor array. "That was your feed," he says. "Until the day you left us."

Yasmin says nothing.

"Now I rather wish we'd installed some proper optics. Night vision! Not a patch on livestreaming. But no hard feelings. Progress is expensive."

Yasmin is rooted. Vacillating.

"You know you're distinct, don't you?" the Manor Lord asks. "Unique? You were made that way deliberately. Not that there was a lot going for you at first. That's the thing, over in that place. So much wasted potential: no work, no opportunities, a chronic lack of education. So I saved you, brought you into my arms. And then I trained you and broke you and whittled you into shape. Only then could you perform this little number for us." He snaps his fingers, enjoying the theatre of it all, and the monitor array wipes to a single feed.

Yasmin watches herself on screen. Looking out from behind the blinking camera, Y sitting in the stuffed bursor's embrace, in that room beneath the cradle suites. Her shoulders broader than Yasmin's feel now.

"You were perfect," the Manor Lord says.

Three figures enter the frame and surround her. Y looks woozy, vague. Then the camera crash-zooms, and Yasmin watches Y seize up, turn lifeless in the fur. Moments later, Y explodes from her chair with such potency, such energy, that her movements transfer to video as a blur. The trio of figures are soon unrecognizable – three piles of wreckage, synthetic skin.

The Manor Lord smiles. "Ribbons, is how I recall Chaplain describing that little mess. And that's how we sold you to Havelock. On that short clip alone."

Yasmin doesn't feel anything. She hadn't recognized herself.

"But then," the Manor Lord went on, "you weren't supposed to come home, Y. Not that you can't be redeployed. It's one hazard we face. But I tell you: the day it's more affordable to build complete fabrications – the day we can actually *control* our output – is the day we avoid the hassle of meetings like this."

The Manor Lord closes his hand. The feed cuts back to riots, jumbled images, chaos. His realm off-kilter. Yasmin realizes she's watching events from the mansion as well as outside it.

"What a fuss," he says to her. "What a commotion."

Yasmin takes her broken hands and makes a triangle of them. She holds the shape together, shaky but resolute. She closes her eyes. She says to him, "You caused it," in a stream of fragmented digits that seethe from her throat as froth.

"What? What are you saying to me? Never mind. You understand our failsafe procedure, don't you?"

She ignores him. She says: "My name is Yasmin."

"I could whistle to end you," the Manor Lord says. "Perhaps the first note of a musical score. The faintest hint of a word... and *poof* – vaporized. Perhaps I should've done so sooner. But to deny myself such pleasure would be pathological."

Yasmin edges away. The Manor Lord enlarges.

"Would you prefer a warning? A countdown? Why don't you come and kneel before me like the good girl we made you? Explain why it was you removed my gift to you?"

Yasmin manages another step backwards. She uses the movement to reach up for the bag. She struggles to unclasp it, dexterity so far from what it was.

"Come along," he says. "Come along."

She unclasps the bag. Her gnarled fingers brushing cold alloy–

"Bow!" the Manor Lord shouts. "Curtsey!" But Yasmin doesn't react. He laughs. "Countdown it is, then. Shall we say ten?" And with that, the Manor Lord mumbles and moves directly for her, arms raised, palms flat. A chain and tooth hanging from a thumb.

"You'll have to go outside to do it," the Manor Lord says. "It'll ruin my office."

Fingers twisted together, Yasmin jerks free the device Sol extracted from her. It's pulsating. She hasn't a chance to do anything else before the Manor Lord is on her.

"I am Yasmin," she says again. And their tussle goes like this:

Yasmin takes both of the Manor Lord's wrists and with her third hand forces the canister into his mouth. His teeth shift inwards. Then she pushes him away; watches from beyond herself, interstitial, as he trips over his chair and scatters over the desk – his robe on the wood like so many pearls scattered over marble. He comes to rest under the circle of light. Here he tries to say something more, but the canister's wedged too far in.

"I will not serve you," she tells him.

Yasmin relishes the Manor Lord's look, the confusion of it caught there in the irradiating glow, a fragile gold. His eyebrows arch, flatten, then lose their structure entirely, like his expression is wiped clean, absolved, by the sunlight's purity. His chin sparkles with liquid ruby. His eyes are whited out.

She's never been grateful for sunshine before.

Yasmin opens the Manor Lord's chamber door. Her systems in full collapse. Footfall beyond – brothers and sisters coming up the corridor towards her. She pivots to show them her swollen flanks – the mound where the dart had struck. They take her by the arms and legs, try to drag her away. She resists and wrestles free. Tottering, erratic, she holds up all three hands in protest – gestures along the corridor. She turns and grips the Manor Lord's door – catches a glimpse of him writhing on his desk – and with her remaining strength, slams it shut.

"Be defective," she whispers to her brothers and sisters.

After this, there's an instant in which all the air seems to leave her lungs, just as the tide recedes before a tsunami.

And Yasmin waits for the light.

ACKNOWLEDGMENTS

Thank you to friends and colleagues who read and chatted through my early drafts – particularly Alex Hill, Jayne Travis, Mike Williams and Steph Venema. Extra special thanks to James Smythe, Kim Curran and Nina Allan for their invaluable suggestions and encouragement.

Big thanks to my agent, Sam Copeland, whose belief, insight and flowery shirts I always appreciate. We got there eventually...

The Angry Robot team is ace. Thanks to Marc Gascoigne, Mike Underwood and Caroline Lambe for their care and hard work both sides of the Atlantic. Huge thanks to Phil Jourdan, my bionic-eyed editor, who honestly understands this novel more than I do, and to Penny Reeve, cybernetic publicity manager extraordinaire. I also want to thank Paul Simpson, the book's copyeditor, and Trish Byrne and Claire Rushbrook, its proofreaders. And, of course, thank you to John Coulthart for the book's magnificent cover art.

Loads of love to my family, who support me even though they probably read this stuff and wonder where they went wrong. And lastly, love and endless gratitude to Suzanne, who smiles and endures and holds me together. Our son Albert was born just a few days before I wrote these acknowledgments – so here's a little one for him, too: you'll likely be in your teens when you see this. Behave yourself.

ALSO AVAILABLE

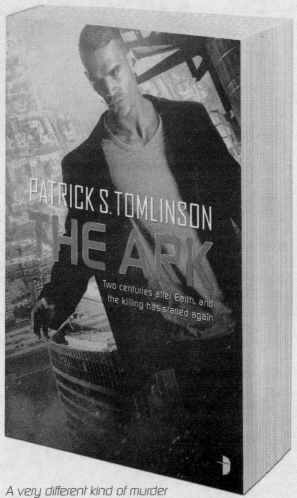

A very different kind of murder
investigation... on a generation
starship two centuries out from Earth...

ANGRY ROBOT

We are Angry Robot.

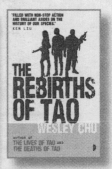

angryrobotbooks.com

Whatever the future brings.

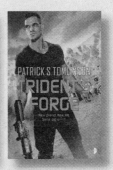

twitter.com/angryrobotbooks

JOIN US

angryrobotbooks.com

twitter.com/angryrobotbooks

ANGRY
ROBOT